Special Thanks

*Ninja Sex Party, for helping remind the world
that unicorns (and wizards) are totally awesome.*

*Starcadian, whose music inspired me to
kick off this entire endeavor, as it inspired
so many others over the years. Rest in peace.*

*Matthew Mercer, whose hosting of Critical Role
helped ignite my passion for storytelling years ago.*

*Jesús Bey, Alberto Garcia, and Katherine C. Neal,
who served as our cover illustrator, map illustrator,
and chapter illustrator, respectively.*

*Ashton Fei, whose software extension
allowed me to format this labor of love.*

*Mom, who was constantly badgered with grisly
equestrian inquiries throughout the entirety
of writing this book. She may never recover.*

*...and YOU!
For reading.
Obviously.*

Contents

Prologue I:
The Siege of a
Thousand Sons

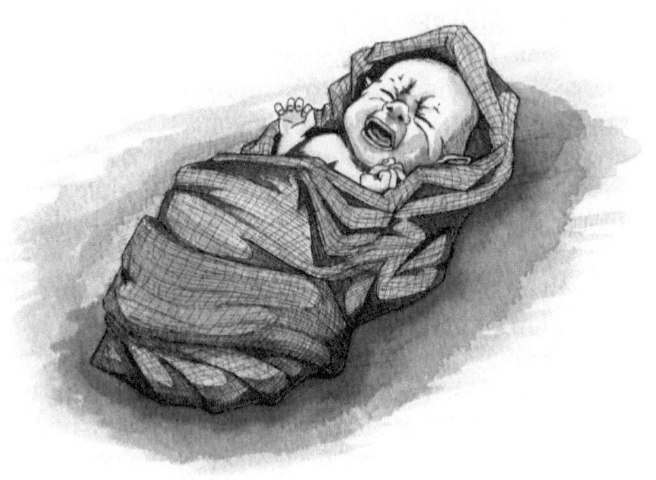

Prologue I: The Siege of a Thousand Sons

The city burns. Flames lick the sky atop charring wood. Swollen clouds blot out the stars. Rain pours down onto blood-soaked streets. Corpses pile in alleyways, spilling out onto main roads. Lightning cracks the sky. A bellowing thunder echoes. It does little to mask the screams of those who wish to be dead.

Amid the chaos, a lone unicorn stands idle at the foot of the castle archway: the centerpiece of the great Kingdom of Man. Her mane — the color of darkness — whips violently in the wind, a stark contrast from her glistening white-gray coat. Radiant blue light spews forth from her eyes. Magical energy *crackles* outward in thin, sporadic bursts. Fresh blood — not her own — drips down the base of her horn. Her armor — fitted metal plating of intricate design, fanciful blue-gray trim around its edges — does little to shield from the rain.

She stares at the shadowed castle ahead.

Further inward, a silhouette moves.

Without hesitation, the eyes of the unicorn lock onto it. From her horn, a thick streak of lightning cuts through the air.

KRAAAK!

It strikes the figure.

In shock, the figure stumbles forward: a grizzled, heavyset man — an older human — long-since soaked by the storm. His right arm hangs low from the place where his shoulder used to be, now tethered to his body by only a ragged clump of flesh.

It swings unnaturally as he staggers forward. Blood spurts from beneath the charred crust of the wound. He stares out at the unicorn before him.

His eyes dart across her features. His mind struggles to form even a single coherent thought. His eyes meet hers.

In a strained voice, he utters a single word.

"Help…"

The man desperately searches the unicorn's face for any sign of remorse.

Of mercy.

Of pity.

He finds none.

With a steady gaze, the voice of the unicorn — powerful and commanding — bellows through the storm.

"You are no help to me."

Another powerful bolt of lightning blasts forth from her horn.

KRAAAK!

It strikes the man's face. His head bursts open. Clumps of hair and wet meat splatter onto the stone walkway behind him. His eyes, reduced to nothing more than globs of viscous pus, hang loose in the bottom half of his sockets. He falls backward, landing in bloody chunks of his own body.

From behind, a masculine voice calls out.

"Queen Marika!"

The radiant blue energy fades from the unicorn. The crackling, too, fades away.

She turns to the source of the voice.

Another unicorn approaches, adorned by armor not dissimilar to hers, though of far less intricate design. His voice carries above the storm with ease.

"We found one."
Queen Marika furrows her brow.
"Show me."

— — — — — — — — — — — — — — — — —

A younger man — elven — breathes heavily, sitting against the stone wall of an alleyway. Two armored unicorns stand on either side of him; blood drips from their front hooves. The man — dressed in long, once-elegant robes, now tattered and covered in dirt — refuses to look at the ground. Where his legs should be sits a pile of torn cloth, mashed together with thick, dark red clumps. They converge at the exposed, throbbing flesh of his lower thighs. Blood spills forth at a worrying speed. Crimson fills the cracks of the cobblestone below him.

Another armored unicorn steps into the alleyway.

Queen Marika follows behind.

At the sight of the cripple, she speaks.

"Is this the one?"

The unicorn who led her there replies.

"Yes, Queen Marika."

Queen Marika approaches the man.

The *clack* of her hooves sends a chill down his spine with every step.

She stops in front of him, looking down at the bleeding mess below her. The man averts his gaze.

Queen Marika's voice booms.

"Look at me."

The man does not.

Queen Marika repeats, now much louder.

Magically louder.

"Look at me."

The volume sends a ringing through the man's ears. He winces briefly, but — with steady control over his breathing — pushes through the pain.

He refuses to look at the unicorn.

Queen Marika shoves her front hoof into the raw, spongy flesh of his thigh.

He jolts upward. A howl of pain escapes his lips on instinct.

Queen Marika jams the point of her hoof further into the wound. The sound of wet, crushing meat echoes in the alley.

The man cries out once more. Tears stream down his face, washed away by the cold sting of the rain.

The queen removes her hoof. Stringy clumps of meat and sinew peel off from its front, plopping down onto the mangled remains of a leg.

The man — with a great reluctance — looks to the unicorn above him.

The eyes of Queen Marika stare down into his.

He can almost *feel* the intensity behind them. The forcefulness. The determination. The danger.

The queen's voice bellows out once again.

"Tell me of the weapon that slays my people."

The man remains silent.

She continues.

"If you do not speak, I will tear your tongue from your body."

The man speaks.

"It's too late. It has already been made. Used."

He takes a heavy, forceful breath.

"You now live in a world where you can be beaten. There is nothing you can do to stop its creation."

The queen remains unfazed.

"I intend to butcher its creator."

At the mention of 'creator', the man's eyes flick to the opposite wall for a mere *fraction* of a second.

Queen Marika notices.

She leans in close. Her warm, wet breath sticks to his face, its unwelcome stench in his pores. The man feels the vibration of her voice in his chest.

"What were you looking at?"

A deep-seated fear flashes behind the man's eyes; something not present before.

Queen Marika maintains eye contact. She flicks her head toward the spot on the wall that the man looked at.

"Check that wall."

The man lurches forward in protest, met with immediate pain.

"NO!"

The three unicorn knights step up to the opposite wall. Their eyes scan the stone, looking for something amiss. Before long, the centermost knight calls out.

"Here!"

The other knights follow his gaze. Their eyes fall to a loose brick in the wall, peeking out by the slightest amount.

The centermost knight focuses intently. A gentle blue glow emanates from his horn. The brick in the wall — now surrounded by an identical glow — floats out. As it pulls free, the unmistakable cries of a newborn child ring out into the alleyway.

The queen looks surprised.

"Oh? What's this?"

The blue glow around the brick dissipates. It *clatters* to the ground.

From within the hole in the stone wall, a newborn baby, wrapped in a burlap swaddle — emanating a blue glow of its own — floats out.

Queen Marika grins wickedly.

"Bring it to me."

The man lurches forward once more.

"NO!"

The three unicorn knights — the centermost still glowing blue — approach their queen. The newborn floats over to her, coming to rest on the wet, blood-covered cobble in front of her.

The glow dissipates.

The queen looks down at the writhing, helpless creature. Its cries — its screams of discomfort — torture the man's ears.

Queen Marika looks back to him.

"The King of Man has lost a thousand sons this day."

She leans in even closer. Her humid breath smothers his skin.

"Is he ready to lose another?"

The man retorts.

"Daughter."

He winces, the true pain of his injuries catching up to him.

"That's my daughter."

Queen Marika locks eyes with him once again, a confidence behind her words.

"Tell me of the weapon, or I crush your daughter's head."

The man quickly responds.

"It's a sword."

The queen raises a threatening hoof.

Not good enough.

The baby continues to cry.

The man hurriedly elaborates.

"It's a sword! Something enchanted! That's all I know, I swear!"

Queen Marika keeps her hoof steady above the child.

"Who wields it?"

The man wastes no time.

"King Astani. He knew you would arrive. He
wanted to slay you himself."

The queen looks disappointed.

"Then he truly has damned his own people."

She places a gentle hoof on the chest of the
newborn. She leans down, covering its wailing head
with her jaws, and clamps shut.

The vocal cries become an indistinct mess of wet
gargles. In a single motion, Queen Marika twists her
head and pulls back, tearing the crushed mess of tissue
from the neck of the body. Blood spills out through her
open lips. A thick pool gathers around the neck of the
tiny, lifeless body below her.

The man's shrieks overtake him. He sobs through
each word, hatred brimming as he speaks.

"Why?! Why are you doing this?! We've done
nothing to you!"

The queen spits the crushed mass of flesh from her
mouth. It hits the center of the man's chest, leaving a
heavy red stain. It peels off and plops into his lap. The
sticky, oozing blood seeps through his clothes, mixing
with his own.

Queen Marika's lips shine with heavy red stains of
her own. Her steaming breath carries the stench of iron.
Tiny flecks of flesh — *his daughter* — stick to her
teeth.

She takes a single step back from the man.

Ever-so-slightly, she lowers her head.

"Give your daughter my regards."

She thrusts her head forward, skewering the man's
eye on the base of her horn.

——— —— —— —— —— —— —— —— —— —— —— —— —— ——

The flames of the kingdom glow through stained
glass. The ambient cries of the dying echo beyond. Rain

pummels wood and stonework above. Intermittent booms of thunder rattle the very walls. Positioned at the rear of the chamber – his back to the trio of decadent thrones behind him – stands a bulky, imposing older man: a human with flowing gray hair, long-since matted from the storm. He holds tight to a massive greatsword in his hands, its blade nearly six feet in length. Donned in lavish robes — a visible suit of leather beneath, dyed purple — he scowls, eyes trained on the grand pair of carved wood doors before him.

A faint blue glow emanates from their handles.

The doors begin to open.

A wooden blockade prevents them from opening further.

The old man's grip tightens around his greatsword. Its leather feels warm in his grasp. He steels his resolve.

The blue glow fades from the door handles.

They gently close.

From beyond them, a deep, low-toned sound pulses rhythmically.

An explosive sound rips through the air.

*KRAAAK-**KOW!***

A massive burst of lightning tears the doors from their hinges. They fall to the ground, wood now dark and charred.

Queen Marika stands at the now-open doorway. Crackling blue energy fades from her eyes. Dozens of armored unicorn knights — donned in heavy combat plating, many covered in splashes of blood — stand behind her. Beyond them, the rain continues its downpour. The fires of burning buildings flicker against the darkness.

Queen Marika locks eyes with the old man.

"It's a pleasure to finally meet you, Alans."

The voice of King Alans Astani bellows, nearly matching the queen's intensity.

"There is no pleasure for you here."
Queen Marika grins, baring her stained red teeth.
"Oh, I assure you, there is."
She steps forward.
The greatsword in the king's hand's *hums* audibly.
Runes — seemingly forged into the metal itself — glow
white with a tense magical power.
The queen stops.
"Is this the weapon meant to slaughter my people?"
The king holds his ground.
"It has already slaughtered your people, and by my
hand, it will again."
The queen responds.
"I am eager to see you try."
The king raises his voice.
"You will pay for desecrating the flesh of our
children."
The queen holds her gaze.
"The flesh of your children catches in my teeth."
The king scowls, eyes burning with rage.
"Then let it rot there."
Queen Marika stomps her front hoof on the
ground. On cue, the battalion of unicorn knights rushes
forth, charging into the chamber.
King Astani tears away his robes, revealing the
series of unicorn horns fastened to his belt. One by one,
each horn charges with a piercing white light,
reminiscent of the runes in his sword.
The unicorn knights draw closer.
The glow of each horn strengthens. The horns
themselves can hardly be seen beneath the brightness of
their light.
The thunderous sound of hooves fills the room.
With a heavy swing, King Astani slashes the air in
front of him. A curve of pure white light jettisons out
from his blade.

FWOOM!

It impacts the front line directly. It splits their armor and carves through their flesh.

The front line falls. The meat of their twitching bodies fathers an ocean of blood where they lie.

The knights that remain charge on.

King Astani slashes the air once again.

FWOOM!

Another curve of brilliant white cuts deep into the knights. Blood sprays out from their wounds, splashing onto the head of the king. He breathes heavily.

The knights that remain charge on. Their hooves splash through the gathering blood.

King Astani slashes once more, an unintended angle to his swing.

FWOOM!

Its curve of light flies out, hitting only several of its targets.

Two knights — missed entirely — flank the king.

He brings his sword down onto the head of the knight in front of him. The heavy blade sinks with a meaty *crack*. Both eyes rupture from the weight of the impact, bursting outward.

The knight behind King Astani jams her horn forward, piercing his back. She lifts the king into the air. He holds tight to his sword, still embedded in the head of the knight; the corpse, too, lifts higher.

The knights that remain charge on.

The king pushes his foot against the head of the dead knight. The sword pulls from its skull. The body falls to the ground.

The king feels the pierce of the horn in his back. He holds tight to his sword with a single hand.

With his other, he firmly grasps a glowing horn on his belt. He tears it free.

Reaching behind, he stabs the horn into the eye of the knight. She recoils.

King Astani drops to the ground.

The horn glows bright within the knight's eye socket. She backs away, violently shaking her head in an attempt to dislodge it.

Lying prone, King Astani watches the army of knights gallop toward him. He forces himself to a knee. With a heavy, one-handed swing, he cuts through the air once again.

FWOOM!

Its curve of light flies out, carving deep through the unicorns closest.

More knights are upon him regardless.

The king swings again with great effort.

FWOOM!

The curve of light barely impacts its targets.

The king's breathing turns heavily labored.

Queen Marika scowls. The tip of her horn *sizzles* with thin cracks of electricity. The pupils of her eyes fade; a vibrant blue glow overtakes them.

The storm beyond grows ever louder.

King Astani stands. Visibly slowing, he swings at the knights again. And again. And again.

FWOOM!

FWOOM!

FWOOM!

With every movement, they surround him further.

The king belts out a war cry. He thrusts his blade through the chin of the knight closest. It skewers the skull, embedding in bone.

He throws the body over his head with near-magical strength. It collides with a cluster of knights, sending them tumbling into the ocean of blood that surrounds them.

A solitary beam of blinding blue electricity explodes from the chamber's entrance.

KSSSSH!

It rips through the bodies of those in front of the king. Broken metal and bloody scraps scatter.

The beam engulfs the king.

The horns on his belt pulse in tandem, deflecting the beam with a wall of translucent white light.

Queen Marika — the massive beam of electricity stemming from her horn — takes a single step forward.

Her voice — magically enhanced — dwarfs the sound of the crackling beam.

"ENOUGH!"

King Astani steadies himself. The force of the beam pushes him back. His feet begin to slide through the layer of blood on the floor.

The queen takes another step forward. The beam from her horn pulses; *crackles*. Her eyes shine bright with intensity.

"You will die."

The king glares at her through the wall of light in front of him.

"You will fall."

King Astani, pushing back against the force of the beam, takes a heavy step forward.

The army of unicorn knights steps aside, giving space to the massive beam of lightning that carves through the center of the chamber. They set their backs to the walls, surrounding the king at a distance.

The king takes another step forward.

Then another.

And another.

One by one, the horns of the unicorn knights *crackle* with a similar blue electricity. Then — one by one — a beam of lightning blasts out from each.

The smaller beams of electricity surround the king, hitting him from nearly every angle. The white glow of the magic shield forms a full barrier around him.

The king takes another step forward.

"You do not know torment."

Then another.

"You do not know suffering."

And another.

"But I will rape it into you."

Queen Marika walks forward, a slow and steady pace. The beam from her horn grows wider. Its crackles, louder. Its pulses, more erratic.

The knights around the room keep their focus on the king. Their own beams, too, press against him.

The king takes another step, reaching the center of the room.

Queen Marika — the massive beam of energy still blasting from her horn — stops her approach. She locks eyes with the king, mere meters now between them.

The king lifts his sword. With strained arms, he slashes the air.

FWOOM!

Its curve of white light collides with the beam, absorbed almost in its entirety. The slivers of energy that manage to escape slice into Queen Marika's skin, cutting her body. She begins to bleed.

She looks back. She sees the blood seep out from her wounds, shallow as they may be. Thin trails of red stain her coat. She looks back to the king, furious.

She takes another step forward. The beam from her horn widens further, nearly filling a third of the chamber. Behind the king, the arrangement of royal thrones shatters from its intensity. Bricks in the wall chip and crack. Chunks of large stone break away from the sheer force of Queen Marika's beam.

The king's feet slide in the blood below him, now unable to hold his ground. Left with few options, he swings his blade once again.

FWOOM!

As before, its curve of light disintegrates into the beam, only its edges finding purchase on the queen.

The knights against the chamber walls step closer.

Queen Marika pushes forward.

King Astani slides through the blood, now fighting to stay upright. The beam continues pushing him back.

He swings.

FWOOM!

Its edges strike the queen, cutting her skin.

The glowing eyes of the queen fill with rage. Driven by calculating fury, she takes note of his shaking hands. The physical strain on his muscles. The blood pouring out from the wound in his back. The splotches of red in his hair. The countless beads of sweat cascading down his body. The rhythmic pulsing of the horns strapped to his belt. The single horn missing from his left side. The weaker, dimmer pulses from each horn on either side of the gap. The strange array of perfectly vertical singe marks along the side of his leather armor, barely the width of a fingernail. The way he actively turns that side of his body away from the smaller beams.

She locks eyes with the king once more. Her lip curls into a terrifying grin.

The beam from her horn withers to nothingness. The piercing blue glow fades from her eyes.

With confusion, the knights surrounding the king follow suit, their own smaller beams dissipating.

Hands still clenching his sword, King Astani breathes heavily. The sweat from his body mixes with blood, leaving thin streaks all over him.

He says nothing. He simply stares ahead at the queen, the shield of bright light still surrounding him.

Queen Marika's grin stirs a nightmare.

"You will rape nothing."

In a single movement, she rushes to the side of the king, jamming the tip of her horn against the gap of his magic shield, its very point just *barely* pressing beyond the translucent white energy. Her eyes flash a deep orange glow; embers spring out from her sockets.

A maelstrom of fire explodes from the tip of her horn. It floods the inside of the magic shield, the barrier wholly confining it. An ear-piercing shriek emanates from the fire itself as it scorches the very air around it.

The silhouette of King Astani crumbles beneath the weight of his own incinerating flesh. And – as Queen Marika watches – she can almost swear the hand of the king bears a prominent middle finger on the way down.

The orange glow of Queen Marika's eyes disappears. The flames subside. The magic shield vanishes. Where the great King of Man once stood now lies a mass of charred flesh and bone. Next to it lies the enchanted greatsword, its runes already fading. Surrounding the ash – in pristine condition — burned patches of leather still clinging to the backs of them — sits a circle of eleven unicorn horns.

Queen Marika straightens her posture.

"General."

From the wall of the chamber, a unicorn knight approaches, his coat a blue roan coloration. Scars busy his face from battles long ago. His armor — unlike that of the others — is far more similar to the queen's.

"Yes, Queen Marika?"

The queen turns to him.

"Gather the corpses. Prepare for us to return to the city at once."

She gestures to the pile of ash with her hoof.

"Ensure that each of these horns is accounted for. If so much as one goes missing before we reach the city, I will personally skin you alive."

The general nods.

"Yes, my queen. But what of the wounded? The dying?"

He struggles to find the proper words.

"Our blood has been spilled before, but… never like this. I am uncertain of the proper procedure here."

The queen does not hesitate.

"Allow them their valiant deaths. They have served me well. They deserve such."

The general continues.

"And what of those that may survive?"

Queen Marika, too, continues.

"Even if we were to heal them, they would never return to their prime. They would be far too weak to serve any purpose."

After a moment, the general replies.

"Then what would you have me do?"

Queen Marika responds.

"Kill them yourself."

The general nods.

Queen Marika walks off.

The general turns to his knights.

"Alright! You heard the queen! Prepare the dead for return to the city! Put down any wounded you find! And make sure each of these artifacts is guarded closely! We will perform a sweep of the kingdom upon exit to wipe out any remaining civilians."

The knights stand idle, many still processing the carnage before them.

The general raises his voice.

"What are you waiting for? *Get to it!*"

On command, the knights calmly disperse. Horns glow faint blue. Corpses are levitated and organized.

Every few moments, a pained gargle emanates from one of the mortally wounded before they, too, are levitated and stacked with the rest of the corpses.

The general steps a few paces, approaching a dead knight nearby. His own horn glows a bright blue, preparing to lift the body.

The muzzle, smashed and torn to pieces, leaves a wet, gaping hole at the front of the face. Thick grafts of skin are torn free from muscle throughout its neck and shoulders. Eerily, its entire lower jaw remains intact… minus a handful of missing teeth.

Poor soul.

The corpse forces a wet cough.

The glow fades from the general's horn in surprise. He takes a step back instinctively.

The bloodshot eye of the knight looks up to him. Speech barely discernible, he utters a single word.

"General…?"

A loud *crash* — the sound of shattered glass — rings out from within the castle.

The general snaps to attention. The unicorn knights do the same. Queen Marika raises an eyebrow.

The sound of footsteps echoes from the hall adjacent, their sound rapidly approaching.

Queen Marika readies herself for another attack. Her knights – and general – do the same.

From the hallway, a young boy emerges. Dressed in a lavish set of travel clothes, he appears no older than ten. His ears — tips sharply pointed — dig into his messy blond hair.

He freezes in place at the sight of the unicorns, unable to comprehend so much carnage. He stands in silent stillness, terrified even to breathe. The gaze of every unicorn in the room rests solely upon him. A dark moisture spreads at the front of his pants.

Queen Marika steps forward, approaching.

"Well, well, well… Who might you be?"
The boy says nothing.
The queen lowers her head toward him.
"What's your name?"
The boy begins to quiver.
She leans closer.
"Don't worry. You'll tell me your name. In fact, I think you're going to tell me a whole bunch of things."
Wordless tears gather at the corners of his eyes.
She turns back, addressing the room.
"I'll deal with this."
She gestures to two knights nearby.
"You two. With me."
They nod, then approach.
She addresses the room once again.
"The rest of you, get back to work. We leave as soon as this business is dealt with."
The commotion of the unicorns resumes. The general turns back to the broken knight before him, still holding on to some small, confused fraction of consciousness. Again, the bloodshot eye of the knight looks up at the general. And again — through globs of muddled flesh — he utters a single word.
"General…?"
The general stares at the wounded knight, not the slightest tinge of empathy. The general raises a single hoof. It — along with his horn — glows green.
"Queen Marika thanks you for your service."
The general stomps on the head of the knight with magical strength, scattering the pulp of his face across an indistinguishable ocean of blood.

Prologue II:
The Torture of
Damon the Prince

Prologue II: The Torture of Damon the Prince

His palms burn. Searing pain courses through them. The weight of his body pulls down hard against the nails that drive through his hands. That keep him bound to the wall. Blood flows down his arms. It gathers at his torso. Drips over the rest of his body. Stains his soiled clothes.

Dried tears taint his cheeks.

Dried snot taints his upper lip.

His upper lip quivers.

His feet do not touch the ground.

He aches.

Queen Marika towers in front of him. A single unicorn knight stands idle each end of the hallway. The flames of torches dance along the stone wall. The boy watches their dance, the moment providing some brief bit of mental escape.

The queen steps forward.

The boy's eyes snap to hers.

She grins.

"I think you and I are about to get *very* acquainted. And I think acquaintances should get to know each other. So, answer me this…"

She leans closer.

"Who are you?"

The boy attempts to speak. The rapid trembling of his body — the incessant quivering of his lip — the sob between every word — forces a stutter.

"I'm… I'm…"

Queen Marika remains unmoved.

"Stop crying, or I make it worse for you."

The boy forces composure. He struggles to hold eye contact.

"I'm Prince Damon. My father is King Astani."

The queen replies.

"Oh, sweet child… your father is dead. I killed him."

An impossible shock takes hold of Prince Damon's face. The sheer disbelief nearly purges the pain from his mind… but after a moment, its heat comes rocketing back, reminding him of where he is.

Queen Marika speaks once more.

"I've always thought parents were close to their children. Fathers and sons, especially. Always telling each other all sorts of things."

She cocks her head to the side.

"Did your father ever tell *you* any sorts of things?"

Prince Damon takes a moment to reply.

"I… don't know."

Queen Marika maintains her uncomfortable closeness.

"Surely you must know *something*. To tell you the truth, I'm really quite fascinated by that sword of his. Where it came from. How he made it. Being that you're his son, well… I find it hard to believe you know *nothing*. I suggest you spill what secrets you know, before I spill *you* all over the floor."

Prince Damon replies, wasting no time.

"I don't know! I promise! He told me only grown-ups could be in the club! He wouldn't let me join!"

The queen raises an eyebrow.

"The club? Do you speak of the Legion?"

The prince nods.

Queen Marika chuckles.

"We hunted them down when we first entered the city. Time was of the essence, you know. So many of them refused to talk. So many of them were eager to die."

She sighs.

"No, my boy, I'm afraid you're the only one left. Your people have been slain. So you're going to have to give me a little more than that."

She wraps her mouth around the hand of Prince Damon. Her slimy, leathery tongue slides across his fingers with intent — with force — almost moving them into place. She pulls his thumb between her teeth. She clamps down hard, pulling and tearing away. He feels — *hears* — his skin *snap*.

Prince Damon screams. Unable to resist, his eyes flick over to his hand: a pulsing, mangled stump where his thumb once was.

Queen Marika spits the bloody thumb onto the ground.

"Like wet clay between my teeth."

The screams of the prince turn to sobs. He forces words.

"I don't know anything! I don't know anything! I don't know anything!"

The queen shakes her head.

"I disagree."

She steps close. She places her bloody lips over the young prince's hand.

He writhes in protest. He begs her to stop. He knows what's to come.

Queen Marika slides his index finger into place with her tongue, holding it between her teeth. She clamps down, pulling away. The wet *snap* of skin follows.

Queen Marika spits the bloody finger onto the ground.

The prince screams.

Amid this, the queen licks the blood from her lips.

"Everyone knows *something*. So… tell me what you know."

The prince struggles to bottle his shrieks. But, after a moment, he does.

"I don't know magic! I don't know swords! I don't know *anything!*"

The queen frowns.

"You are testing my patience, young prince."

She takes a breath.

"I will count down from eight to one. I suggest you jog your memory."

She leans in close, her voice dropping below a whisper.

"You won't like if I get to one."

She leans over to the prince's hand, wrapping her mouth around it.

The prince shrieks.

Muffled only slightly, Queen Marika speaks.

"Eight."

She bites. Skin and bone *snap* like an apple. She spits out the finger disgracefully. Blood spills from the stumps on the prince's left hand, its position locked to the wall by the nail that pierces it.

The queen wraps her lips around the prince's bleeding hand.

"Seven."

She bites. Flesh *snaps*. She tears away. She spits the finger to the ground.

Blood cascades down the prince's palm.

The queen wraps her lips around the prince's bleeding hand.

Futily, he bends his pinky away. The queen forces it between her teeth with her tongue.

"Six."

She bites. The *snap* is almost deafening. The blood of the prince paints his palm a deep, unsettling red. The queen spits the finger to the ground.

The prince continues to scream.

The queen walks to his other hand, intentionally drawing out the moment. The sound of her hooves echoes. With a mere moment of respite, he forces himself to speak.

"I don't know anything! Stop, stop! *Please!*"

The queen wraps her lips around the prince's other hand. She slots his thumb between her teeth with her tongue.

"Five."

She bites. She tears the thumb away. Blood pours from the place where it once was. She spits it onto the ground.

The prince — more frantic — forces speech again.

"Stop! Please! I'll do anything! I'll do *anything!*"

The queen wraps her lips around the prince's bleeding hand. Her viscous saliva mixes with his blood. She forces his index finger between her teeth with her tongue, it, too, now coated in the blood of the prince.

"Four."

She bites. It *snaps*. She rips it away. She spits it onto the floor.

The prince speaks, hysterics taking over.

"Please, please, please! Stop! Stop! *Stop!*"

There is no one to listen.

The queen wraps her lips around the prince's bleeding hand. She forces his middle finger between her teeth.

"Three."

She bites. The skin *snaps*. The prince howls in anguish. The queen spits the finger onto the floor.

The prince — desperate — speaks again.

"Please! I'll help! I'll help you! *I'll do anything!*"

The queen wraps her lips around the prince's bleeding hand. She forces his ring finger between her teeth with her tongue.

"Two."

She bites. The finger *snaps*. The prince howls.

Sanity cast aside, the prince screams.

"STOP!"

The queen wraps her lips around the prince's bleeding hand. The blood pouring out from his ragged stumps trails down his arms, painting both a deep red. She forces the prince's pinky between her teeth.

"One."

She bites. The finger *snaps*. The prince weeps.

Queen Marika takes a step back. She locks eyes with the prince. She spits the finger onto the ground.

"You've caught me in a good mood. All things considered, today has been a pretty good day. So, I'm going to give you one last chance. *Tell me what you know.*"

Through rapid, pained breaths, the prince speaks.

"I told you, I don't know anything…"

Snot — fresh — drips from his nose.

"No one told me anything…"

The queen shakes her head.

"Shame. And we were just getting to know each other."

She looks to her knights.

"Take him down and hold him to the floor."

The prince wails in protest. The bleeding stumps of his hands flex slightly, a subconscious attempt to form fists.

The two unicorn knights approach. Their horns glow blue, as do the nails holding Prince Damon to the wall. The nails tear from his flesh.

He drops to the floor.

He scrambles to his feet. He runs. His empty palms clasp together, an attempt to wrap his fingers around his wounds.

Queen Marika's cold voice chills him.

"Running will get you nowhere."

The air around Prince Damon glows blue. His legs yank out from under him. His face impacts the heavy stone with a loud *crack*. Blood pours from his nose.

The prince's body drags across the floor. He returns to the unicorns, the knights with their horns glowing blue. The prince paws at the floor to no avail. Against his own will, his body flips over, placing him onto his back. He stares up at the unicorns above him.

He is *mortified*.

The blue glow fades. Each knight places a firm hoof on the prince's chest, pinning him down.

His arms and legs flail violently.

He does not move an inch.

Queen Marika stares down at him.

"Let's make sure you don't run off again."

She leans down toward his kicking legs. Prince Damon throws a pitiful kick in her direction. She catches his foot in her mouth. She clamps down, splintering bone. She slides higher up the leg. She stops at his lower thigh, gripping it tight with her teeth. With all of her strength, she pulls.

Prince Damon feels the heavy strain of his muscles doing everything in his power to resist.

Then he feels the tear.

A thunderous wet *rip* echoes through the hall. Blood — rapidly pooling — gathers around the prince's waist. His mind rings, a mental static overtaking conscious thoughts. Looming over him – just a few paces away – Queen Marika holds the dismembered leg of the prince in her mouth.

She drops it to the ground.

"I don't suppose we want you hobbling off either, now do we?"

With his frantic vitality greatly diminished, the queen grips the prince's remaining leg in her mouth.

The knights continue keeping weight on the chest of the prince.

The queen pulls.

A thunderous wet *rip* echoes once more. Prince Damon hardly notices more than the heavy strain — the burning, pulling pressure — quickly followed by the lack of it. The blood around his waist creeps up, the pool now drenching his back.

Queen Marika drops the leg of the prince from her mouth. Blood paints her lips. It spills between them as she speaks.

"It's a shame, really."

She walks over to the side of Prince Damon. Her hooves lightly *splash* in the blood, dotting the prince in red speckles.

"I thought we were *great* acquaintances."

She leans down, wrapping her lips around the forearm of the prince. She pulls once again. The heavy wet *rip* rattles the prince's ears.

He can almost feel himself floating. Floating softly in a warm, red ocean. Nothing but the water and the breeze. The water and the breeze.

The breath from Queen Marika feels almost like a breeze. At his other side now, she firmly clamps her mouth around his other forearm. Another forceful, heavy pull. The muscle begins to fray. The skin begins to tear. Queen Marika's back hoof slips in the blood.

She steadies herself at once, but drops the arm from her mouth.

She shakes her head.

"Little ones are always such a mess."

She places her mouth back over the broken, bloodied arm. She pulls, This time, it rips free, leaving the prince with nothing more than a mangled, twisted stump.

Queen Marika drops the arm from her mouth. She stares down at the bleeding prince below her.

She frowns.

"I thought I told you to stop crying."

That phrase rattled around in the prince's head. Stop crying? She told him to stop crying? *Was* he crying?

The prince realized his mouth was wide open. He realized a primal, guttural shriek was belting out of it. The pain of his torment had been so great, the prince failed to realize he had been screaming.

Queen Marika leans down, sticking her face up to the prince's. She forces her snout deep within his mouth, stretching it far beyond normal capacity. The prince feels the texture of her muzzle under his teeth; the taste of her breath in the back of his throat. The cuts on her face pass under his lips. The smallest bit of blood from her wounds enters his own body. Prince Damon — barely clinging to consciousness — notices a sudden taste of cotton candy.

The queen grips the boy's jaw in her own. In a slow, forceful motion, she tears it away from his face. His tongue rips out behind it.

She drops it to the ground. It splashes in the blood below. The young prince — soaking in a pool of his own blood, surrounded by the ragged flesh of his own torn limbs — closes his eyes.

Queen Marika – face drenched in blood – turns to her knights.

"Our work here is done. Inform the general of our lack of intel from the boy. If you find any survivors on departure, have them brought to me. Alive is mandatory. Whole is optional. Let us not waste time. We have a kingdom to return to."

She takes a breath.

"…and I'm told my daughter wants gingerbread."

She sighs.

"Again."

Both knights nod. They walk off, heading back toward the throne room.

Queen Marika takes one last look at the broken, bloody prince.

"Long live the king."

She leaves, following her knights.

The dying mind of the young prince drifts away on the warm, welcoming waves of a comforting red ocean, its breeze lulling him to rest.

— — — — — — — — — — — — — — — —

Warmth. A gentle, pleasing warmth. Warmth on the eyelids. A light. A soft light. A warm light. Light on the eyelids. Warm light on the eyelids. Eyelids. Eyes closed. Bird sounds. Bird sounds far in the distance. Iron. An iron smell. A stale iron smell. A bad smell. More bird sounds. Pretty bird sounds. Warm light on the eyelids. Getting warmer. Brighter. More bad iron smell. Stone. Stone below. More bird sounds. More light. Sunlight.

Prince Damon opens his eyes.

He wishes he hadn't.

He looks down. Far below him — far away from him — he sees his arms. His legs. Their skin, dried from the sun, is mostly red. Crusted red. Even from here, he can see flies. Flies buzz around them.

He looks to his left. He can see the thick, crusty red residue that surrounds him. The bad iron smell. Against the far wall, he sees his fingers. What are likely his fingers, anyway. It's hard to tell. His vision is blurry. Mostly blurry. Why? What happened?

He can't move.

He *tries* to move.

But he can't.

Why?

He looks down again. He sees his arms. His legs. He looks to his own body. He has no legs. He looks to his left, his right. He has no arms. But the bleeding stopped. He isn't bleeding. But he has no arms. He has no legs. What is this?

He calls for help. But there is no call for help. He tries again louder. A soft popping noise — barely audible — comes from his throat. But no words. No volume. Why? What is this?

He tries once more. Another quiet popping noise. He tries again. Another popping noise. He tries again. The noise repeats. He can't feel his tongue.

He looks back to his left. He sees a crusty red clump of flesh.

He looks back to his right. He has an arm.

No.

Not an arm.

He focuses on the spot. His vision — by the smallest amount — begins to clear up.

Not quite an elbow. That's what he has. Not an arm. And not quite an elbow. But it's *something*.

He tries to move it. It twitches.

He tries to move it again. It twitches more dramatically. More precisely.

He tries once more. It moves.

It's not an arm.

Not even up to the elbow.

But it *moves*.

He pushes it against the floor. He feels the thick, crusted surface at the end of it.

He pushes against the floor harder.

He moves.

It was barely noticeable. Barely perceivable. Maybe to other passersby, sure, but not to him. He notices things that others don't. Perceives things that others don't.

Why? What happened? What is this?

He pushes against the floor with his appendage once more. He moves again. Very slightly. Very, *very* slightly. Quite possibly the smallest movement a living thing could possibly make. But he *did* move. Is he a living thing? Is he alive?

He pushes against the floor again. His body turns by a fraction of a fraction of the smallest of smallest movements. Is he alive?

He pushes again.

At the far corner of his vision — not visible before, but visible now, thanks to the slightest of turns of his body — he sees the rancid remains of his lower jaw.

And he remembers.

He pushes against the floor, making the first of a thousand movements toward the throne room at the end of the hall.

He remembers his father telling him to leave. To say his goodbyes. To never speak of him again.

He pushes against the floor.

He remembers sneaking back into the castle. He remembers hearing screams. He remembers being scared. He remembers hiding in his room.

He pushes against the floor.

He remembers seeing a unicorn break into his room. He remembers being terrified. He remembers the horn buried deep within its eye. He remembers it, too, being terrified. He remembers it leaping through the window. He remembers the sound of breaking glass.

He pushes against the floor.

He remembers fleeing from his room at the sound. He remembers the fear of what might happen if his father found him. He remembers running down the hall. He remembers seeing the room full of blood. He remembers seeing the room full of unicorns.

He pushes against the floor.

He remembers the vile stench of iron. He remembers the uncomfortable feeling of pissing himself. He remembers being told to be brave. He remembers his father telling him to be brave. He remembers not being brave.

He pushes against the floor.

He remembers being nailed to the wall. He remembers the stench of the breath of the unicorn. He remembers wanting to have known something. He remembers losing all of his fingers. He remembers the torture.

He pushes against the floor.

He remembers trying to run. He remembers breaking his nose. He remembers being dragged across the floor. He remembers his legs being ripped from his body. He remembers his arms being ripped from his body. He remembers the torture.

He pushes against the floor.

He remembers the unicorn sticking its mouth into his. He remembers the unicorn clamping its jaw around his. He remembers his lips feel the cuts of her face. He remembers the taste of cotton candy.

He pushes against the floor.

He remembers the taste of cotton candy. He remembers the sweetness. He remembers the surprise at tasting it. He remembers the taste of cotton candy.

Why? What is this? Is he alive?

He pushes against the floor.

Someone would find him. He knows someone would find him. No, someone *will* find him. He knows someone will find him. He just has to get to the city. If he gets to the city, someone will find him. Someone will help him. This will all be over when he gets to the city. This nightmare will end when he gets to the city. Someone will find him. Someone will help him.

No.

He pushes against the floor.

He remembers the screams. He remembers the fire. He remembers the bloodshed. He remembers the sounds of the dying.

The city is dead.

The kingdom is dead.

His father is dead.

The Legion is dead.

He is not dead.

Why? What is this? Is he alive?

No one will help him.

No one will find him.

No one will ever find him.

No one will ever come looking for him.

He is not dead.

He pushes against the floor.

He remembers the unicorns. He remembers the screams. He remembers the fire. He remembers the bloodshed. He remembers the sounds of the dying. He remembers the torture. He remembers waking up with no arms or legs and not being able to move.

He remembers the unicorns.

He pushes against the floor.

He hates the unicorns.
He pushes against the floor.
He hates the unicorns.
He pushes against the floor.
He hates the unicorns. He hates the unicorns. He hates the unicorns. He hates the unicorns. He hates the unicorns. He hates the unicorns.

He pushes against the floor.

Prologue III:
The Flight of the Coward Petunia

Prologue III: The Flight of the Coward Petunia

King Astani feels the pierce of the horn in his back.
More knights approach from the corner of his vision.
With his free hand, he firmly grasps a horn from his
belt. He tears it free.

He reaches behind him, stabbing the horn into the
eye of the knight that pierced him.

Petunia recoils, dropping the king. The horn glows
within her eye socket. She backs away, shaking her head
violently in an attempt to dislodge it. But it remains.

The horn — its magic — *burns*.

Petunia stumbles away, heading down the nearest
hall she finds.

Anything to get away from the chaos. From the
danger. From the blood of her people.

Behind her, the battle rages on. Its ambience rings
in her ears. She feels the deep pulse of the horn in her
eye. It fills her with dread. With *panic*.

Unicorns are fearless. Nearly invincible.
Long-lived, and well-known for it. As long as she has
been alive — as long as *any* unicorn has been alive —
there has *never* been carnage like this.

Disbelief carried her to the front lines, but the
searing heat from the horn in her eye would allow it to
carry no further.

Behind her, the sound of an electric blast *explodes*
out. Crackling blue light spills into the hall.

She takes a single, panicked glance. She sees the king's magical defenses at work. She sees the frightful blue beam of what must be her queen.

And it scares her.

She turns back around, stumbling ever forward.

Dizziness fights to take hold of her. She fights it back. Nausea arises. She pushes through. All the while, she hears a subtle, sourceless *hum*, seemingly deep from within her own skull.

How did the king — a human man — come to possess a weapon that can kill the unkillable? That can slay those who cannot be slain? Did he forge it? Did he find it? Did he steal it? How many unicorns died by that blade? How many did it take to acquire those horns? How did he know how to use them?

She continues down the hall. Disoriented, she bumps into the stone wall. She quickly corrects herself.

Her heart jumps at the thought of falling here. Of falling *now*. The glowing horn pulses in her head. It *burns*. But she continues.

Unicorns do not tolerate weakness. In knights, it is trained out of them. But through all recorded history — *their* recorded history — unicorns have never been mortally wounded. Never been challenged. Never been killed. Not like this.

And it scares her.

Unicorns do not tolerate weakness.

Queen Marika does not tolerate weakness.

What will they do if she cannot be healed?

They will kill her.

Surely, they will kill her.

Death feels more like a myth. A distant landmark. An idea of an idea, separated by an ocean of time. Something talked about. Something acknowledged. But never feared. Not by unicorns. Not before today. Not before now.

Petunia does not want to die.

She gallops down the hall. Her eyes dart frantically. She needs a hiding place.

No. Not a hiding place. The knights will surely sweep the castle. They have their tactics of preference, and she knows them all too well. Hiding will do nothing. She will be found. She will be killed.

She needs to escape.

Echoing from the throne room — far behind her now — she hears the powerful voice of her queen.

"ENOUGH!"

She does not dare look back.

The voice of her queen is rarely enraged. Hearing it terrifies her. She knows not the state of the battle, but it is behind her now.

It will be farther behind her soon.

The horn still glows. Still pulses. Still hurts.

She needs to run.

So she runs.

She stops at the end of the hall.

There is no grand staircase. No quick escape. No clear means of descent. Only more halls. More locked doors. More useless rooms with no ways out.

The ambient warfare continues. Even with that weapon — even with those horns — the human king cannot win. Surely, he knows this is suicide.

Though, just a few hours ago, she was certain no unicorn could ever be slain by mortal hands.

She is running out of time.

She can feel it.

She can *sense* it.

She kicks the door nearest. It does not open.

She kicks it again. Its wood *creaks*, bending out of shape. But it does not open.

She kicks it again. The hinges *snap*. And it opens.

Nothing but storage.

She kicks the next door, more weight behind her
hoof. Its wood splinters. It swings forcefully.

Useless fucking storage.

More blue lights spills into the hall from the throne
room. Petunia does not bother to look. She moves to the
next door, desperate. Even from where she stands, the
voice of the king carries down the hall.

"You do not know torment."

She kicks the door. This one is locked. Barricaded.

"You do not know suffering."

She kicks it again. The wood *cracks*. It bends out
of shape.

"But I will rape it into you."

Her horn — her own horn — begins to glow the
same color as the one in her eye. For the briefest
moment, her hooves, too, glow white.

She does not notice.

She kicks again.

The door flies off its hinges, clattering to the floor,
masked wholly by the battle raging on. The glow from
her own horn — from her hooves — fades.

This room looks larger. Safer.

Without hesitation, she runs inside.

But there are no stairs here. No exits. No clever
hiding places. With her one good eye — her *only* eye —
she hurriedly scans the room.

She sees a large bed built low to the ground. She
sees an intricately carved wardrobe against the far wall.
She sees the heavy wooden nightstand — now thrown
to the floor, chipped at its edge — that was formerly
blocking the door. She sees an excessive stained glass
window in the wall of the room. She sees a tiny human
boy — no older than ten — trembling in the corner of
the room, eyes glued firmly to her. He wears a set of
travel clothes, as if dressed for a comfortable journey.

His arms — trembling — point the blade of a wooden toy sword her direction.

The two stare at each other wordlessly, both deathly afraid of the other.

The glowing horn throbs in Petunia's eye socket. She wishes it would stop glowing. She wishes it would stop hurting.

But it throbs. And it glows. And it hurts.

Petunia's ears perk up.

The sounds of war have stopped.

How long has it been? Has the king been slain? Have her people been slain? Do they know she is missing? Do they know she is alive? Are they looking for her? Are they going to kill her?

Yes.

Petunia leaps through the stained glass window.

It *shatters.*

The noise echoes throughout the walls of the very castle. She does not look back. But she does look down. And she realizes that the stairs to the throne room do not do the height proper justice.

She is very high up.

Was very high up.

She crashes to the ground.

Her legs buckle and fold under the weight of her body, all breaking and *snapping* on impact.

Broken bones dig through her skin from inside of it. Blood seeps out through the tears.

She has never seen her own blood before.

And it scares her.

She feels the pain from the breaks. She feels the horn in her eye. She feels the rain on her body.

She is cold.

She looks to her legs. Hard to see with just one eye, but the glowing horn provides some light. She wishes it would glow brighter. Just a little bit brighter.

Then it would be easier to see. And in this moment, she almost swears that it does. But it matters not. The rain continues to fall around her, chilling her body with every drop.

She is colder.

Her horn — the one she was born with — glows a soft, embracing yellow. She focuses intently on her leg. Her front left leg. Healing magic takes longer. Always does. She needs to focus.

She hears commotion from the open window of the castle. She needs to hurry. They will kill her. Magic does not hurry, but she wishes it would.

The horn in her eye socket mimics the glow.

She hears an unnatural *snapping*, like the sound of the break in reverse. She feels the broken bones force their jagged edges back into place. She watches the bits of bone move under her skin, each fragment slotting back into position.

It should not have been this fast.

But it was.

And it is.

Petunia's leg is healed.

Her ears perk up. She hears distant screams from above. She does not know who they belong to. But it does not concern her. She needs to run.

She feels the chill of each raindrop smack against her body. She feels the tips of her mane stick with the cold, clammy moisture. She needs to focus. She needs to heal. She needs to run.

She feels colder.

Her sense of touch begins to dull.

She focuses intently on her leg. Her front right leg. She hears more screaming within the castle. She hears the unnatural *snapping* again. She watches — *feels* — the broken bones' movement within her.

Petunia's leg is healed.

The screaming from the castle has stopped. She does not know when it stopped. She hears commotion, but no screaming. Not anymore. She is running out of time. She knows it.

She needs to run.

She focuses intently on her leg. Her back left leg. Both horns glow soothing yellow. A clearly visible yellow glow. One that could be seen from great distances in this darkness, even if dim from afar.

She needs to focus.

She needs to heal.

She needs to run.

She feels the broken bones rearrange under her skin. Hears their sounds. Feels the relief at their healing.

Petunia's leg is healed.

But she feels ever colder.

She needs to run.

She hears movement at the front of the castle. The steady *clack* of hooves. The gentle clattering of worn armor. Muffled notes of conversation.

The knights are emerging.

She wishes the horn in her eye would stop glowing so brightly. But it does not dim.

She hears knights converse. More of them now. Outside of the castle.

She digs her horn — the one in her eye — deep into the dirt. She feels the pressure push against her skull as she forces it into the soil. She feels it scratching at the inside of the top of her head.

She forces it further into the wet ground. The horn sticks deep into the mud, its glow masked almost completely. The yellow glow of her own horn — the one in her head — fades as she relaxes her magic.

Now she waits.

For the voices to leave.

For the commotion to pass.

She feels colder.

She is so close to freedom.

So tantalizingly close.

And still, she feels colder.

The rain on her skin dulls her senses even further.

Oh, how she wishes to flee. To simply run from here. From her death. From the cruelty of this great power she inherited. She wants to run. She needs to run. She wishes to run.

She feels colder.

Her broken leg *snaps* back into place.

It hurts. It hurts greatly. It hurts far more than it did to break it.

But it is healed.

Petunia does not understand.

But she does not need to understand.

So she stands.

And she runs.

And the mud does not fall from her horn — the one buried deep in her eye — until she is miles beyond the valley. And she does not rest until she is more than a day's journey beyond that. And the horn in her eye continues to glow.

And she lives.

Chapter I:
Princess Pipsy's Dreamland

Chapter I: Princess Pipsy's Dreamland

White nothingness. An endless expanse. Air, but no sky. Wind, but no ground. A cool, distant softness, almost like a heavy blanket. Far beyond the nothingness, a sourceless, muffled voice. It does not speak aloud. Its words enter the mind without speech. Its speaker — masked by the thick veil of nothingness — has no identity. No face. No cadence.

"We will rest."

Nothingness fades to somethingness. The sound of the wind grows closer.

No, not wind.

Waves.

A lone unicorn rests on the sand. The foam of a soft wave rolls over her body; its water brushes across her white-gray coat. With the water's recession, the black hair of her mane, too, pulls back, only to be returned as the next wave washes over her. Her prominent horn — silver, like the purest metal — glistens in the sunlight.

Another wave washes over her.

Her eyelids flutter. She opens them.

Sluggish, she stands.

She feels the warmth of the sun on her skin. The streaks of cool water falling from her body. The grains of sand beneath her hooves.

The dream has repeated.

Further down the beach — the sands of which seem to spread for eternity — a figure moves. Something small. It almost matches the color of the sand.

The unicorn approaches.

The small figure trudges forward. Its tiny feet leave footprints in the sand. Waving lines of white border the edges of its body. Three small circles of solid color — blue, green, and yellow — stick tight to its chest in a vertical line. The features of its face — eyes and mouth, but no nose — are, too, made of white.

This is a gingerbread man.

It pays the unicorn no mind. It hums tunelessly to itself. Strangely, not a single grain of sand sticks to its surface. It trudges onward.

The unicorn — as she always does — speaks.

"Who are you?"

The gingerbread man does not reply. It trudges onward.

The unicorn speaks again.

"Where am I?"

The gingerbread man does not reply. It trudges onward.

The unicorn — anger building in her voice — speaks once more.

"Answer me!"

The gingerbread man does not reply. It trudges onward.

The unicorn frowns, irritated beyond measure. She kicks the back of the gingerbread man with her front hoof. It shatters instantly. Pieces scatter across the sand.

Somethingness fades to nothingness. A white expanse engulfs all.

— — — — — — — — — — — — — — — —

White nothingness. An endless expanse. Air, but no sky. Wind, but no ground. A cool, distant softness, almost like a heavy blanket. Far beyond the nothingness, a sourceless, muffled voice. Its speaker — masked by the thick veil of nothingness — has no identity. No face. No cadence.

"Time is not an issue."

Nothingness fades to somethingness. The sound of the wind grows closer.

No, not wind.

Waves.

A lone unicorn rests on the sand. The foam of a soft wave rolls over her body; its water brushes across her white-gray coat. With the water's recession, the black hair of her mane, too, pulls back, only to be returned as the next wave washes over her. Her prominent horn — silver, like the purest metal — glistens in the sunlight.

Another wave washes over her.

Her eyelids flutter. She opens them.

Sluggish, she stands.

She feels the warmth of the sun on her skin. The streaks of cool water falling from her body. The grains of sand beneath her hooves.

The dream has repeated.

Further down the beach — the sands of which seem to spread for eternity — a figure moves. Something small. It almost matches the color of the sand.

The unicorn approaches.

The small gingerbread man trudges forward. Its tiny feet leave footprints in the sand. It pays the unicorn no mind, humming tunelessly to itself. Strangely, not a single grain of sand sticks to its surface. In its arms — outstretched — it carries a small bundle of tiny, chopped firewood.

The unicorn — as she always does — speaks.

"Who are you?"

The gingerbread man does not reply. It trudges onward.

The unicorn speaks again.

"Where am I?"

The gingerbread man does not reply. It trudges onward.

The unicorn — anger building in her voice — speaks once more.

"Answer me!"

The gingerbread man does not reply. It trudges onward.

The unicorn frowns, irritated beyond measure. She kicks the back of the gingerbread man with her front hoof. It does not shatter. The firewood in its hands does not fall. As though having kicked an immovable wall, her hoof simply stops at its back.

The gingerbread man stops walking. Its humming silences. It turns, facing the unicorn. Its voice — a deep, heavy voice — speaks into the very mind.

"You are mistaken. You are forgotten. You are without burden."

It continues.

"I am on this beach."

It continues.

"You cannot answer what has not been asked."

The gingerbread man turns back around. It trudges forward once more, heading further down the beach.

Somethingness fades to nothingness. A white expanse engulfs all.

— — — — — — — — — — — — — — —

White nothingness. An endless expanse. Air, but no sky. Wind, but no ground.

No, not wind.

Waves.

Far beyond the nothingness, a sourceless, muffled voice. Its speaker — masked by the thick veil of nothingness — has no identity. No face. No cadence.

"As long as it takes."

Nothingness fades to somethingness.

A lone unicorn rests on the sand. The foam of a soft wave rolls over her body.

Her eyelids flutter. She opens them.

Sluggish, she stands. The smell of smoke wafts in her direction.

The dream has repeated.

Further down the beach — the sands of which seem to spread for eternity — a large figure sits by a roaring campfire. The figure — a gingerbread man — pokes at the campfire with a long wooden stick.

The unicorn approaches.

Now at the figure, it matches the unicorn's height, if not surpasses it. The campfire, too, seems quite large. Or, perhaps, the unicorn is small. It is impossible to tell.

The gingerbread man pays the unicorn no mind. It pokes and prods at the campfire, its eyes watching the dance of the flames.

The unicorn — as she always does — speaks.

"What is this?"

She stares at the gingerbread man.

The voice of the gingerbread man — a deep, heavy voice — speaks into the very mind.

"This is a dream."

The gingerbread man pokes at the fire.

The unicorn speaks again.

"Why can't I remember anything?"

The gingerbread man replies.

"I have no memory."

The unicorn — anger building in her voice — speaks once more.

"What's your fucking problem?"

The gingerbread man stops poking the fire. Its eyes meet the unicorn's.

"Anger management."

The unicorn blinks a few times.

"I'm sorry?"

The gingerbread man replies.

"I will be."

The wooden stick catches fire. The flames spread rapidly along the length of the stick, reaching the arm of the gingerbread man. At once, its body ignites. Its frosting slowly melts, dripping from its form. Eyes still trained on the unicorn, the frosting of its lips falls away as it speaks.

"I will not know. I will not remember."

Irritated, the unicorn speaks.

"Can you stop with the riddles?"

The gingerbread man burns. His body chars. Blackened fragments of cookie crumble away. He responds.

"I will not know."

The head of the gingerbread man *snaps*, falling forward into the raging campfire. Its flames climb ever higher.

The world around the unicorn, too, climbs higher. Grows taller. Larger. Farther. Grander. Expansive. Incomprehensible.

The sands below the unicorn swirl. She sinks. Her knees lower into the shifting sands.

The beach grows longer. The sands grow coarser. The flames grow higher.

Within the fire, the head of the gingerbread man speaks again.

"I will not know."

As if pulled, the unicorn sinks below the sands in an instant. The waves of the beach crash onto each other. The head of the gingerbread man crumbles to ash. The world folds in on itself.

— — — — — — — — — — — — — — — —

Princess Pipsy's eyes shoot open. She jolts forward. The armor on her body — a fitted chestplate, bracers on her legs, thin rings of metal around her neck — *rattles* with the movement. Her eyes dart around the room. She takes in her surroundings.

A tall, imposing window on the wall in front of her. Sunlight shines through. Walls of beautiful, flush stonework around her. Wooden stands behind her, all adorned with various intricate armors, excluding a couple farthest to the left. A grand wooden door seals this chamber away from whatever lies beyond it. Next to the window, a tall, ornate mirror — gorgeous silver — rests.

Princess Pipsy walks up to the mirror.

She stares into her own eyes.

"What the *fuck* just happened?"

Chapter II:
Unicornicopia

Chapter II: Unicornicopia

The sound of commotion — of conversations; of confusion; of movement — enters the chamber from the barely-open window.

Princess Pipsy peers out of it.

The sun sits high in the sky. Its light reflects off the wondrous curvature of buildings below. Magnificent domes of illustrious silver cap the tops of many such buildings. Smooth stones — white-gray in coloration, perfectly flush — make up the wide roads of the city, staircases connecting them to each other. Rounded edges appear on every structure.

Princess Pipsy — wherever she stands now — seems to be placed at the very center of it all.

Around the city, a fortified wall of metal and stone forms a barrier. At the far end, two massive metal gates seal off the city from a long, descending stone bridge that touches down to the beach of the shore, its resemblance striking to the one from her dream.

Hundreds of feet below the city, the sound of crashing waves endlessly repeats. A pristine base of gorgeous stone holds the city high above such waves.

From within buildings, unicorns wander into the streets, most aimless. The sound of worried conversations grows louder. Few notice the face of the princess in the window.

What happened?

Knock, knock, knock from the bottom of the chamber door. Princess Pipsy steps back from the window. A familiar feminine voice — a learned wisdom behind its words — speaks from beyond the door.

"Hello? Is anyone in there?"

Princess Pipsy responds.

"Yes. I'm here."

The door pushes open. An older unicorn stands on the other side. Her braided brown mane curls behind her neck. Subtle brown speckles dot her coat, itself a muted rose gray. From the center of her forehead, her horn protrudes, a light gray-brown color. She stands considerably taller than the princess.

Princess Pipsy voices her concern.

"Aster? What's going on?"

Aster — the other unicorn — speaks.

"We need to talk."

She steps into the hall beyond the door.

"Please, come with me."

Princess Pipsy follows.

Decorative displays of elegant armor and weaponry line the walls. Sunlight illuminates the space from tall, open windows looking out to the city below. The two unicorns continue ahead, each at a hurried pace reserved for uncertainty.

Aster speaks.

"I've been looking all over for you. The queen is nowhere to be found."

The princess replies.

"That's impossible."

Aster responds.

"I thought the same. But it seems we are living in times of impossibility."

Aster turns the corner. The princess follows.

The two descend a beautiful interior staircase of near-white stone, each of its steps much longer to allow its inhabitants ease of use.

Aster continues.

"I was one of the first to awaken. I witnessed firsthand the paralyzed state of our people. Of our city. Only a few of us were conscious at first, but it quickly became exponential. I imagine the whole city will be awake soon, if they aren't already."

The two continue their descent.

The princess speaks.

"Do we know what happened? Do we know who's done this?"

Aster gently shakes her head.

"We do not. No one can recall anything that happened before… whatever this is. From those I spoke to, there are very concerning gaps in our memories."

Princess Pipsy speaks.

"How long?"

Aster responds.

"Months. Years. Possibly more. We aren't sure."

Princess Pipsy exhales sharply.

"Fuck."

Aster turns to her.

"On that sentiment, we can agree."

The two step off from the staircase and enter the wide atrium of the building's main floor. A long, smooth wooden table sits at the center of the room. Banners of various muted designs hang from the tops of the walls. More displays of armor — worn with scuffs and scratches — rest prominently along the far wall. Maps and scrolls sit strewn across the table, not a speck of dust in sight. Aster and the princess arrive at a towering set of wooden doors.

Aster speaks.

"I've yet to find any other members of the guard, nor any other hands to the queen. For the time being, you and I will have to address the city. Even an acknowledgment of shared confusion should put them at ease."

Princess Pipsy nods.

"To the square, then?"

Aster responds.

"Unless you have any objections, princess."

The princess shakes her head.

"None."

Aster pushes against the doors with her snout. Slowly, they open, creaking gently. More sunlight spills in from beyond, the sound of worry and confusion along with it.

Princess Pipsy raises an eyebrow.

"Why so archaic?"

Aster looks back.

"Our magic, princess. It's gone."

Aster steps out into the city.

The princess follows.

The two walk through the wide city street with intent, heading eastward in the direction of the gates. Unicorns around them watch closely, most holding conversations of their own. Some – from a respectful distance – begin to follow.

Princess Pipsy voices concern.

"Our magic can't be gone. Just think of what you're saying."

Aster replies.

"I welcome you to try, princess. And I hope you prove me wrong."

Princess Pipsy stops walking.

Aster, too, stops.

The princess focuses intently on the open air in front of her. She furrows her brow. She holds her focus. And she waits.

And nothing happens.

The princess relaxes. A look of shock takes over her face. She makes no attempt to mask it.

"That's impossible."

Aster speaks.

"As I said, princess, it seems we are living in times of impossibility."

Aster resumes walking.

Princess Pipsy forces the shocked expression from her face, recapturing her steady look of determination. She follows. Behind her, more unicorns trail at a distance, whispers of concern growing frequent. Aster and the princess descend a brief staircase, stepping out onto a lower city street.

A masculine voice — gruff; familiar — calls out from somewhere beside them.

"Aster! Princess!"

The two turn.

A unicorn approaches. Several large scars streak down his body from battles long prior. He wears an armor — far more concealing than Princess Pipsy's — adorned with magical runes.

The princess speaks.

"General."

The general continues.

"Do either of you know what's going on?"

Aster shakes her head.

"We do not. None of us can remember what happened. And beyond that, none of us can use any magic."

The general sighs worriedly.

"Fuck."

Aster and the princess — in unison — reply.

"Agreed."

The general looks to the both of them.

"What should we do?"

The princess responds.

"We're heading to the square to give a formal address. Something needs to be said, even if only in acknowledgement."

The general nods.

"Understood. I'll come with you. Should we pass any knights on the way, I'll have them join us."

The trio — Princess Pipsy leading the way, with Aster and the general on either side — makes their way to the city square. As they walk through the main roads of the city, more unicorns, all in varying degrees of worry, follow behind them, now forming a decent crowd.

Every few moments, the general shouts to those around him.

"The princess will be giving a formal address at the city square! Do not panic! Keep your wits about you, and stay alert!"

Another moment passes.

"The princess will be giving a formal address at the city square! Do not panic!…"

The sunlight above would make the streets a beautiful sight, were it not for the confusion and alarm of the unicorns that populate them.

Before long, the trio — Princess Pipsy, Aster, and the general — are followed in their march by a cluster of unicorn knights. And, further beyond that, the growing crowd, too, follows.

The city square, even in times of confusion, seems to radiate beauty and splendor. The white stonework of adjacent buildings surrounds it, the wide roads of the city giving it separation. Short walls of white stone — subtle metalwork incorporated into their designs, the walls themselves no more than a few feet tall — form a series of square barriers, each housing a number of flourishing plants, flowers, and trees, lending the city a splash of refreshing greenery amid the overwhelming white of its architecture. At the center of the city square, an intricately carved fountain of white stone — depicted in which is a triumphant unicorn, its front hooves raised — burbles endlessly. The sound of its flowing water provides a small semblance of calm.

Princess Pipsy enters the square. She stops at the base of the fountain. Aster and the general stand at either side of her. Unicorn knights — a few dozen — step up to position, taking posts along the lining of the city square, facing inward.

The crowd of unicorns — of civilians — enters the square. Their numbers easily reach beyond the hundreds, with more and more joining them every few moments. They fill the square, hushed whispers sporadic among them.

After a few minutes – what seems like an eternity – their voices settle, all eyes on the princess.

She steps forward.

"By now, I'm sure you've all realized something has happened. Something that none of us can seem to remember."

Murmurs of agreement. Some nod.

Princess Pipsy continues.

"And, as I'm sure some of you have noticed…"

She hesitates.

"…we seem to have no access to magic."

Gasps from the crowd. Comments of pure disbelief. Side conversations heavy with concern.

Princess Pipsy raises her voice a bit, speaking above their astonishment.

"I know this is worrying. And having no memory of whatever happened certainly doesn't help. But our people — we, as unicorns — are strong. And I like to believe our magic is merely a bonus.”

The crowd settles a bit.

The princess goes on.

“I assure you, we *will* get our magic back. The power of our people *will* be returned. And we *will* get to the bottom of this.”

A voice from the crowd — feminine; distantly familiar; an irksome quality that the princess can’t quite place — speaks out.

“How do you know?”

For a brief moment — a split second — Princess Pipsy looks taken aback.

She quickly regains her composure.

Most of it, anyway.

“I’m sorry, I don’t get what you mean.”

The crowd parts just a bit. A unicorn steps to the front — dapple gray coloration; her mane a soft white hue, neatly trimmed; an average height for a unicorn, standing a bit taller than the princess — bearing a look of deep discontent.

She locks eyes with the princess.

“How do you know we’ll get our magic back?”

Princess Pipsy frowns.

“For a student of the archives, I’m surprised you have such little faith. I’m sure the rest of us don’t feel the same.”

The other unicorn goes on.

“Throughout all time, this has never happened to us before. There has been no record of any loss of magic. And we have *never* had a problem with our memories. Why are you so confident? If we’re truly in trouble, we have a right to know.”

The general steps forward. He leans close to the princess and whispers in her ear.

“Should I have her apprehended?”

Princess Pipsy — quickly — responds.

"No need. I'll handle this."

She clears her throat.

"As I'm sure you already know, we have some of the greatest mortal minds among us. Throughout history, it's true, this has never happened to us before. But it's *also* true that we have been faced with equally impossible problems. And we have always — *always* — overcome them. I assure you, by the honor of the queen, the problem *will* be solved."

The unicorn at the front of the crowd speaks up once more.

"Where *is* the queen?"

Murmurs from the crowd echo variations of the question. Princess Pipsy hesitates to respond.

Aster and the general exchange a brief glance.

The crowd — ever-so-slightly — begins to stir.

From atop the city wall, stationed next to the closed, imposing gates of the city, a younger voice shouts: one of many stationed knights.

"Unwelcome visitors at the gates! Royal family requested at once!"

———————————————————————

Princess Pipsy stands before the magnificent gates of the city. Aster and the general stand beside her. Behind them, a now-larger battalion of unicorn knights stands at the ready, horns trained forward. Atop the wall, a half-dozen unicorn knights stare down at the unwelcome presence on the other side.

Princess Pipsy calls out to them.

"Open the gates!"

The heavy, rhythmic *shunk* of chains fills the air, their movement hidden by some unseen mechanism.

The city gates — slowly — begin to open.

On the other side, a large group of horses — *not* unicorns — stands idle, sets of light battle armor draped over them. On each horse, a humanoid knight sits — most human, though the clammy, gray skin of elven lineage is clear among some of them — wearing their own set of armor, sword sheathed at the side.

The humanoid knights gasp at the sight of the angry unicorns in front of them, wholly speechless. Whispers and murmurs of astonishment float among their ranks.

Though the unicorn knights remain speechless themselves – as trained – the civilians further behind share similar hushed discussions of their own.

Unable to fully disguise it – or, perhaps, unwilling to – both sides appear genuinely shocked at the presence of the other.

Princess Pipsy speaks.

"I am Princess Pipsy. You stand at the gates of the great city of Unicornicopia. Visitors are not welcome. But you've caught us on a good day. If you leave now, we won't slay you where you stand."

On cue, the battalion of unicorn knights stomps their front hooves, lowering their horns in unison.

From the front of the humanoid knights, a lone rider takes a few paces forward, cautiously approaching atop his horse.

The unicorn knights take a single step.

The princess speaks.

"That's quite far enough."

The lone rider stops.

Now closer, his features are much more visible. He wears a fairly light set of metal armor, its plates only protecting some portions of his body. Beneath it, a set of fine leather armor — though horribly damaged and dirtied — peeks through the plates. Further beneath that, his darker cloth wear shows itself in numerous places, it, too, visibly worn.

Even through his armor, the physical strength of this rider makes no attempt at concealment, his stocky build clear. Flecks of dirt speckle his short brown hair, length coming to rest just below the bronze skin of his ears. A wide scar streaks across the side of his nose, so wide, in fact, that he appears to be missing a portion of his nose entirely. A prominent mustache springs from his upper lip, masking small scars across the front of his face, these far less noticeable. Affixed to his back, a heavy weapon rests.

The gruffness of his voice matches his appearance.

"I am Maus, mercenary of the Silver Coast. I have been hired by the king, on behalf of the Kingdom of Peace, to investigate the disturbance you've caused."

Princess Pipsy scoffs.

"Your lies are weak. There is no Kingdom of Peace."

The humanoid knights seem… confused.

Maus speaks again.

"I do not lie. We — my compatriots and I — come directly from the Kingdom of Peace, not far to the east. The beaches of the Silver Coast have been vacant long before the king took the throne, but not long ago, your city…"

He pauses.

"…*appeared*. And it has caused quite the disturbance among the kingdom."

That was not the right answer.

The princess speaks.

"You have trespassed into our territory. Moreover, you continue to lie to our faces. You will be put to death for your transgressions."

She stomps her front hoof.

"Seize them!"

The battalion of unicorn knights darts forward.

The humanoid knights attempt to flee. Their horses race down the stone bridge, heading back toward the beach… but the unicorns are no mere horses.

Before their steeds can even reach the halfway point, the unicorn knights encircle them, a hundred angry horns pointed sharply in their direction.

Toward the back of the group, one of the humanoid knights — a younger fellow with pointed ears, thin, dark hair, sweat collecting on his pale skin — looks frantically between each unicorn knight surrounding them. Briefly, he makes eye contact with Maus, still at the head of the group.

Maus — frowning — shakes his head.

Don't do it.

The rider's horse kicks up in a whinny. Its rider, now panicking, whips the reins.

The horse attempts to charge through the line of unicorn knights. It fails. Their horns leave deep gashes across its body. The unicorn knights closest lunge forward, their horns spearing into the horse's flesh. It cries out, head whipping wildly. Its rider falls, landing square on his back against the hard stone of the bridge.

With the horse held in place by the horns piercing it — blood now pouring from its wounds, tainting the beauty of the stonework — another unicorn knight lunges forward, shoving its horn through the eye of the horse, stabbing into its skull with a meaty splatter.

The horse's body falls limp. The unicorn knights pull their horns free, each an unsettling *squelch*, their horns now slick with its blood.

The unicorn knights snap their attention to the elven man on the ground.

Still on his back, he scoots away from the towering, blood-stained unicorns before him.

His head bumps into the leg of another unicorn knight. The man looks up, terrified. Worried noises escape his lips, none of them words.

The unicorn knight raises its front hoof. It swiftly brings it down onto the man's face, stomping his nose.

Blood spews out with the *crunch*, painting more of the bridge. A jagged, crumpled mess of broken bone sits where the man's nose was. The skin below his eyes — torn — bathes his face in red. His upper jaw now folds inward at the center, numerous teeth knocked free. He forces wet, strained coughs, small bits of skin and bone falling out of his face with each one. Hardly able to breathe, he raises his hands to his face on instinct.

The unicorn knight stomps again.

The man's hands shatter from the impact, their skin and bone mushed into the concavity of his face. He twitches.

The unicorn stomps again.

Blood erupts. Bone *cracks*.

The unicorn stomps again.

More blood. Fewer *cracks*.

And again.

Less blood. The dense sound of meaty impact.

And again.

Less blood. No cracks. Only the sound of pitiful wet slop, like rotting food thrown from its storage.

The unicorn knight rests its blood-soaked hoof on the ground, thin strands of muscle still clinging to its surface. He stares down at the fresh corpse below him.

The rear of the man's skull – like a cracked egg – collects the vile soup of his face within it. Thick blood spills over its sides, stringy clumps scattered all over. His arms reach deep into his head, hands stomped into his brain, their splintered bones buried deep in the pile of gore.

The unicorn knight — still staring — exhales sharply.

———————————————————————————————

The corpses of a dozen horses sit in a bleeding mountain, their bodies crudely stacked on top of each other. Leaned against the side of a nearby building, their blood washes over its architecture. Large streaks and splatters across the wall serve as the only proof of struggle, however pointless it might have been.

Hundreds of unicorns – nearing the thousands – surround the city square, forming a massive crowd. Shouts of anger — of confusion; of excitement — echo in the air. Within the square itself, dozens of unicorn knights stand at the ready, their focus entirely on the square's center.

Princess Pipsy stands before the beautiful fountain, looking out toward the grand audience that surrounds her. Aster – accompanied by several other unicorns of visible import – stands farther back, keeping a watchful eye on the crowd.

Princess Pipsy — voice naturally rising above the crowd — speaks.

"Bring the trespassers forward!"

From behind a line of unicorn knights, the general steps forward. In front of him, the group of humanoid knights walks forward, now stripped of their armor and weapons. Unicorn knights surround them in a tight cluster, keeping them bunched together.

The general kicks the nearest with his hoof.

"Keep walking."

The figure — Maus — looks behind him, flashing a scowl at the general.

The general kicks him again.

"I said keep walking."

Maus turns back around. His scowl holds steady.

Guided by the unicorn knights, the group stops next to the princess. All eyes of the crowd rest upon her.

Princess Pipsy holds up a hoof.

The crowd quiets.

She speaks.

"The fools who stand before us have trespassed on our land. Lied to our faces. And we will bring them to death."

Cheers and shouts erupt from the audience.

The princess continues.

"It seems that the world is starting to forget to fear us. But we will *gladly* remind them."

Maus raises his voice, speaking up.

"We did not fear you because we did not know you!"

The eyes of the crowd drift to Maus.

The unicorn knight directly beside him kicks him in the leg.

"Do not speak to the princess unless spoken to!"

Princess Pipsy walks up to Maus. The sound of her hooves reaches his ears even among the noises of the crowd. She leans in close, her eyes trained on his.

"I don't believe you."

From the crowd of unicorns, one pushes to the front. Her soft white mane comes into view, the sight of her gray coat striking a sense of irritation in the princess yet again.

The unicorn speaks.

"We can use them!"

Princess Pipsy responds.

"Are you questioning our methods of punishment?"

The unicorn speaks again.

"These trespassers clearly know something we don't. Killing them too quickly would only rob us of their knowledge."

The princess steps toward her.

"I prefer to kill things quickly."

The unicorn speaks once more.

"Liars or not, they could be useful to us."

Princess Pipsy steps closer.

"Being a keeper of knowledge may grant you wisdom, but it does not grant you the power to make decisions."

The princess leans in close. Her voice drops to a forceful whisper.

"If you keep being such a bitch in my side, I'll have you killed next."

The unicorn shrinks back into the crowd, nearly disappearing among the sea of other unicorns. Princess Pipsy returns to the front of the fountain, addressing the crowd yet again.

"I think it's time we get this show started. I assure you, the mystery of recent events *will* be solved. But for now, why don't we enjoy the entertainment of an execution?"

The crowd cheers, excited.

Princess Pipsy speaks again.

"Bring their leader forward!"

Two unicorn knights bite into the clothes around Maus's shoulders. They drag him forward, dropping him beside Princess Pipsy.

The two knights take a step back.

Maus looks up as the princess steps up to him.

She speaks.

"Don't worry. I'll make it quick."

She pauses.

"Well, as quick as I can, anyway. After all, we've got a crowd to entertain. I'll probably just have you disemboweled. Nothing too fancy."

Maus spits on her face. It hits her nose.

The princess changes her mind.

"On second thought, I think we *will* make it fancy."

From the gates of the city, muffled shouts echo briefly, then stop abruptly.

A strange sound — like a herd of running dogs — approaches from the street adjacent.

Princess Pipsy turns her head toward the sound. The crowd of unicorns does the same.

Without averting her gaze, the princess speaks.

"General? What is that?"

The general takes a step forward.

"I don't know. But it seems we may have more company."

Aster, too, speaks to the general.

"Why didn't the guards alert us?"

The general says nothing.

The strange, unnatural noise — the rapid, thudding movement — stops *just* around the corner of the building nearest.

Silence falls over the crowd.

From around the corner, a set of long, clawed fingers wraps around the stone.

Below that, a set of fingers from a tough, burly man wraps around the stone.

Above them both, a set of rotting feminine fingers wraps around the stone.

A voice speaks from around the corner. Or, more accurately, a collection of voices. Speaking in unison, all overlapping each other: a deep, gravelly voice; a wispy, light voice, reminiscent of a ghost; an older woman's voice, strained and dry with age; the boisterous cadence of a heftier man; a voice that belongs to a child.

"After all this time, the blight of your violence remains. How… despicable."

The general calls out to his knights.

"Horns at the ready! *Now!*"

Every unicorn knight abides. Their horns — many still red with blood — lower in the direction of the voices. Members of the crowd do the same.

As evident on the face of every unicorn, adrenaline — mixed with fear; uncertainty — rushes through their bodies. Courses through their veins.

Maus speaks.

"What the fuck is that?"

Princess Pipsy keeps her eyes trained on the series of hands.

"I was thinking the same thing."

The cluster of voices speaks out once again.

"Sorry about killing your guards. Well, I'm not sorry, actually. I enjoyed ripping them apart. But it's a shame. They're going to miss the rest of this."

The voices continue.

"I'm so glad you've brought everyone together for me. I do love a dramatic entrance."

The source of the voices — the ominous figure just beyond the wall — emerges.

The stench of long-rotten flesh poisons the air.

The crowd steps back.

Each arm from the wall attaches to a body: the long-clawed arm, covered in scales, that could have very well been from a young dragon; below it, the arm of a muscular, heavyset man; above both, the arm of a human woman, large portions of skin rotting, specks of bone visible. On the other side of the misshapen body: a long, spindly arm, its skin a pale white; above it, in the middle, the larger arm of an orc, its skin an aged, vile green, like that of a rotting olive; above those both, the shorter, stockier arm of a dwarf, its sunburnt skin dry and leathery.

A massive rib cage forms the torso. Large patches of flesh form a cover, but leave the majority of its center exposed. Layered below that, a translucent purple shell — its magic sparkling in the light — seems to hold the piecemeal body together.

The waist of a large humanoid creature — what could have been from a massive orc, perhaps something even larger — serves as the base of the lower body. Ragged clothing, all made of long-stained cloth, covers portions of the creature's form. Two legs — both clawed, their true origins masked completely by the rotting and fraying of their flesh — hold the figure upright.

No, not legs.

Arms.

Where feet should be are hands instead.

Those are more arms.

The head of the creature comes together through hideous layers: the upper half of the head of an orc, skin dried from the sun; patches of various scalps affixed to the orc skin, a disgusting collection of thin, matted black hair; the eye sockets, physically empty, but filled with blinding purple light from further within; the oversized lower jaw of a younger dragon, its teeth stained an ancient color, the skin of its inside a pale, sickly brown; a smaller jaw nestled within that, likely that of a dwarf; the nose of the face wholly absent, revealing more of what lies beneath; deep within the outer head, the smaller, jawless, tongueless head of a boy, eyes glowing a dark, steady purple.

With every movement of the jaws, the head of the boy peeks through the mouth, if only for a moment.

The monstrosity speaks.

"It's been such a long time since I've seen you. Such a very, *very* long time."

Princess Pipsy speaks up.

"Who are you? What do you want?"

The eyes of the creature — or, rather, its glowing purple sockets — turn to Princess Pipsy. It speaks.

"Well, that's a bit of a loaded question, isn't it?"

The creature cocks its head — an oddly familiar inquisitive motion — and takes a step forward.

The unicorns of the crowd take *many* more steps back. They have seen monsters before, but they have never seen this.

The creature continues, its voices chilling.

"Let's start with the easy one."

In near-perfect mimicry of Princess Pipsy's voice, the creature repeats the question.

"Who are you?"

The eyes of every unicorn grow wide.

The imitation drops.

The creature's many voices return.

"As you can see, I'm kind of a lot of things. In fact, most people are kind of a lot of things. Everyone's personality has layers. I've just got a few more."

It takes another heavy step forward, its true height now coming into view.

The unicorns of the crowd step back even further.

As it stands, the creature seems to be well over ten feet tall.

The creature speaks again, its cadence slow and meticulous.

"But you want to know my identity. That's what you really mean, right?"

It pauses.

"People have called me just about everything you can think of. The monster. The zombie. The boogeyman. But to you, I'm something better. Something *worse.*"

It takes another step.

"I am your Damnation."

And another.

"But you wanted to know why I'm here. What I want."

And another.

"I want to slaughter. And *you,* my friends, are at the top of the list."

The crowd continues to distance themselves from the creature.

Princess Pipsy — sensing the rising panic, hoping to steady it — speaks up.

"We are not friends. We have no business with you."

The creature takes another step.

"You see, that's where you and I disagree. I'd consider us well acquainted. And I say we have plenty of business. Unfinished, if you can believe it."

The creature spots the general standing among the unicorn knights. It points to him.

"*He* should know plenty about it. What do you think, general? Do I seem familiar?"

Nervous sweat streaks down the general's face.

The creature notices.

"Good."

The creature steps forward again.

The crowd of unicorns continues making space.

The creature addresses the crowd.

"My father was a very wise man. See, he realized that power unchecked… that was a bad thing. And he realized that you — *all* of you — would never change. Would never stop."

He continues, moving closer.

"My father fought you. My father slaughtered you. Showed you damage that you had never even fathomed before. Damage that you would do to us a thousand times over, given the chance. Turned the butchers into pigs. All in the name of self-defense, mind you. Of protecting his family. Keeping his people safe."

The creature looks off into the distance momentarily.

"And for the crime of loving his own kind — of questioning your violent, unchecked dominance — you killed him."

Towards the back of the crowd, several unicorns turn, preparing to flee.

The creature notices. It wags a finger on its three left hands.

"Nuh, uh, uh."

The unicorns freeze in place.

"I've waited a hundred lifetimes for this. If you leave before I finish, I skin you alive and wring your flesh."

The unicorns dare not move.

The creature continues.

"See, the thing is, you didn't stop with the father. You found his son. You bit off his fingers. You ripped off his limbs. And he begged you to stop. So you ripped off his face and you left him to die."

Its voices grow angrier. The purple glow in its eye sockets flickers vibrantly, turning to flames.

"But he didn't die! He lived! He wanted to die, but he lived! He felt the ache of his form, but he lived! He felt himself *starving*, he felt himself *rotting*, but he *lived!*"

The anger drops from the creature's voices. The flames in its sockets recede to their prior glow.

"Do you know what unicorns taste like? Because I do."

It steps closer.

"I had a lot of time to think. A lot of time to feel. A lot of time to tap into magic that I didn't even know was possible."

He points several playful, accusing fingers at the unicorns.

"And you. It took so long before I could find the rest of you. Before I could smell you again. You've clearly got *something* going on, considering I see a face I recognize, and I *know* you don't live forever."

Princess Pipsy — finally — responds.

"Do you really expect us to sit here and die?"

The creature looks to her.

"Oh, no. I expect you to run. I expect you to scream. I expect some of you to escape. But I'm very patient. Very persistent. And I *will* rip you from existence. After that, I think I'll kill everything else, too, just to make it even. But, like I said… you're at the top of the list."

The creature looks down at the crowd, spotting a younger-looking unicorn near the front. It points to her.

"You."

With its oversized arm, it reaches out, grabbing the young unicorn by the neck. It raises her up. Her legs kick wildly in the air, head thrashing at an attempt to break free.

The creature looks at the unicorn in its grasp.

"You're clearly in peril. You're clearly in danger. Why don't you use your magic? Defend yourself?"

The creature twists its fingers.

The neck of the unicorn *snaps*, skin tearing at the motion.

The creature — the one that called itself Damnation — drops the twitching corpse to the ground.

Blood spews from the neck, staining the road.

With a tinge of disappointment, Damnation speaks.

"You break easy."

He looks back to the other unicorns, a misshapen grin on his patchwork face.

"I'll go as slow as I can."

Chapter III:
Damnation

Chapter III: Damnation

Damnation gallops into the crowd. His heavy, misshapen body swings as he moves. His arms strike out, claws and nails digging through the bodies of unicorns. Blood flies through the air. Unicorns flee. Screams erupt from the wounded. Damnation cackles, his arms lashing out at every unicorn nearby. He reaches for the face of a wounded unicorn lying below him, still alive. He digs the claws of his dragon hand into the front of its face. The unicorn cries out in futile protest. With a meaty twist, he rips the snout of the unicorn from its body. He picks up the unicorn with several arms, holding it high above his head. He opens his jaws, blood pouring into his mouth from the wet hole at the center of the unicorn's face.

Damnation's voices speak, a hint of disappointment.

"You taste so sour. What a shame."

He casts the dying unicorn aside.

Unicorns continue fleeing from him, racing through the streets of the city, all in disorganized panic.

Princess Pipsy turns to Maus.

"You will take us to your kingdom. You have no choice."

Maus responds.

"What about the rest of us?"

The princess speaks.

"No time. They run or they die."

With that, the rest of the human knights — the mercenaries — take off, sprinting down adjacent city streets.

Maus speaks.

"I can't outrun that fucking thing!"

The princess sighs.

"Yes. I know."

She bites onto the scruff of Maus's clothes. With an impressive strength, she swings him around onto her back. He lands awkwardly, having to reposition himself.

The princess continues.

"If you mention this to anyone, I'll feed your eyes to your children."

Maus touches the back of his neck.

"You broke skin."

The princess replies.

"Shut up."

She takes off, running full speed down the nearest street. Aster and the general — accompanied by a couple of terrified unicorn knights — follow.

Behind them, Damnation's rampage continues. The crowd has since dispersed, but numerous unicorns remain within unfortunate reach, unable to flee from the monster. Blood flies into the air. Pained whinnies echo down the streets. After a few moments, the unicorns left alive have all fled. Damnation looks around, taking note.

He speaks, a playful tone in each of his voices.

"You cannot run from me!"

He gets down on all eight arms once again. He spots Princess Pipsy fleeing with Maus on her back. He grins.

"So be it."

He takes off, galloping after the princess.

Maus looks back. He sees Damnation rapidly approach.

Maus speaks.

"He's gaining on us!"

Princess Pipsy continues to run. Aster and the general match her speed. Further behind, the unicorn knights — visibly tiring, now unable to keep up — begin to fall back.

Damnation leans his head out, his jaws clamping around the head of the nearest unicorn knight. It explodes in a burst of blood and broken metal. Damnation throws the carcass against a building, its bones breaking on impact. His glowing purple sockets stare at the unicorn knight closest.

"You're next."

The unicorn knight screams.

Princess Pipsy speaks.

"We need to lose him!"

Aster responds.

"We have to get to the bridge. It's our only way out."

Damnation's teeth rip through the head of the next unicorn knight. Its blood scatters through the air, much of it hitting Maus.

Maus complains.

"You gotta be fuckin' kidding me."

Damnation speaks, its voices thunderous.

"You cannot escape your Damnation!"

Princess Pipsy turns the corner, running farther into the city. Aster and the general follow close behind.

The princess shouts.

"Stay close!"

The general responds.

"Planning on it!"

At the sharp turn, Damnation — heavy; unable to adjust so quickly — slides into the wall of a building.

The wall cracks. He pulls himself away, retraining his focus on the clearly important trio of unicorns. He speeds ahead, giving chase once again. The blood of slain unicorns trails behind him as he runs, dripping from all over his grotesque body, smearing across the beautiful architecture of the city. The sound of running hooves — of screams — echoes all around.

Princess Pipsy shouts.

"Here!"

She turns sharply. Maus holds tight to the rings of armor around her neck, nearly falling off. Aster and the general follow the turn. They speed down another lavish city street, breathing heavy, hearts beating fast.

Damnation attempts to follow the turn. He fails, sliding into another wall. Chunks of stone and glass cascade down from the force.

He speaks.

"Clever girl."

Still atop the princess, Maus flashes a glance behind. Damnation is nowhere to be seen.

Maus voices concern.

"He's gone!"

Aster responds.

"What do you mean he's gone?"

The trio continue to speed down the street. A handful of other unicorns spot them, joining in the run.

One speaks up, his brown mane flowing behind him, the blood of others staining his muted beige coat.

"Princess! Where do we go? What do we do?"

The princess replies.

"Find the Kingdom of Peace! If you cannot find it, run to wherever you can! Tell the others! Evacuate the city!"

The other unicorn nods.

"I will!"

From the next street over, a heavy, rapid thudding sound echoes. The buildings themselves seem to quiver on one side of the street. The thuds trail upward. Several moments pass. A massive shadow leaps high into the air from atop the dome of a building nearby.

Damnation lands directly on top of the beige unicorn, instantly crushing him in an explosion of blood. He now gallops alongside the princess and her allies.

He looks over to them, grinning.

"Found you."

Princess Pipsy frowns.

"You've gotta be fucking kidding me."

Damnation closes the gap, attempting to crush the unicorns against the wall.

Princess Pipsy, Aster, and the general drop their speed. The several other unicorns — the ones that had joined in running with them — attempt to pick up speed.

They do not.

Damnation hurls his body into the wall, crushing the cluster of unicorns against it, their mangled bodies pressing into the stonework, blood pouring down. Several legs twitch.

Princess Pipsy — sensing an opportunity — quickly turns around. Maus nearly flies off, but manages to hold on.

The princess shouts.

"Follow me!"

Aster and the general comply.

Almost at once, Damnation notices, his glowing purple sockets trained behind him.

"Have it your way."

Princess Pipsy turns a corner, her hooves briefly slipping in the blood below her. Aster and the general follow close behind.

The princess speaks.

"Split up! Spread word to the others, whoever you can! Meet us at the bridge!"

Sounds of carnage in the distance. Screams. Breaking bones. Breaking stones.

Aster nods.

"You have my word, princess!"

She pauses.

"Good luck."

Aster splits from the group, running down another street in the same direction.

The general speaks.

"As you command."

He, too, splits off, running down another street parallel.

Princess Pipsy continues to run. As she does, she speaks.

"How far is your kingdom?"

Maus — holding tight to her armor — replies.

"Not three days' travel. To the east."

The princess speaks.

"Let's hope we can make it."

She runs further ahead, moving as fast as she can. Other unicorns — all running in wildly different directions — spot the princess. Quickly, they change paths, attempting to follow. In the distance, thin plumes of smoke rise up into the sky. Before long, a small crowd forms, all tailing after the princess, many covered in blood.

Princess Pipsy races down a set of stairs leading to another street, this one more familiar to Maus. Another sharp turn. The growing crowd of unicorns — panicked and terrified — follows.

Princess Pipsy speeds ahead. She enters the city square. Sounds of screams — of unmistakable destruction not too far away — chill the air.

All around them, the shredded, mashed bodies of unicorns litter the square. Thick blood pools all over. The princess races through it, blood splashing as she speeds onward. Mangled corpses of unicorns — these more intact — lay sporadically before her, nearly blocking the path.

She speaks.

"Hold on!"

Maus leans forward. He grips onto the armor tighter, knuckles white.

Princess Pipsy charges forward.

She weaves through the mess of bodies, wholly maintaining her reckless speed. Her hooves lose traction in the blood, but she corrects herself, keeping balance.

Unicorns in the crowd behind her are less lucky. Several fall into one of the countless piles of sinewy mess. Still, many press on.

A cluster of deep, guttural roars — all in perfect unison — rings out from somewhere deep within the city.

Princess Pipsy continues to run.

The unicorns behind her do the same.

She looks ahead. Now within view, she spots the open gates of the city, the beautiful expanse of the stone bridge beyond it.

Aster emerges from the city street parallel, her own cluster of unicorns following behind her. She rejoins the princess, now running at her side once again.

Somewhere in the city — perhaps in several places at once — fire audibly crackles to life.

Still running, Aster speaks.

"I gathered everyone I could. Have you seen the general?"

The general — almost on cue — emerges from another parallel street.

"Right here."

He, too, rejoins the princess, running at her side. Numerous unicorn knights — and civilians — follow him. The three small crowds converge, forming one, their gaze fixed on the trio leading their escape. Only a few blocks away, the princess stares at the city gates ahead.

She addresses her people.

"Split up as soon as we get to the beach! If you cannot get to the Kingdom of Peace, get to wherever you can!"

Eerily familiar, the sound of rapid thudding approaches. At a building close to the gate, Damnation crashes through its corner, large chunks of stone scattering across the ground. He gallops through the open gates, beating the unicorns to the bridge. He rushes to its halfway point. He stops, standing upright, and turns to face them.

His voices shout to the unicorns, all still heading for the gates.

"You have nowhere to run!"

The general speaks to the others.

"Don't back down! If we do, we all die!"

Aster replies.

"And what if we don't?"

The general speaks.

"Then some of us may live."

Hearing this, a number of unicorns in the crowd turn back, vanishing into the blood-soaked streets of the city. Still, many remain, following their princess.

The general races to the front, now leading the charge.

Princess Pipsy speaks.

"You better know what you're doing."

The general — eyes locked on Damnation — replies.

"I do."

The unicorns approach.

Damnation grins.

The general shouts.

"Your father was a coward!"

The grin falls from Damnation's face.

"What did you say?"

Princess Pipsy and Aster share a glance. Both slow their approach, giving the general more room.

The general continues.

"Your father was weak!"

The unicorns continue to close the distance. Those in the crowd grow wary.

Damnation pounds the stone of the bridge with six fists. The stone cracks.

"My father was *strong!* He was a *hero!*"

The general presses on, now even closer.

"You are nothing more than his bastard son! The product of him and his whore! He was weak, and you are weaker!"

Damnation pounds the bridge again, now much more forceful. It cracks further. His voices — though speaking in unison as always — carry the cadence of a child throwing a tantrum.

"NO!"

The glow of Damnation's sockets burns, purple flames now radiating from within them. His attention drifts away from the other unicorns, his focus resting exclusively on the general.

He continues.

"I'LL KILL YOU!"

Damnation charges, galloping toward the general. He reaches out with several arms, attempting to grab him. The general races around his body. Damnation spins, making frustrated attempts to grab the unicorn encircling him.

The general calls out.

"Go!"

Princess Pipsy and Aster maintain their speed. They race underneath the standing Damnation, making it through to the other side. Without looking back, they keep running.

Unicorns from the crowd do the same. Too overwhelmed to catch them all, Damnation swats at them; punches the ground; reaches out to crush them. He kills many — their bodies being crushed and broken into bloody messes — but not all.

Enraged, his voices speak.

*"No, no, no, **NO!**"*

In a single motion, he grabs hold of the general's body, swings him through the air, and slams his back against the wall of the bridge. A meaty crack follows. The limp body of the general — blood pouring from wounds unseen — tumbles off the bridge, landing in the water below.

Unicorns continue rushing past. Damnation throws them back toward the city with a single arm, sweeping them back to where they began. Many hit the stone hard, spots of blood left behind, though they manage to force themselves back into the city.

Damnation's jaw opens wide. A purple light sparks violently within. The flames of his eye sockets grow brighter. He digs his hands into the stone of the bridge, holding steady.

A massive beam of purple light blasts out from his mouth, pulsing and cracking with erratic energy. The beam carves through the center of the bridge, its stones shattered and blasted away. The unicorns that remain flee into the city.

The purple beam carves through more of the bridge. Several unicorns fail to move fast enough. The beam carves through their bodies, disintegrating large chunks of their flesh, any tissue not destroyed by the beam rapidly rotting away.

One unicorn — back leg cut by the magic of the beam — races back toward the city gates. As he runs, the skin of his body begins to turn a stale, putrid color, spreading from the site of the wound. His muscles grow weaker, starting to fail him. As he reaches the gates, large clumps of skin slough off, revealing the already rotting muscle beneath. By the time he enters the city, his body collapses under its own weight. His consciousness fades as he falls apart into a pile of rotten meat and ancient bone.

The purple beam cuts through the other side of the bridge, leaving the city isolated. Unicorns continue rushing back into it, hoping to hide, some already knowing they cannot.

The beam vanishes. Damnation fixes his gaze on the countless unicorns now running deep into the city. Some jump from the city walls, landing in the water below.

Damnation — feeling the bridge begin to give way below him — leaps onto the fragment of bridge still connected to the city. The other half of the bridge falls, its massive stones splashing upon hitting the water, several hitting unicorns attempting to swim. Damnation slinks back into the city. Smoke rises more rapidly from the city, numerous fires now burning within its walls.

Screams continue.

The unicorns on the beach escape into the forest, scattering in all directions.

Chapter IV:
Don't Be
Interesting

Chapter IV: Don't Be Interesting

The forest smells damp. The air feels humid. Princess Pipsy walks through the thick clusters of trees, many of them oak and ash, the occasional thorn tree appearing every so often. Spots of blood and soot tarnish her armor. On her back, Maus rides, silent by choice. Aster walks alongside them, bits of sand and dirt in her mane. In the distance, the steady sound of a babbling brook resonates, a gentle ambience cloaking the forest. Rays of evening sun filter through the treetops, birds singing their songs. Farther ahead, the forest begins to visibly thicken.

Princess Pipsy speaks.

"We should pass the threshold before nightfall. We can rest once we do."

Maus responds.

"Do you really think he won't find us?"

Aster pokes Maus in the arm with her horn. Very slightly, he bleeds. She shouts at him.

"Do not speak to the princess unless spoken to!"

The princess speaks.

"It's alright, Aster."

Maus speaks.

"I am no prisoner."

Princess Pipsy frowns. She stops walking and bucks Maus from her back. He flies off, landing upside-down against a heavy tree. He puts a hand to his head on instinct. He opens his eyes, seeing the unicorn princess towering over him.

She leans in closer.

"In light of the current situation, we have elected to keep you alive. We have *allowed* you to lead us to your kingdom. But make no mistake, you *are* our prisoner. Even without our magic, we are stronger than you. *Bigger* than you. *Faster* than you."

She continues.

"If you try to run, we kill you. If you try to fight, we kill you. If you try to hide—"

Maus interjects.

"I get it. You kill me."

The princess grins.

"So he *does* learn. Good."

She takes several steps back, giving Maus room to stand. He gets to his feet, one hand on the center of his back.

The princess continues.

"But, to answer your question, no, I don't think he'll find us. The heart of these woods is one of the many homes of the fairies. As much as I despise the pests, the places they reside are tainted by their magic over time. They become hard to navigate. Hard to find. We can use that to our advantage."

Maus speaks.

"We've always been told to avoid fairies. That their magic makes them unpredictable. Dangerous."

Maus walks ahead, now leading the way on foot. The unicorns follow.

Princess Pipsy speaks.

"And that's why the journey from your supposed kingdom took three days."

Aster chimes in.

"They *are* unpredictable. They live on a whim by their very nature. But they're hardly dangerous."

The princess speaks again.

"We will leave for your kingdom in the morning. Thanks to us, we should arrive before tomorrow's end."

Maus pushes a thicket out of his way.

"What do you plan to do once we get there?"

The princess thinks for a moment.

"I'm not sure."

Nearby, branches *snap*.

The trio frantically look around them, Aster and the princess especially.

Maus speaks.

"Did you hear that?"

The princess — immediately irritated — responds.

"Of course I fucking heard that."

Aster comments.

"Far too heavy to be an animal."

More branches snap, closer now.

Princess Pipsy lowers her horn in the direction of the noise.

"Whatever it is, we kill it."

Aster, too, lowers her horn.

"As you command, princess."

Maus simply watches.

From the thinner trees, a gray unicorn emerges, her soft white mane flecked with dirt. Dried blood patches her body, origin unknown. The sense of a sour recollection hits the princess.

The gray unicorn speaks.

"My name is Delphi. There is no need for that."

Aster and the princess relax.

The princess speaks.

"How long were you following us?"

Delphi responds.

"Long enough to know you don't know where you're going. Or what you're doing."

The princess replies.

"You will address me properly when you speak to me."

Delphi stands her ground.

"Etiquette in speech is not the highest of my concerns. And as far as I'm aware, the two of us are on pretty equal footing, princess."

The princess — begrudgingly in agreement, but unwilling to admit it — frowns.

Delphi continues.

"Besides, the only ones who know anything useful are the Keepers of Knowledge and the queen. Maybe the general. But the queen is missing, and the general is dead."

Aster speaks.

"What do you know?"

Delphi replies.

"Who Damnation is. Where he came from. And — maybe — how we can kill him."

———————————————————————

Deeper in the forest, Maus marches forward, pushing thorns out of his way more frequently. Princess Pipsy walks behind. Aster and Delphi walk in tandem on either side of her. Above them, the treetops converge as they continue, forming more of a canopy.

Delphi speaks.

"Before the princess was born, Queen Marika led an attack on a place called the Kingdom of Man. That's where the First Casualties happened. I wasn't around yet, either, but... uh..."

She pauses and looks to Aster.

Aster speaks.

"Aster, right hand to the queen."

Delphi continues.

"...*Aster* might remember it."

Aster nods.

"I do. I wasn't there on the day, but I remember hearing word of it."

Delphi speaks.

"Records talk about the king of that place. An older human man. After he was killed, the queen found his son and tortured him. He didn't know anything useful, so she left him to die. Based on what he was saying — and how he was saying it — I'm going to assume that's Damnation. Or it used to be him, anyway."

Princess Pipsy ducks below a branch of thorns.

"I thought you said you knew something useful."

Delphi replies.

"Knowing your enemy is half the battle."

The princess retorts.

"And the other half is killing them."

Princess Pipsy and Delphi glare at each other.

Aster breaks the tension.

"How can we kill him?"

Delphi responds.

"The king had a sword. Enchanted with something powerful. We don't know what. We *also* don't know how he got it. The only people that did were his Legion, but they were all killed when the kingdom was attacked."

The princess scoffs.

"*That's* your plan? To look for the sword someone stole from us years ago?"

Delphi replies.

"We don't *know* that it was stolen. That's just an assumption. All we know is that it was lost. If we can try to get to the ruins, we might be able to look for it. If we find someone who has it along the way, even better.

The princess shakes her head.

"The chances of finding that thing are ridiculously small. If my mother couldn't do it, why do you think *we* can?"

Delphi steps over a clump of twisted roots.

"I think we *could*. Until we find a way to get our magic back, it's the best idea we've got."

The princess looks to Maus, still marching at the front of the group.

"Prisoner! Do you know how to get to the Hundrian Valley from your kingdom?"

The group moves deeper into the forest. The trees become less distanced. The branches and thorns become thicker. Maus pushes large vines and thorns out of the way, watching his steps.

"I do, yes. But the things you're describing…"

He pauses.

"What you're talking about sounds like ancient history."

Delphi speaks.

"Do you know how long it's been? Since the battle, I mean."

Maus replies.

"Specifically, no. But long enough that most people haven't heard of it. And long enough that most people believe you never existed at all."

A large thorn pricks Maus's arm. He recoils slightly. Annoyed, he pushes it further to the side, pressing forward.

In the sky, the sun begins its descent, the world growing just a bit darker. The gentle songs of the forest birds fall silent. The air cools.

Maus speaks again.

"Are you sure we're going the right way?"

The group pushes through a large brush, stepping under thorns and vines. They enter into an expansive forest clearing, almost entirely guarded from the sky by its canopy. Vines hang low from numerous branches. Wide, ancient trees sporadically fill the space, generous room between each of them. Lush green fauna springs up in dense patches among the blades of soft grass. Far from where they stand, a wide stream wraps around one of the large trees, having flowed to this clearing from somewhere else in the forest. As the sun continues to set, the sky growing darker, tiny holes — now visible in many of the clearing's trees — light up from dim sources within.

Princess Pipsy speaks.

"I'm sure."

She walks ahead. Aster and Delphi follow. Maus stands at the edge of the clearing for a moment, taking in the sight before him.

The princess continues.

"We can rest here for the night. They're mostly nocturnal, so I doubt they've seen us. Stay away from any of the trees that they live in. Don't encourage any of their antics. If they don't find you interesting, they'll leave you alone."

Maus steps into the clearing.

"Yeah? And what if they do?"

The princess looks over to him.

"Don't be interesting."

— — — — — — — — — — — — — — — —

Nightfall. A subtle breeze blows. The sound of distant chirping bugs surrounds the clearing. Maus feels hard bark against his back. Against his head. He feels the cool grass beneath his legs. He stirs to consciousness and opens his eyes. He rests on the ground against one of the many large trees here, his devoid of any flickering little lights within. Not far off, the three unicorns — Princess Pipsy, Aster, and Delphi — stand upright next to a similarly dark tree. Their eyes rest shut, each asleep. They all look incredibly tired, even now. Maus should know, being exhausted himself.

He could run now, but what would he run back to? Not only did he fail to get the job done, but all of his hired hand compatriots were killed. Even if he did return, there's a pretty good chance he'd be killed, too. And even if he wasn't, the unicorns would surely find him eventually, and they would *definitely* kill him. And even if Damnation killed them before they got the chance, he was pretty sure Damnation would kill everyone else eventually.

Maus sits up. He feels the dryness of his mouth. The cracked texture of his lips. The staleness of his tongue.

Deeper in the clearing, more towards the center, many of the trees now exhibit dozens and dozens of small, carved holes, gentle lights flickering within. Balls of colored light float through the air around these trees, many floating quite low to the ground, their various colors a mix of blues and greens and purples. The distance is too great to make out any details. Nonetheless, Maus is no fool, and he does not feel the need to investigate further. They do carry a feeling of intrigue and wonder, but it would be a mistake to provoke them directly. The unicorns might know what these creatures are capable of, but Maus does not.

He spots the stream, its water flowing deeper into the clearing, disappearing under bramble beyond that. Even for a simple stream, it appears quite deep in some places. Reflections of the colored lights dance along its surface.

The previous day was one of the most stressful, chaotic days he ever had. His worst job as a mercenary — the one that gave him the distinctive hole in his nose — seems like an afternoon nap by comparison. And —

as Maus begins to realize during this brief period of reflection — it has been a long time since he has had anything to drink.

His eyes follow the curve of the stream. Much of it is very close to the illuminated trees further in, but one particular bend — not incredibly far from where he rests — stretches into a much darker part of the clearing. A part where no tiny flickering lights seem to be present. A part where he'd be unlikely to be seen.

Maus stands. Quietly, he approaches the bend in the stream.

The gentle flow of the water becomes more audible. He stops at the bend and crouches down. Before anything else, he takes another look at the colorful lights farther away. They continue flittering about, as they had done before. A few disappear into the bottom of a tree now and then.

He hasn't been noticed.

Maus cups his hands in the stream, collecting water. He leans closer and takes a sip. Almost immediately, he feels the cool temperature of the water run down the back of his throat. He feels much better. He cups his hands a second time, collecting the water, taking another sip. Although his perception is likely influenced by his prior dehydrated state, this water may be the freshest he's ever had.

Not one to waste much time, he decides he's had enough.

Maus looks up. Floating directly in front of him, mere feet away, is a glowing ball of blue light. Within the light — or, rather, *emitting* the light — is a small humanoid figure, no more than a few inches tall. Its form is unmistakably feminine, but where clothing might be expected, the body seems wholly smooth. Her head — small as it is — cocks to the side, staring at the mysterious burly man in front of her, soft golden hair hanging down. From her back, blue wings flutter rapidly, keeping her aloft. They seem too fortified to be similar to a butterfly's, yet not fortified enough to be reminiscent of a bug or a beetle: something in-between.

In a shrill, high-pitched voice, the fairy speaks.

"Hello."

Maus stays silent.

The fairy flies a bit closer.

"Hello."

Still, Maus does not respond.

The fairy flies directly into Maus's face. She zips around his head, poking at it.

"Hello, hello, hello! I'm talking to you, dummy! Hello, hello, hello!"

Maus swats at his head. Hushed, he speaks.

"Fuck off!"

The fairy hovers in front of his face.

"You *do* talk!"

She frowns and crosses her arms.

"So you're just an asshole, then."

Maus maintains his hushed tone.

"I'm not supposed to talk to you."

The fairy responds.

"Why not?"

Maus speaks.

"That's none of your business."

The fairy flies closer.

"Is too my business!"

She zips around Maus's head once more, jabbing him with her fingers. Maus swats at her to no avail. She continues.

"Why not? Why not? Why not? Why not?"

Maus stands, stepping away from the stream. The fairy follows, continuing to zip around his head, poking at his face.

After a moment, she stops and hovers in front of his nose. She points at the large scar.

"What's that?"

Maus frowns, losing his control over his hushed tone.

"None of your business!"

The fairy lands on his nose.

"Is too my business!"

She reaches an arm through the scar, wiggling her tiny hand around in the hole of Maus's nose.

"Tickle, tickle, tickle!"

Maus coughs, exhaling forcefully. The fairy springs from his nose, hovering in front of him once more. He speaks again, this time just a bit more forceful; just a bit louder.

"Fuck... off!"

The fairy crosses her arms.

"Asshole."

Behind Maus, the hushed voice of Princess Pipsy speaks.

"Prisoner. What are you doing?"

Maus turns around. Princess Pipsy — now very much awake — stares at him from her resting place. Aster and Delphi slowly blink to consciousness. The fairy — previously hidden by Maus's body — turns to look at the same time. The second she spots the unicorns, she gasps.

She zips away, flying toward the trees at the center of the clearing.

Princess Pipsy scowls.

"What did you do?"

Maus replies.

"I didn't *do* anything. That little shit wouldn't leave me alone."

One by one, all of the floating lights at the center of the clearing recede into their trees.

Watching this, Delphi speaks.

"Oh, boy…"

Maus sees the last of the fairies disappear from view. He looks back to the unicorns, a bit more confidence behind him now.

"See? It's fine. They're probably scared of you."

Thousands of colored lights explode out from the trees at the center of the clearing. They all rush at the unicorns, swarming them in an instant. Through chaotic shouts of excitement, the fairies declare — individually, all talking over each other — their amazement at the sight of the unicorns.

Maus swats at the air. He accomplishes little, missing most of the fairies. They taunt him, flying around his face, poking at his head. The blue fairy from earlier flies back onto his nose, wiggling her arms around in the hole.

"Tickle, tickle, tickle!"

Maus shouts angrily, all patience lost. He smacks at his own face.

"Stop digging in my fucking nose!"

The unicorns whip their heads around, attempting to push the fairies away. Their tails swing wildly. All of this, of course, does nothing. The fairies continue to fly around the unicorns, poking and prodding and pulling.

Princess Pipsy kicks up. The fairies move back for a moment, then resume their incessant swarming. Several fairies yank on Princess Pipsy's ears, inspecting them closely. More tug at her lips. Even more poke at her horn. The princess actively loses composure.

"Enough!"

But the fairies continue. They repeat what the princess said, openly mocking her; continuing to poke; continuing to prod. Aster and Delphi kick at the air.

Maus swats at his head.

"Do something!"

The fairies mock in repetition.

"Do something!"

"Do something!"

"Yeah, come on, do something!"

Princess Pipsy's eye twitches. Her brow furrows. Her upper lips curls into a snarl. She glares at the swarm of fairies around her. They continue to chant. To mock. To enrage.

"Do something!"

"Do something!"

"Do something!"

Princess Pipsy wraps her lips around a little green fairy in front of her face. She pulls him into her mouth, sealing her lips around him. All of the fairies freeze in place. They hover in the air, all eyes on the mouth of the princess. Inside, the fairy zips around, attempting to push free. Muffled, high-pitched shouts cry out. Still glaring at the fairies around her, Princess Pipsy moves her tongue around in her mouth.

She bites down with a tiny wet *snap*. The muffled cries stop abruptly. She exhales forcefully. Sparkling green mist floats down from her nostrils, which quickly dissipates. The princess swallows. The fairies around the group hover and stare, saying nothing.

The princess speaks.

"Could've been sweeter."

All of the fairies frown, angry eyes trained on the princess. Many start to growl. From their hands, each brandishes a set of tiny little claws. One particular fairy — visibly buffer than the others, emitting a radiant green glow — floats directly in front of the princess. He cracks his knuckles. The cracks are very, very tiny.

Aster speaks.

"Good news, prisoner. We're leaving ahead of schedule."

The fairies scream angrily, flying forward.

The unicorns take off. They head for the center of the clearing.

Maus runs after.

"Hey!"

Princess Pipsy rolls her eyes.

"Pathetic."

She turns around, heading back toward Maus… and the approaching mass of angry fairies.

She bites onto the nape of Maus's clothes and throws him onto her back. He quickly repositions himself. The princess races ahead, catching back up to Aster and Delphi. They continue forward, the lit trees of the clearing not far from them now. The fairies give chase, quickly gaining ground.

Maus, noticing them, speaks.

"Where do we go now?!"

Princess Pipsy focuses ahead.

"There."

Straight ahead — a considerable distance away — is a gap between two large thorn trees at the edge of the clearing. Just enough room to squeeze through.

The princess continues.

"The fastest way is through. We can leave the forest beyond it."

The fairies continue gaining ground. Several from the front of the swarm latch onto Aster's back. They sink their claws into her hide, just barely piercing it. Aster yelps. She swings her tail at them. They fall off, but quickly recover, landing on her back once again.

More fairies land on Delphi's back. They claw at her. She shakes her body, knocking a couple down. Most remain unaffected.

Maus turns to get a look at the swarm. The little blue fairy — the same one from earlier — leaps onto his nose. She claws at his scar with her tiny hands. Her voice sounds distorted. Angry.

"Tickle, tickle, tickle!"

Maus grabs her with one hand and throws her behind. She collides with Princess Pipsy's horn. Her body falls, limp and bleeding. More fairies land on Princess Pipsy, hitching a ride on the rear of her armor. Maus swats a heavy hand at them. He knocks several off. More land in their place. The main swarm continues to approach.

The group races ahead. They enter the fairy village. Even now, the insides of the trees remain lit. A handful of fairies emerge from within them, immediately joining in the assault.

The swarm gains considerable ground. Dozens land on the backs of Princess Pipsy and Aster. The two exchange a brief glance.

The princess shouts to Maus.

"Watch your legs!"

Maus lifts his legs.

Princess Pipsy and Aster knock their bodies together. Many of the fairies crush between them. The two unicorns separate. Tiny corpses peel from their hides, falling off as they run. Maus lowers his legs. He takes a displeasing note of the dozens of teeny bodies pressed into the grooves of Princess Pipsy's armor. The group continues racing through the village.

Aster looks to Delphi.

"I don't suppose you studied how to kill these things?"

Delphi winces, more fairies stabbing at her back.

"No, but I think I know a way!"

Delphi whips her head around, the swarm now beginning to overtake them. She catches numerous fairies in her mouth. She bites down hard. Spittles of blood cover her teeth. A strange mix of blue and green sparkles spews from her nose and mouth, dissipating immediately.

Aster catches on.

She, too, whips her head around. She catches several fairies in her own mouth. She crunches.

The gap at the edge of the clearing draws closer.

The unicorns continue racing through the village.

Fairies fly into Maus's hair, clawing at his scalp. It bleeds. He smacks hard against his own head, nailing several, feeling their fragile little bodies shatter under his palm.

Three fairies fly onto Princess Pipsy's snout. They claw at the skin inside her nostrils. She thrusts her nose into the air. The fairies bounce off. She whips her mouth up toward them, catching them inside. She crushes them between her teeth.

Breathing heavier — now angrier — she speaks.

"I've had enough of these little shits."

She shouts to Maus.

"Watch your legs!"

Maus lifts them.

Still running, Princess Pipsy slams her body into one of the many large trees the fairies live in. The thin outer layer of the tree crushes under the weight of the impact, breaking inward. Tiny broken furnishings tumble down, some small bodies tumbling out down with them. In the wreckage, teeny, tiny candles and lanterns — having been knocked over quite violently — spread their teeny, tiny flames to bits of the broken wood.

Pressing on, Princess Pipsy slams herself against another village tree. As with the first, its outer layer of wood breaks inward. Tiny furnishings fall. Tiny corpses along with them. Tiny fires spread.

Aster and Delphi continue to whip around. They catch fairies between their lips. Crush them between their teeth. Feel the little pops of blood on their tongues. Blow clusters of sparkles from their noses.

Princess Pipsy slams hard into another fairy tree. Its wood breaks. More of the swarm lands on her armor.

Maus continues swatting at them. A few land on his arm. He swats at them with his other arm. More fairies land on his other arm.

The swarm fully surrounds the group, easily keeping speed. They swoop in sporadically, attacking the unicorns — and Maus — from all angles. The fires of the broken trees spread further, a crackling backlight behind them.

Aster spits several bodies from her mouth.

"There's too many of them! We can't kill them all!"

Maus speaks.

"They're gonna pinprick us to death!"

A teeny fairy flies in front of him, baring her teeth and claws.

"Heeyah!"

Maus punches her out of the air. Her shattered carcass flings through the swarm, colliding with numerous fairies, tiny droplets of blood spraying out.

Princess Pipsy speaks.

"Hold on! We're almost there!"

Aster replies.

"We'll never make it out if we can't lose them!"

The gap of the clearing approaches. Beside it, however, the princess now spots a deeper extension of the stream.

"There!"

Aster and Delphi nod.

The unicorns continue charging forward. The fires climb higher, smoke curling into the sky. The full swarm lands on the group, all fairies clawing at once.

The unicorns splash through the bend of the stream. Their bodies submerge into the water. They dip their heads below the surface. Maus ducks along with them, rinsing the water over his body. The fairies fall off, floating on the surface of the stream.

The unicorns — and Maus — emerge on the other side. Simultaneously, they rush through the opening, a single thorn scratching the sides of Aster and Delphi. The group disappears beyond the thorn trees.

The fairies — all floating in the stream, looking quite displeased — stare angrily at the gap of the clearing. A purple fairy near the front speaks.

"I liked you better when you were extinct."

The buff fairy — floating farther back — calls out. "Yeah! That'll show 'em!"

One of the burning fairy trees collapses into ash and flame, tumbling to the ground in large, charred pieces.

— — — — — — — — — — — — — — — — —

The sun rises on the horizon. The unicorns — and Maus, clothes now soaked — stand atop a hill at the edge of the forest. Across the grassy fields before them, visible in the distance, sits a massive cluster of buildings. A kingdom. A rickety-looking castle breaks the sky at its center.

Maus shakes water from his head.

"There she is. The Kingdom of Peace."

The unicorns look surprised.

After a moment, Delphi speaks.

"This… wasn't here before."

Princess Pipsy walks on.

"Come on. We've got work to do."

Aster and Delphi follow.

— — — — — — — — — — — — — — — — —

The light of early morning fills the sky. Damnation walks upright along the sands of a beach. Thick layers of blood drip from all over his body. Far behind him, the ruins of the city of Unicornicopia burn on the water.

He sniffs the air, likely through magical means.

Nothing.

He sniffs again. And again.

Still nothing.

He sighs, irritated.

A moment passes.

Suddenly, he sniffs again.

Something.

He turns toward the scent, facing further inland.

In the distance — just barely visible at such a long range — tubes of dark smoke billow into the sky. Something burns at the center of the forest.

Damnation grins.

"Gotcha."

Chapter V:
The Kingdom
of Peace

Chapter V: The Kingdom of Peace

Without looking back, Maus speaks.

"This would go a lot faster if I didn't have to walk."

Aster responds.

"The princess has already stated her disdain for being ridden. So stop bringing it up."

Maus sighs.

"Whatever you say."

Maus continues on foot, leading the unicorns down the worn dirt path, its winding route connecting to the Kingdom of Peace. Around them, long grasses sway in the breeze. Weeping willows speckle the landscape. Farther still, mountains pierce the sky along the horizon, much of their visibility masked by fog. The sky mellows into its bright, familiar blue. And — now somewhat closer, though a great distance remains — the outskirts of the kingdom stand ahead.

Delphi speaks.

"The valley is still quite far. Once we enter the kingdom, I suggest we get our bearings. Collect whatever supplies we may need. Plan for the travel ahead."

Princess Pipsy scoffs.

"Collect supplies? We're *unicorns.*"

Delphi replies.

"Your point being what, exactly? Our power *was* immense, yes… emphasis on *was*. Right now, we're as vulnerable as anything else alive. And we need to adjust accordingly."

The princess challenges her.

"Do you really think a wild goose chase is still our best idea?"

Delphi continues.

"Yes, I do. We don't know how to get our magic back, so I think it's safe to assume it may take a long time, which means Damnation would probably kill us before we ever figured it out. Until we get any other leads, we need to plan around the only one we have. And unless you want to cross the shale plains up north, we need a better route."

Princess Pipsy shakes her head.

Delphi speaks.

"No?"

Princess Pipsy shakes her head again.

Harder.

She speaks.

"Not that. I think…"

She flinches.

"I think there's a bug in my hair."

She shakes her head again, trying to knock something loose.

"It's driving me *crazy.* I've been feeling it the whole walk over."

She gives one more wild shake.

From the back of her mane, the small, wiggling body of a fairy flies out. The fairy screams, sailing into the tall grass.

Princess Pipsy frowns.

"You've got to be fucking kidding me."

The others stop walking. They turn to look.

The fairy flies out from the grass, now emitting a blue glow. Her appearance — and her shrill voice — is unfortunately familiar to the group. She hovers above the eye line of the unicorns.

"Wow! Talk about a fairy knot!"

She looks down to Princess Pipsy.

"You ever think about washing your hair, princess?"

Princess Pipsy chomps at the fairy. The fairy flies up higher, easily dodging the unicorn's mouth.

The fairy continues.

"Nice try! Maybe if you brushed your teeth, I wouldn't smell you coming from a mile away!"

Aster speaks.

"Get lost. We have no business with you."

The fairy responds immediately.

"You ate my uncle, you son-of-a-bitch!"

The princess speaks.

"And you're testing our patience. What do you want?"

The fairy blinks.

"What do I want?"

She flies in a bit closer, careful to stay out of biting range.

"I want to kill you! *And* your dumb-looking friend!"

Maus crosses his arms.

"I am no friend of theirs."

The three unicorns turn to Maus. They speak simultaneously.

"Shut up."

The fairy shouts again.

"Doesn't matter! I'll kill you all!"

Princess Pipsy — unamused — raises an eyebrow.

"And how do you intend to do that?"

The fairy thinks for a moment. She shrugs.

"I dunno."

She continues.

"But if I follow you long enough, I'll figure it out. And when I do…"

She cackles dramatically, tilting her chin to the sky, her arms raising upward in celebration.

Maus turns back toward the kingdom. He continues his walk.

Wordlessly, the unicorns follow.

The fairy continues cackling to herself. Even after a considerable length of time, she fails to notice that her audience has long since departed.

— — — — — — — — — — — — — — —

Without turning around, Maus speaks.

"They aren't going to like you."

The group continues forward. The long, swaying grasses become shorter. The ramshackle huts previously dotted across the hills give way to more proper housing. And, though the road is still very much made of dirt, its path is far more worn. As evident by the wooden houses and farming fields around them, they now break the outskirts of the kingdom. Taller, more refined structures — most made of heavy stone — stand farther ahead, still some distance away.

Princess Pipsy speaks.

"They don't *need* to like me. They just need to do what I say."

In the distance, solitary farmers turn their heads, immediately spotting the unicorns. The farmers rush back into their homes, shutting their doors. The braver among them peek out at the group through drawn curtains and cracks in their walls.

Maus speaks.

"No one has seen you for hundreds of years. As far as I know, anyway."

The princess replies, losing patience.

"Get to the point, prisoner."

Maus continues.

"My *point* is that getting through here — getting supplies, information, whatever you're trying to do — it's not gonna be easy with so many people watching your every move. And there's gonna be a *lot* of people watching you."

Delphi chimes in.

"I think he has a point. If we cause too much trouble, we're only going to draw more attention to ourselves."

The princess disagrees.

"We *already* drew attention to ourselves. We lit a fairy forest on fire."

Delphi shoots her a look.

"All the more reason to limit any chaos."

An older elf man walks across the dirt road, dressed in simple cloth attire. He holds a bundle of chopped wood in his arms. Before he can reach the other side, he sees the three unicorns led by a gruff man, all still blood-stained in various places. He stops.

The princess speaks.

"What do you want?"

The farmer drops his wood. He staggers back, tripping on his own feet. He lets out a brief, scratchy scream.

Aster takes a step forward.

"Be gone. We want nothing to do with you."

The man shrieks again. He points a long, wrinkled finger at the unicorns.

"You can *talk!*"

He pushes himself back with his hands.

He moves very, very little.

"You're… you're *real!*"
Princess Pipsy rolls her eyes.
"Thanks for the insight."
Maus shakes his head.
"I told you they wouldn't like you."
The farmer — still on the ground — looks to Maus.
"You *know* them?!"
Everyone ignores the farmer.
Aster turns to Maus.
"If all of your people act this way, we're going to have to kill a lot of them."
The farmer shouts.
"You're going to *kill* me?!"
Maus replies.
"I wouldn't really call them 'my people'. I just live here."
The princess raises an eyebrow.
"I thought you were working with the king."
Maus corrects her.
"Working *for* the king. He rounds up the toughest mercenaries he can find when he needs a job done. I just happen to be one of his regulars."
The farmer — still on the ground — gasps dramatically.
"You're *mercenaries?!*"
Maus stares down at the farmer.
"You live outside one of the most crime-infested cities on the entire continent. You shouldn't be surprised."
Princess Pipsy looks up to Maus.
"The Kingdom of Peace is one of the most crime-infested cities on the entire continent?"
Delphi speaks.
"The name would lead me to believe the opposite."
Maus responds.

"Peace is the name of the kingdom's royal family. They've been killin' people for years."

Aster glares at him.

"Watch your tone, prisoner, or we'll gore you where you stand."

Maus sighs.

"You'd be putting me out of my misery at this point."

The farmer — still on the ground, though he's managed to move a pitiful few inches back since he first fell — stares at Maus in disbelief. In shock. In *horror*.

"You'd let them *kill* you?! What kind of masochist are you?!"

Maus responds instinctively.

"I ask myself the same thing every morning."

The princess speaks.

"We clearly can't let him live. He's just going to cause trouble."

The farmer — yes, *still* on the ground, despite having more than enough time to have fled by now — gasps. Dramatically, of course.

"You're going to *kill* me?!"

Maus speaks.

"You already said that."

Delphi looks to Aster and the princess.

"If we kill everyone who does this, we'll never make it out of the city."

Aster responds.

"What are you suggesting? We disguise ourselves?"

Delphi nods.

"If that's what it takes."

The princess butts in.

"We're *unicorns*. How do you suppose we do that?"

Delphi looks over to her.

"Maybe a shawl or something. Maybe some cloth."
She pauses.
"Or a really big hood."
Princess Pipsy looks down at the pathetic farmer below.
"Do you have any shawls? Cloth scraps? Really big hoods?"
The farmer's eyes — a look of defiance; of shock; of *horror* — lock on to the princess.
"I'd rather die than surrender my cloth scraps to the likes of you."
Princess Pipsy replies without hesitation.
"Alright."
She steps closer to the farmer. Instinctively, he raises his hands in protest.
"No! Wait! I was bluffing!"
Princess Pipsy thrusts her head forward.
Shunk.
The tip of her horn just barely pokes through the back of his head. His jaw slacks, as does the rest of his body. Dark blood pours out from the puncture, steadily draining onto the dirt.
Maus shrugs.
"That's one way to do it."
Princess Pipsy pulls back. Her horn, however, remains stuck.
"Ah, shit…"
She pulls back harder. The limp, bleeding corpse of the farmer jolts with her.
Aster takes a step closer.
"Do you need… help, princess?"
Princess Pipsy quickly responds.
"No, no. I got it."
She pulls back again. The corpse follows her motion. Blood flicks into the air. Limbs wiggle from the movement.

She tries again. Her horn pulls out *just* the slightest bit. The farmer's arms and legs flop.

Aster, already losing faith in the princess, speaks.

"Princess… are you sure?"

Princess Pipsy holds the bottom of the corpse down with her hoof. She tears her head away, her horn finally — *finally* — pulling free. Thick spurts of blood bubble out of the hole in the farmer's head.

Princess Pipsy shakes her horn, successfully shaking some of the blood off.

"I told you I had it."

A pause.

"Well… now what?"

The corpse continues to slowly bleed.

Delphi speaks.

"We should probably search his house. Take whatever we need."

The princess looks to Delphi.

"I still say it's a stupid idea. I don't know how you expect to gather supplies if we're disguised. If we can't even *talk* to these people."

Delphi replies.

"If you've got a better plan, I'm all ears."

The princess frowns.

Maus turns to the unicorns.

"I assume there's no way you're letting me go once we get into the city."

Aster speaks.

"Absolutely not."

Delphi chimes in.

"Not only are you our prisoner, but you know more about this age than we do. There's no way we're letting you run off. Ever."

Maus sighs.

"Yeah. Had a feeling."

Princess Pipsy looks to the other unicorns.

"How do you suppose we pull it off? If we walk in posing as unattended horses, we'll be chased away. Captured. Sold, maybe. And that defeats the whole purpose of the disguise."

Wordlessly — in unison — the three unicorns look over to Maus.

He returns their gaze.

"What?"

Princess Pipsy exhales forcefully.

"I hate this plan."

———————————————————————————

Maus, riding atop Princess Pipsy once again, leads the other two unicorns into the city. Each unicorn wears a burlap sack over their horn, tied off at their foreheads. Their horns are not well hidden in the slightest. They are, however, not immediately visible.

Princess Pipsy speaks, hushed.

"If you mention this to anyone—"

Maus interjects.

"You'll kill me. Yeah, I know."

Delphi — also hushed — speaks.

"If you keep talking, princess, we're going to be discovered."

The princess replies, maintaining a low volume.

"Some things require talking."

Delphi — also maintaining a low volume — replies.

"And some things don't."

Princess Pipsy huffs.

Maus leads them on. The dirt road they traveled previously gives way to mismatched cobblestone. Clusters of buildings surround them, many old and rickety, though a few appear more structurally sound than others. Little bits of debris — dirt, cloth scraps, rotten food, pebbles and stones — litter the places where the buildings meet the roadways. Townsfolk mill about, some with carts or horses of their own, though many simply walk to wherever it is they're going. As Maus and his 'horses' pass by, they flash unwelcome glances in his direction. Every single one of them looks like they've had the worst day of their lives. And — though confirmation bias may very well be involved — it seems like every other person has a hideous scar on their face. Even the children.

Maus speaks quietly, ensuring only the unicorns can hear him.

"First thing to do is get you into the stables. Or any stable, really. I can take one of you around no problem, but that becomes tougher to pull off when there's three. And if you really want to avoid getting caught, stolen, or killed, it's time you do a bit of listening to *me*."

Aster responds in a low whisper.

"Remember your place, prisoner."

Maus — without looking to Aster — speaks.

"Remember yours."

Sounds of scuffles and brawls float through the distant air, giving the city a chaotic, dangerous ambience. Every so often, loud cries or shouts ring out, always falling on deaf, uncaring ears. And every so often, one of the unicorns is fairly confident they spot a finger or two in the road.

A scratchy voice calls out from the alleyway adjacent.

"Oi! You there!"

Maus slows his ride to a stop. Aster and Delphi do the same.

A tall, scraggly-looking man leans against the wall. Dirt and grime pepper his already unkempt appearance. Thin gray hair falls over his face, though he looks no older than thirty.

He continues.

"What's with all them horses?"

Maus thinks for a moment.

"Selling them. None of your concern."

The scraggly man takes note of their heads.

"What's with all them bags?"

Maus replies.

"Like I said, it's none of your concern."

The two take a long look into each other's eyes, each failing to get a proper read on the other.

Maus speaks again.

"A man like you should know not to ask too many questions around here. Could lead to trouble."

The scraggly man holds Maus's gaze a moment longer.

He smirks, barely noticeable.

"Have a nice day."

The scraggly man walks deeper into the alley, disappearing around the bend.

Maus waits a moment to see if he returns. Quickly, he realizes the man is not coming back.

Hushed, Maus speaks.

"We'll post up for the day. Maybe spend the night. But if my life is tied to your success, I don't want to stay here a second longer than we have to."

Maus walks on.

Aster and Delphi follow.

— — — — — — — — — — — — — — — — — —

It doesn't take long to find a stable. Even in the heart of the city, they seem to be everywhere. Same to be said about all the private armories along the way; all the blacksmiths; all the weapons shops; all the run-down, ramshackle homes, all squeezed too tightly together and forced into uncomfortable placements.

Three full-sized unicorns — or, *horses* — are tough to move through the city streets easily. But Maus knows where he's going. Besides, they aren't the only beasts of burden on the streets. The oblong bags on their heads might be a strange sight, but they themselves are not.

Maus — having already spotted the stable — speaks.

"We'll need to leave two of you here. I think I should take Aster with me. Leave you two behind."

He gestures to Princess Pipsy and Delphi.

Delphi speaks, hushed.

"Fine by me."

The princess disagrees.

"You don't speak for me."

Maus responds.

"You two talk too loud and too often. Like I said, if my life is tied to you not getting caught, we're gonna do a few things my way."

Aster looks to the princess.

"I have to say, I agree with our prisoner. I think this is the right move."

Princess Pipsy frowns.

Briefly, Delphi speaks.

"How long will you be gone? What should we expect?"

Maus replies, careful of his volume as the group nears the stable entrance.

"Since you so mercifully stole my *everything,* I'm gonna need armor. A good weapon. Basic rations and supplies. Shouldn't take more than a few hours at most."

The unicorns stop in front of the stable.

Maus hops down from Princess Pipsy. His boots *thud* as he lands. He pushes through the doors of the stable. The unicorns walk on, entering single file… and watching Maus *very* closely.

Inside this more well-built part of the stable, a simple desk sits on the creaky wooden floor further into the room. An open wall connects this room — almost like a foyer — to the actual stables where the horses are kept. Bits of hay and muck speckle the floor.

As soon as they enter, Maus and the unicorns are hit with the pungent stench of wet hay, stale grains, and old shit.

Behind the counter, a wrinkled man cranes his neck over an open book, lamplight catching in the tufts of white hair around his head. Possibly dwarven in lineage, though one can't be certain what elements of his person would come from that over simply being a wiry old man. Based on his abrupt surprise at the sight of visitors, it doesn't seem like he was expecting any customers. He quickly straightens his posture — which makes almost no difference in his height — and shuts his book.

His strained, scratchy voice speaks.

"What can I do ya for? Lookin' to board these horses?"

Maus opens his mouth to speak.

The old man cuts him off.

"I gotta say, those are some *strange* lookin' horses ya got there. Why they got those bags on their heads?"

Maus takes a breath.

The old man cuts him off.

"Say, don't you live around here? I've seen your face before. Ain't ever seen you with no horses, though."

Finally, Maus speaks.

"Just need to put two of these in for the night. Maybe all three. Double your rate if you stop asking questions."

The old man nods.

"Deal."

He hops down from his seat behind the desk, now clearly a stool. He disappears below the desk, trotting around to the front of it. *Definitely* a dwarf. Either that, or the shortest human man Maus has ever seen.

He stops in front of Maus and extends a hand.

"That'll be… ten gold."

Maus thinks for a moment.

"You hesitated."

The old man retorts.

"No, I didn't."

So does Maus.

"Yes, you did."

The old man shakes his head, doing a horrible job at feigning ignorance.

"Uh… no, I don't think so."

Princess Pipsy mutters under her breath.

"Yes, you did."

The old man snaps to attention.

"Did that horse just talk?"

Delphi kicks the back of the princess's leg with her hoof.

The old man speaks again.

"Did *that* horse just try to subtly tell the other one to shut up by kicking her leg?"

Maus drops a small leather pouch into the old man's still outstretched hand.

"Twenty gold. No more questions."

The old man pockets the pouch. Coins clink together. He chuckles lightly to himself.

"Big spender, big spender! I like the way you think!"

He walks off into the stables.

"Follow me!"

Maus sighs.

"I'll be broke before this is over."

Even quieter, Princess Pipsy replies.

"We'll break you if you aren't."

Maus sighs again, far more emotionally exasperated than he was mere moments ago.

Chapter VI:
Horses Can't
Get Drunk

Chapter VI: Horses Can't Get Drunk

Princess Pipsy upturns her nostrils.

"If I could vomit, I would."

She stands in the center of a grimy stable, old hay and dry grass scattered all over the floor. Her head barely manages to peek above the wooden dividers. Seeping in from all around her, the stench of working animals stains the air.

Delphi stands in the stable next to her, hers, too, in an undesirable state.

"Keep it down. We don't want anyone to hear us."

The princess rolls her eyes.

"Yeah. Right."

She locks eyes with Delphi.

"That crusty old man can't hear for shit, and the only other life around us is — *exclusively* — a pair of regular, dumbass horses."

Across from Princess Pipsy, two stallions — one younger and one much older, both a shade of muddled brown — stare at her.

The older one wiggles his upper lip in an unwelcome smile.

The princess scowls.

"Keep it in your sheath, or I'll fucking kill you."

The older stallion — understanding her tone, though not her words — backs down, head hung low.

Delphi speaks again.

"The language use is a little excessive."

The princess replies.

"So are you."

Delphi remains unbothered.

"I think you let yourself become far too angry far too easily. You should really work on that. It could get us killed."

Princess Pipsy responds, the slightest growl in her voice.

"I'll add it to my list."

The sound of clattering metal cuts through the air. Princess Pipsy and Delphi — and the pair of regular, dumbass horses — turn toward the source of the sound.

Standing at the far end of the stable — slack-jawed, face full of absent-minded horror — is a pudgy peasant boy in simple clothing. Next to his muck-stained boots, an empty metal bucket rolls across the floor.

Delphi and the princess speak in unison.

"Shit."

— — — — — — — — — — — — — — —

The sound of Aster's hooves on the cobblestone remains audible, even at this busy hour. As busy as a city of criminals can really be, anyway.

Clip-clop. Clip-clop. Clip-clop.

Maus rides atop her, his focus steady. His gaze remains fixed ahead of him, looking out at a building further down the street. He leans closer to Aster's ears, keeping his voice hushed.

"I've got some spare equipment back at my house. Armor, that is. Assuming nobody stole it, anyway. But I've only got a few weapons on standby, and the ones I do got are rusted to shit. So a weapon's my top priority.

And since I like 'em big, there's only one place around here worth going to."

Aster — in an even quieter tone — responds.

"I don't care why you need it. Just make it quick. We have important things to do."

Maus grunts in acknowledgment. It isn't worth it to respond to that.

He stops Aster at the front of an oddly charred storefront. Thin layers of soot seem to cover the outside of the windows, a particularly large patch spreading out from under the front door. Above it, a hanging wooden sign juts out from the building. In faded, long-worn lettering, it reads: "THE POKING PONY".

Further within, metal on metal *clangs* repeatedly. Even from here, the distinct musk of forging — of metalworking — is impossible to ignore.

Maus takes another look at Aster.

"Stay here. This shouldn't take long."

Barely audible, Aster responds.

"It better not."

Maus enters the shop.

The heat hits him at once. Inside, a massive stone furnace burns, built into the very brick of the far wall. Tables and tools of all sorts clutter the room, anvils of numerous sizes placed throughout.

The steady sound of metal on metal continues.

Clang.

Clang.

Clang.

Clang.

At the base of the forge stands a tall, green-skinned figure, their skin wrinkled, almost leathery. Pointed ears stick out from the sides of the head, their shade a touch lighter than the rest of the skin. Thinning gray hair comes together in a ponytail at the back of the head. An untidy gray beard of decent length covers the jaw and chin, the tips of two large, pointed teeth poking out. The figure wears a set of dark leather goggles over the eyes, the glass pitch black in color. The reflections of the forge's flames dance along the lenses. In their right hand, the figure brings a heavy hammer down onto the metal blade in front of them, the blade itself glowing a soft orange hue. Sparks fly out with every swing.

Clang.

Clang.

Clang.

Clang.

On the torso, the figure wears a ragged cloth shirt, its sleeveless edges frayed from age, its color an unsightly cream-brown color. Over the shirt, the figure wears a scuffed leather apron; small metal tools sit in its pockets. Around the hands and forearms, the figure wears a set of thick leather gloves, though their formidable construction makes them seem more akin to gauntlets. Simple pants of unknown material — and a pair of dirty work boots — cover the rest of the figure. Despite visible signs of age, the figure stands at what must be seven feet tall.

Along the walls of the room, all manner of heavy weapons are displayed — greatswords, battle axes, war hammers, pikes — all at varying degrees of completion. Each one, however, is noticeably larger than usual.

Maus approaches the figure.

Clang.

Clang.

Clang.

Clang.

Maus calls out, his voice just barely rising above the noise of the blacksmith.

"Hey! Taking any requests?"

The hammering stops.

The figure slips the hammer into a deep pocket. They turn around — now facing Maus — and lift up their goggles, revealing the face of the elderly orc man beneath. The eyes flash with recognition. The figure speaks, the bass of his voice easily projecting in the space.

"I thought I smelled a mouse!"

The blacksmith steps forward. With one arm, he gives Maus a brief hug.

"How's my favorite customer?"

Maus replies.

"I've heard you say that to all of 'em."

The blacksmith chuckles.

"Yeah, but for you, I mean it."

He takes a couple steps back, returning to his work at the forge, though still clearly continuing the conversation.

"So, what can I do ya for? Cashing in from the latest gig, I assume?"

Clang.

Clang.

Clang.

Maus speaks.

"Sure. Close enough."

The blacksmith replies.

"I thought you wanted to hold on to your last girl for a while. You lose her in a scuffle or somethin'?"

Maus exhales silently.

"Somethin' like that."

Clang.

Clang.

Clang.

The blacksmith pulls the heated blade — now far more shapely — from the heat of the forge. As he does, he faces Maus.

"So, you lookin' for another 'Big Barric' special?"

Maus nods.

"Yeah. Somethin' like the last one, if you can. Really didn't mean to lose it so soon. And I've never been a big fan of the other stuff."

Barric chuckles again.

"Everybody says their weapon's the best 'til they get killed by somebody else's."

He continues.

"But yeah, I can do that for ya. Matter of fact, I been workin' on this hunk'a metal for a while now. Might as well make her yours. I know she's not much to look at now, but don't worry…"

He stands before a tall wooden barrel, filled about halfway with murky water.

"…I'll make her beautiful for ya."

Barric submerges the metal blade into the water. Immediately, steam rises up with an audible *hiss*. Frantic bubbles break the surface of the water. Their fervor slows to a halt as the hiss of the steam quickly dies down.

"A'course, the speedy delivery's gonna cost ya."

Maus can't help but frown.

"I was afraid you might say that."

Barric shrugs, a knowing amusement in his eyes.

"You know I can't help it. Man's gotta eat. If there's money to be made, then I might as well make it."

He pulls the cooled metal blade from the water. Already, it looks far more refined than it had previously… though that could be attributed to Maus only now seeing it up close.

Barric brings the blade back to the forge, its metal slowly heating up once more.

"Let's make you somethin' big."

Clang.

Clang.

Clang.

Clang.
Clang.

— — — — — — — — — — — — — — — — —

The peasant boy stares.
Princess Pipsy stares back.
Delphi does the same.
And so does the regular horse.
And so does the other regular horse.
They all just stare at each other.
Unblinking.
Unmoving.
Each afraid to break the tension.
Quietly — without moving too much — Princess Pipsy whispers to Delphi.
"I've got an idea."
Another tense, silent moment passes.
Delphi responds.
"He can still hear us. He hasn't moved."
The peasant boy gulps.
He can still hear them.
He hasn't moved.
Princess Pipsy takes a single step forward. She keeps her gaze steady on the boy, a confident power behind her eyes. Her voice breaks the stillness in the air.
"Hey."
The boy looks to Princess Pipsy.
She continues.
"Don't move. Or we'll fucking kill you."
The boy takes off, running out the back of the stables at full speed.
Delphi gives the princess a judgmental look.
"I told you the language was excessive."
Princess Pipsy sighs.
"Fuck."

Delphi cranes her neck over the top of her stall door. With a careful (yet hurried) precision, she touches the metal latch with her snout. Her upper lip deftly fiddles with the hook, attempting to pull it free. She picks it up with her lip, moving it ever-so-slightly… then drops it. The hook falls perfectly back into place.

Delphi groans, frustrated.

"He's getting away!"

Princess Pipsy turns around, squaring her hind legs up to the stable gate. She lifts both legs, and—

WHAM!

She kicks the stable gate. The metal latch snaps off, clattering to the ground. The gates flies open violently, slamming into Delphi's stable.

Princess Pipsy flashes a cocky look.

Delphi exhales.

"Shut up."

Princess Pipsy charges out of the stables. She runs through the open back door, speeding into the alleyways. Her hooves *clack* rhythmically as she runs across the cobblestone. Behind her, a sound rings out from inside the stables.

WHAM!

Delphi races out of the stables, catching up to Princess Pipsy.

Ahead of them both, the peasant boy runs. He turns his head around. Immediately, he spots the two unicorns — 'horses' — charging right for him. He shrieks.

Princess Pipsy and Delphi continue gaining ground.

The princess speaks.

"This should be easy."

Frantic, the boy runs faster, a vain attempt to outrun them. Were he as wise as he is slow, he might know better than to try and outrun two horses in a straight line.

Nearly upon him, Delphi speaks.

"Don't underestimate happenstance. Better keep your guard up. At least until we kill him."

Princess Pipsy chuckles a singular chuckle.

"He's about to be dead by our doing. What could possibly happen?"

The unicorns continue running. As they do, Princess Pipsy feels more… cramped.

The alleyway begins to narrow.

Princess Pipsy groans in frustration. With the tighter space, both her and Delphi slow down. Their charge gives way to a focused trot. Their reckless speed gives way to careful steps. The princess's certainty gives way to frustration.

What was once a speedy chase is now the slowest, tensest race of all time.

The peasant boy continues sprinting — stumbling? — down the narrow alley. In a quick glance, he looks back at the "horses" following him.

Princess Pipsy growls.

The peasant boy yelps. He climbs over another crate — this one much larger — and continues. He breathes heavily, clearly not used to this level of physical exertion. He wobbles a bit as he runs, struggling to keep a steady balance in favor of moving even faster.

The princess narrows her eyes.

"Back up."

Delphi — momentarily confused — responds.

"What are you talking about?"

Princess Pipsy barks.

"I said *back up.*"

Delphi backs up. She drops her speed, intentionally falling behind. With the extra space, Princess Pipsy picks up speed.

Farther ahead, the boy continues stumbling on.

"Dad! Dad! Help me!"

Princess Pipsy runs even faster.

She arrives at the large crate. She jumps, soaring through the air in a powerful arc. She clears the crate without issue, landing on the other side with a heavy *clack* and *thud*. She continues racing forward, her chase unbroken.

Delphi, too, leaps over the crate. She lands, slightly less graceful than the princess.

The boy catches another glimpse of them. He yelps, reaching for a door, clearly the rear entrance to some local business. Before he can touch it, two looming shadows cast over him from behind. Frozen, the boy says nothing.

Princess Pipsy speaks.

"Gotcha."

She grabs the scruff of his shirt with her mouth. She throws him to the ground. The boy looks up at the towering animals in front of him.

Stuttering, he speaks.

"I- I- I won't tell anyone, I swear! I swear!"

Princess Pipsy steps closer.

"I think it's a little too late for that. Don't you?"

She takes another step.

The boy backs up, bumping into the wall behind him. He lets out a concerned whimper.

Princess Pipsy takes another step.

"I always love this part."

She looks to Delphi.

"Hold him down."

Delphi responds.

"You can't handle him yourself? He's a *boy*."

The princess groans, frustrated.

"Just do what I say, and we won't have a problem."

Delphi responds.

"Just kill him already, and we *really* won't have a problem. Who knows who could've heard us. That chase wasn't quiet."

More frantic, the boy cries out.

"Dad!"

The princess looks back to the boy.

"Shut up."

Behind her, the door opens. She, Delphi, and the boy all snap their attention to the sound. From the open door, a stocky peasant man — a little on the shorter side — steps into the alleyway. He wears a simple cloth shirt and a leather vest, a strap across his chest holding a large pouch to his side. A short beard wraps around his face.

"Oi! What's goin' on out here?"

He spots the first 'horse'.

Then the second.

Then the boy on the ground, trembling in fear.

"My son!"

The man runs over to the boy. He pulls him to his feet, embracing him briefly.

"What happened? I thought you were working the stables. What's goin' on here?"

Still frantic, the boy attempts to explain.

"I- I- There was talking, and the horses, they were talking, and I ran away, and they chased me all the way here and they followed me and they said they were going to *kill* me!"

The father blinks a few times.

"...Right."

He walks his son toward the open door.

"Come on, then. I think you need to rest up for a minute. Must'a hit your head somethin' nasty."

Princess Pipsy looks through the open door as the two step through it. Inside, dozens of others — likely customers of some kind — stare into the alleyway, some with various tools or antiques in their hands. Even if she ran in and killed them both, she'd never be able to kill the rest of them. *Someone* would survive. *Someone* would get away. And then she'd just have the same problem all over again, albeit worse than it is now.

The son looks up at his father.

"What about the horses?"

The father continues inside.

"Fuck 'em."

Princess Pipsy scowls.

The door closes.

She exhales forcefully.

From behind her, Delphi speaks.

"And now he got away."

Princess Pipsy's upper lip twitches.

Delphi continues.

"You should've killed him when you had the chance. No point in doing anything now."

Princess Pipsy stares ahead at the closed door in front of her.

And Delphi continues.

"Well, we should probably head back. Aster should return soon. Unless you have anything else you want to say, *princess.*"

Princess Pipsy's lip stops twitching.

She kicks behind her.

Hard.

Her hooves impact Delphi's body, the force breaking skin.

She kicks again.

And again.

And again.

And again.

And again.

Delphi falls to the ground.

Princess Pipsy turns around to face her. Her back hooves feel wet. Delphi bleeds from numerous gashes on her barrel.

Finally, she speaks.

"What the *fuck* are you doing?"

Princess Pipsy shouts.

"Stop! Talking!"

She stomps down onto Delphi's body. Bones crack in her chest. Her head lurches out in response.

Delphi opens her mouth to speak.

The princess doesn't let her.

Again, she stomps, her hooves piercing Delphi's flesh. More cracks. More blood.

She stomps again.

And again.

And again.

Thick holes — wounds torn open across Delphi's body — pour red. Splatters stain Princess Pipsy's face, all four of her hooves now drenched. She breathes heavily, anger still evident on her face, even now.

Weakly, Delphi looks up at her.

"I know so much more than you. Now we're all going to die."

Princess Pipsy glares at her.

"I said stop talking."

With a single, heavy kick, Princess Pipsy stomps Delphi's snout into the corner of the stone wall. Bone snaps and shatters on impact. Several teeth fall out. Delphi pulls her head from the wall, already losing consciousness. Her skin sticks to the wall, some peeling off in small bits. Half of her snout has caved into itself. With a steady outpour of blood from the mashed, mangled wound, she falls limp.

Princess Pipsy continues breathing heavily, anger finally subsiding.

Blood drips down her hooves.

Her legs.

Her face.

She exhales.

"I need a drink."

Blood now seeping into the burlap on her head —
and into several other parts of her body — Princess
Pipsy walks out of the alleyway, searching for the
closest place to acquire such a thing. And in a city like
this, it doesn't take long.

— — — — — — — — — — — — — —

It doesn't take long at all.

Princess Pipsy stands before the sign of a tavern,
its grandiose lettering carved into a panel of dark wood,
grafted onto the stone of the building itself. It reads
"Bald Man's Gate". Below it, in considerably smaller
lettering: "Tavern, Inn, and Eatery". The door sits
slightly ajar. The sounds of conversations and laughter
spill out from within. Even though the day has barely
begun to darken, firelight flicks through the doorway.
Princess Pipsy pushes the door open with her snout and
walks inside.

The interior — while certainly cramped to some
extent — is far more spacious than the exterior would
leave one to believe. A long wooden bar stretches the
length of the room, various drinks and glasses on
display behind it. In the main chamber, chairs and tables
of mismatched wood fill most of the space, the patrons
themselves, in turn, filling most of the tables and chairs.
Most of the patrons appear human. Or at least
half-human, though a number of dwarven and elven
figures are visible. In the farthest corner of the room, a
staircase leads up to the second floor balcony above.
The balcony itself, however, is quite small, and only
seems to host a handful of patrons, acting as more of an

accessory to the rooms behind it. Next to the staircase, a pair of hooded figures quietly converse, likely negotiating something unbecoming. Near wholly obscured, a handful of large feathers poke out from under their cloaks.

Lanterns and torches light up the space, all supplemented by the fire roaring in the fireplace. The entire space is cast in a soft yellow glow, relying almost exclusively on its flames to light its interior, with few windows to be seen.

At the bar, a pair of human men — both a bit older — make no hurry to serve drinks to those at the counter. Between them, a much larger fellow — an older orc man, bald, with a braided gray beard — cleans a number of large glasses.

When Princess Pipsy enters, the conversations stop.

The laughter disappears.

The room falls deathly quiet.

Nobody makes any moves to stop her. While the patrons all certainly have *questions* — especially after watching a horse walk into a bar — they know better than to *ask* those questions. It could lead to trouble. It could get them killed. So, instead of *stopping* the blood-stained horse with a bag on its head, they simply watch.

But they *all* watch.

Very, very closely.

Princess Pipsy approaches the bar.

Clip-clop. Clip-clop. Clip-clop.

A couple patrons step to the side.

Clip-clop. Clip-clop. Clip-clop.

One scoots her chair closer to the table.

Clip-clop. Clip-clop. Clip-clop.

A drunken woman with dark, frazzled hair stumbles out in front of Princess Pipsy.

Princess Pipsy stares at her.

The drunken woman stares back. And hiccups.

Princess Pipsy furrows her brow.

The drunken woman staggers forward, clutching tight to the handle of her empty mug. She reaches her free hand to Princess Pipsy's face, gently stroking her jaw as she stumbles past. Almost incoherent, she mumbles to herself.

"Good horsey… Pretty little pony…"

The drunken woman wanders out of the tavern.

Princess Pipsy inhales.

Princess Pipsy exhales.

Princess Pipsy walks forward.

Clip-clop. Clip-clop. Clip-clop.

The three bartenders exchange silent glances of notable confusion.

Princess Pipsy stands at the bar, head poking between two patrons on stools. Both patrons scoot aside, giving Princess Pipsy more space. She stares ahead, eyes locked onto the orcish bartender.

The orcish bartender scans the room. His voice bellows.

"Alright, who did this? This some kind of joke?"

Nobody answers.

He continues.

"I don't care *who* this thing belongs to, but *somebody* better get it outta my bar."

Silence.

The fireplace crackles.

Princess Pipsy kicks the bar.

THUD!

Everyone looks to her, orcish bartender included. She kicks it again.

THUD!

The orcish bartender steps forward.

"Hey! Stop kicking my bar!"

Princess Pipsy pokes a nearby glass with her snout, holding eye contact. She huffs.

One of the human bartenders — his voice shrill — speaks up.

"I think she wants a drink, Boss."

Princess Pipsy huffs again.

Affirmative.

The orcish bartender crosses his arms, skeptical.

"The horse wants a drink?"

A deep voice from the tavern calls out.

"Come on, Boss, give 'im a drink!"

Another voice — a woman's — follows.

"Give it a drink, Boss!"

More patrons begin to stir.

Boss — the orcish bartender — grunts in thought.

After a moment, he uncrosses his arms.

"Yeah. Alright. Horse walks into a bar, guess he better have a drink. Why the hell not."

Murmurs of amusement among the patrons.

Princess Pipsy keeps her eyes focused ahead.

Boss pulls a cork from a tall bottle. *Tunk!* He pours it into a fresh glass. The drink is a deep, murky brown color. He sets the bottle on the counter and pushes the drink to Princess Pipsy.

The patrons all lean closer.

Princess Pipsy looks down at the fresh drink in front of her.

She leans across the counter and grabs the open bottle with her lips. She tilts her head back, chugging the rest of its contents with ease.

She flicks her head to the side, throwing the bottle to the ground.

It *shatters.*

She looks back to Boss.

She kicks the bar.

THUD!

One of the human bartenders — the one with the shrill voice — speaks up again.

"I think it wants another drink, Boss."

Boss — halfway between irritated and amused — responds.

"That was one of our strongest liquors. I mean, it's a horse, for fuck's sake. And it drank the whole bottle. We don't *got* much else. That's as strong as it gets."

From the crowd, another patron calls out.

"What about Last Drink?"

Murmurs of shock and intrigue among the patrons. A few folks in the back voice their agreements. The human bartenders look surprised at the mention.

Boss shakes his head, waving his hands dismissively. He addresses the patrons.

"No, no, no. Look… I think this is as funny as the next guy, but I got a business to run. Not only has that drink killed most'a you who tried it, it's *also* expensive as shit. So unless someone's payin', I say it's time this horse goes home."

Another voice calls out, speech slurred.

"Whaddya kickin' 'im out for? You cuttin' 'im off already?"

Quieter, another voice follows.

"They should'a kicked *you* out *yesterday.*"

A moment passes.

A patron near the bar chuckles: a middle-aged elven woman with tattoos along her arms, head completely shaved. She pulls a single gold coin from her pocket and raises it into the air.

"One gold, down payment!"

She tosses the coin in the direction of Princess Pipsy. It lands directly in front of her, quickly falling still. Unflinching, she continues to stare ahead at Boss, eyes locked onto his.

Another patron — a shorter human man near the front, dirty brown hair tucked behind his ears — staggers forward. He holds a small leather pouch in his hand.

"Aye! Put this on the horse's tab!"

He tosses the pouch. It, too, lands in front of Princess Pipsy, giving a gentle *clink;* clearly not packed with gold, but definitely more than a few coins inside.

One by one, other patrons raise their hands, each one clutching a coin or two, almost all of them gold. Shouts ring out.

"I got a couple!"

"Take mine while yer at it!"

"Here, here!"

"Few'a these outta do it!"

"Coin for the horse!"

As they shout, many chuckle. A few among them can't help but laugh already. One by one, in relatively quick succession, patrons of varying levels of drunkenness walk up to the "horse" at the bar, dropping their coin on the counter. Princess Pipsy continues staring ahead, focus unwavering as the pile of coin collects in front of her. Before long, every willing patron drops a coin or two on the pile, most gold, though a few copper pieces are visible.

Boss looks at the collection of gold on the counter, too dumbfounded — too surprised — to say anything.

Holding eye contact, Princess Pipsy pushes the pile of coin toward Boss with her snout.

She huffs.

Boss looks back to her.

Then to the pile.

Then back to her.

Silent for a moment, he thinks.

Then, he speaks.

"Yeah. That'll cover it."

— — — — — — — — — — — — — — — —

Princess Pipsy stands at the bar. Around her, most of the patrons have gathered to watch. Those that remain in their seats very much watch from afar, joining the crowd in spirit. The pile of coin has since been taken. The bar itself has been cleared of any other glasses or drinks near the equestrian customer.

Boss sets a heavy corked bottle down on the table. *Thunk.*

A thin layer of condensation wraps around the entire bottle. Its body seems considerably larger than a more traditional wine or liquor. Its glass is a dark, foggy red, almost impossible to see directly through. Around its center, an intricate metal relief — affixed to the bottle itself — depicts a jawless skull surrounded by roses and thorns. Inside, a dark-colored liquid sloshes gently, its true color masked by the glass of the bottle. A soft red mist — barely visible to the naked eye — seems to gather around the cork.

The temperature of the surrounding air drops.

Boss speaks.

"This is what we call the Last Drink. Most expensive thing we got. It's the strongest, too. Killed every hard-nosed drunk that's tried it, except for one."

He looks to the crowd, addressing them.

"And if this thing kills this fuckin' horse, every last one of you is helping drag it outta my bar."

He isn't asking.

He looks back to Princess Pipsy. Despite talking to her directly, it's clear he's still addressing the crowd.

"When this bar first opened, we had a wizard stop by. Real affinity for drinking himself blind. When we didn't have anything strong enough for 'im, he made us a bottle'a this. Left before we had a chance to try it. And — like I said — it's killed almost everyone since."

Boss uncorks the bottle. *Tunk!*

A phantom *hiss* comes from within. The red mist — while still faint — does not diminish. An oaky, burning scent spreads through the air. It stings the nostrils of the patrons closest, several recoiling slightly.

Boss grabs a shot glass from under the counter. It *clinks*.

He places the glass on the counter. He grabs the bottle, and — with patrons holding their breath in anticipation — he pours.

The bottle — or, rather, the liquid within — *hisses* louder as it pours. It fills the glass, its reddish-brown color unnatural in hue. Boss stops pouring. He corks the bottle and sets it aside.

Princess Pipsy looks down at the drink before her. Even now, its contents swirl in a gentle motion, as if still being poured. Like the bottle itself, a soft red mist gathers above it, almost imperceptible.

She takes a sniff. It stings.

She looks back to Boss.

Boss nods.

"You wanted a drink. *There's* your drink."

Princess Pipsy looks back down to the drink. The eyes of every conscious person in the tavern rest upon her.

She leans forward and wraps her mouth around the glass. She flicks her head back, downing the drink in one go. Numerous onlookers gasp.

At first, she feels nothing.

Then the burning starts.

Fumes from the drink scorch her throat. Her chest tightens, a growing heat within it. Her nose twitches. Her mouth aches. She exhales. Light red mist blows out from her nose, dissipating immediately. *And it burns.*

She rears back, front legs kicking the air. The patrons around her step back, giving space. She feels the heat rise to her face, now spreading to the rest of her body. Her head feels lighter. Her body feels less present.

And it all burns.

Instinctively, Princess Pipsy shakes her head.

Wildly.

The crowd backs up even further. Princess Pipsy kicks the air a few times, entirely unaware of her own movements, eyes squeezed shut. She continues shaking her head. The tie at the base of her horn comes loose. With another shake, the burlap flies off. It lands on the head of a drunken peasant man passed out against the wall.

Princess Pipsy stops. Her breathing returns to normal. Her head retains some of the effects — a gentle dizziness; a soothing buzz; a softer, more welcoming warmth — but the burning subsides. And, as it does, Princess Pipsy realizes that every single person in the tavern is staring right at her.

Or, more accurately, her horn.

Still feeling the effects of the drink, she speaks.

"What the fuck are you looking at?"

Realization sets in.

"Oh."

Boss steps forward, a careful concern in his voice.

"Who or *what* are you? And what the *fuck* are ya doin' in my bar?"

Princess Pipsy sighs.

"My name is Princess Pipsy. What I'm doing here is getting drunk. The 'why' is none of your concern."

Boss keeps a steady eye on Princess Pipsy.

"Well, now, I gotta be honest… a talking horse? A *unicorn?* That's got me *mighty* concerned. I suggest you talk fast or run faster."

Princess Pipsy frowns.

"Are you *threatening* me?"

Even the drunkest patrons among them can sense the growing tension in the room.

Boss holds his ground.

"I think we're way past conversation."

He whistles.

From within the crowd, two burly figures — both human, a man and a woman, each wearing heavy cloaks — step forward. Princess Pipsy notices them, but elects not to move. The two figures — slowly, but not stealthily — approach.

Whispers and hushed conversations spring up from the crowd.

"I knew something was weird…"

"Horses don't usually do that. Drink, I mean."

"Someone should kill it."

"I don't buy it. Probably belongs to some wizard. Magic types are always up to weird shit."

"Yeah. Probably just a regular, dumbass horse."

Princess Pipsy's ears pin back.

Her upper lip twitches ever-so-slightly.

She snaps her attention to the source of the last comment.

A shorter man — clearly dwarven in lineage — sits at a table near the bar, seated by himself. His scraggly gray-brown hair comes together in a half-assed ponytail, his beard wholly unkempt, flecks of foam caught in it. He wears a simple cloth shirt, sleeves pulled up to his elbows, a leather chestplate of some kind overtop it. Judging by the scratches and bruises across his face — and the cocky, taunting expression he now bears — this is a man who frequently gets into trouble. Several empty tankards crowd the table he sits at.

Princess Pipsy approaches.

"What did you say?"

Clip-clop. Clip-clop. Clip-clop.

Murmurs from the crowd. Those in the way step aside. Boss flicks his head toward the unicorn. His two bouncers trail behind her carefully.

The man at the table chuckles to himself, unclear whether he's too drunk to notice the tonal shift or simply too cocky to care.

"You got trouble hearing, or you just wanna hear it again?"

Princess Pipsy stops in front of the man. Even at her shorter height, she still towers over him.

"I want you to say it again."

Boss nods to his bouncers: *That's enough of that.* They close the distance.

The man at the table leans in closer.

"You don't scare me. You're just a regular, dumbass—"

SHUNK!

Princess Pipsy jams her horn through the center of the man's nose. He coughs, blood pouring from his mouth… and the hole enveloping most of his nose. In shock, he reaches up to touch the horn. Princess Pipsy shoves it deeper, the tip of her horn just barely poking through the back of his head. With a heavy throw, she tosses the limp body to the floor. It lands with a *thud.*

Immediately, both bouncers unsheathe shortswords. Patrons shout in frenzied panic. Several draw weapons of their own. Dozens rush the unicorn.

Boss shouts above the chaos.

"Kill it if you have to, but get that thing *out* of my bar!"

A bottle soars through the air. It shatters against Princess Pipsy's body. She ignores it, focused on the bouncers. She charges.

Both take wild swings. Their blades cut her skin, but not deeply. Princess Pipsy slams into them at full speed. The three of them fall to the ground.

Princess Pipsy lands on their faces.
CRUNCH!
She feels the warmth of blood. Quickly, she gets up, kicking several people away. Mounds of blood and fleshy clumps lie scattered across the floor where the bouncers' heads were, facial features smashed into the floor beyond recognition. Their muscles twitch.

Princess Pipsy runs around the angry crowd, weaving through tables and chairs. She spots an elven woman standing against the wall, pulling out a small war hammer of some kind. The woman raises the weapon as she approaches. Princess Pipsy jumps off the ground, throwing herself into the wall full-force. The elven woman brings down the hammer a moment too late: it impacts Princess Pipsy on the shoulder, but not before the weight of the unicorn's body crushes her chest, popping her lungs.

The elven woman falls.

Princess Pipsy continues to run through the tavern.

The crowd catches up to her, attempting to surround her. She kicks up violently, knocking her front hooves into several faces, bloody teeth knocked loose and *clacking* as they hit the floor. A few folks at the back of the crowd run out of the tavern. Before long, even more rush back in. People that weren't here before. People that seem excited. People that are looking for a fight.

A wiry woman — likely human — *smashes* a wine bottle against the side of Princess Pipsy's head. Bits of broken glass cut her skin, deep purple wine now covering her face. Princess Pipsy whips her head to the woman and bites her nose. With a twist and a pull, she tears it off. The woman screams, cries gurgled.

Princess Pipsy slashes her horn wildly. It cuts a number of bodies. Blood sprays into the air. The pained cries of the wounded are drowned out by the sounds and shouts of chaos.

Boss — now speckled with the blood of his patrons — speaks above it all.

"Kill that fucking horse!"

He reaches below the counter, grabbing a heavy crossbow. He loads a metal bolt into it.

Princess Pipsy continues slashing violently. Thick curves of blood fly through the air. Around her, dozens of bodies — most wounded, but many dead — clog the available space. Slowly but surely, more townsfolk rush in, all eager for the chance to kill a unicorn.

A stocky dwarven woman runs in, battleaxe in hand.

"I heard there's killin' in here!"

She bumps into a human man, a heavy cloak masking his identity. He turns to look at her, a dagger in each hand.

"Watch where you're fuckin' going!"

The dwarven woman grunts.

"Watch *this!*"

She swings her axe upward. The blade buries itself in the man's chin. He spews blood. In response, he swings both hands around, jamming his daggers into the sides of the dwarven woman's head. Both fall to the ground, bleeding all over each other.

More criminals rush into the tavern. Seeing the scuffle, more begin to attack each other in a fury. Blood splatters onto every surface it can.

CHOOM!

The crossbow fires.

SHUNK!

The bolt sticks into Princess Pipsy's shoulder. She recoils immediately, already feeling limitations in her movement. All around her, the tavern radiates chaos.

Shouts and cries blend with the sound of breaking wood and breaking glass.

Princess Pipsy swings her horn through the air, forcing more space between herself and the people around her.

At the bar, Boss loads another bolt into his crossbow.

Princess Pipsy charges ahead, a hobble in her gait.

Frantic, Boss fires the crossbow.

The bolt misses. It flies into the violent crowd, piercing the arm of a tattooed older man, pinning him to the wall. The criminal next to him — a younger man with an eyepatch — calls out.

"Hey, thanks!"

The man with the eyepatch stabs a large knife repeatedly into the other man's cheek.

Princess Pipsy leaps onto the bar.

Boss reaches for another bolt.

Princess Pipsy — bolt still very much stuck in her — runs across the countertop. Her hooves *thud* against the thick wood. Glasses fall off, shattering on the floor.

Boss shoves a bolt into the crossbow.

Princess Pipsy jumps onto him, knocking him to the ground. She lands on his chest, standing atop it, pinning him down. With a single hand, he fires the crossbow. The bolt misses the unicorn's head and flies into the ceiling.

Princess Pipsy stomps on his dominant hand. He feels the bone shatter, pointed fragments tearing into his own muscles. Blood pools around it. Before he has a chance to speak, Princess Pipsy stabs her horn into his jaw, digging deep.

Boss falls limp.

Princess Pipsy pulls her horn from his flesh. Blood spurts out from the fresh hole. Boss feebly reaches toward the wound, still conscious.

Princess Pipsy stares down at him, almost entirely covered in blood.

"I really should thank you for the drink. It was almost as strong as I'm used to."

From the corner of her eye, she spots the infamous bottle on the shelf beside her.

"Why don't *you* try it?"

She grabs the top of the bottle with her mouth, lifting it from the shelf. She swings it down, bashing it into Boss's face. It shatters. The liquid burns his broken skin, a *hiss* emanating from it. Steam — light red in color — rises into the air. He claws at his peeling skin.

Princess Pipsy slams the broken bottle back into his face, almost flattening his nose. *THWACK!* More liquor and blood scatters across the floor.

She brings it down again. *THWACK!*

And again. *THWACK!*

And again. *THWACK!*

And again. *THWACK!*

Breathing heavily, she drops the broken bottle onto the floor. (Or what's left of it, anyway.) She stares at the indiscernible bleeding mass below her.

"That one's on the house."

What she doesn't see, however, is the shadow from the towering figure behind her.

Something blunt — something *heavy* — hits the back of her head.

She falls.

Chapter VII:
Right Where
We Aren't

Chapter VII: Right Where We Aren't

Delphi's eyes shoot open. Overwhelming pain radiates through her body, almost impossible to even comprehend. She feels the crushed, jagged bone at the front of her snout, swaths of skin pulled taut or torn off entirely. She feels the holes in her side. The crusty residue of dried blood all over her body. And in the distance, she hears screams. Crackling fires. Heavy impacts. And somewhere in the distance, a cluster of deep, guttural roars — all in perfect unison — echoes through the city.

Along the horizon, the sun begins to set.

Delphi tries to move her body. She feels it react — she feels it *try* to move — she feels her muscles tense and spasm — but she does not move, unable to even lift her head.

Then the pain grows.

And grows.

And grows.

Now more conscious, the pain in her body — *throughout* her body — does not allow itself to be ignored.

And Delphi feels it all.

— — — — — — — — — — — — — — — — — — —

Damnation stands at the center of a wide city street. Rubble and debris lie strewn about. Various corpses — all humanoid — speckle the road in pieces. Heavy streaks of blood taint the surfaces around him. Nearby, several fires burn, dark smoke rising into the sky. Distant screams continue.

Damnation roars.

"Where are they?!"

He tears his arms into the building adjacent, ripping stones from the wall. He *cracks* the structure of the building with his force. Dust kicks up in response.

He looks to the sky. His jaw opens wide. A purple light sparks within. The flames of his eye sockets grow brighter.

SHOOM!

A massive beam of steady purple energy blasts forth, pulsing and cracking with erratic fervor. It carves through the sides of buildings, obliterating whatever it comes in contact with.

From further down the street, figures approach.

Damnation's beam dissipates. With a hint of amusement under his rage — perhaps of curiosity — he stands idle. And he waits.

The figures continue to approach, now coming into view.

Nearly a dozen knights — all clad in battle-worn armor — ride atop horses, each holding a weapon at the ready.

The knights stop, a hundred feet between them and the monster.

The front-most figure rides forward. Against the other knights, his armor is far more fitting. Looks to be a human, though his helmet obscures much of his face, only a sliver of his eyes visible through the gap in the metal. He holds a simple longsword at his side, gripping it tight.

The knight speaks, a practiced gravitas in his voice.

"Stop, in the name of Peace!"

Damnation tilts his head. His voices reply.

"And who the fuck are *you* supposed to be?"

Hearing the monster speak up-close, the knights shudder.

The front most knight catches a notable whiff of Damnation's rotten stench. He holds back a gag. Then, he speaks.

"I am Captain Kell, and we are sent on behalf of the king. We are your first and only warning."

With these words spoken, the rest of the knights train their swords on the monster. Several at the back of the group tremble lightly.

Damnation speaks.

"I'm not here for you. I'm here for the unicorns. Working on tying up a whole lot of loose ends."

He leans closer, a subtle grin spreading over his face.

"If you tell me where they are, I promise I'll only kill most of you."

Captain Kell's horse shifts nervously. He runs a hand across its mane, calming it.

"We are the Knights of Peace. We do not—"

From the back of the group, a young male knight calls out.

"I've seen one, aye!"

Damnation shifts focus.

"Oh, *really?*"

Damnation takes a few steps forward, gaze fixed on the young knight.

Captain Kell moves in front, blocking his way.

"Halt! By order of the King, you will come no closer!"

Captain Kell raises his sword, blade pointed at the monster.

Damnation sighs, disappointment in his voices.

"You talk too much."

Damnation gallops forward, his lopsided body
weight swinging as he moves. He reaches out with his
large, scaly hand.

Captain Kell raises his sword to strike.

Damnation wraps his heavy claws around Captain
Kell's helmet. He crushes it in his palm. It *pops*. An
explosion of blood, flesh, and metal spurts out from the
gaps between Damnation's fingers.

The other knights take off, speeding down the
ruined street.

Damnation throws Captain Kell's horse against the
building adjacent. It whinnies in panic as it flies through
the air. Its spine *snaps* on impact, a splash of blood left
behind.

Damnation refocuses on the fleeing knights ahead.

"I always love this part."

He gallops ahead at full speed, all eight of his
limbs supporting his hulking form. In almost no time at
all, he catches up to the knights, now running alongside
them.

His arms reach out, tearing riders from their horses.
He slams their heads into the ground, mashing their
faces and helmets into the stones of the very street they
traverse.

Blood sails through the air. Horses cry out. Metal
scrapes against stone. In a fit of pure strength and
violence — one by one — Damnation rips through the
bodies of the knights, taking their horses down with
them.

And then there was one.

Still riding atop his horse, the lone knight looks
back, terror in his eyes.

Damnation reaches out with his clawed hand once
again, blood now running through his fingers, sparse
bits of flesh stuck under his nails. He pulls the knight
from his horse and throws him to the ground.

The horse attempts to flee, still in a panic. Damnation sinks his claws into the horse's back. He pulls with heavy force, splaying it open. The horse tumbles to the ground. It skids along the stones, body twitching, sailing across a pool of its own blood.

Damnation stops galloping. Now calmer, he stands upright. He walks back over to the knight on the ground, each step leaving a bloody footprint behind him.

He reaches down, his large hand wrapping around the helmet. He rips it away, revealing the face of the knight. Clearly a younger man, his features are sharp and pointed. Matted blond hair sticks to his head. Splotches of blood — true source unknown — stain his face. Thin streaks of tears water down the deep red on his cheeks.

He speaks, voice trembling, much like the rest of his body.

"Please don't kill me… Please don't kill me…"

Damnation steps on his chest, pinning him to the ground. He leans in close. The sour stench of his body burns the knight's nose. The knight wretches, struggling to hold back vomit.

Damnation leans in even closer.

"You said you've seen one."

The knight nods.

Damnation stares down at him.

"Show me."

— — — — — — — — — — — — — — — — —

Panicked crowds flee from the city. Maus — atop Aster, a large weapon slung across his back — fights against the current, pushing through the frenzied townsfolk. Every so often, a grizzled fighter charges forward, weapon held high, disappearing down a random street. Large fires continue to burn, their plumes of smoke almost encasing the kingdom. Shouts and cries hang heavy in the air, sourceless; constant; fading to the background amidst the chaos.

Maus — not bothering to hide his voice — speaks.

"We can't stay much longer. He'll find us."

Aster continues to push through the crowd.

"I lost the queen before I even awoke. I am *not* going to lose the princess."

She continues.

"Besides, we need all the help we can get. Who knows how many of our people survive. I'd rather not lose any more."

A loud burst of screams from around the corner. Heavy, irregular thudding swiftly approaches, quickly growing louder.

Before Maus or Aster can react, Damnation comes barreling through the street, clutching a bleeding, whimpering knight in one hand. Dozens of civilians run ahead of him, attempting to flee. He continues forward, crushing them under the weight of his movement, stomping their bodies into the stone. He spots Maus and Aster in the corner of his vision. The two simply stand idle, not bothering to flee, but not wanting to draw much attention to themselves.

Damnation skids to a halt. His claws and nails *grind* against the stone, making a hideous sound. The knight in his grasp yelps at the sudden stop.

Damnation stares down at the odd horse and its rider, not quite making the connection.

His gaze locks with Maus's. Flames lick the sky behind him.

"I've seen you before."

Suddenly, a flurry of arrows flies in, most piercing Damnation's body, many still falling to the ground. Two arrows fly into the arm of the held knight. He shouts, pained.

Damnation snaps his attention to the source of the arrows. Not far off, a cluster of archers stands at the far end of a connecting street. A lone knight stands at the front, barking orders.

"Ready!"

The archers each knock an arrow into their bow, pulling it taut.

The knight — in near-immediate succession — calls out once more.

"Aim!"

Damnation's voices let out a frustrated groan. He gallops over to the archers. Their arrows fly through the air as he approaches.

Aster charges on, the monster now distracted.

"Come on!"

She continues racing through the abandoned streets, making her way back to the stables.

— — — — — — — — — — — — — — — —

The city burns. Dark smoke continues rising into the sky, the flames now providing light as the sun begins to set. Sporadic groups of townsfolk remain — and, every so often, a cocky mercenary eager to fight — though most have long since fled the city, many running on foot, each one focused purely on survival. Muffled sounds of distant violence — the kingdom's limited troops defending their land — give a tense, unstable ambience to the city. That of which, at this point, is a burning ghost town.

Maus and Aster ride into a thin alleyway, a faint trail of uneven hoofprints leading them. They follow the path wordlessly, each of the two focused and sharp, both keeping eyes out for any other leads. Any other trails. Any other clues on where Delphi and the princess went.

At the center of the alleyway — right in the middle of their path — sits a large crate, bits of stone and debris since fallen around it.

Aster picks up speed.

Maus holds tight.

Aster leaps over the crate, clearing it.

Barely.

Her back hooves clip the top of the crate. She lands a bit rougher than expected. Her footing falters. Maus nearly slips off. Quickly, however, both regain their balance, easily correcting in the moment.

Aster spots a large lump on the ground, a heavy pool of blood collected around it, its features just barely visible in the dimming light.

Delphi.

Aster shouts.

"There!"

She runs to the body.

Lying on the ground — a thin layer of soot now blanketing her — is the unmoving body of Delphi. Deep puncture wounds dot her barrel. The front of her snout, now crushed in on itself, resembles nothing more than an indiscernible clump of bloody meat.

Maus sighs.

"Well, shit…"

Aster speaks, directed at no one in particular.

"Who… *did* this?"

In the distance, a cluster of deep, guttural roars — all in perfect unison — echoes throughout the city.

Maus looks down to Aster.

"We have to go."

Aster says nothing. She simply stares down at Delphi.

She exhales.

"Alright. Let's go."

Aster turns away to leave, preparing to take off, when—

A wet, burbling sound from Delphi.

Breathing.

Aster and Maus look back to her.

With slow, struggled movement, her eye looks over to them.

Then her eye widens.

Her pupil dilates, quickly becoming a mere sliver.

Aster takes a step back.

A subtle yellow glow builds in Delphi's eyes.

It continues to grow brighter.

And brighter.

And *brighter.*

Then it becomes blinding.

The glow overtakes Delphi's eyes completely. From her eyes, the yellow glow travels through her veins, a web of light spreading across her entire body. It glows vibrantly beneath her skin. Her blood, too, slowly loses its natural red color, it, too, overtaken by the glow. Even the blood around her body shares the effect.

The entire alleyway brightens with the glow of Delphi, light now cast all around her.

Maus covers his eyes with one arm, unable to look directly at her.

Aster squints heavily. She takes several steps back. Delphi's body lifts into the air. She hovers, nearly ten feet off the ground, her legs and head hanging limp, her glow now even brighter than before. Its light now casts beyond the immediate space of the alleyway, brightening more of the city. Somewhere nearby, a pulsing hum resonates.

The hum grows louder.

It emanates from Delphi herself.

She rises higher into the air.

Her yellow glow strengthens, a radiant cascade of blinding light.

Aster shuts her eyes.

Maus does the same.

Delphi cries out.

Her whinny pierces the skies.

Then the glow dims.

The light dissipates.

Moments pass.

Aster and Maus open their eyes.

Delphi gently floats down, the glow continuing to fade. Her eyes return to normal. The hum fades to nothingness. And — as Aster and Maus quickly realize — the blood in the alley is gone. The gore on the wall has vanished. Delphi stands upright before them. The wounds that were present have vanished, and with no obvious signs of repair. *Not even a scar.* Her face, too — her snout, in particular — is just as it was the day prior.

By all accounts, Delphi now stands in perfect condition.

She blinks a few times, regaining proper consciousness. The glow of her body finally vanishes. A handful of sparkles — yellow in color — gently fall over her, each fading into nothing as it touches her skin.

Delphi takes note.

"Am I fucking sparkling?"

Maus speaks.

"And I thought the princess had a mouth."

Aster steps forward, ignoring Maus.

"We have to go. Whatever that was, it wasn't subtle."

Once again, a cluster of deep, guttural roars echoes through the ravaged city streets.

Delphi nods.

"Then let's go."

Maus grunts in agreement.

Aster takes off, speeding out of the alleyway, Maus steady atop her. Delphi follows, matching her speed.

As they run, Delphi speaks.

"I thought I was really going to die. That we were *all* going to die."

She thinks to herself for a moment, continuing to run.

"I… don't know what happened."

Aster responds.

"I don't know what happened, either. But whatever it was, I think it means something."

Aster looks over to her.

"I think you just got your magic back."

The group continues, galloping through the empty streets, breaking for the hillside as fast as they possibly can. Before long, they breach the city limits. The packed buildings around them give way to wooden shacks and farming fields once again.

Townsfolk — those who successfully fled, anyway — continue walking through the hills, many going in wildly different directions. Some form larger groups, a handful of ramshackle encampments already set up farther into the countryside.

The fires rage on. The kingdom burns.

From somewhere deep in the heart of the city, Damnation roars, the frustration in his voices — the *irritation* — carrying for miles.

Aster — still running — looks to Delphi.

"Who attacked you? What happened to the princess? Where is she?"

Delphi frowns.

"We have much to discuss."

— — — — — — — — — — — — — — — —

Da-dunk. Da-dunk. Da-dunk.

Movement. Continuous movement. Uneven, continuous movement.

Da-dunk. Da-dunk. Da-dunk.

There's a feeling. A cold, heavy feeling. It wraps around the legs. It wraps around the neck. It feels uncomfortable. Unwelcome. Restricting.

Da-dunk. Da-dunk. Da-dunk.

Princess Pipsy opens her eyes.

Around her legs, heavy metal chains keep her bound. Still coming to, she looks around, examining the space.

Fairly cramped, all things considered. A few draperies. Some spare clothes. The occasional light weapon hanging from the wall. Her armor sits in a pile nearby, hastily thrown to the corner. But nothing else of note. Even lying down, Princess Pipsy takes up most of the available space. Looks like the back of some ramshackle storage cart.

Da-dunk. Da-dunk. Da-dunk.

No… it *is* the back of some ramshackle storage cart. That's the sound of wooden wheels moving. Of a rickety cart wobbling along some unseen path.

Princess Pipsy tries to move.

Shink! Shink!

The chains rattle. She gets nowhere.

She tries again.

Shink! Shink! Shink!

It's no use.

A muffled chuckle comes from the front.

After a moment, a wooden slat in the far wall slides open. The face of an orcish figure peers through, only the eyes and top of the head visible. Thinning gray hair comes together in a ponytail at the back of the head. Even from here, Princess Pipsy can see the age in the figure's leathery green skin.

Farther behind the head, Princess Pipsy can just barely see the darkening sky overhead, the sun almost wholly below the horizon.

The figure speaks, a deep, masculine voice.

"Well, well, well! Look who's finally awake!"

Princess Pipsy attempts to speak. She finds herself unable to, only capable of muffled, indiscernible sounds. She feels a tight cloth wrapped around her snout. She's been gagged.

As much as a talking unicorn *can* be gagged, anyway.

The orcish figure chuckles.

"Save your breath. You're gonna need it."

Princess Pipsy stops struggling. She stares at the figure, eyes brimming with hatred.

The figure continues.

"I don't believe we've formally met. The name's Barric. And you killed my brother."

Da-dunk. Da-dunk. Da-dunk.

"Heard a lotta commotion down at his place. Figured another big fight broke out. Figured I'd help 'im clean it up. And boy howdy, did I *not* expect to see *you* in there. Always thought y'all were a myth."

Da-dunk. Da-dunk. Da-dunk.

"A'course, once I saw you kill 'im, I knew you'd have to be dealt with. Certainly could'a killed ya myself, but there's no money in that. And if there's money to be made, I better be makin' it."

Da-dunk. Da-dunk. Da-dunk.

"I got some friends of mine up north. Friends that run a *real* special business, just for the sake of us orcish folk. And they pay a *real* pretty price for anything… unique. Anything dangerous. And you seem like both."

Da-dunk. Da-dunk. Da-dunk.

"Don't get me wrong, I'm all torn up on the inside. Promise. My brother's gone for good, and I hope you die a horrible death. But once I'm done with this, I get to retire. And after that, I get to watch you gored in person. And I won't lie, that *does* make me feel a little better."

Da-dunk. Da-dunk. Da-dunk.

"Rest up. Or don't. Either way, you won't last long."

The wooden slat *slams* shut, leaving Princess Pipsy alone with her thoughts.

She doesn't know exactly where she's going. She doesn't know exactly how much time is passing on the way. But she knows that she's probably going to have to kill something soon. And for the transgression of kidnapping royalty, she really wants that something to be Barric.

Chapter VIII:
Shit-Eating Lamprey

Chapter VIII: Shit-Eating Lamprey

The cart stops abruptly.

Princess Pipsy lurches forward.

Her head collides with the wall.

She wakes up.

She feels the dull, throbbing pain in her head. Then she feels the cold weight of her chains, still keeping her bound. Then she feels the tight fabric keeping her jaws clamped together.

Outside — beyond the walls of the cart — a steady wind blows; light, but audible. Muffled voices speak. She raises her ears, attempting to hear *just* a bit more. Enough to make out any details of the conversation. Enough to glean any useful anecdotes that might help her now.

No luck. The speech is too muffled. Sounds like more than one person — likely two — though she can't be certain. It's too hard to tell.

Laughter. The two voices are laughing.

So it is two people.

Heavy footsteps walk around the side of the cart.

Very heavy footsteps.

They stop at the rear.

Muffled, a lock *clicks*.

The back doors of the cart open outward.

Blinding light spills in. Instinctively, Princess Pipsy squints. She can't make out any details. Not really. And, as she realizes this, she *also* realizes it's cold. *Bitingly* cold.

A towering shadow stands in front of her. It chuckles. Then, it speaks, its deep feminine voice a touch too loud for comfort.

"There she is."

The shadow reaches out, wrapping its large, heavy hand over the princess's chains. The figure yanks her from the cart and throws her onto the ground.

She lands hard. Chipped bits of shale scratch her body. Somewhere on her side, light trickles run down. Feels like she's bleeding a bit.

Her eyes slowly adjust to the light. She's still forced to squint, but she can see a bit more now. She can see the shale plains all around her, the flat, gray rock stretching for miles. She can see the heavy mist on the horizon. She can see the stone construction of a city not too far off in the distance. She can see the edges of some grand structure behind her, *just* beyond the limits of her vision. She can see the storage cart, its doors still open, two horses standing idle at its front. She can see an older orc man, a thin gray ponytail at the back of his head, a smug look on his face, his hands holding tight to a hefty leather pouch. *Barric.* She can see a few more orcish figures around them, possibly standing guard.

And she can see the towering orcish figure that threw her from the cart: a smooth mask of black leather wraps around her head, a loose cowl draping over the top of her shoulders, only her eyes visible; a studded dark outfit, likely leather as well, no sleeves to cover her arms, countless scars visible across the muscle; some sort of hide-like material poking out in several places, likely padding of some kind, either for warmth or protection, if not both.

The cold air continues to bite. Already, the princess feels her body temperature falling.

Next to the cart, Barric grins.

"She's a real handful. Try not to have *too* much fun with her."

The masked orc looks down to the unicorn.

"Oh, I think we will."

She reaches down and grabs hold of the chains. She walks toward the tall structure — the one Princess Pipsy can't quite see — and drags her prisoner along the ground.

On either side, the other guards follow, the princess now clearly able to see their identical leather masks. In their hands, they carry familiar shapes of metal.

Her armor.

The metal chains grind against the shale. Chips and fragments of the rock dig into her skin, piercing her hide as her body scrapes along the ground. She wriggles, attempting to lessen the pain.

The one holding her chain notices. She yanks them hard. Bits of stone dig deeper into the princess's skin.

The guard speaks.

"Stop moving."

Princess Pipsy abides. The guard continues to drag her along, her body continuing to scrape the ground. In several more places now, she feels the trickle of blood. Behind her, the faintest trail of red marks her path.

Now farther away, she watches Barric's cart ride off, pointed toward the stone city in the distance. Princess Pipsy adjusts her head, getting a better look at where she's being taken. It's hard to see all the details.

What she *can* see, however, is the massive wall of the building, clearly some sort of oblong shape. This wall alone must be at least five stories tall. But no windows of any kind. Not ones she can see, anyway. A large metal gate — currently open — leads inside. Two more orcish figures — very similar masks and outfits — stand guard on either side. Between those at the gate and those taking her in, that makes seven guards, each one as strong as she is, if not stronger. Even at her best, she'd struggle to best them in physical combat, let alone when she's bound and gagged. No use trying anything now.

What is this place?

The guard pulling her chains looks back to her.

"Most of the new ones gotta wait weeks before a show. Most of 'em get roughed up before then. Some of 'em get killed. But you're just in time for the next one. Coming up *real* soon."

She continues dragging the princess across the ground.

"Let's see if you make it that long."

— — — — — — — — — — — — — —

The masked orc hurls Princess Pipsy through the open cell door. She impacts the damp stone with a heavy *thud*, skidding along the floor.

The cell door slams closed.

CHANG!

The lock *clicks*.

Now free of her chains, Princess Pipsy clambers to her feet.

The voice of the masked orc echoes in the chamber.

"I'm only gonna say this once, so listen up. You been caught, and now you been bought. We *own* you now. So if you wanna live, you do *what* we say, *when* we say it. Do anything we don't like, and we make it worse for you."

She smirks, her eyes giving it away.

"But don't worry, we love a good fight. No punishment for killing a cellmate. Just try not to make a big mess."

She walks off, thumping the metal bars of the cell on the way.

"Welcome to the All Hells Tournament. Greatest in orc entertainment the last few hundred years. We hope we'll enjoy your stay."

She heads further down the hall, disappearing from view.

Still within earshot, she calls out.

"Say hi to your cellmate for us! I hear he's a *real* ladykiller."

With that, another metal door closes, this one at the end of the hall.

CHANG!

She's gone.

Princess Pipsy pulls down her gag with her hoof, finally free of it. She throws it to the ground in disgust.

"Fucking amateurs."

She turns around, getting a better look at the cell.

As a whole, the chamber seems to be twenty feet tall, easily. Light illuminates the space from a small, square metal grate in the ceiling. In perpetual consistency, a single drop of grimy water falls down from it, landing on the stone.

Plink...

Plink...

Plink...

The carved stone of the ceiling curves downward, becoming the walls. Metal chains with empty clasps — some rusted; all far too large for a normal humanoid — are affixed to the far wall, embedded into the stone. To her right, two shallow alcoves push further into the wall, each a few feet deep. Short, stubby bed frames poke out, one in each. Their wood looks old and beaten. A dirty stretch of burlap material covers the surface of each.

Beyond that, a few miscellaneous adornments populate the space — an old wooden pallet; a mostly-intact wooden chair; a couple moldy buckets placed against the wall — but it remains fairly empty, all things considered. Even for a prison cell, it's oddly spacious… as if its usual occupants are generally larger.

Beyond her own cell, Princess Pipsy can hear echoes of commotion from others. Not too close, of course — on the way in, she noted how much stone separated each cell in the grid — but close enough.

Conversations bounce around the walls. A shout or two, every once in a while. A punch. A rattle. A thud. A loud threat. A quiet scream.

And with it all, the steady drip of the grate continues.

Plink…

Plink…

Plink…

Then—

Skitter skitter skitter…

Princess Pipsy whips back around.

The noise came from somewhere in her cell.

Her eyes scan the space. She doesn't spot anything that catches her eye.

Skitter skitter skitter…

There it is again.

That sounded *much* closer.

She looks around once more, growing wary.

"I can hear you. Stop hiding."

She adds on.

"Don't make me find you."

A voice speaks out, coming from the prison bed nearest. The voice sounds… strange. Light and wispy — almost shrill — yet rough and scratchy at the same time.

"Oh, I'm *terribly* sorry. Yes, terribly sorry. Hm."

Skitter skitter skitter…

From above the prison bed — hiding on the underside of the stone alcove — a lanky figure crawls out, hugging the wall. Its four arms grip the stone with long, spider-like fingers. Its legs — noticeably shorter — rest against the stone, doing nothing to hold it up. It wears a scrappy outfit of torn fabrics, discarded leathers, and mismatched clothing. Across the pasty cream skin of its body, numerous cuts, gashes, and minor scars are visible. It wears a large, singular goggle over its bald head, held in place by a dirty leather strap. Its oblong, pitch-black eye — its *only* eye — stares right into Princess Pipsy's.

The creature smells stale. Grimy. Like a gross, wet cloth left in the sun for too long.

It speaks again.

"Looks like we're stuck here together. At least for a day or two, anyway. Hm. Before the next fight. Yes. At least until then."

The princess keeps a watchful eye on the creature.

"Tell me who you are. And make it quick, before I do something about it."

The creature climbs down from the wall. It stands upright in front of the princess, its height far shorter than its arms would lead one to believe.

"My name is Eckle. I've been here for a long time. A long time, yes. Not so good at fighting. But good at being fast. And that's good enough. Hm."

Princess Pipsy can't help but take a whiff.

Repugnant.

"Can you stand farther back? Your body reeks of mildew."

Eckle steps back.

"Oh, yes. That would be the mildew. Hm."

He continues.

"Don't bother trying to escape. Useless. Never works. Never works."

The princess responds.

"Every prisoner in every prison has been saying that ever since prisons were built. They have to open these cells at some point."

Eckle shakes his head.

"Never. No. Not like that. Only for the tournament. Fight to the death. Or live long enough to get thrown back. Do that 'til you die. Hm."

Princess Pipsy takes a breath. This creature is *horribly* irksome.

"How often?"

Eckle glances toward the locked door.

"Once a month. No more than that. Next in a couple'a days. Sometimes they start early. Hard to tell. Place like this. Hm. Hard to keep track."

He continues.

"Lucky for you. You'll see the sky again soon. Hm. Most people wait longer."

He skitters forward a few paces, walking on his hands more than his legs. He examines the princess closely.

"You look strange."

She frowns.

"You're one to fucking talk."

Eckle smirks.

"Hm. Feisty. More than most. Good. Might have a chance. We'll see how you do. Don't count on it."

The princess looks around once more. Her eyes lock on to the grate in the ceiling.

"What's up there?"

Eckle, too, looks up.

"That's the floor of the battleground. Hm. The coliseum. Where they take us. Not all at once. Just a few at a time. Spread it out. Make us wait."

The princess speaks again.

"You've never tried climbing up there?"

Eckle scoffs.

"I can. I do. Easy for me. Hm. No point. Grate stuck in the rock. Too weak to break it. Useless. Hm. Just like I told you. Not all bad, though."

He looks back to the princess, meeting her eyes.

"Sometimes we get lucky. Fighters get stuck. Lose a weapon. Lose a finger. Lose a face. Falls into our cells. We get to keep it all. Even the meat."

He smiles. Just barely visible between his cracked lips, Princess Pipsy catches a glimpse of the countless little teeth inside. Hundreds, if not thousands.

Revolting.

She tries to ignore his face.

"I assure you, I won't be staying long."

Eckle cocks his head.

"Oh. Suicide by battle. Giving up easy. Not uncommon. Bold choice. I respect it. Hm."

The princess stammers.

"No, I— That's not—"

She sighs.

"Forget it."

Eckle grunts.

"Forgot it already. Hm."

Princess Pipsy takes another glance around the room, this time looking for something. Based on her expression, she doesn't find what she's after.

She looks back to Eckle, hesitant to even speak.

"I don't see any chamber pots in here. Surely, even the lowest of places like this would supply them."

Eckle snickers. Even his laugh sounds jagged and uncomfortable.

"Astute observation. Hm. That's what the buckets are for. Empty now, though. Thirsty. Finished before you arrived."

He turns around, making very obvious motions to cover his eye.

"I won't look. Some privacy for you. Hm. Just let me know when you're done. Not much food here. Need all the nutrients we can get."

Absolutely vile.

In endless repetition, the grate above drips on.

Plink...

Plink...

Plink...

Princess Pipsy sighs.

"This is going to be a very long day."

Chapter IX:
Solitary Fairy

Chapter IX: Solitary Fairy

Hovering in the air, a small humanoid figure — glowing with a steady blue light — cackles maniacally. As she does, the sun begins to set along the horizon.

After a moment, she stops.

She wipes a single tear from her eye.

"I'm just too funny."

She adds on.

"And smart."

She continues.

"And beautiful."

She sighs contentedly.

Her eyes scan the space in front of her. She looks… confused.

"Huh?"

She spins around, getting a look at everything around her. She sees the winding dirt road below her, one of many leading to the kingdom ahead. She sees, further in the distance, the kingdom itself. She sees the rolling grasses, the farmhouses nearby, the willow trees that speckle the hillsides, the edge of the forest behind her… but no unicorns.

"They were just here a minute ago…"

It's been hours.

From within the Kingdom of Peace, a cluster of deep, guttural roars — all in perfect unison — echoes through the hillside.

The fairy snaps her attention toward the source.

Even from here, she can see the teeny flames on the tops of the buildings, all tickling the slowly dimming sky.

Wait. No. *Not* teeny.

Right. That's how distance works.

Those flames are probably regular-sized.

It's all about perspective.

But the unicorns lit the forest on fire. Maybe they lit *that* on fire. It would make a lot of sense. The pattern doesn't lie.

Not nearly as clever as they think they are.

She grins.

"Ooh-hoo-hoo… I'm gonna *find* you!"

She zips off, flying toward the kingdom.

— — — — — — — — — — — — — — —

The city burns. All around her, fires paint the sky. Screams and shouts echo through the streets. Every so often, she flies over pools of blood or bits of bodies.

What a mess!

The roars fill the air once more. The ones in perfect unison. The ones that she heard before.

She giggles.

"How interesting…"

She zips away, heading further into the city.

The chaotic noise around her only grows more chaotic as she continues. She keeps her focus steady as she flies, intent on finding the source of those roars. A few fleeing townsfolk catch a glimpse of her flight, but they quickly move on from the awe, turning back to their paths of escape; they have more important things going on.

The fairy spots a large group of lumps in the street. Curious, she flies to it.

Now closer, the lumps are clearly bodies. All humanoid, though it's hard to tell for sure, since most of them are torn to pieces. Broken bows and bloody arrows litter the area, mixed in with chunks of wet meat and muscle.

Nearby, a cluster of voices — all speaking in unison — shouts in frustration.

"What do you mean *you don't know? Tell me everything!"*

A cowardly, pitiful whimper follows.

The fairy turns toward the voices.

Not far off.

Surprisingly close, actually.

She goes to them, determined to see whoever it is — *whatever* it is — for herself.

And it doesn't take long.

———————————————————————————

Damnation stands before the entrance to Bald Man's Gate. Dust and ash swirl through the air, partially obscuring the sign for the tavern, inn, and eatery. In his largest hand, he clutches the young knight.

Damnation glares at the knight, the purple of his sockets glowing bright. He brings the knight's face close to his own. *Uncomfortably* close.

"What do you mean *you don't know? Tell me everything!"*

The knight whimpers.

Damnation brings his face even closer.

"Now."

The knight — trying to avoid eye contact — forces speech.

"I was here not too long ago. Evening drink. A little early, I know, but it was a long week. Sometimes, you just—"

Damnation's voices growl, losing patience.

"Get to the fucking point."

The knight shivers.

"I saw a horse walk into the bar. Had a bag on its head. A disguise, I guess. But then it came off. We all saw it. Me and the other folks there. It wasn't just *any* horse… it was a *unicorn.*"

Damnation shakes the knight a bit.

"And *then?*"

The knight continues.

"She went berserk. Killed a man for no reason. Started trashing the place. Got people riled up. I ran when the fighting got bad — wanted to let the other guards know — but, uh… then you showed up. And I got a bit… distracted."

Damnation stares at him for a moment.

"So you don't know where it is now? The unicorn?"

The knight freezes up. He struggles to reply.

Damnation exhales, irritation building.

The knight stammers.

"She could still be inside!"

He flashes a nervous smile, hardly believing his own words.

Damnation does *not* smile.

Holding the knight, he steps up to the front door, only slightly ajar. He pushes it open with two of his free hands. And, gently, it opens.

Creak...

The interior sits in absolute disarray. Tables and chairs lie on their sides, some chipped, their edges scratched or broken. Drying blood covers most of the surfaces. Numerous bodies — most indiscernible — sprawl across the floor. Slumped against the farthest corner of the room, a horribly drunken figure snores quietly, a bloody burlap cloth over their head.

Slowly, Damnation looks over to the knight.

The knight shrugs, a fearful grin on his face.

Damnation presses his fingers against the sides of the knight's head. He twists.

Crunch!

His neck snaps.

Damnation drops the limp body of the knight.

Thump!

He sighs.

"I had a feeling."

Then he feels something else.

Senses something else.

Something else behind him.

He turns.

From the corner of his vision, he sees a small blue glow duck behind a small pile of rubble, just barely beyond his direct line of sight.

He approaches.

"I can feel you. I can *sense* you. Reveal yourself, and I might not kill you right away."

From behind the rubble, the blue glow floats back up, revealing itself. Now much closer, Damnation can make out the details.

A fairy.

And a weak-looking one, at that.

Damnation stares at it.

"Speak."

The fairy does.

"You seen any unicorns?"

Damnation cocks his head.

"Elaborate."

He adds on.

"Now."

The fairy flies up a bit higher, now meeting Damnation's eye line. With a near-comical mischievous grin, she speaks.

"I'm gonna kill 'em."

Damnation takes a step back, immediately disinterested.

"So am I. But I work alone."

He turns and walks away.

"I respect the common goal, so I won't crush you between my fingers. I suggest you leave before I change my mind."

The fairy grunts, unhappy.

"Wow. I try to help, and this is the thanks I get?"

She crosses her arms.

"Asshole."

Damnation stops.

He turns back around.

Slowly.

His sockets burn brighter than before.

"What did you say?"

The fairy scoffs.

"What, you hard'a hearing? Or you just want me to insult you again?"

Damnation's voices growl.

Suddenly—

Many blocks away, a blinding yellow light shines, illuminating the city around it. A steady, subtle hum accompanies it.

Damnation's anger drops. Immediately, he turns.

He speaks, voices thick with disdain.

"Unicorns."

He leaps, bounding into the air. He hooks onto the side of a building, landing with a heavy impact. Bits of stone tumble downward, clacking against the wall as they fall. From there, he leaps again, hooking onto the next building.

The fairy gasps.

"Hey! Wait for me!"

She flies after, moving as fast as she can.

Damnation leaps again, landing on the next building. He keeps his gaze fixed on the source of the light.

The fairy catches up.

"Slow down, dummy!"

Damnation turns to her, now irritated.

"Get out of here!"

He leaps to the next building, returning his focus to the light.

The fairy follows.

Damnation lands askew. He digs his hands deeper into the wall, adjusting himself to avoid falling. More chunks of stone tumble downward.

The fairy follows.

He swats at it.

"I told you to *leave!*"

The fairy dodges his heavy, clumsy swing.

"I'm not leaving until I find those sons-a-bitches!"

Damnation's voices groan, frustration evident.

"That's what I'm trying to *do*, but you keep *distracting* me!"

The fairy scoffs.

"Distracting you? Yeah, right."

The blinding yellow light begins to fade.

Damnation notices.

"No!"

He leaps onto another building, trying to follow the source.

It dims further.

He leaps to the next building.

Its light begins to vanish.

He leaps to the next building.

It fades into nothingness.

He looks around, now more frantic, trying to see where it might have come from. All around him, rooftops burn with fires of varying sizes. Their flames cast a warm yellow glow on whatever their light can reach.

It's no use. The radiant yellow glow is gone.

Damnation shouts from his perch.

"No, no, *NO!*"

The fairy speaks, more distance between them now.

"Some help *you* were! I'll just find 'em myself."

She flies just a bit closer, taunting him.

"And I won't tell you where."

Before he can take another swipe, she zips off.

"Thanks for nothing, numbnuts!"

She flies into the ruined streets below, disappearing from view.

His irritation builds, getting the best of him. Damnation roars. The frustration in his voices — the *rage* — carries for miles.

"I will find you, unicorns!"

He looks out to the darkness of the night, now fast approaching.

"You can never escape your Damnation."

— — — — — — — — — — — — — — —

The fairy soars through the air. Her eyes scan the land below her. She flies high above the streets, leaving ample space between her and the chaos below. Every so often, she sees another few townsfolk fleeing the city. But she doesn't see any unicorns. And she doesn't see their dumb friend, either.

She moves on.

She flies outside of the city, entering the farmlands beyond. Here, fleeing townsfolk seem more frequent. Many continue walking into the countryside. Some still run, though they appear to reach their limits, movements now slow and exhausted. Every so often, one or two folks look up to stare at her blue glow speeding away into the night. Far behind her now, the sound of Damnation's continued destruction carries.

What a baby.

Farther ahead — much farther than any townsfolk have gotten — she spots a wooden cart riding down a wide dirt road. The two horses pulling it move quickly, clearly in a hurry. She hovers in place and watches it from a distance, realizing it's the only cart on the road. At least this far out, anyway. Most of the townsfolk fled on foot. Those who had horses got farther than others. But this cart — the one riding further into the distance — seems *very* far away.

It must have left hours ago. Before Damnation even arrived.

The fairy thinks.

"Hm…"

She flies to it.

The cart wobbles as it moves. Its wheels look poorly attached, in need of some serious maintenance. At the front, an older orcish man sits upright, eyes fixed ahead of him.

The fairy lands on the back of the cart, standing on the lip of it. She pushes her hands against the bottom of the cart's door, trying to push it open.

It doesn't budge.

She looks up. She sees the lock and chain on the door, keeping it shut.

Bummer.

She examines the door again.

Closer to the bottom, she spots a tiny little hole in the wood, just barely big enough to see through. She gasps excitedly.

"Jackpot."

She gets low and peers through the hole.

"Let's see what you're hiding, mystery man."

Inside, it looks fairly cramped. A few draperies on the wall. A handful of light weapons. Some weird-looking armor in a pile in the corner. A white horse chained up and gagged with some bloody spike on its head.

Wait a minute…

She looks closer.

The cart hits a pothole in the road.

THUNK!

It bounces from the impact. Knocked off, the fairy arcs through the air, falling to the ground. She tumbles in the dirt, kicking up dust.

She coughs a few times. Then, she stands.

She watches the cart ride off, its horses leading it toward the gray mountains in the distance.

She thinks for a few moments. She watches the cart get smaller and smaller, riding further and further away.

"Where are the other guys?"

She flies off, heading back out into the night.

— — — — — — — — — — — — — — — — — — —

Aster charges on through the hillside, heading deeper into the thick patch of forest. Maus rides steady on her back. Delphi runs alongside them, keeping pace. In the far distance, the remnants of the Kingdom of Peace burn, the fires still going strong. Above them, stars peek through the crowded canopy.

Delphi looks over to Aster.

"How much farther do we have to go?"

She sounds exhausted.

Aster responds.

"As far as we can."

She, too, sounds exhausted.

She continues.

"But this should be far enough for now."

Aster and Delphi slow to a stop. They both breathe heavily.

Maus hops down from Aster. He stands beside her.

"We should find somewhere to camp for the night. We need the rest."

Aster looks to him.

"But no fires."

Maus nods.

"No fires."

Delphi looks between them.

"Now we talk?"

Aster thinks for a moment. Then, she speaks.

"We should set up camp first. Make sure we're well hidden, just in case he looks for us out this way. Then we can talk."

From somewhere above — just barely within earshot — a familiar voice calls out.

"There you are!"

The trio looks up, immediately ready to run.

The fairy descends from above the canopy, surrounded by her consistent blue glow. At the sight of her, the trio relaxes, though they each bear a look of annoyance.

The fairy flies closer.

"You're a real pain to find, you know that?"

Aster replies.

"We'd be dead if we weren't."

The fairy smirks.

"Sure, sure. Looks like that's working well for ya."

Maus glares at her.

"What do you want?"

The fairy flies over to Maus.

"Aw, somebody still mad I tickled his nose?"

Maus frowns.

"I am *not* mad."

The fairy reaches a single hand toward Maus's nose. Immediately, he swats her away. She flies around the swing with ease.

She giggles.

"Uh-huh! *Sure* you aren't."

Maus grunts, just a little bit mad.

The fairy flies back a bit, giving more space.

"Like I told you before, I want to kill you."

She sighs.

"But it's no fun if you're all beaten and miserable. And that big guy's an even bigger buzzkill than you are."

Aster steps closer.

"You survived against Damnation?"

The fairy nods.

"Yeah. He's a real asshole."

She looks back to Maus.

"You'd probably like him."

A moment passes.

"Asshole."

Delphi speaks.

"So what do you *really* want? Why are you here?"

She flies over to Delphi and kicks her ear.

"I said I want to *kill* you, dummy!"

Delphi shakes her head.

The fairy backs off.

"Listen before you open that smelly mouth next time!"

Aster speaks.

"That's *not* what she meant."

The fairy shrugs.

"Yeah, I know. I just wanted to kick her ear."

Delphi groans.

The fairy flies over to Aster, a sing-song tone in her voice.

"I know where your friend is! I know where your friend is!"

Aster's eyes widen.

"You know of the princess? Where is she?"

The fairy flies even closer.

"I'll never tell!"

The fairy spins around in the air, dancing and taunting the trio. She continues to sing, regrettably off-key.

"You need me now! You need me now! You need me now!"

Delphi's horn glows blue, her hue darker than the fairy's.

The fairy stops dancing, frozen in place. She finds herself engulfed by the darker blue glow. And she finds herself unable to move.

She stops giggling.

Delphi focuses intently.

The fairy — through magical means — pulls closer.

The two lock eyes.

Delphi speaks.

"You *will* tell. And if you try to leave before you do, we'll kill you."

Delphi's horn stops glowing.

The dark blue glow around the fairy vanishes. She falls, a soft *thud* as she hits the grass below.

Delphi walks off, heading further into the dense patch of forest.

Aster looks down at the fairy.

"We leave at first light. Until then, you're with us."

She leans closer.

"We've got a *lot* of talking to do. And you're going to tell us everything you know."

Aster walks off, following Delphi.

The fairy crosses her arms and pouts.

"Well, maybe I'll just sit here forever, since you wanna be so mean to me. How about *that?*"

Maus leans down and picks her up. She yelps.

He walks behind the unicorns, following their path.

The fairy sighs.

"Assholes."

Chapter X:
Self-Inflicted Trauma Bonding

Chapter X: Self-Inflicted Trauma Bonding

Aster glares at the fairy, the latter of which sits on a tree stump, arms crossed, pouting vehemently.

The fairy groans.

"Don't make sense to me."

Aster speaks.

"Your opinion is irrelevant. I trust Delphi. She speaks first, then you."

The fairy whines.

"But what I gotta say is *really* important!"

Maus stands nearby, back leaned against a tree.

"Just let her say *somethin'*. If you don't, she'll never shut up."

Delphi stands in front of him, closer to the group.

"I hate to agree with him, but he's probably right."

Delphi watches the fairy's leg bounce impatiently.

"I can wait."

The fairy gasps, demeanor instantly changing.

"Really? Ooh, you're gonna *love* what I gotta say!"

She jumps up and lands on her feet, still atop the stump. She looks at Aster, clearly the voice of authority.

"Please? Come on! Lemme say it!"

Aster sighs.

"Get it over with. Short and to the point. No dancing around the subject."

The fairy raises an eyebrow.

"Oh? You mean like… *this?*"

She dances on the tree stump.

Aster steps closer, unamused.

"Speak."

The fairy stops dancing.

"Whatever."

She straightens up.

"I saw some dinky storage cart. Riding out of the city. It got *way* farther than everyone else. Even the people on horseback. Had to've left way before then. Seemed real strange. *Real* interesting."

She continues.

"So, naturally, I flew right up to that thing, took a peek inside, and… *BAM!*"

She gestures outward with her hands in overly dramatic fashion.

"There was the princess. All chained up, too. Could've been dead. Could've been sleeping. Who knows?"

Aster leans closer.

"Where were they headed?"

The fairy looks to her.

"Up to the mountains. Or somewhere else, I guess. But they were definitely headed that way. Don't really know what's over there."

Maus furrows his brow.

"You've never been past the mountains?"

The fairy looks over to him, visibly annoyed, hands on her hips.

"Of *course* not, ya big stupid dummy!"

Maus grunts, irked.

Aster clears her throat.

"Are you sure that's where they were headed?"

The fairy looks back to her.

"Yeah. I'm sure."

Aster sighs.

"Then we have less time than I thought."

The fairy cocks her head.

"Huh? Why?"

Delphi speaks.

"The Dreadrock Mountains are what you're talking about. Beyond the Foothills, to the north. And they're in orc territory."

The fairy speaks again.

"What's with the silly name? Call 'em that yourself?"

Delphi shoots a quick glare at the fairy, then continues.

"The mountains were named after the lack of life within *and* beyond them. And yes, our people *did* name the range ourselves."

Maus looks surprised. Shocked. A little impressed.

"You… *named* the mountains?"

Delphi replies, very matter-of-factly.

"Of course we did. We're unicorns. You've been using our names on your maps for centuries."

Maus blinks a few times, her words sinking in.

"Wow."

Delphi, ignoring Maus, addresses the group once more.

"Beyond the Deadrock Mountains are the Shale Plains. Most of the orcs live up there. At least, they did before we were all put to sleep. And I assume not much has changed. They tend to be a… *stubborn* people."

Aster speaks.

"You don't think…"

Delphi meets her gaze.

"That's exactly what I'm afraid of."

The fairy pipes up.

"Uh, *hello?* Mind sharing with the class?"

Delphi speaks.

"Before we were put to sleep, there was a tournament held there. Happened once a month. They put their toughest fighters in a battle to the death. Other peoples competed, of course, but it was tough to match the brute strength of an orc. They were usually killed. And the orcs would always be victorious."

She continues.

"We didn't care much. Wasn't our business. And there was never a shortage of foolhardy warriors, so the competition never ended. Granted, it's been quite some time since then, so we can't be sure of any changes… but if it *is* still ongoing, then the princess will likely be slaughtered in combat."

The fairy smiles.

"How *interesting!*"

Aster sighs.

"I was hoping we'd get at least a few hours of rest. Leave at the first break of dawn. But assuming this sprite tells the truth, we can't afford to take that luxury. We'll have to leave as soon as we can."

Maus groans.

"Figures."

Aster looks back to the fairy, still standing on the tree stump.

"Anything else to say?"

The fairy thinks for a moment.

"Nope!"

She plops back down.

"Go on! Say *your* thing, other horse! I'm sure it'll be *really* exciting."

She makes a shooing motion with her hands.

Delphi deliberately ignores her. She focuses back on Aster.

"You weren't separated from us for too long, but…"

She pauses.

"A lot happened. Are you sure you want to know *everything?*"

Aster nods.

"Yes. Whatever happened, it resulted in you getting your magic back. And if we want our people to have the best chance of survival, we need to share that knowledge. Make use of it."

Delphi exhales.

"The princess and I were overheard in discussion. No one notable, just a simple stable boy. So, we chased him down. Planned to kill him, just to tie up the loose end. But he got away. Then the princess beat me to death."

Aster looks… alarmed.

"What? Why?"

Delphi responds, irked.

"Why do you *think?* Her whole fuckin' *family's* had anger problems ever since we've fuckin' *existed.* I'm surprised she hasn't killed us already, the angry piece of shit. At least the *queen* was fucking *stable.*"

She takes several deep breaths, calming down. Her composure returns.

"Sorry. Still getting over it."

The fairy snorts.

"Wow! *Somebody's* mad!"

Maus smacks her on the back. She stumbles forward.

"Shut up."

The fairy scrunches her face at him. She mumbles under her breath.

"Asshole."

Aster stares at Delphi, momentarily speechless.

A moment passes.

She speaks.

"Well… I should remind you that this is the princess you're talking about. The daughter of our ruling queen, assuming both still live. And as the family's right hand, it *would* be my duty to inform her of what you said…"

She pauses, choosing her words carefully.

"…but considering the circumstances, I think we can forget about it for now."

Delphi breathes a soft sigh of relief.

"Yeah. Thanks."

Aster continues.

"What about the magic? Have you regained all that was lost?"

Delphi shakes her head.

"I don't think so. I mean, obviously I can use it again, but it feels… different. More limited. I'm not sure how or why."

Aster thinks.

"Clearly its strength lies within you. You brought yourself back from the brink of death. Perhaps even from beyond it. That's more power than our people have accessed before."

Delphi speaks.

"Yes, but…"

She pauses.

"I only feel *part* of it. It *is* there, and it's clearly strong. We agree on that much. But it still feels different. Not quite the same as it was."

She looks around briefly. Not far off, she spots a frail-looking tree. Its thin, spindly branches look ready to fall at any moment.

"Alright. Let's try something."

Aster watches.

"Alright."

Delphi focuses on the thin tree in front of her. Slowly, her horn glows a subtle blue, much like before. The tree, too, emits a soft blue glow of its own. It shakes gently. From its canopy, small fragments of branches fall to the ground.

The glow around the tree dissipates. It stops shaking.

The glow around Delphi's horn vanishes as well. She breathes a bit heavier, slightly more exhausted than before.

"At our full strength, I should've been able to rip that tree from the ground. But I could barely shake it."

She sounds disappointed in herself.

Aster continues looking at the tree.

"I… don't quite understand. What we saw you do in the city should have been impossible. I assumed you would have access to all the magics beyond it."

She looks back to Delphi.

"Do you think you're stuck this way? With this… limitation?"

Delphi speaks.

"I don't know. Obviously, *some* of what I can do is powerful. Maybe more powerful than before. I just can't do it all. Not like I used to."

She exhales.

"Whatever the case, I don't think I'd have *any* magic back if I hadn't been attacked by the princess. Maybe something from our… *extended* slumber… blocked something within us. Or maybe whoever put us to sleep did that on purpose. I have theories, I guess, but none based on empirical evidence. I may have studied our history, but nothing like this has happened before."

Aster steps closer.

"Then I need you to kill me."

Delphi looks shocked.

"What?"

Maus raises an eyebrow. He says nothing.

The fairy chuckles on her stump. She leans forward.

"Now it's getting interesting!"

Aster elaborates.

"You gaining access to magic was clearly related to physical trauma. At least to some degree, anyway. Even if it wasn't the direct cause, it triggered whatever was. Much of your magic appears to be limited, yes, but clearly your healing capabilities are not. So I want you to kill me. Or bring me close to death, anyway. If luck is on our side, I may regain magic myself, just as you did."

Delphi speaks, hesitation in her voice.

"And if it doesn't work?"

Aster replies.

"Then someone takes out some anger, I'm healed, and we move on."

Maus comments.

"You sure it's a good idea? If this messes up, or it takes too long, or we get caught at the wrong time… that's it."

Aster looks to him.

"By all accounts, this is a terrible idea, and, frankly, is in the running for the worst I've ever come up with…"

She pauses.

"…but Damnation is distracted. He's as dangerous as he is childish, and right now, he's throwing the most destructive tantrum of all time. Even if he *wants* to hunt us, he can't. He's too blinded by his rage. But he won't be forever. And if we wait too long, we'll lose this opportunity."

Delphi voices concern.

"If you really want to do this, I don't think I should be doing both. The hurting and the healing, that is."

Almost on cue, both unicorns look to Maus.

He grunts in understanding.

"So be it."

He straightens up.

"Lemme know how you want it."

Aster nods. She looks back to Delphi.

"Be ready."

Delphi says nothing. Her eyes begin to glow yellow, brightness building until it overtakes her pupils in its radiant light. The veins around her eyes, too, glow the same. The glow materializes around her horn rapidly. While not as blinding as it was in the city, the strength of the magic here is evident.

Delphi speaks.

"Ready."

Aster looks to Maus.

"You're going to have to hit me with all you've got. Like you really mean it."

Maus stifles the hint of a smirk.

"Yes, ma'am."

He takes a few steps forward. With both hands, he reaches to the weapon sheathed on his back. He grabs the hilt.

Aster exhales.

"Good."

Slowly, she kneels to the ground, then rolls to her side. Immediately, she feels the cold texture of the grass. The draining feeling of the ground sapping her body heat. But she ignores it.

"I will tell you when to strike. Delphi will heal me after each."

She pauses for a moment.

"We stop when we succeed."

Delphi takes a few steps back, giving more space.

"Are you sure you want to do this? I can heal your wounds, but I won't be able to stop the pain. We don't know how long this could take."

Aster looks over to her.

"I'm sure."

She closes her eyes and exhales.

"For the good of our people."

Then she looks to Maus.

"Approach me."

Maus replies.

"It would be my greatest pleasure."

With effort, he pulls the weapon from his back. The blade glimmers faintly, reflecting the starlight, nearly five feet in length. The guard above the hilt seems to be made of identical metal. Around the hilt, bands of aged brown leather coil over each other, the hilt itself long enough to fit both of Maus's hands. Even with his strength, the sheer weight of the sword is apparent. Were he a much weaker man, he might not be able to pick it up.

He approaches Aster, as instructed. He holds the weapon steady. Its blade looms over her.

She meets his gaze.

"Hit me."

Maus brings the weapon down with force.

Its heavy metal *chops* into Aster's chest. Blood flies out. The sword *cracks* her ribs, digging deep into her lungs. Her head lurches out. She screams, her voice quickly shriveling away. Blood spills from her body. She coughs endlessly, a pained whine in her throat. Thick globs of blood fall from her lips.

Maus pulls the sword from her body. Blood runs down its edge. He holds it above her, keeping it still.

Delphi stares down at Aster. A subtle, steady hum emanates from her horn.

Aster emits a yellow glow of her own. The breaks in her flesh fold back together. Yellow light mends the muscle and skin. Her broken bones *snap* back into place.

She screams instinctively… then calms. She takes forceful breaths. The yellow glow around her body dissipates.

She takes a deep breath in.

She exhales.

"I feel no different."

She looks up at Maus.

"Again."

Blood still on his blade, he brings it down once more. It *chops* into her body again, its blade ripping into her chest a second time, tearing through muscle, crushing her organs under its weight. Bones *crack* from the impact. Blood flies, splattering Maus's face. Aster's head lurches. She screams. Her cries fade to gargles.

Maus pulls the sword from her body. Her muscles *squelch*. More blood runs down the blade. It drips over his fingers, warming his hands. He holds the weapon steady above her.

The yellow glow appears around Aster once again. The tears in her muscles undo. The rips in her skin mend together. Her organs *push* and *force* themselves back into place. Her broken bones *snap* back to position.

She cries out, instinctual, but brief. Her voice tapers off to a pained whimper. She breathes heavily, forcing herself to regain composure.

"Again."

Maus strikes. Aster screams. Delphi heals.

"Again."

Maus strikes. Aster screams. Delphi heals.

"Again."

"Again."

"Again."

Chapter XI:
All Hells
Breaks Loose

Chapter XI: All Hells
Breaks Loose

The cold sting of morning air wakes the princess.

Then again, the air *always* has a cold sting here. If such a celebrated slaughter fest were any further out, she'd probably die from the cold before it even began.

She feels scratching along her back. A shifting weight. Not a lot of movement, but enough to be bothersome. Enough to be *irritating*.

Princess Pipsy shakes her body. The weight falls.

Thud!

Eckel grunts as he hits the floor.

The princess looks down at him.

"I told you to be off when I awoke."

Eckel — now awake — stands upright. He puts a hand to his head.

"How would I know. You sleep standing up. Hard to tell. Hm. Your idea anyway. You made the deal. Hm."

The princess replies.

"I *allowed* you to sleep on my back so I didn't fucking freeze to death. I still think you're a disgusting creature, and I don't want you anywhere near me when I'm conscious."

Eckel adjusts the goggle over his eye.

"Hm. Not the first one to say that. But you might just change your mind."

He flashes an unwelcome grin.

The princess scrunches her face, disgusted.

"I think you've got shit in your teeth."

Eckel's thin, pointed tongue dances around his mouth, flicking each of his teeth.

"I hope so. Hm. Some for later. Since you don't want to share."

She looks him dead in the eye.

"I'd rather kill myself."

Eckel crawls over to his bed.

"Message received."

He slinks into the alcove.

Abhorrently repugnant.

Princess Pipsy looks up. She stares at the heavy grate embedded in the ceiling. In perpetuity, the steady drip continues.

Plink...

Plink...

Plink...

She can just barely hear the sound of the wind outside. Maybe some shuffling beyond that. It's too hard to tell for certain.

"How soon until they bring us out?"

Eckel remains in the alcove, almost hiding.

"Any minute now. Always in the morning. Hm. Could be any one of us. Yes. But they'll get to us all eventually. Only a matter of time."

Eckel wretches, a wet sound coming from deep in his throat. He coughs a thick glob of phlegm into his own mouth, then chews, eating it.

The princess turns away.

"I wish you'd stop doing that."

Still chewing, Eckel responds.

"And I wish you'd share. I guess we all have wishes unfulfilled. Hm."

From the wide hall beyond the cell, a massive door opens.

CREAK!

Murmurs start from the cells nearby. Hushed conversations. Speech, barely audible. Words wholly unrecognizable. Whether born from excitement or panic, it's unclear.

A deep, thunderous feminine voice calls out from the end of the hall, echoing throughout the prison.

"Good morning, prisoners! This is not a test. It's almost time to roll."

She continues.

"I hope you're having a *wonderful* day, because it only gets worse from here. It's almost *showtime!"*

Princess Pipsy steps up to her cell door, peering through the bars.

Eckel does not, electing to tremble in the corner instead.

Many of the other prisoners — at least the ones the princess can see, anyway — peer through their own bars, attention hooked on the voice of the guard. She spots a hefty dwarven fellow, what could be burn marks across his face and arms. She sees a couple human-looking figures, one missing an arm, both with shaved heads and runic tattoos. In the far corner of another cell, she spots a massive shell leaned against the wall, clearly from some kind of animal. From the cell directly next to her — the one to her right; one that she can't see into — she spots a towering shadow, its edge peeking *just* beyond its cell bars. And — from somewhere *far* off, possibly the very edge of this prison — she almost swears she hears a gentle rumbling before it vanishes entirely.

The guard at the end of the hall enters. As the princess thought: it's the same guard who dragged her in a couple days ago. There's no mistaking that voice. Must be more than *just* a guard, though. Especially if she's the one making announcements.

The orcish guard slowly walks through the hall, shooting daggers at all the prisoners through her mask.

"If you've been here a while, you know the drill. If you haven't, follow the ones you have, and pray you live long enough to become one yourself."

The prisoners start getting rowdy. A few call out, threatening their peers in the name of bloodlust and excitement.

The orcish guard continues walking past the cells. Behind her, more than a dozen other guards follow, all dressed in similar garb.

She smacks cell bars as she walks past.

Thunk… Thunk… Thunk…

"When you are called — *when,* not *if* — your cell will be opened. You will exit single file. You will be escorted to the gates of the battlefield. You will not struggle. You will not argue. You will not speak. Anyone who gets fussy will be killed without remorse. You are expendable, and you are here to be expended."

She stops in front of Princess Pipsy's cell. She locks eyes with Eckel through the cell bars.

"Don't make us expend you early."

Eckel shirks away, whimpering.

The guard continues, addressing the full body of prisoners once again.

"Good luck! I hope you survive until next month. Don't forget to give us a good show."

On cue, the guards behind her disperse, teams of two approaching various cells in the prison. Their selection *seems* random at first, but it can't be. They're moving too deliberately. To the princess's surprise, there seems to be no defiance from the prisoners. Not from the ones she can see and hear, anyway. Everyone selected is just… going along with it.

Directly across from her, a single guard approaches the cell with the tattooed human figures. The one with the missing arm stands *very* close to the bars.

The guard looks at the two of them.

"You have been selected for the first round of the All Hells Tournament. Follow me."

He unlocks the cell door.

Click!

He opens it.

Creak...

The two tattooed figures step out. Now a bit closer, Princess Pipsy can make out some more of their details. The one missing an arm looks taller. Clearly an older man. Likely elven, at least in part. But no ears attached. Just crusted, misshapen skin where his ears used to be. The other figure does, indeed, appear to be human. An older woman, by the looks of it, but not quite as old as her counterpart. Both wear simple rags, dirt and stains all over.

The guard escorting them closes the cell door.

CHANG!

He locks it.

Click!

He shoves the tattooed prisoners forward.

"Start walking."

They do.

Briefly, the one-armed figure — the one walking up front — flashes a glance at the figure behind him. No mouthed words. No emotions. No expression. Just a glance.

The guard notices.

"Hey! Eyes to yourself."

He shoves both of them again.

"Keep walking."

They do.

For a moment.

They whip around, each wielding a crude shank made of shale. They stab the weapons into the sides of the guards head, piercing through his leather mask. The weapons penetrate, but not as deep as they hoped. Blood spurts out from the guard's head. He staggers back, hands on his wounds. He trips over his own feet, falling backward.

Immediately, all guards on duty charge toward the tattooed prisoners.

The one with the missing arm looks to the woman.

The woman speaks.

"Don't worry! We can do this! Just—"

A heavy stone war hammer swings down onto the woman's head. The back of her skull caves in from the impact. Blood explodes in all directions. Her neck *crunches* in on itself, folding into her chest. Her ribs push out, making space for the meat and bone cannoned into them. Both eyes bulge out, blood seeping from her sockets. The body falls.

The one-armed figure has no time to process. In a split-second, another stone hammer swings around. Its blunt force caves in the center of his face with a thick, wet *crunch*. The body falls.

The guards wielding the hammers affix the weapons back to their sides, now dripping onto the ground. They each grab a body, dragging the corpses back toward an unseen chamber.

The guard in charge — the woman in front of Princess Pipsy's cell — shakes her head.

"There's one every month."

In groups of two, the other guards bring their prisoners forward, marching them to the metal door at the end of the hall. At least a dozen prisoners are being walked out. Didn't they say this was for the first round? How many prisoners are really down here? How many cells *are* there?

The female guard walks past Princess Pipsy's cell. *Slowly.*

Eckel trembles on his bed, hardly hidden, but choosing to believe that he is.

The guard locks eyes with Princess Pipsy.

The two stare at each other.

The guard grunts.

She moves on. She stops at the cell adjacent.

Eckel breathes a sigh of relief.

Princess Pipsy keeps a careful eye on the guard.

The guard speaks, looking at whoever resides within the next cell.

"You have been selected for the first round of the All Hells Tournament. Follow me."

She unlocks the cell.

Click!

She opens it.

Creak...

The hulking figure — the one casting the massive shadow — steps out of the cell. Each footstep carries a great weight behind it.

Thud. Thud. Thud.

The figure walks in front of Princess Pipsy's cell. She gets a close look.

The figure stands at what must be almost nine feet tall, nearly at Damnation's height. He reeks of piss and sweat. He stands at a slight hunch, shoulders up. He wears a ragged shirt full of stains and holes, some rope or belt around his waist holding up the moth-eaten scrap of his pants. His skin looks a sickly pale grayish-green, old scabs and bruises all across his body. Heavy metal chains cuff his hands together, keeping him partially bound, though it feels like more of a formality than anything. Judging by all the fat and muscle that makes his stocky form, he could easily break out if he wanted to.

As he walks by Princess Pipsy's cell, he looks into it. The wide eye at the center of his forehead studies the princess, the white of it stale yellow instead. Two small tusks poke out from behind his lower lip, just barely cresting past his philtrum. With intent to intimidate, he growls.

Despite the fetid stench of his breath, Princess Pipsy does not flinch.

The cyclops chuckles.

"I like you."

He leans closer.

"I'm gonna pop your head like a fruit."

He marches onward, heading for the door at the end of the hall. The other guards hardly pay any mind, all more focused on the other prisoners. Like the cyclops has done this a thousand times before.

He probably has.

The female guard remains in front of Princess Pipsy's cell.

"That's Shorty. He's a real favorite 'round here. They just can't get enough of him. *Real* nasty son-of-a-bitch, too. Likes to play with his food."

Eckel trembles.

The guard abruptly changes cadence.

"Congratulations. You have been selected for the first round of the All Hells Tournament."

Eckle whimpers.

She unlocks the cell.

Click!

She opens the door.

Creak...

She continues.

"Follow me."

With no other choice, Princess Pipsy steps out from the cell. Eckel follows behind, jittery and nervous.

The guard shuts the cell behind them.

CHANG!
She locks it.
Click!
"Start walking."
Both do.

As the princess walks on, more prisoners — many still in their cells — peek out to get a better look at her. They murmur and converse quietly. Even some of the orcish guards can't help but whisper between each other, staring at the unicorn in front of them.

Farther ahead — but not *that* far ahead — Shorty glances behind him. He spots the unicorn trailing behind. He grins, yellow teeth showing.

"I wonder what you taste like."

He turns back around, marching onward.

"I look forward to finding out."

———————————————————————————

The crowd roars. Hundreds of orcish folk — no, *thousands* — fill the seats of the coliseum. A flat stretch of gray shale — likely hundreds of feet across — sits at the center of the oblong structure. Dried bloodstains blend into the ground, disappearing in its texture. Small grates form a grid across the field.

There are *hundreds* of them.

Stone walls elevate the crowd above the battlefield, the closest seats still forty feet above the ground. Various weapons and armors sit on display at the center of the field. Heavy iron bars block off dozens of entrances, likely where the prisoners are held.

Somewhere within the stadium, a steady, rhythmic drum beat fills the air.

At the center of the coliseum, a humanoid figure floats high above the ground, at least a hundred feet in the air, if not more. His flowing robes hang loose, their deep pink fabric starkly contrasting the drab world around him. Large, flashy jewelry hangs from his body, oversized gems catching in the sunlight.

The eyes of the figure glow bright pink. Short gray hair sits at the back of the head, despite the man looking no older than forty. Yet something about this figure feels… different. Unlike any that have been encountered before. Something that the princess has never had the displeasure of meeting.

He's an entertainer.

He bears a bright, beaming smile, looking out at the crowd.

He flies in a circle, showing off.

The crowd claps and whistles in response.

Loving the attention, he spins again, this time a wider maneuver.

Again, they whistle. They clap. They cheer.

They *love* him.

He speaks, some sort of magical enhancement behind his voice allowing it to carry throughout the arena.

"Good morning, Ulrag! It's been *so long* since we've all seen each other. I'm *so* glad you've decided to join us today. We've got some *real* contenders this month, and I *can't wait* for you to meet 'em all. Those in the splash zone, get ready, because we're gonna get messy."

In the lowest few tiers of seats, the orcish folk within them go wild. One orc at the front — a young woman with large tusks, hair in a ponytail — shouts as loud as she can, pulling against the stone barrier in front of her.

"YEAH!"

The flying figure chuckles.

"Hey, alright! I know *she's* excited."

The figure soars above the crowd. He extends his arms dramatically.

"Welcome… to the *All… Hells… Tournament!*"

The crowd erupts. The sheer volume of their chaos is overpowering.

For weaker folks, it probably is.

Princess Pipsy stands behind one of the many metal gates built into the coliseum. Around her, numerous prison guards stand at the ready, ensuring she makes no effort to escape. She watches the movement of the flying figure, repulsed by his gravitas.

To no one in particular, she speaks.

"Who the fuck is that?"

The guard directly behind her — the orcish woman in charge — replies.

"*That* is your announcer. Been our resident showman for years. Don't bother trying to kill him. You won't."

She kicks Princess Pipsy in the leg.

Hard.

"And stop talking."

Princess Pipsy takes a deep, calming breath.

She feels her upper lip twitch ever-so-slightly.

She feels the heat of anger rising in her chest.

She feels her heart begin to quicken.

She feels her muscles tense.

And she does nothing.

Even if she *did* manage to kill that guard, she'd never stand a chance against the others. Not only was she considerably outnumbered, but she was powerless. Lesser-than.

Weak.

So she stands.

And she stares.

And she waits.

The announcer spins once again. He laughs.

"Like I told you folks, we've got some *real treats* lined up for you today. I think it's time we get this slaughter started. Whaddya say?"

The crowd roars.

Pleased, he continues.

"Our *extra special guest* hails all the way from the gorgeous sunny shores of the beach-lined Silver Coast! Folks, this rampaging beauty slaughtered a whole *tavern* full of dirty, rotten criminals, and by golly, that was just the other day! Before we bought her, lemme tell ya, I didn't even think she *existed,* and now you get the chance to watch her die before your very eyes. Ladies and gentlemen, orcs of all ages, bloodthirsty vagabonds and slap-happy ne'er-do-wells…"

He pauses dramatically.

"…please welcome your *very first* contender… the *stampeding psychopath* herself… *Princess… Pipsy!*"

The metal gate in front of the princess raises up.

Ga-chunk… ga-chunk… ga-chunk…

She walks through the open gate, stepping onto the battlefield. As soon as she does, it shuts behind her, sealing her in.

Ga-chunk… ga-chunk… ga-chunk… CRASH!

She looks around at the countless onlookers, each one practically foaming at the mouth. Seeing a unicorn step onto the battlefield certainly doesn't help.

Like a tidal wave of vocalizations, cheers sweep across the crowd.

Far above the princess, the announcer chuckles, savoring the energy.

Princess Pipsy examines the field before her. As with the rest of the landscape beyond the city of Ulrag, the ground is exclusively shale. Small metal grates form a spacious grid pattern over the arena. At the center of the space — *dead* center — is an elaborate display of various weapons and armors. Many of the pieces are coated in rust or blood. Among the sets of wildly varying armors, she manages to spot her own.

Her eyes lock onto its haphazard display.

That is *her* armor.

It belongs to *her.*

And she's going to take it back.

Her eyes narrow with determination.

The announcer flies toward her, a wild grin on his face. He lowers rapidly, now floating just a few feet above the ground.

"Now, I don't wanna know your life story, and, frankly, I don't care. But if you got anything you wanna say to these *stunning* people, now's the time!"

Despite his voice projecting throughout the arena, the volume at this distance — while certainly loud — isn't painful, as the princess imagined it would be.

But he could probably shatter her eardrums if he really wanted to.

Princess Pipsy says nothing. She simply glares.

He extends his palm toward her. Its skin glows a faint pink, the same shade as his eyes.

"Go on, don't be shy! Talk to the hand."

He brings it closer, taunting her.

The princess does nothing.

The announcer shakes his head, pulling away.

"Bah! Who am I kidding? It's a *horse*, people!"

He laughs. Similar chuckles ring out from the audience.

"Can't wait to see her get massacred, though."

Princess Pipsy speaks, her own voice now carrying through the arena thanks to the announcer's magic.

"Your walls cannot hold me!"

The crowd quiets.

A moment passes.

Then they cheer, even louder than before.

The announcer looks surprised. *Genuinely* surprised.

"Well, *fuck me!* **Ladies and gentlemen, she can** *talk!"*

More noise from the crowd.

The princess speaks again.

"The longer I'm here, the more of you will die."

The audience has no reaction. Just more cheers.

The announcer chuckles.

"Well, I sure *hope* **so!"**

The audience agrees.

Princess Pipsy shakes her head.

"A creature that calls itself Damnation hunts my people. The longer I'm here, the more time he has to find me. And if he does, he'll kill you *all."*

She locks eyes with the announcer.

"Even you."

The crowd groans. The cheers die down.

That wasn't very exciting.

The announcer rolls his eyes.

"And *that,* **folks, is why you never give the floor to a mythical creature just because it can talk."**

He flies off, taking his place high above the crowd once again.

All eyes are on him.

"Now, it's not often we've got a dead species with a sob story — oh, who am I kidding, it happens twice a year — but ladies and gentlemen, we're starting off *strong* **today! Yes, by special request of the reigning champion himself... the only one who loves bloodshed more than I do... an eyeball not even his mother could love... please give it up for** *Shorty!"*

At the opposite end of the arena, the farthest gate rises.

Ga-chunk... ga-chunk... ga-chunk...

Shorty steps onto the battlefield.

As soon as he appears, the crowd goes wild. Upon hearing the cheers, he can't help but grin. His eye locks on to the unicorn hundreds of feet away. He cracks his knuckles and licks his lips.

The announcer flies over to him. As with the princess, he floats closer, extending a glowing palm.

"Well, champion? Any big, wise words of wisdom you'd like to extend to the self-appointed princess?"

Shorty keeps his eye trained on the unicorn.

"I'm gonna skullfuck your eyes with your spine."

The crowd goes ballistic.

That's what they wanted to hear.

The announcer takes off, flying high above the crowd yet again.

"Talk about a killer opener! I think our champion may just keep his title after all."

He looks across the thousands of cheering crowd members.

"Like every month, I'm gonna give you the rules. When fighters enter, *nobody* leaves until *somebody* dies. Other than that, get creative. Equipment's in the middle there, if you think you can get to it. And for the spell suckers on our roster, magic *is* on the table."

He looks down at the arena below him.

"Ladies and gentlemen... *are... you... ready?*"

The audience roars.

The announcer grins.

"Let the All Hells Tournament begin."

— — — — — — — — — — — — — — — —

Shorty charges forward, eye locked on the unicorn ahead of him. He moves slow, but he's gaining ground.

Time to move.

Princess Pipsy races forward, heading for the middle of the arena.

She feels the stark, cold dampness of the shale under her hooves. She feels the wind nip at her skin as she runs. She feels —

Her front hoof catches on a grate.

She loses her footing completely, tumbling forward. Her body collides with the shale. Chips from the rock fly up from the impact, poking into her skin.

The crowd laughs.

Floating high above, the announcer comments.

"Ooh, *that's* gonna leave a mark! Looks like *someone* forgot about the eager beavers down low!"

Princess Pipsy looks back.

Through the grate in the ground, the fingers of some ashy humanoid hand poke through.

She groans angrily.

The announcer continues.

"Hey, buddy… you forget about the *fight* happening?"

The princess stands. She feels thin trickles of blood along her body.

Stupid fucking shale.

Across the way, Shorty continues his approach.

The princess takes off, faster than before.

In a few moments, she reaches the center of the arena.

Shorty gives a battle cry, now less than a hundred feet away.

All around the princess, old wooden tables host a wide array of weapons: swords, axes, hammers, shields — even some sort of daggers she doesn't recognize — all displayed in clear view. Next to the tables, wooden dummies wear mismatched sets of armor, most pieces hardly fitting their forms at all. No doubt confiscated. Or stolen.

On the farthest dummy, the princess sees a set of armor that looks *far* too big. It can barely sit on the dummy without falling off, its shape clearly meant for another type of creature. Dried blood sticks to its side, almost distracting from the dark blue trim around the metal plating.

Her armor.

She runs to it.

Above, the announcer speaks.

"Looks like a defensive play from the unicorn that has no hands or arms to defend with! I'm sure this will work out *great*."

Princess Pipsy grabs hold of her armor — one piece of it, anyway — with her mouth. She pulls, trying to free it from the dummy.

The dummy falls, pulling her armor with it.

Crash!

The announcer chuckles.

"Well, that's about what I expected."

He spots Shorty fast approaching, now reaching the center of the arena.

"Uh-oh, look out! Here comes trouble!"

The princess turns.

Thud… thud… thud… thud…

Shorty stands less than twenty feet away.

He roars.

"Get over here!"

The princess scrunches her nose.

"Absolutely fucking not."

She takes off.

Shorty plows through the tables of weapons, knocking them aside on his direct path to the unicorn. The weapons *clatter* to the ground, spilling across the immediate space. Below several grates nearby, hands of various prisoners reach up, all hoping to grab hold of a weapon.

Princess Pipsy runs circles around the center, keeping her distance.

Shorty stands in place. He spins, trying to keep his eye on the unicorn.

The princess continues to circle him.

He continues to spin.

His movement slows.

He puts a hand to his head.

He falls back, landing on his ass…

…and on the blade of a rusty broadsword.

The blade presses into him, cutting his flesh right at the cheek.

He gives a pained cry in response. He leans over, putting a hand to the wound.

Blood.

He looks back up at the unicorn encircling him.

He grins.

"I like it when I bleed."

He stands.

"Your turn."

He reaches down, grabbing the sword that cut his ass cheek.

He hurls it toward the unicorn.

It flies *just* below Princess Pipsy's barrel, nearly sticking into her. Close call. It *clatters* to the ground.

Shorty picks up a battleaxe. He grips the handle with both hands. He reaches up, brings it behind his head, and hurls it.

The axe soars through the air. *SHUNK!*

It sticks into the stone wall directly in front of the princess, its bladed edges very much exposed.

She tries to slow down. Her hooves skid across the shale, unable to get enough traction. She trips over her feet, tumbling right into the blade.

The curve cuts deep into her face. It forces its way into the side of her jaw with a loud *crack.*

She falls.

The crowd 'oohs'.

The announcer speaks.

"Talk about *jaw-dropping!* That did *not* look pretty."

Princess Pipsy stands. She feels her head pulse and throb with pain. Warmth runs down the side of her face. Luckily, it didn't seem to permanently break anything. Not that she can tell, anyway. But it *did* cut deep.

She looks up, glaring at Shorty, still standing at the center.

He shouts to her, now cocky.

"An eye for an eye. A cheek for a cheek."

He picks up a war hammer from the ground. He raises it high behind his head.

Princess Pipsy takes off, a bit slower than previously.

Shorty hurls the hammer.

It *smashes* into the ground in front of the princess, scattering bits of shale into the air. She runs around it, pressing on.

Shorty groans, frustrated.

The princess arcs back around, now running in Shorty's direction.

He smirks.

"You're gonna make this easy."

Princess Pipsy charges toward him.

She leaps over the scattered weapons on the ground.

She lowers her head.

She doesn't slow down.

Shunk!

Her horn digs deep into Shorty's thigh. *Deep.*

She feels the warm blood splatter her face.

Shorty shouts in pain.

The announcer speaks.

"Ooh, and Shorty takes a blow to the leg! How will he *ever* recover?"

Shorty's shout turns to laughter.

The princess tries to pull back. To free her horn from his flesh. But her horn doesn't budge.

Shorty looks down at her.

The princess looks back, a panic in her eyes.

Oh, shit.

Shorty speaks.

"Thanks for making it easy."

He balls his hands into fists. He brings them high above his head.

Princess Pipsy pulls back again. But it's no use.

Shorty slams his fists down onto her neck.

Thoom!

Her breath rockets out of her body. Her neck flexes in on itself for the briefest moment. Searing pain explodes from its muscles. Her skin holds… but it burns. And she chokes.

She coughs blood onto Shorty's feet.

The announcer speaks.

"And *there* she goes, ladies and gentlemen! I gotta tell ya, I'm starting to see why these guys went extinct."

The princess *pulls*. But her horn doesn't move. Blood from Shorty's thigh drips over her face. The rotten stench of his crotch is apparent.

He laughs.

"Don't worry… I'll make sure you're alive to feel the skullfucking."

Shorty raises his fists once again.

The princess *pulls*. But her horn still doesn't move.

Shorty slams his fists down onto her neck, even harder than before. The force of the fists breaks her skin.

The wall of her throat pushes inward. She feels its lining *snap* somewhere within. Blood runs down her throat. It's almost suffocating. She wheezes hard. Blood sprays out with her breath. She screams, voice strained beyond measure.

The announcer speaks.

"*What* a *shame.* I thought she'd put up a fight! Can't say I'm surprised, but I *can* say I'm disappointed. *What* a *shame.*"

The crowd leans in, watching closely.

Princess Pipsy struggles harder, moving frantically, trying to pull free from the flesh.

She *pulls* and *pulls* and *pulls*.

The muscles of her neck scream in pain.

Her horn begins to pull free.

Shorty wraps his thick hands around her head. The sweat from his palms sticks to her skin.

He *pulls* her head closer, shoving her horn back into the fresh wound.

Squelch...

She tries to fight back to no avail. Her neck *strains*. Muscles tense throughout her body. But she doesn't move an inch.

For the first time in her life, she feels uncertainty.

Panic.

Fear.

But she feels something stronger than all of that.

Something *much* stronger.

She feels *anger.*

She looks up at Shorty, renowned fury in her eyes.

He looks… surprised.

Far off in the distance — somewhere *very* far away
— gentle thunder rolls.

Shorty takes note of the princess's rage.

"Looks like you got somethin' to say. Too bad you
won't—"

Everything flashes red.

An explosion rocks the stadium.

— — — — — — — — — — — — — — — — —

Ears ring. Vision blurs. Then — *slowly* — it all
returns to normal.

Meaty clumps fall from the ragged remains of
Shorty's thigh. Blood gushes out, painting the ground.
He falls to the side. He screams, putting pressure on the
wound with his hands.

"You *bitch!*"

Princess Pipsy stands above him. Her eyes glow
bright red. They *crackle* with electricity. The same glow
surrounds her horn, it, too, *snapping* and *popping* with
energy.

In the distant sky behind her, thunder clouds roll in.
Quickly.

The crowd takes a moment to process what just
happened.

Then they roar.

The announcer speaks, shock and glee on his face.

**"Ladies and gentlemen, I *don't* believe it! Our
reigning champion just got his *whole fuckin' leg*
blown off!"**

Shorty pushes against the ground, crawling away,
putting just a bit of distance between himself and the
angry unicorn.

Princess Pipsy approaches, thunder clouds still
rolling in behind her.

"You are *disgusting.*"

Shorty — frantic — grabs a shortsword from the ground. He chucks it at the unicorn.

A bolt of thick red lightning arcs out from her horn.

KRAAAK!

It collides with the sword in mid-air, knocking it aside. It *clatters* to the ground.

Princess Pipsy continues forward, closing the distance.

"You are *pathetic.*"

Shorty takes a swing with an open, bloody palm, attempting to grab hold of the unicorn.

She notices.

Another thick bolt of lightning *shoots* from her horn. It strikes in the center of Shorty's palm. His hand explodes in a slurry of flesh. Only his thumb and pinky remain attached, the center of his hand now a gaping, bleeding hole.

The dark clouds in the sky draw near. The audience begins to notice.

The princess steps onto his body, pinning him down.

Shorty looks up at her, a mix of surprise and shock. He opens his mouth to speak.

She sticks the very tip of her horn into the roof of his mouth, pressing gently. He feels a slight pressure, his mouth just barely bleeding from the poke. His tongue goes numb from the warm, electric tingles of the energy.

Princess Pipsy stares into his bulbous, yellowed eye.

Her horn *hums*, energy building. The *crackles* in her eyes grow more erratic.

"Fucking amateur."

KRAAAK!

Heavy red lightning explodes from her horn.

Shorty's head erupts into a rain of blood, bone, and sinew.

The ragged remains of Shorty's neck bleed gently, much of the muscle and tissue now charred. The body falls limp.

The audience screams in delight.

The announcer shares the sentiment.

"Holy fucking *shit*, ladies and gentlemen! Shorty's head just got *obliterated!*"

He flies down closer, still keeping a safe distance. He gestures to the princess with both hands, as if presenting her to the crowd.

"Please give it up for your *new* reigning champion... *Princess... Pipsy!*"

They cheer.

The princess looks across the audience, taking in their reactions. Blood covers her horn, dripping down her face.

The announcer flies back up, regaining the crowd's attention.

"That was one of *the* most surprising deaths I have *ever* seen. But it only gets better from here!"

Princess Pipsy looks up at him, red energy still crackling.

Where is he going with this?

The announcer continues.

"First of all, why don't we get the *real* show started?"

All around the arena, the other gates rise up.

Ga-chunk... ga-chunk... ga-chunk...

Ga-chunk... ga-chunk... ga-chunk...

Ga-chunk... ga-chunk... ga-chunk...

From behind each one, a prisoner steps forward. The princess spots a large humanoid beetle, at least six feet tall. She spots a figure wholly clad in jet-black armor, identity wholly obscured. She sees a grizzled dwarven man with heavy scars, one eye missing. She sees a long, smooth-scaled snake-like figure, only two arms on its torso. Further off, she watches more figures step forth, warriors and prisoners of all kinds entering the arena. And at the back, she notices the familiar, skittering movements of Eckel.

There are nearly twenty fighters here, if not more.

Immediately, combatants turn on each other, many attacking with nothing but themselves. Others take off, running toward the weapons at the center of the arena… and toward the princess.

The crowd cheers with excitement.

She sighs.

"Fuck."

She runs over to her armor. The red energy fades, morphing into solid blue. The *snaps* and *crackles* fade from her eyes. The armor emanates a blue glow of its own.

One by one, each piece of the armor flies to the princess with harrowing speed. It affixes itself to her body, its metal components interlocking as it does.

Chunk! … Chunk! … Chunk!

The armor hugs her form, together once again.

A shout rings out from beside her.

"Aaaargh!"

She turns.

The dwarven fellow — the one with a single eye — charges at her, wielding the axe that got stuck in the wall.

She steps to the side, dodging just in time.

As the axe falls, its blade clips her armor, leaving a heavy scratch.

Chink!

She scowls.

"My *mother* gave me this, you bastard."

The dwarf raises his axe immediately, preparing another strike.

The princess charges into him, piercing through his upper lip with her horn, It knocks out his front teeth, pressing deep into the roof of his mouth. He gargles incoherently, blood spilling from his lips.

The eyes of the princess turn red once again, the *crackles* and *pops* reappearing. Her horn, too, glows the same red.

KRAAAK!

The dwarf's head explodes in a gush of blood and lightning, scattering across the shale. Bits of flesh *plop* down from above.

At the front of the crowd nearby, remains of the dwarf sail into the audience. One orcish woman in particular — seated at the *very* front — beams with delight, blood and skin bits *splatting* onto her face. She cheers, absolutely *thrilled.*

"YEAH!"

The other prisoners continue to fight each other, many still racing toward the center.

High above the chaos, the announcer speaks.

"Now, I'd be lying if I said I *didn't* love this… but we've got *one* more surprise for you folks. Tell me, do you think we should bring it out?"

The crowd cheers.

The announcer feigns consideration.

"Hm, I dunno… you *sure* you can handle it?"

They cheer even louder.

The princess rolls her eyes.

The announcer chuckles.

"Alright, alright, I hear you! Guards… *let's bring her out!"*

The other prisoners close in, reaching the center of the arena.

The princess takes off, making as much distance as possible. Almost immediately, those at the center pick up weapons, all turning on each other.

From the far end of the arena, Princess Pipsy hears a deep, heavy *rumbling*. It sounds like the same one she heard in the prison below.

No.

Not just *like*.

It *is*.

And it sounds *big*.

The crowd turns to the rumbling gate.

The announcer continues.

"Ladies and gentlemen, this piece of work has been on our minds for the last seven years, and thanks to the hundreds of valiant sacrifices, we *finally* got her clipped. And *that* means she's ready for *you!*"

The crowd goes wild. Clearly they know something.

The heavy gate begins to rise. The princess, now arcing toward it, keeps a steady gaze.

Ga-chunk... ga-chunk... ga-chunk...

The announcer continues, more ecstatic.

"We're kicking it up a notch, and we're doing it for *you!* Ladies and gentlemen, hailing all the way from mountains up north, a kidnapping years in the making, please welcome... *Carly!*"

From behind the massive open gate, a dragon steps out. Its bronze-red scales look grimy and disgusting, all caked with dirt. It stands on all fours, at least fifteen feet tall, if not more. Thick spikes protrude along its body, a spare few snapped off at the base. It hunches over, an unending fury in its eyes.

It enters the arena, each step shaking the ground. It rolls its shoulders, flexing. Now visible, it has no wings, only wide, ragged clumps of flesh on its back, clearly the aftermath of a horribly botched clipping.

The massive gate closes behind, sealing it in.

Ga-chunk... ga-chunk... ga-chunk...

It *roars.*

Its throat rumbles from the vibrations.

The crowd goes ballistic.

Princess Pipsy's eyes go wide.

"Fuck!"

She turns around, speeding away from it as fast as possible.

"Fuck, fuck, fuck, fuck!"

Carly — the dragon — pursues.

She *roars* once more, eyes locked on the unicorn.

The dragon shouts, her voice blazing with anger.

"I will kill you all!"

She clambers after the unicorn, gaining more ground. Her heavy tail swings behind her, knocking into combatants. One human warrior gets flung into the air. He sails into the arena wall and splatters against the stone, only a chunky, bloody pulp left behind.

Princess Pipsy races on.

"Shit, shit, shit, shit!"

A figure leaps onto her back, grabbing hold. It speaks, its voice familiar.

"Wait! Wait! Hm. It's me!"

Eckel.

She looks back to him, still rushing ahead.

"What the *fuck* do we do?"

He responds.

"Keep—"

Carly roars, cutting him off.

He continues.

"Keep running!"

So she does.

And Carly follows.

Suddenly, the announcer's voice rings through the stadium.

"Ladies and gentlemen, I have *one* more surprise for you!"

But the announcer isn't speaking.

He looks confused; concerned; alarmed. He gives a nervous chuckle, looking around the space.

"Sorry, folks! I don't know what that is. I think someone's—"

His own voice cuts him off, continuing to speak, seemingly sourceless.

"Lemme tell ya, folks, you've got *no* idea what you're in for! There's no one else like him, and frankly, he's gonna kill you all."

The crowd doesn't consider his words. They just cheer.

The real announcer stammers.

"That is *not* me!"

But the crowd doesn't listen.

They simply cheer.

And the copied voice continues.

"Please give a warm, dramatic welcome to..."

The announcer's voice fades, replaced by an eerie cacophony of voices, all speaking in unsettling unison.

"...your Damnation."

The large gate that the dragon stepped through *explodes* into the arena, chunks of twisted metal scattering across the field.

Damnation gallops into the arena.

Eckel catches a glimpse, mortified.

"Hm! What do we do now?!"

Princess Pipsy charges onward.

"Keep running."

The crowd screams in excitement.

Carly sniffs the air twice, attention breaking from the unicorn.

She slows to a stop.
She licks the air.
She sniffs once more.
She growls.
The prisoners on the ground shudder.
Carly turns around, eyes locking onto Damnation approaching.

"You reek of my brother!"

Damnation continues charging. The shadows at the corners of his mouth curl into a grin.

"It was a pleasure to rip him apart."

Carly roars.

Her roar turns to fire.

From her mouth, heavy flames spew forth, a whirling inferno.

The flames impact Damnation. They engulf his body entirely, obscuring him from view.

Within them, a bright purple spark flickers to life.

CHOOM!

A steady beam of crackling purple energy explodes forth, pushing back the flames.

Now visible once again, Damnation hunkers down on all eight limbs, his claws and fingers digging into the shale. His larger jaw hangs slack, the ferocious beam originating within it.

The purple beam — unstable as it appears — continues to push back the flames.

Carly's breath burns hotter. Her flames grow brighter. They push the purple beam back. Embers flick about the air.

Damnation digs his hands deeper into the ground, chipping the shale. His jaw opens wider. The purple beam expands, its pulses more erratic. His eyes glow brighter with it.

The purple beam dissipates the flames, cutting through them. Surprise flashes in Carly's eyes.

KA-BOOM!

Another explosion rocks the arena.

Damnation's purple beam dissipates. He relaxes, his jaw sliding back into place. He stands upright.

Carly — still very much alive, but reeling from the explosion — coughs up black smoke, flecks of blood along with it. Her lips are cracked and bleeding, the edges of her face now singed.

Next to Carly — at the wall of the arena, where the explosion occurred — a crumbling pile of corpses, blood, and rubble covers the ground. Beyond it?

Freedom.

All at once, the prisoners race for the hole in the wall, complete and total disregard for the warring behemoths in front of it.

Audience members near the site of the explosion scream. Many start to flee.

The gates all around the arena rise.

Ga-chunk... ga-chunk... ga-chunk...

Ga-chunk... ga-chunk... ga-chunk...

Ga-chunk... ga-chunk... ga-chunk...

From behind them, dozens and dozens of masked orcish guards charge into the arena, attempting to control the chaos.

The announcer is nowhere to be seen.

Still atop the princess, Eckel spots the gap in the wall. He pulls on her mane, getting her attention.

"Look! Look!"

She does.

And she sees it.

"Hold on!"

She pivots, whipping her body around. Eckel nearly falls. The princess runs toward the two titans. Thankfully, neither seem to notice, each too focused on the other.

The humanoid beetle reaches the gap in the wall first. It leaps into the air. From its back, two insectuous wings emerge, *whirring* to life. It arcs through the air, attempting to land on the rubble.

Carly's tail whips it.

THWACK!

The beetle sails into the corpses and stones. Its body shatters upon impact, green blood *splatting* out.

Carly doesn't notice. Her eyes remain locked on Damnation.

She growls.

"You killed my brother!"

Damnation replies.

"Yes, I thought we went over that. If it makes you feel better, he'll be with me forever."

He gestures to his larger jaw with his scaled dragon hand.

Carly scowls.

"You will *pay* for what you've done! And so will *everyone* else!"

Damnation groans, frustrated.

"I'm not here for *you*. I'm here for the *unicorns*. I can smell them. I *know* they were headed here. And I know that they're likely here already."

Carly speaks again, ignoring his words entirely.

"Your body will *rot* with my brother!"

Damnation, in turn, ignores *her.* He turns, looking at the slew of prison warriors rushing toward him. Among them all, he spots Princess Pipsy, some hideous little thing hitching a ride on her back.

"Gotcha."

Princess Pipsy notices.

"Fuck."

Damnation leaps, all six arms on his torso outstretched.

In mid-air, Carly tackles him, knocking him aside. Both tumble to the ground, immediately tearing into each other. Horrific shrieks ring out, no way of knowing which one they truly come from.

Princess Pipsy charges onward.

She leaps over the limp, dirty remains of Shorty.

She jumps onto the rubble.

Then onto the next pile of rock.

Then across the corpse of the beetle.

Then to freedom.

She lands on the flat shale expanse beyond the arena.

Behind her, more prisoners reach the rubble, all sprinting furiously. A number of them successfully clear the carnage. Those that do continue running. They vanish beyond the fog of the plains, disappearing from view. Inside the arena, sporadic bursts of white-hot fire and bright purple energy flash. The dueling titans *roar.* In the sky, the thunder rolls, dark clouds drawing near.

Now much farther beyond the arena, Princess Pipsy stops.

"Get off. *Now.* "

Eckel does, albeit nervously. If she was really going to kill him here, there'd be nowhere to go. Nothing to do.

As puny as he is, he stands upright, facing the princess.

He says nothing.

The princess looks down at him.

"Go."

Eckel gasps. Unable to hold it back, he grins. His rows of tiny teeth show between his lips.

The princess steels her resolve, not wanting to visibly react to his *disgusting, revolting, hideously vile* body.

She scrunches her nose *just* a little. But Eckel doesn't notice.

She continues.

"Get out of my sight before I change my fucking mind."

Eckel looks at her for a moment. He blinks. Or doesn't. It's hard to tell with his goggle. And his stomach-churning, beady little eye.

Eckel scampers off, running on all four arms.

Skitter skitter skitter…

He vanishes beyond the fog.

Princess Pipsy stares out at the fog for a moment, eyes fixed on the point where he disappeared. She isn't sure why.

He was *disgusting.*

More freedom-bound prisoners rush past her, her mane catching in the breeze they create. One calls out, running onward.

"Move!"

She snaps back to reality. The chaos in the arena — now far behind her — continues.

She nods.

Right.

She takes off, running away from the coliseum. Away from the city. Away from the orcs. Away from Damnation.

She speeds into the fog.

— — — — — — — — — — — — — — —

The coliseum fades to gray behind her.

The sounds of its chaos disappear into the growing wind.

The city, too, disappears.

Before long, she runs across nothing.

To nothing.

From nothing.

And she sees nothing. Nothing but the endless expanse of the shale plains before her. Every so often, she spots chips and divots in the rock, giving her some kind of visual reference. Were it not for the texture of the ground, she's not sure she'd be able to tell she was moving.

She isn't sure precisely how long she's been running.

Minutes, likely. Perhaps a little longer. Surely no more than an hour.

Right?

It's no wonder people get lost here. That they *die* here. Most of the prisoners probably will, anyway. Escaping from one hell, just to be caught up in the next.

Running across this expanse, she thinks back to Eckel's scraggly, *repulsive* face. How he looked just before he ran off. And despite it all, she still can't shake the feeling of… *something.* She isn't sure what it is.

Is this what mercy feels like?

She lingers on the questions she asks herself. She doesn't answer it. And, truthfully, she doesn't think she *could* answer it.

But she thinks about it.

Then she sees silhouettes in front of her.

Distant, but approaching.

And they continue to approach.

Rapidly.

Princess Pipsy stops moving.

The shapes continue to draw closer.

Not far behind her, thunder rumbles.

She furrows her brow, standing at the ready.

The blurry silhouettes begin to sharpen.

The first shape steps through the mist.

Aster.

Maus rides atop her, a heavy weapon slung across his back.

The princess — surprised — relaxes. She exhales.

"Aster."

Aster gives a firm nod, something… *off.*

"Princess."

She says nothing else.

Maus grunts. He and the princess lock eyes for but a moment. No words need spoken between them.

Another shape comes through the fog, this one much smaller. And glowing blue.

The *fairy?*

She giggles.

"There she is. Took long enough!"

She crosses her arms.

"We had a whole prison break plan and everything. You just *had* to ruin it, huh?"

Then another shape steps through the fog.

Delphi.

And she looks… perfectly fine. If not better than usual.

Delphi squints just a bit.

"Princess."

The princess stares back, hiding her shock.

"Delphi."

She pauses.

"Good to see you again."

Delphi says nothing.

Thunder rumbles once again, clouds now gathering overhead.

Maus looks up at the sky.

"Gonna rain soon. Looks like it, anyway."

Aster, too, looks at the sky.

"It doesn't usually rain here. This is… peculiar."

The princess replies.

"I believe that was me."

Aster steps closer.

"You have your magic back?"

She pauses.

"All of it?"

The princess shakes her head.

"Not all of it. Not yet, anyway. But I can finally feel my connection to the storms again. I think I called one by accident when I was fighting."

Maus grunts.

Impressive.

The princess continues.

"I *did* use some simple motion magic, too. So… it's *something.* But it's not *everything. "*

She glances up to her own horn.

"And my lightning has never been *red* before."

Delphi says nothing, simply staring at the princess.

Aster speaks.

"What do you think it means?"

The princess shrugs. As much as a unicorn can shrug, anyway.

"I've got no fucking idea."

A quiet moment passes.

Then, from deep within the fog, a voice calls out.

Or, more accurately, a cacophony of voices.

They all speak in unison.

And — somewhere below all the vocal layers —just *barely* discernible — the princess swears she can hear the voice of the dragon she just escaped from.

"Thank you all *so much* for waiting."

A towering shadow approaches from the fog. The end of a heavy tail — a *dragon's* tail — whips around.

Damnation steps into view.

His skin looks singed in patches all across his body. Two new arms — both torn from a bronze-red dragon — protrude from Damnation's back. They arc over his shoulders, their hands dangling in front of him.

And — affixed to his lower back — the swinging tail of Carly *thwips* against the fog.

The fairy mumbles.

"Ah, shit."

Aster doesn't take her eyes off him.

"Get ready to run."

Delphi replies.

"Way ahead of you."

The princess stares at him, unyielding. A red glow overtakes her eyes, thin strands of electricity arcing out. Her horn, too, glows the same.

Damnation stares at them gleefully.

"You are, by far, the most organized unicorns I've ever seen. When I kill you, the rest of your people will be child's play. You won't even be a *smear* on the map."

He raises up the arms on his torso, taunting them.

"Have at me."

Chapter XII:
Fractal Rainbow
Vomit Fest

Chapter XII: Fractal Rainbow Vomit Fest

Red lightning explodes out of Princess Pipsy's horn.

KRAAAK!

It strikes Damnation's chest. Purple sparks fly out, casting the dimmest of light on the gray rock around him. He staggers back, feeling the force behind the impact.

His voices chuckle.

"You'll have to do better than that."

The princess charges forward.

Another bolt of red lightning strikes out.

KRAAAK!

Damnation holds his three draconic arms in front of him. The lightning strikes their scales, most of the energy nullified… but not entirely.

Aster and Delphi follow her lead, approaching Damnation. The fairy flies behind, staying close, her blue glow shining through the fog.

As Aster runs, Maus reaches for the weapon on his back. With a single arm, he unsheathes it, holding it before him with both hands. Dried blood paints the edge of its blade, fairly fresh. He keeps a close eye on Damnation, as do the others.

Delphi's eyes glow a magnificent, blinding yellow. Her horn, too, glows the same, casting its light onto the gray expanse around her.

"I've got us covered! Don't be afraid to get close! Just try not to die!"

Aster's eyes glow blue, the centers nearly white with intensity. But her eyes don't *crackle,* they *pulse.* Her horn glows the same, thin waves of blue energy rippling outward.

"We cannot kill him, but we can fend him off. We can do enough damage to escape."

Damnation stares down at the unicorns approaching him.

"Cocky."

The shadows at the corners of his mouth bend into a grin.

"I like it."

In the sky above, the dark clouds gather further. Light rain falls.

KRAAAK!

Another bolt of red lightning strikes his chest. Purple sparks scatter out. He groans, a hint of pain behind his voices.

Princess Pipsy runs around him, keeping distance.

With his orcish hand, he reaches under the princess.   With a bit of effort, he lifts her up into the sky. Her legs flail.

Delphi draws near.

A yellow glow surrounds the body of the princess.

Damnation slams her down into the shale.

Her bones *crack* all over. Blood flies out in all directions. Skin *snaps* and *tears* and *rips* from the impact. She screams, consciousness already slipping.

Damnation turns to the others.

On the ground, lying in a pool of her own blood, the princess feels a fiery warmth spread within her. In an instant, the holes in her flesh fold back together. Light mends the muscle and skin. Her broken bones *snap* back into place. She cries out instinctively. Then she stands, brought back to the present moment.

Eyes and horn still *crackling* with red energy, she takes off again, encircling the monster once more.

Aster and Delphi, too, encircle Damnation, running opposite the princess.

Aster fires a perfectly cylindrical beam of thin, blue energy.

Pew!

It plunges through Damnation's purple shell, piercing his true body. He winces at the impact, clearly feeling some semblance of pain, even if it isn't a lot.

Aster fires again.

Pew!

Damnation raises his hands. He takes heavy swipes at the unicorns racing around him, fingers outstretched. His claws tear into Aster's side, not taking hold, but digging deep enough to penetrate. Blood spurts out from them, his claw marks running deep across her barrel. Her run falters, her body attempting to adjust to the wounds. Not a moment later, her body glows yellow. Her wounds repair themselves. And, as soon as it appeared, the yellow light around her dissipates.

Her strength returns.

Her sprint resumes.

Now closer, Maus takes a heavy swing at Damnation. The blade of his greatsword digs into the back of Damnation's orcish arm, embedding itself in its flesh.

Damnation's voices groan, a mix of pain and frustration.

Aster rides on.

Maus pulls the weapon back as she rides.

Shunk!

It pulls free.

Damnation follows their movements. Quickly, he takes another swipe. He misses, striking the ground. Flecks of broken shale fly into the air.

Directly behind him — his back now exposed — another red bolt shoots out from the princess's horn.

KRAAAK!

It strikes Damnation's back. No blood spills from the wound. It leaves a charred mark at the impact, more of Damnation's purple glow now visible from within, just a bit more of the rotting flesh blasted away.

Damnation's voices cry out.

Not in pain, but in anger.

He swings around, arms outstretched. His hands collide with Delphi, knocking her to the ground.

She skids along the surface, sliding across the broken bits of shale, leaving a thin trail of blood behind her.

The yellow light strengthens for a moment. Delphi's wounds close. She stands, now almost a hundred feet away.

The light returns to its prior steady brightness. She runs back toward the chaos, closing the distance with ease.

Princess Pipsy fires another bolt of lightning.

KRAAAK!

He buckles, nearly falling to a kneel.

His voices growl.

Aster races across the front of him. Maus takes another swing, cutting across the exposed bone of his rib cage. Small chips of bone fly off.

Damnation lashes out, striking Maus with his claws. They tear through Maus's shoulder, pulling off most of his arm with a wet, meaty *rip*. Blood explodes out from the wound. The weight of the greatsword *pulls* downward, ripping his arm even further.

Maus screams.

Aster runs on.

Around Maus's body, the bright yellow light appears. His flesh folds back together. His broken bones *snap* back into place. He screams out in pain once again.

The glow dissipates. He is healed.

Delphi's yellow glow — her eyes; her horn — dims ever-so-slightly. She takes note and shouts to the others.

"We need to go! I can't keep up with this much healing forever!"

Princess Pipsy's eyes flash to white, her horn now glowing the same. She changes trajectory, now running right for Damnation, his focus still locked onto Maus.

The princess picks up speed. The white of her eyes glows even brighter. She steps into the air, her hooves racing across an invisible staircase. Each hoof steps onto a platform of brilliant white light, each one vanishing as soon as she steps onto the next. She rises further and further above.

Damnation looks back, sensing movement behind him. And he sees her.

Nearly thirty feet above his head, Princess Pipsy gallops through the air, her white glow still very much present.

She stares down at him, righteous anger in her words.

"Fuck you."

The white glow dissipates. The *crackles* and *pops* of the red energy return, filling her eyes, surrounding her horn.

And Princess Pipsy falls.

Delphi watches closely, eyes focused.

Aster and Maus can't look away.

The fairy soars through the air nearby, unsure what to do.

The light rain continues to fall, its cold drops peppering everyone's skin.

And Damnation scowls.

The princess's horn *crackles* more wildly, an audible *hum* of a building charge.

And — her horn pointed directly below, aimed at the center of Damnation's patchwork face — she falls.

And as she falls — as her horn *just* about touches the rotting skin and bone of his head — she fires a bolt of lightning.

*KRAAAK-**KOW**!*

The explosion knocks Damnation away. He staggers back, clutching his face with several hands.

For the first time in a *very* long time, his voices cry out in pain.

And he *growls*.

Princess Pipsy lands askew. Her body weight slams hard onto her front hoof.

Crack!

Her leg snaps. She falls, skidding along the shale. The bits of cracked rock bite into her.

Without delay, the yellow glow surrounds her. Her broken leg *snaps* back into place. She winces. She stands. And she runs.

Damnation — still covering his face — spews a mess of hot flame from his mouth, burning the very air around him. He turns rapidly, painting the ground around him with fire. It's almost as if he merely hopes to burn a place where they might be.

He doesn't know where they are.

The princess races past the others, calling out.

"Run!"

Aster and Delphi follow.

The rain from above strengthens the fog, making it even thicker than before. As the unicorns run, their brilliant light trails behind them, the glow of the magic hardly diffused by the fog: Delphi, a bright yellow streak behind her; Aster, a wondrous blue following; Princess Pipsy, a sparking, electric red trail. Among them all, the fairy's blue glow flies adjacent.

Aster speaks.

"We don't know the way! We'll never escape if we're lost!"

Maus speaks, attention half-focused behind him.

"To *hell* with the way! We need to get out of here! It doesn't matter where we end up, as long as it isn't here!"

The fairy catches up, wings beating feverishly.

"Pick a direction and stick to it! Just keep going!"

The group races on, putting distance between them and the monster.

Almost wholly obscured thanks to the fog and the distance, Damnation's flames die down. His voices *roar*, anger and rage in their sound. He shouts, no magical projection behind his voice. Despite the distance, the fleeing group hear him perfectly.

"I will unmake you!"

He looks out toward them, the purple in his eye sockets flaring bright. He gallops ahead, moving fast, gaining ground at a concerning pace.

Maus notices.

"He's gaining on us!"

The fairy speaks.

"What do we do?!"

Aster replies, voice firm.

"Get ready."

Her horn pulses brighter.

Delphi keeps an eye on the group, her radiant yellow eyes watching closely.

Maus holds tight to his greatsword, all muscles tensed.

Red sparks flick out from the princess's horn.

Damnation approaches.

Tha-thump... tha-thump... tha-thump... tha-thump...

He arrives.

Thick scars of charred skin cover the center of his face, even more of his rotting flesh blasted away.

Aster turns her head toward him. She looks back to Maus, still atop her.

"Watch your arms!"

Maus leans to the side.

Aster's horn blasts energy into Damnation, a perfect cylinder of beautiful, sparkling blue.

Pew!

It misses.

Damnation draws closer.

She fires again.

Pew! Pew!

Both hit, impacting Damnation's torso.

But he doesn't flinch. He doesn't wince.

And he doesn't slow down.

Aster calls out.

"Need a little help here!"

The fairy glances over at Damnation.

"I don't suppose you wanna talk this out?"

Damnation glares at her, now running parallel to the group, his fury evident.

"I will rip out your cunt with my teeth!"

Princess Pipsy turns her head, horn aimed at Damnation. Brow furrowed, she lets loose another red bolt.

KRAAAK!

It strikes his shoulder, offsetting his balance. Skin *singes* at the point of impact. Nonetheless, his gait remains unfaltering.

Princess Pipsy — eyes still *crackling* red — looks up to the fairy.

"Can't you do fucking *anything?!*"

The fairy responds.

"Oh, shit! Yes! I forgot!"

She flies over to the princess, latching onto her mane. Through her tiny, glowing blue hands, the princess feels the slightest pulse of energy at the back of her head.

The princess's horn glows brighter. *Crackles* faster. *Hums* louder.

Both Aster and Delphi give space, wary of the intensity.

Damnation starts to close the distance, focus locked on the princess.

The fairy calls out.

"Now!"

The princess stares at Damnation, horn pointed squarely in his direction.

"Rip *this.*"

*KRAAAK-**KOW!***

The massive explosion knocks Damnation aside. He flies across the shale, nearly knocked prone, now more than a hundred feet away. He lands on his new draconic arms, forcing himself back up. His tail pushes off the ground, launching him back into a gallop.

More distance now lies between them.

But not for much longer.

The princess looks back toward the fairy.

"You could do that *the whole fucking time?!*"

The fairy responds.

"Sorry! Kind of a lot going on right now!"

Damnation's voices roar.

Galloping onward, his jaw opens wide, almost stretching to its limit. Within his mouth, a bright purple spark flickers to life.

The fairy points to it.

"What the hell is *that?!*"

Aster looks. She sees it.

"A really bad way to go!"

She starts running more erratically, trying to become a tougher target.

Delphi notices. She does the same.

"Don't let it touch you!"

The princess, too, runs erratically.

"Wasn't fucking *planning* on it!"

The purple spark in Damnation's mouth ignites. A massive beam of steady purple energy blasts forth, *pulsing* and *cracking* chaotically. A sickly *hum* emanates from it. Damnation wobbles, struggling to keep a steady gait against the force of his own beam.

The beam sails between the unicorns, carving into the shale.

Aster leaps over it. She lands on the other side of the beam, running faster.

Princess Pipsy and Delphi drop their speed, falling behind just enough to avoid running into the beam.

The beam dissipates.

Damnation huffs and groans, his voices laced with exhaustion. He pushes through, keeping speed with his enemies.

Maus calls out to the others.

"We have to lose him! We can't let him follow us!"

The princess — annoyance in her voice — calls back to him.

"If you've got any great ideas, I'd *love* to fuckin' hear 'em!"

Beside the unicorns — opposite to where Damnation runs parallel — a streak of glowing white light brightens into visibility, obscured by the fog.

The fairy sees it first.

"And what the hell is *that?!*"

The unicorns — and Maus — all look to it.

Aster speaks.

"I don't know! But we've got bigger problems at the moment!"

The purple spark in Damnation's mouth flickers once again.

Princess Pipsy fires into it.

*KRAAAK-**KOW**!*

The impact pushes against Damnation. It does nothing to quench the spark in his mouth.

Aster, too, shoots at his head.

Pew! Pew!

Yet they, too, do little.

The streak of white light emerges from the fog, appearing alongside the unicorns. A four-legged being of some kind — clearly a horse, if not a unicorn — gallops alongside them, matching their speed. The being's entire body shines with a radiant white glow, their form far too bright to look at for long, let alone discern any details. It's as if they are made purely of light.

The spark in Damnation's mouth flickers brighter.

Delphi races over to him.

Blinding yellow light flashes from her horn.

FLASH!

Damnation stumbles. Instinctively, he holds his new draconic hands in front of his face. The purple beam does not fire.

Delphi calls out to the group.

"Keep running! I can distract him!"

The white being races ahead of the unicorns, their white glow still trailing behind them. They move over to Delphi, now running right alongside her.

Delphi looks to the being. She opens her mouth to speak.

Blinding white light brightens the space.

FLASH!

It dissipates.

Both Delphi and the being are gone.
Aster calls out, already panicked.
"Delphi! Delphi!"
The fairy mumbles.
"Oh, shit…"
Aster breathes heavily, almost panting.
"Where did she go?! We can't lose anyone else!"
Maus looks around.
"I don't fuckin' *know* where she went! I don't see
her *anywhere!"*
The spark in Damnation's mouth flickers back to
life. His focus recovers. The intensity of the purple
spark grows.
The princess fires another bolt into his mouth.
*KRAAAK-**KOW!***
The electricity flows into the spark, its energy
absorbed entirely.
Now directly in front of the oncoming blast — now
without any distractions — the princess groans.
"Well, fuck me."
The purple beam blasts forth, its *pulses* and
crackles impossibly erratic. Its uncomfortable *hum* fills
the air.
The beam carves into the ground behind the
princess, just *barely* missing its target. Large chunks of
rock fly up, pieces scattering all across the ground. The
princess slips, hooves catching on the rubble. She
manages to stay upright, running forth, the crackling
beam close behind her… but her leg falls too far back.
The edge of the beam nicks her back leg.
A *wrong* sensation spreads through her.
She looks back, seeing the point of impact. She
watches dark, surface-level rot spread from the back of
her leg, reaching upward. It moves slow… but it doesn't
stop spreading.
She feels her back leg beginning to weaken.

"Fuck."

She presses on.

Damnation's beam dissipates.

He huffs and groans again, the exhaustion in his voices impossible to ignore. His gait slows just a touch, now starting to lose ground.

Aster looks back to the princess.

"Fight it off! Forget the lightning! Protect yourself!"

The princess feels the rot push in deeper.

"I *can't!* I have no healing magic!"

Aster responds.

"Neither do I!"

The fairy lets go of the princess's mane.

"Hold on!"

Carefully, she approaches the site of the rot.

She puts her hands down onto the princess's body. They glow a soft, gentle yellow, like a dimmer version of Delphi's light before… but the rot continues to spread.

"It's not working!"

The princess feels her bones start to ache.

Without warning, the blinding white being emerges from the fog once again, cutting in front of Aster and Maus.

Aster speaks, concerned and confused.

"We're running out of time! Who—"

Blinding white light brightens the space.

FLASH!

It dissipates.

Aster, Maus, and the being are gone.

Damnation's voices roar.

"You cannot escape your Damnation!"

He gallops onward, picking up speed just as the princess starts to lose it.

She feels the rot push in deeper.

Her back leg buckles a moment, struggling to keep her upright.

Damnation catches up to her, running parallel once again.

He says nothing. His jaw opens wide. The purple spark brightens inside his mouth.

The princess frowns, simply staring at it.

What a waste.

Directly in front of her, the white being appears once more. It drops its speed, getting incredibly close to her.

In her mind, the princess hears a voice not her own.

"We must go."

Through the brightness of the being's glow, the princess can barely make out the shape of a horn at the front of its head… and a second one protruding from where its eye would be.

She has no time to speak.

No time to quarrel.

No time to even comprehend what she heard.

Blinding white light brightens the space.

FLASH!

It dissipates.

The princess, the fairy, and the being are gone.

Damnation's beam blasts forth. It strikes nothing but shale.

Chapter XIII:
Amputation
Station

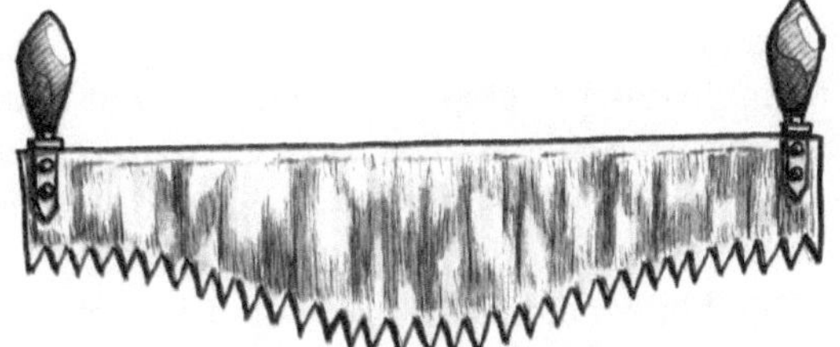

Chapter XIII: Amputation Station

The farmhouse door swings open.
Hard.
A single unicorn steps through. Her skin looks leathery and wrinkled, almost to an excessive degree, its color faded to a not-quite white, like a palomino horse that lost its color over time. A long white mane hangs down from her head, her pristine white horn poking through it. And — embedded deep within her right eye socket, the bottom end facing outward — a second horn sticks out from her head.
The being.
She speaks to unseen figures behind her, an urgent authority in her voice.
"In here. *Now.*"
She enters the farmhouse proper.
Princess Pipsy hobbles through the doorway, Aster and Delphi pushing against her, supporting her from behind.
Maus enters after, the fairy hovering next to him. He shuts the door behind them, the muffled sounds of rolling thunder now distant.
Wooden planks make up the floor; the walls; the ceiling. Thick beams support the structure, a half-dozen placed around the room. Barrels, crates, piles of spare wood, and various workman's tools crowd the space further.

Princess Pipsy whimpers — *cries* — as she hobbles. The magical rot has infected most of her leg, the now-putrid skin of it starting to sag. The noxious stench of it soaks into the air.

Aster wastes no time.

"What can I do?"

The white unicorn responds, already walking off toward a collection of supplies.

"We need to restrain her. Tie her down. Ropes, chains, whatever you can find."

She bends down, her teeth latching onto something. She pulls a thick chain from the ground with her mouth. She runs it back to the center of the room. She drops it. It *clinks*.

She looks back to Aster.

"Quickly!"

Aster nods.

She runs off to the far wall. Her horn glows blue, as do her eyes. Another long stretch of metal chain floats up from the ground, it, too, glowing blue.

The white unicorn turns to Delphi.

"Lay her down. Here. Center of the room."

Delphi walks the princess to the center.

The princess winces, pain coursing through her.

"I can't…"

The white unicorn glares at her.

"Lay down!"

Pushing through the pain, Princess Pipsy kneels onto the floor. She rolls to her side, exposing her rotting leg.

The white unicorn turns back to Delphi.

"Tie the chains around her legs and neck. Leave the rotting one free."

Delphi hesitates.

"I can heal her! We should at least *try!*"

The white unicorn barks back at her.

"There will be *nothing* to heal if we don't cut that off!"

Aster returns. She drops several piles of heavy chains onto the floor. They *clink* against the wood.

The princess cries out.

Aster levitates a chain, a blue glow around it.

Delphi's eyes, too, glow blue, as does her horn.

The two begin levitating chains, wrapping them tight around the uninjured legs of the princess.

The white unicorn turns to Maus.

"How heavy is your sword?"

Maus responds.

"Very."

The white unicorn gestures to the floor beside the princess.

"If she thrashes too much, it could kill her. She needs support. Bury the blade in the floor. Ensure it does not move."

Maus grunts.

You got it.

He pulls the greatsword from his back. He walks to the side of the princess, glowing blue chains still fastening around her. He looks down at her. Ever since this insanity started, he has never seen her falter. He has never seen her panic. Even at the assault on her own city, she exuded some sense of control. Some sense of confidence. Of dominance.

Now, he sees nothing but fear.

"Watch your head."

Humph!

He swings the greatsword down. It buries itself into the floor with a resonant *thwack*, its lengthy blade now supporting the side of the princess.

She leans against it. The cold metal touches her skin. For the briefest moment, it almost feels refreshing.

Metal chains wrap around each front leg of the princess, their ends floating in the air, all still untethered. Aster and Delphi flash a look to the white unicorn.

Now what?

The white unicorn gestures to the wooden beams nearby.

"Tie them around the beams. Use the rafters if you have to. But for gods' sakes, *keep them tight.*"

They nod.

Each chain floats to a beam. They curl around its base, looping in on themselves numerous times.

The front legs of the princess pull taut, now restrained.

She winces at the sudden change. She cries out.

Her cry morphs into a scream.

It dies as a whimper.

The white unicorn looks over to Maus.

"There are some barrels by the entrance. All carpentry supplies. Take the heaviest one and roll it over here. Prop it up against her back legs. She needs more support."

Maus nods. He trots back to the entrance.

Indeed, there are several barrels here, the top of each sealed tight.

He shakes the first. Tools inside *rattle.*

Not heavy enough.

He shakes the second. Its contents *rattle* quietly, as if overstocked.

That's the one.

The white unicorn yells out.

"Hurry!"

Maus rolls the heavy barrel onto its side. It *thunks* onto the floor, wobbling a bit. He pushes it into the center of the room, stopping at the rear of the princess.

She cries.

He glances down at the rotting leg. Its flaying skin looks a vile, sickly mix of brown and gray, the kind of color reserved for dead things.

With some effort, he props up the barrel.

The princess feels the wood panels of it press against her, the sword still firmly in the floor beside her.

The white unicorn looks to the others.

"Finish her restraints."

She runs off, eye locked onto an array of tools on the wall.

In the distance, the muffled storm draws closer.

More chains float up from the floor, glowing blue.

One wraps around the uninjured back leg of the princess, pulling tight. Its other end flies out toward the nearest wooden beam. It coils around it, as the other chains did before it.

The back leg of the princess pulls taut. She cries out once more.

The other chain wraps itself around the princess's neck. She wheezes uncomfortably, trying not to fight the restraint.

The end of the chain flies into the ceiling. It curls rapidly around one of the wooden beams of the rafters. It pulls tight, coming to a knot.

Restraints now complete, Aster and Delphi drop their blue glows.

The princess *chokes*, her head pulling back from the chain. She forces herself to relax. To not fight against her chains.

Her breath returns to normal. She feels the cold links of metal wrapped around her body, each one pulling a different part of her in a different direction.

The rot pushes deeper.

The princess cries out. Instinctively, she flails. Her chains shake from the movement.

Shink! Shink! Shink!

Thanks to her restraints — and the atypical supports around her body — she hardly moves at all.

But it still hurts.

The white unicorn rushes back, eyes and horn glowing blue. A two-man crosscut saw floats in front of her, emanating an identical glow. She floats the tool down to the ground. Its glow — and hers — dissipates.

"We'll cut off the affected leg with this. But we need to cut down to bone first, or we'll never make it in time."

She looks to Maus.

"Do you have a dagger? Shortsword? *Anything?*"

Maus pulls a hunting knife from his boot.

The white unicorn nods.

"Good. Come here."

She steps up to the writhing body of the princess.

"Stop moving. You're going to get yourself killed."

The princess whimpers.

"I *can't!* It *hurts!*"

The white unicorn looks back to Aster and Delphi.

"Tighten her restraints."

Their horns and eyes glow blue. Both unicorns focus on the chains that bind the princess, the links of which glow blue as well. All at once, they *pull,* further restraining the princess.

She chokes.

Maus approaches.

The white unicorn hears him. She points to the magical rot with her hoof.

"Anything rotten is tainted. We need to cut into healthy flesh."

She leans closer to him.

"Use as much force as you have to. We need to reach bone."

Maus grunts.

She continues.

"Hurry."

He drops to his knees before the rotting leg of the princess. Unlike the rest of her body, its movements seem delayed. Less responsive. *Weak.* More akin to muscle spasms than intentional control.

He places the edge of the knife against the lower hip of the princess. Its serration pricks her hide.

He cuts.

The princess screams.

Maus cuts deeper.

Blood leaps out with every motion of the blade. The smell of heavy iron fills the air. But the cut isn't deep enough. Not yet.

Maus cuts.

The princess screams.

The meat gets darker.

Good. Getting closer.

Blood gathers in a heavy pool around them. It pours out from the worsening wound, soaking into the floor.

Maus feels its warmth on his knees.

The white unicorn turns to the other two.

"No healing magic can counter Damnation's, but we can still use it on the untainted parts of her body. Try to slow the bleeding, but *do not* heal the wound. We must wait to cauterize. If a *speck* of that rot spreads into her living tissue, she will die as her body falls apart."

Aster and Delphi nod.

Their eyes — and both horns — glow bright yellow, Delphi's the brighter of the two. Both focus on the body of the princess below, eyes locked on the flesh being cut. Almost imperceptible, a gentle yellow light flows into the cut.

The blood continues to jettison outward… but it slows.

It's working.

The rot pushes deeper.

Maus forces the blade in further. His hands press into the tender meat within, his fingers drenched in the blood of the princess. He forces the blade *even deeper,* exerting his full strength to do so. The princess's blood coats his forearms.

She wails.

A muffled sound comes from the blade.

Scrunch... scrunch... scrunch...

Maus calls out.

"I think I got it!"

The white unicorn steps closer.

"Move. Let me see."

Maus pulls his arms from the wound. Thick blood drips from them, as if he plunged both into a bucket of paint.

The white unicorn looks into the cut. Her eyes and horn glow bright white, illuminating the immediate space. Between the bleeding clumps of muscle, she catches a glimpse of something further in: thick, off-white strands.

She drops the glow, turning back to Maus.

"It's not bone. But it's close enough."

From behind her, Aster speaks, still glowing.

"Are you sure we can do this?"

Without looking, the white unicorn responds.

"No. And we're running out of time."

The princess wails once more.

The white unicorn continues, looking to Maus.

"Pick up the saw. You grab one end, I'll take the other. Don't stop until I tell you to."

Maus grunts. He picks up one end of the heavy saw, lifting it up.

The other side glows blue, lifting with him.

With the white unicorn's help, he places the saw into the cut. Its teeth dig into the princess with its weight.

The princess pulls against her chains, going nowhere.

Maus grabs one end of the saw, holding it tight. "Ready?"

The white unicorn bites down on the other end. "Ready."

Maus pulls.

The saw cuts.

The white unicorn pulls.

The saw cuts deeper.

Blood surges out with each motion. It splatters their bodies with color. The rotting leg of the princess sags, far less attached than before. Skin at its hoof begins to slough off. Clumps fall into the growing pool of blood. Vile *snaps* and *squeaks* ring out from the wound.

Maus pulls.

The white unicorn pulls.

The saw cuts even deeper.

The eyes of the princess glow red. Her horn does the same. Violent sparks of *crackling* red energy arc outward. She cries out.

The white unicorn shouts above it.

"Keep cutting!"

So they pull.

And they pull.

And they pull.

The blade *scratches*.

And *scratches*.

And *scratches*.

Krrrnch...

Krrrnch...

Krrrnch...

The white unicorn shouts again.

"Almost there!"

The storm beyond draws much closer.

The red eyes of the princess glow brighter.

The electricity *snaps* out more violently.

Thunder *rumbles* in the dark sky outside.

The blade pulls once more.

The princess shrieks.

Everything flashes red.

An explosion rocks the farmhouse.

———————————————————————

Maus flies back, colliding with the wall. His head *slams* against it. He falls to the ground, unconscious.

The white unicorn tumbles away. Her body rolls through the massive collection of blood on the floor.

Aster and Delphi fly back, pushed towards the door of the building.

The fairy hides behind a barrel near the entrance, her shaking blue glow obscured.

Princess Pipsy thrashes violently, pulling hard against the links of her chains. The wooden beams *groan* and *strain* with the force of the movement.

The eyes of the princess glow brighter, their centers now white with intensity. Massive arcs of powerful red lightning *crack* from her horn.

Directly above her, a charred hole sits in the center of the ceiling, easily ten feet across. Heavy rain pours through it, soaking into the massive pool of blood. Spread by the rain, the light red fluid washes across the floor, coating the room in its entirety.

The princess thrashes once more. She wails. Screams. Shrieks. Her rotting leg shakes with every motion, now hanging on by limp, bleeding tissue.

The white unicorn stands, taking in the crackling red maelstrom before her. She shouts above the chaos, voice magically enhanced.

"We need to finish that cut! Her leg is still attached! This is our only chance!"

The air swirls around the princess, the rain falling in a vortex around her.

The white unicorn approaches the princess.

"Come on!"

Aster and Delphi stand. They, too, approach her.

A red bolt of lightning arcs through the air with a *crack*.

The bolt strikes the barrel of the white unicorn, burning her skin. She winces, still stepping closer.

Now she can see the cut.

The blade of the saw still sits in it, now embedded in the ragged flesh that remains. Its handles have been snapped off, the blade itself bent and warped beyond use.

Aster and Delphi stand behind the white unicorn. Tendrils of electricity whip at their skin. Blood trickles down from the points of impact, small clusters of hair singed by each mark. They push through the pain, still wincing instinctively.

The white unicorn speaks.

"The saw is destroyed! We have to rip it off! It's the only way!"

Delphi feels a sourness at the back of her throat. She speaks, voice barely audible among the storm.

"Are you sure?"

The white unicorn shouts back.

"There is no time!"

She wraps her mouth around the rotting leg of the princess. Her nostrils flare, burning from the stench. Her very mind seems to fight against the decision.

But she pushes through.

She bites down hard on the leg.

Aster and Delphi do the same.

Clumps of flesh slough off in their mouths. Slick, grimy layers peel back as they clamp down. The leg feels soft in places it shouldn't be, a sour sponge between their teeth.

But it doesn't give them leverage.

Not yet.

They bite down harder.

Pus bursts under the surface, coating their lips in its rotten cream. Sickly blood seeps into their mouths.

Their teeth hook onto something more solid. Likely a tendon or bone, the likes of which hasn't rotted yet. Not entirely.

They have leverage.

The *pull*.

The princess shrieks. The sound of her voice fills the air like the thunder above.

And they *pull*.

She shrieks again, growing louder.

And they *pull*.

A thick bolt of lightning *cracks* out from the tip of her horn, arcing downward. It strikes the floor next to the white unicorn, the sound ringing in her ears. The fluid below *splashes* up on impact, hitting her face.

So they *pull*.

The rot seeps deeper in, nearly reaching healthy flesh. The princess feels its ache pushing deeper. She screams out yet again. Another thick bolt of lightning *cracks* out.

And they *pull*.

The princess flails wildly, shaking her chains in the storm. A flurry of little red sparks flick out from her horn, as if calling to the dark clouds above her.

And they *pull*.

Numerous wet *snaps* ring out in sequence.

The rotten leg tears free.
The three unicorns fall back.
The princess blacks out.

— — — — — — — — — — — — — — —

Warmth.
Light.
The gentle sound of birds.
Princess Pipsy blinks awake.
She lies on her side, some sort of fabric blanket beneath her. Sunlight shines in through a square glass window next to her, incredibly simple in its construction.   The white unicorn stares out of it, not yet noticing the princess.

The room itself is almost wholly made of wood, the chamber no larger than twenty feet across. Blankets pile high, other cloths and scraps piled with them. Her armor — having been taken off and set aside — rests against the wall adjacent to the open doorway. Whether the doorway has no door or it's simply open too far, she cannot tell.

The white unicorn notices the princess. She turns to her.

"Good. You're finally awake."
The princess responds, still in a daze.
"What… happened? Where are we?"
She looks right at the white unicorn.
"And who the fuck are *you?*"
The white unicorn walks over.
"Damnation attacked you at the Shale Plains. His magic struck your leg. We had to amputate before the rot spread."
The princess looks back to her leg. Or where it used to be, anyway. Thick bandages wrap around the

amputation, layered over the rear of her body for durability.

It really is *gone.*

The white unicorn continues.

"We are in my Sanctuary, not far from the western side of the Dreadrock Mountains. I built everything here myself. Made this place into a home. I teleported you here during the fight. Which is an *exhausting* thing to do, mind you."

...teleport?

Since when could unicorns fucking teleport?

"This place is protected by my magic. It has been for a long time, ever since I've lived here. My family—"

She stops, like she said something wrong.

Then she continues.

"...well, we keep to ourselves."

Family...?

"As for who I am, I'm not surprised you don't remember. It's been a *very* long time for you. Even longer for me. You were just a foal, if I recall."
The white unicorn stands tall. The horn jutting from her eye socket catches stray rays of sunlight, deflecting them outward.

"My name is Petunia, former Knight-Captain of the Queen of the Unicorns."

She walks off, leaving the room through the open doorway.

"Rest for now. I will return shortly. Then we'll see what to do about that leg."

Princess Pipsy leans back, resting on the blanket beneath her.

She inhales.

She exhales.

"Fuck."

Chapter XIV:
The Sanctuary

Chapter XIV: The Sanctuary

Petunia steps outside.

The morning air greets her, as it always does. A light breeze brings it closer, the air itself otherwise still. Birds chirp in the distance, some barely audible. The grasses of the clearing and the hills around it soak up the sun. Trees gather like miniature forests, sporadically clumped about the space, worn dirt paths and trails winding into them. Farther out, more prominent arrangements of the trees almost form a natural barrier, the mountaintops beyond even moreso. Over it all, the faintest white light shimmers.

She steps off the wooden porch — basic in its construction — and onto the grass. She feels the unusually wet soil under her hooves. It doesn't usually rain here, no, but the Sanctuary will recover.

There, on the grass before her, stands Aster and Delphi. The fairy floats above them, hovering in the air.

All three stare at Petunia.

She speaks, breaking the silence.

"I hope you all slept well, despite your choice of resting place."

Aster replies.

"We have no way of knowing your intentions. Arguably, we still don't. It was safer for us to sleep out here. Only a fool would sleep in the home of a stranger."

The front door of the house pushes open. Maus steps onto the porch. His boots *thunk* as he walks. He

stifles a yawn, leaning against the wooden barrier of the
porch.

Aster glares at him.

He doesn't notice.

Petunia speaks to the group, looking between them.

"The princess has only just awoken. She's still a bit
confused, and rightly so. She's been through a lot of
physical trauma, and I assume there may still be some
shock from it. But she's alive."

The fairy gasps.

"I wanna see! I wanna see!"

Maus rolls his eyes.

"You weren't excited to see last night."

The fairy flies onto the porch. She shouts
impatiently.

"Move!"

She pushes past Maus's shoulder, despite the ample
space to fly around him.

She zips into the simple house, disappearing from
view.

Aster speaks again.

"Right... well, we can't go anywhere until the
princess can walk again. In the hope of not being killed,
I suggest we find a solution before *Damnation* finds
us."

Petunia responds.

"As I told you before, my magic protects this
place. It protects me. It protects my children. And, by
extension, it will protect you. That monster cannot find
us here."

Aster shakes her head in disbelief.

"We don't *know* you. We can't *trust* you. Even if
you believe what you say, how do you know that it's
true?"

Petunia's expression softens.

"This is unlike any other place. I promise you, we won't be found."

Aster doesn't buy it.

"We simply cannot take the risk. The sooner we can leave from here, the better."

Delphi chimes in, looking to Aster.

"Based on the magics I've studied — and the history that comes with all of it — there *are* ways she can walk again. But—"

Aster interrupts.

"No. We have no idea what her magic could do to her."

Petunia chimes in.

"I have to agree with your friend here. There *are* things that can be done, yes, but no others are nearly as swift."

Aster shakes her head.

"No. You said it yourself. There's chaos in your magic. That means we can't trust it."

Petunia frowns, disappointed in her defiance.

"Then you'll be staying here longer than you intend. There are very few magics in the world that can do something so dramatic so quickly. If you want her to run again — not just *stand,* but *run* — it's quite likely the only way."

Aster looks to Delphi.

Delphi shoots her a look.

She's right.

Aster frowns. She turns her focus back to Petunia.

"The princess can make her own decisions."

Petunia replies.

"I agree."

Maus, having been silent this entire time, says nothing. He avoids looking directly at any of the unicorns. He's trying *very* hard to enjoy what little peace there is.

From inside the house, the angry voice of the princess carries.

"I told you to *fuck… off!*"

Delphi speaks.

"That's our cue."

She walks up to the porch and enters the house. Petunia follows after.

"She really has a mouth on her."

She, too, enters the house.

Aster walks behind. She mutters to herself.

"You have no idea."

She enters the house.

Maus leans against the wooden railing of the porch, looking out to the trees; the hills; the mountains.

He sighs.

"There goes my one decent morning."

He notices a horse standing no more than thirty feet from him, the front of its body poking out between some shrubbery. Patches of murky gray skin dot its light yellow coat, a dark mane hanging from its head. A pointed lump sticks out from the center of its forehead, almost reminiscent of a unicorn's horn… but very clearly *not* one.

It stares at Maus idly, like a doe caught in the lamplight.

Maus stares back.

Then he speaks.

"Hello?"

The horse — or whatever it is — says nothing.

Maus tries again, a bit louder.

"Hello?"

The horse simply stares back, unblinking.

Then it darts off through the shrubbery.

Ksh ksh ksh…

It gallops away, vanishing from sight.

Maus shakes his head.

"Why do I bother?"
He heads inside.

———————————————————————————

When Petunia was the only other unicorn in the room, it didn't feel all that small to the princess. When she was joined by not only the other two unicorns, but Maus and the fairy as well, the room felt *very* small.

It also doesn't help that the fairy keeps poking her bandages.

"I just wanna *see* it!"

The princess snarls.

Maus swats at the fairy.

"Knock it off."

She backs away, hovering in the corner. She crosses her arms and pouts.

"Assholes."

Aster speaks, looking to the princess.

"How are you feeling?"

The princess responds.

"Like I just got my fucking leg cut off."

The fairy giggles.

"I didn't know you had a leg for that!"

Nobody laughs.

Maus swats at her again.

"Adults are talking."

The fairy groans. She zips over to the windowsill and plops down on it. She stares down at her feet, swinging her legs, mumbling indiscernibly.

Delphi speaks.

"Do you remember what happened?"

The princess looks over, irked.

"I remember my body fighting back without my control or permission, yes. Thanks for reminding me."

Delphi steps back, saying nothing.

The princess looks to Petunia.

"And — by the way — are we not going to acknowledge the fact that you *fucked* a *horse?* Do you understand how serious of a crime that is to our people, let alone to *nature?"*

Petunia does not shy away.

"His *name* was *Artie."*

The princess snaps back.

"I don't care what his fucking name was. How do you even *know* that? He couldn't talk."

Petunia continues, largely unfazed.

"He was a retired work horse. I followed his caravan in the early days. For safety. I heard his people talk. When they set him loose, we simply found each other again. He was smart enough to know what he wanted."

The princess feels sourness at the back of her throat.

"There are reasons we have laws against this. That *horse* was hardly intelligent. What you did was nothing short of bestiality and heresy."

Petunia raises her voice. Not by a lot, but by enough.

"I had been alive for hundreds of years by that point. Longer than the natural lifespan of any unicorn. I had not even *seen* another unicorn since my accident."

She gestures to the horn stuck in her eye socket.

"You disappeared. *You* vanished from the world. Even if I *was* found before you disappeared from existence, I would have been slaughtered for treason. For fleeing from the field of battle. For being weaker than the rest."

She continues.

"Before I saved your lives, the only unicorns I had seen were the ones Damnation got his hands on. I have been alive just as long as that monster. Be thankful I did not turn out like him."

She straightens up, regaining her composure.

"I don't expect you to understand. We are two *very* different unicorns in just about every sense of the word. But the actions of Artie and I blessed me with children. With *company.* Something I missed for a *very* long time."

The princess speaks.

"Your children are inferior."

Petunia responds.

"They are my children nonetheless."

She takes a moment to breathe.

"As I said, I don't expect you to understand. But you are not in Unicornicopia. You are in *my* domain. I am *allowing* you to stay here. I have saved your life *twice.* So, while you may not understand, let alone empathize, you *will* show me respect. That is not up for discussion."

Princess Pipsy leans away. She says nothing.

Aster interjects respectfully.

"I should remind you, Petunia, that you are speaking to Princess Pipsy, sole heir to the Queen of the Unicorns."

Petunia looks to her, a kind of pity in her eyes.

"I left behind the formalities of our people long ago. And, considering the circumstances, I'd say we're all on equal footing."

Aster says nothing more.

Maus leans against the wall.

The fairy still stares at her feet, swinging them out.

A tense silence hangs in the air.

Delphi steps forward and breaks it.

"Well, now that we've gotten *that* out of the way — and I do hope you'll try not to stir up any more conflict, princess — I suggest we address the leg problem."

The princess exhales, calming down.

"Agreed."

Maus speaks.

"Can't you just… I dunno, levitate yourself? *Fly* or something?"

Princess Pipsy scoffs.

"Fly? What do you think we are? We're *unicorns,* not miracle workers."

Aster perks up, as if remembering something. She turns to Petunia.

"In that regard, I'd like to discuss some things with you, Petunia. Delphi would benefit as well, as would the princess. I think we could all do with some… *exchanges* of information."

Petunia nods.

"I agree. But there will be time for that later. For now, we should address — as Delphi so aptly put it — the leg problem."

— — — — — — — — — — — — — — — — — —

The princess stares with conviction.

"Then do it."

Aster steps forward.

"Princess, I have to protest—"

Princess Pipsy looks to her.

"It's *my* decision."

Aster replies.

"But her magic is chaotic. *Unstable.* She said that much herself. Even with her level of control, there's no telling the extent of what it could do to you."

The princess speaks.

"I… am lucky to be alive."

She flashes a look of hesitant gratitude to Petunia.

Petunia gives a subtle nod.

The princess returns her gaze to Aster.

"If I'm not back to full strength, we'll be too weak to bring down Damnation. You heard what he said. The rest of us that are still alive — that are still *out there* — aren't organized. We're the best of what we got. Who knows how many of us are even left? As far as we know, Unicornicopia was the last city of unicorns in the world."

She breathes.

"The longer we wait, the longer Damnation has to kill what's left of our people."

Delphi speaks.

"There *are* other options."

The princess replies, nearly cutting her off.

"Are there? Are there *really?* Nothing we could do on our own would ever be fast enough, magic or not. This *is* the only option."

She looks back to Petunia.

"Whatever you're going to do, I want you to do it."

Petunia steps forward.

"Very well."

Still facing the princess, she speaks.

"We're going to need some space. This room will work fine, but I'll need everyone else to clear out. It's going to take some time. Hopefully no more than an hour or two. Three, at the most."

Maus pushes off the wall.

"Fine by me."

He walks out of the room, leaving the house.

Aster speaks.

"What are you going to do? Specifically, I mean."

Petunia turns to face her.

"It's going to be painful. Incredibly unpleasant. But — to answer your question — I'm going to force her leg back into existence."

Delphi cocks her head.

"In everything I've studied, I have *never* heard of anything like that."

Petunia responds.

"There are more primal magics than ours. Older ones. You'd be surprised what you can do, if only you have the willpower. And the means to tap into it."

She steps closer to the princess.

"Now, if you wouldn't mind…"

Aster nods.

"Of course. I'll be waiting just outside the door."

She leaves the room. Indeed, she stops just beyond the open doorway.

Delphi, too, leaves the room.

"I suppose I'll return shortly. I have no reason to stay behind."

Petunia speaks as she exits.

"Don't be afraid of my children, should you meet them. They tend to be a bit shy. But they're wiser than they look."

Uncertain how to respond, Delphi says nothing more. She leaves the house.

Petunia looks to the fairy.

"You are quite small. You can stay. Just be careful not to get in the way."

The fairy perks up, demeanor instantly shifting.

"Ooh, *okay!*"

She leans closer, giggling mischievously.

"I bet she's gonna *squirm!*"

Princess Pipsy looks up at Petunia.

"Well? Are you ready?"

Petunia's eyes glow a stark, radiant white. Her horns — both the one in her head as well as the one in her eye socket — glow the same. Subtle white light pulses outward from her form.

"I am."

She steps even closer, aiming her horns toward the princess.

"Let us begin."

— — — — — — — — — — — — — — — — — —

The leaves on the path *crunch* under Maus's boots. He walks quietly along the forest trail. Not quite aimless, per se, but certainly with no destination in mind. Walking to enjoy some brief piece. Walking for the sake of the walk.

He looks up at the canopy above him. A few leaves float down, joining those he already stepped on. The screams of pain were too much to deal with back at the house. And for *two hours?* Possibly *more?*

Fuck that.

This entire journey has been one whiplash after another. First, his worldview was shattered, since, apparently, unicorns have *always* been real. Then they *kidnapped* him. He almost got executed. Wouldn't be the first time someone tried that. Lots of unhappy customers over the years. But at least mercenary work had an order to its chaos. The mess he's in now has no order. And *then* — and here's the kicker — a *giant fucking monster* starts killing them all and threatens to murder the *world?*

He sighs.

This ordeal is exhausting.

His entire *life* is exhausting.

Good thing he doesn't have a family. Imagine trying to explain any of *this* to a sane person.

Accepting this insanity at face-value is probably what's kept him alive.

Rustling comes from nearby.

Maus stops.

He listens close.

291

Ksh ksh ksh…

He tenses up.

He looks around, trying to spot the source.

Ksh ksh ksh…

There it is again.

His eyes drift to a large bush — an overgrown hedge, maybe — that wriggles.

Ksh ksh ksh…

He unsheathes his greatsword, holding it in both hands.

Cautiously, he approaches the bush.

The rustling continues.

Ksh ksh ksh…

Then—

It stops.

He furrows his brow, somewhat confused.

A squirrel *leaps* out from the bush, sailing right past his head.

Maus jumps back, dropping his sword. It *thuds,* kicking up dirt from the path, no doubt gaining another scuff mark.

The squirrel lands on the ground, quickly skittering into the trees behind him.

He shakes his head.

"Stupid animal."

He picks up his sword. He shakes off the dirt, then puts it back into its sheath.

He looks up.

A horse stands inches from his face.

He jumps back again, very much startled. He lands on his ass.

Frustrated, he groans.

"You can't *do* that to people! What the hell is wrong with you?"

The horse stares down at him, a vacant expression in its eyes. A fuzzy stump protrudes from its forehead.

Gray splotches dot its light yellow coat, a dark mane giving contrast. Looks like the same… *thing* that he spotted earlier.

Now up close, it looks a bit taller than a normal horse, but certainly not as tall as the unicorns.

Except Princess Pipsy. She's short as shit.

Maus grunts, standing up.

"Hello? Can you understand me?"

The horse says nothing. Its eyes look completely glazed over, as if staring *past* Maus, not even *at* him.

Maus steps closer.

"Can you even *hear* me?"

The horse's eyes snap to his.

It certainly heard him that time.

It stomps a single hoof on the ground.

Thump!

Maus doesn't understand.

"Do you… want something? I don't have any food. I'm all out."

It stomps again.

Thump!

Maus sighs, a mix of pity, frustration, and intrigue.

"I'm gonna need a little more than that."

It stares at him for a moment.

A moment too long, perhaps.

It darts off, running down the path.

Maus shakes his head.

"Stupid animal."

Then the horse stops.

Still on the dirt path — now a bit further away — it turns around to face Maus.

It stares directly at him.

It stomps the ground.

Thump!

Maus speaks, uncertain of his own words.

"Do you want me to… *follow* you?"

The horse does not move.
It simply stares.
Then it stomps the ground again.
Thump!
Maus exhales.
"Better than doing nothing…"
He approaches the horse.

———————————————————————

Delphi stands on a hill, face pointed up to the sky. She watches the slow movements of the clouds. Around her, the breeze starts to pick up just a bit. It doesn't feel cold, but it doesn't feel warm, either. It's the kind of ambient, neutral breeze that simply makes you aware of its presence. It's the kind she most enjoys.

She almost wasn't here to feel this. Not long ago, she was brought to the brink of death. Maybe even beyond it.

By the *princess,* no less.

The queen was cruel, sure, but only because she had to be. Leading the most powerful civilization of all time — *governing* it — it always required a certain level of ruthlessness. It's why they were never bothered. Never pursued. Never hunted.

Not until now, anyway.

And they're far weaker now than they were then. Some of their magic is back, yes, but only in strange limitations. *New* limitations. It doesn't feel like they beat whatever restricted their power… it feels like they're playing along with it.

And Delphi doesn't like it.

If the queen were here, they'd likely be back home by now. Damnation would've been killed already. They would've gotten to the bottom of this mystery and restored their legacy in the world.

But the queen isn't here.

Hopefully she's still alive.

She's probably not.

Only her *daughter* is here.

Her daughter, who inherited all of her rage with none of the self-control.

The queen could've led them to war.

The princess will lead them to slaughter.

From the corner of her vision, Delphi spots a horse step onto the hill adjacent. Its coat is an odd patchwork mix of light gray and golden tan. A pointed nub sticks out from its forehead, almost completely obscured by a mane of matted brown.

Must be one of the children.

It stares at her, unmoving.

Delphi stares back, trying to get a read on its nearly expressionless face.

It stomps the ground.

Thump!

Delphi approaches.

— — — — — — — — — — — — — — —

Maus shoves a cluster of branches aside, stepping between a number of large trees.

"How much farther we going, buddy?"

The horse ahead of him says nothing. It continues walking, almost like it didn't hear him.

Maybe it *didn't* hear him…

It steps over masses of roots and flora clumsily, somehow managing to never lose its footing.

A bug flies into Maus's head. He swats it away, annoyed.

"Look, we've been walking a *while.* I'm sure you got something *really* cool to show me, but I gotta head back. Maybe next time, yeah?"

The horse freezes in place ahead of him, still facing forward.

Maus, too, stops walking.

"This it?"

The horse stomps the ground.

Thump!

It stomps the ground again.

Thump!

Maus walks ahead.

"Alright, hold on. Lemme see."

He steps up to the side of the horse, pushing through more brush. It takes but a moment to pass it. In this brief stretch of forest, more of Petunia's children stand. *Dozens* of them. Their coats are all mixes of gray, tan, and white, their manes either darker or lighter, each one with a nub on its forehead. They all stare out at something beyond. Each one stomps the ground, no true rhythm between them.

Thump! Thump! Thump!

Among them, he spots Delphi, her gaze, too, fixated on something beyond, her face filled with some sort of horror.

Not far ahead, the shimmering wall of white light — the barrier of the Sanctuary — comes to a stop on the ground, much like the side of a dome.

This is the edge.

Damnation stands on the other side.

The half-breeds continue their warning.

Thump! Thump! Thump!

Damnation peers inward, looking past them. Looking *through* them. Like he can't even see them at all.

But he knows he's found *something.*

He just isn't sure what.

Not yet.

Maus's eyes drift over to Delphi. The two spot each other, sharing a glance.

The wind picks up, the strength of its breeze now apparent.

The half-breeds continue their warning.

Thump! Thump! Thump!

Chapter XV:
The Death of
the Coward

Chapter XV: The Death of the Coward

Princess Pipsy screams.

She hardly understands what's happening. What's *really, actually* happening. She understands that Petunia is tied to some sort of ancient magic, or so she claims. She understands the end goal, which is, obviously, to get her leg back. But she doesn't understand how it's working. She doesn't understand *why* it's working. And she doesn't understand how a brand new leg is forcing its way out of her body, pushing through her freshly wounded skin.

Petunia shouts above her screams.

"We're almost there! Hold on!"

The princess glares at her.

"You said that an hour ago!"

Her biting remark devolves into another scream.

Under her bandages, something firm pokes out, pushing from behind her skin. It *pushes* and *pushes*, almost… *growing*.

She feels her skin start to tear just a bit. Blood trickles out from several points.

The shape continues to push.

The skin splits. Blood soaks into the bandages. The shape pushes out even farther.

The bandages *snap* away.

The leg of a young foal pushes out from Princess Pipsy's body, forcing its way through her cauterized skin, as if it had been stuck inside her.

The leg continues to push.

The skin around it *rips* further, forced to accommodate.

Blood pulses out from the steadily growing wound.

The princess screams.

The leg forces itself out even further.

And it *grows*.

The injured skin of the princess *rips* even more.

The princess shrieks. Her horn begins to *crackle* with red energy. Her pupils begin to fade as the same red glow overtakes her eyes. A subtle *hum* builds.

Petunia shouts above the chaos.

"We're almost there! Keep it under control!"

Through searing pain, the princess responds.

"I'm *trying!*"

Her eyes glow brighter against her will.

Petunia's own glow shines brighter in response.

The very air around them seems to ripple with magical energy.

Princess Pipsy feels her lungs begin to struggle.

Her heart beats faster.

Petunia's glow grows even stronger.

The princess cries out.

Then—

CRUNCH!

The leg completely forces itself through her skin.

She exhales.

The pain begins to subside. Not all of it, but enough. For now.

The red glow fades from her body.

Petunia's white glow, too, dissipates.

From the hall, Aster steps into the doorway.

"Did it work?"

She leans into the room.

"Please tell me it worked."

For a moment, the princess simply breathes.

Petunia breaks the silence.

"I'd call that a success."

She turns to the princess.

"What do *you* think?"

The princess looks down at her body.

Bloody bandages pile on the floor beside her, blood now pooled around her lower body. Where her leg was amputated just one night before, a fully grown leg juts out, *covered* in her own blood.

Despite the magically messy procedure, the skin at the base of the leg seems to have healed, like the skin was never broken in the first place.

She tries to bend the leg.

It bends.

With effort, she stands.

The white glow fades from Petunia, her horns — and eye — returning to normal.

"How do you feel?"

The princess raises the leg a few times, staring at it.

"Like I just got a new fucking leg."

Aster breathes a sigh of relief.

Princess Pipsy looks back to Petunia. Her expression softens just a bit.

"Thank you."

Petunia nods.

"I'm glad I could help. And I'm *very* glad it brings you closer to killing that monster."

The fairy zips over to the princess's new leg, positively entranced.

"Woah! It really worked!"

Petunia comments.

"I was hoping it would."

Aster looks at Petunia, dumbfounded.

"Hoping?"

Petunia glances over.

"Of course. There was never a guarantee. The magic I tap into is not always easily controlled. But it looks like it worked out just fine."

Aster's eyes widen with shock. She says nothing.

The fairy pokes at the new leg. The fresh blood sticks to her finger.

She giggles.

"EW!"

The princess kicks at her.

"Knock it off."

The fairy dodges with ease, flying higher up.

"Rude!"

Petunia exhales.

"Well, I don't know about you, but that was exhausting. I say we rest for the day. I think it would do every one of us good."

Aster hesitates.

"That… sounds like a risk."

The princess, too, seems reluctant.

"I don't know if we should. Time that we aren't moving is time that Damnation has to—"

Petunia interrupts.

"I assure you, he cannot find you here. Ancient magics protect this place. We have *safety* here. We have *peace.*"

The front door opens.

SLAM!

The wind outside — heavier now — blows in.

Aster backs up, turning toward the door.

"What's going on?"

Petunia walks over, equally wary.

"I have no idea."

The princess stands behind them.

The fairy hovers above, simply watching. Happy to be here.

Delphi races in through the open door. Maus rides atop her. Both look incredibly concerned.

Princess Pipsy steps forward.

"What is it?"

Delphi responds.

"Damnation is here."

Petunia looks mortified.

She leans forward.

"That should not be possible."

Maus meets her eyes.

"We saw him. Somewhere by the edge. So did your children."

Petunia breaks eye contact. Her eyes dart about the room. She paces.

"It should not be possible. My barrier protects this Sanctuary. It *always* has. I have been here for *hundreds* of years. I *know* that this place is protected. Only the very clouds…"

She trails off.

Her intensity fades.

She finds herself deep in thought, like she's finally connecting the dots. Like she's finally recalling the obvious.

She looks back to Princess Pipsy.

"You brought him here."

Everyone else looks to the princess.

She exhales.

"Fuck."

— — — — — — — — — — — — — — — — —

Petunia — eyes fixed ahead — crosses the small field in front of the house. The rest of the group follows after, Maus still set upon Delphi.

The wind swirls around them, the scent of dampness in its folds.

The princess — wearing her armor once again — speaks.

"I didn't know any of that would happen, let alone reach above your barrier."

Without looking back, Petunia responds.

"It doesn't matter what you thought. It doesn't matter what *any* of us thought. That storm appeared above my protection. No wonder that monster saw it."

Aster calls out.

"What do we do?"

Petunia hurries ahead. She runs onto a worn dirt trail.

"I am going to protect my children. I will do what it takes to defend my home."

Delphi speaks, not far behind her.

"What about us?"

Petunia picks up speed.

"You run. I've been a thorn in his side for a very long time. If nothing else, I know he holds a grudge. That means I should have his exclusive attention."

Maus shouts out to her.

"How do you know?"

Petunia calls back.

"I don't."

She diverts from the path, running into the trees.

The others follow.

To Maus, this route seems familiar.

Princess Pipsy gains ground, now closer to Petunia. Her armor *clinks* with her speed.

"I thought you could *teleport.*"

Petunia responds.

"I *can.* But as I said, it exhausts me. Doing it for *one* of you would have been a challenge. Doing it for *all* of you was a miracle."

The princess frowns.

"We don't have the luxury for you to feel exhausted."

Petunia glares in her direction.

"Everything has its limits. Even magic."

Her focus shifts ahead. She runs on.

"We won't have much longer. He's bound to get inside eventually. When that happens, your party *must* flee."

She takes a breath.

"There is no alternative."

Maus takes it in.

"I don't like it."

Petunia responds.

"I'm not telling you to like it."

Maus grunts.

Whatever you say.

Delphi speaks.

"How far into the mountains are we? Can we get to the valley from here?"

Petunia takes a sharp turn.

"Head east through the hills. Pass through the mountains. Keep going until you reach the Loftwood. If you want to find your artifact, the Varsii will know where it is."

Maus calls out.

"And what if they don't?"

Petunia calls back.

"Then nobody does."

She takes another sharp turn.

The group follows.

The fairy smacks into a branch headfirst.

"Ow!"

She recovers instantly, keeping pace.

Petunia shouts to the others.

"We're almost there!"

She pauses.
"Be ready."

— — — — — — — — — — — — — — — — — —

The half-breeds stomp their hooves on the ground, terrified.

Thump! Thump! Thump! Thump!

They all stare ahead, eyes fixed on the edge of the barrier.

Centered among them, the group stands.

On the other side of the barrier, Damnation *presses* his body into it. The light *bends* with the force, like a fabric that's stretching too thin. Purple sparks fly out from within him.

Petunia speaks to the others.

"He can't see us yet — nor can he hear us — but he knows that we're in here. He *must*. He may be unstable, but he isn't an imbecile."

Damnation *pushes* further in. The light continues to bend.

Petunia continues.

"Something in his magic is allowing him to touch it. I do not know what. It's holding for now, but it *will* break eventually."

Damnation continues to *push* into it. His face presses against the light.

The princess speaks.

"We should attack from within. Push him back."

Petunia shakes her head.

"It would be useless. He can't touch us until that breaks, but we can't touch him, either. The protection goes both ways."

Maus comments.

"Meaning we can't do *shit* 'til he comes for us."

Petunia replies.

"Correct."

Maus sighs.

"Lovely."

Damnation lurches forward just an inch, as if nearing some sort of threshold.

Petunia turns to the group.

"That's your cue."

She pauses.

"Good luck."

Damnation lurches forward again. The light of the barrier *cracks*.

Petunia shouts.

"GO!"

Delphi takes off, Maus still atop her.

The fairy waves, then zips away, trailing behind Delphi.

Aster gives a firm, thankful nod, then runs after.

Princess Pipsy looks into Petunia's eyes for just a moment.

And for that moment, Petunia looks back.

Neither one speaks a word.

The princess looks… conflicted.

Then she takes off, running after the others.

Petunia turns to the barrier, gaze fixed on the monster pressing against it.

Damnation lurches once more.

The barrier *cracks*.

And it *shatters*.

Fragments of light cascade down in broken shards, each piece completely dissipating before it hits the ground, all fading into nothing.

The barrier is gone.

Damnation steps forward.

"Well… isn't *this* a surprise?"

He looks around, taking note of the half-breeds…
and of Petunia. The shadows at the corners of his face
curl into a twisted grin.

"Oh, my. You've been *quite* busy. No *wonder* I
wasn't invited."

Petunia's eyes glow white. Both horns do the same.
Waves of light ripple outward from her body. All around
her, the half-breeds stomp wildly, a sense of panic in
their movements.

Petunia glares at the monster.

"You are not welcome here."

Damnation meets her gaze.

"I know."

———————————————————————

Princess Pipsy gallops between the trees, catching
up to the others. Her hooves *clack* softly against the
forest floor, as do those of her allies. At least for those
who have them.

She says nothing.

The rest of her group glances over to her,
acknowledging her presence. They continue racing
along the trail. In the distance, the central house is just
barely in view.

Far behind them, a thunderous *crackling* echoes
through the trees, like the sound of breaking glass.

Above them, the shimmering light of the barrier
splits into thousands and thousands of fragments. It
falls, each piece simply vanishing before it gets close to
hitting the ground.

The fairy notices.

"That's not good!"

Damnation's voices *roar.*

The fairy continues.

"That's *really* not good!"

Maus frowns.

"Shut up and keep moving!"

The princess speaks.

"Agreed."

Sounds of chaos ring out far behind them. Echoed shouts. Muffled impacts. Distant crackles of energy. Nearly indiscernible whinnies.

They charge on.

They cross through the final few trees, emerging in front of the central house.

Delphi takes the lead. She shouts back to the others.

"This way!"

She runs off toward the hills adjacent.

The others follow.

As she runs, Princess Pipsy spots the farmhouse nestled among the first few hills. She stares at it, running past. She notices the charred, gaping hole that she put in the roof.

She runs on.

Delphi calls out to the group.

"If we keep this direction, we should be on course!"

The fairy responds.

"Should be?!"

Maus concurs.

"I was thinking the same thing."

Delphi groans.

"I'm making some assumptions! We're on a bit of a time crunch at the moment!"

White light *explodes* from deep within the trees. The ground shakes. Purple light *flashes* repeatedly. Another white light *flashes* after. Flames *roar* to life, only to vanish. Another purple light *flashes*. And *another* white light after.

Damnation's voices roar. His words carry on the very wind.

"You cannot escape me! And neither can your bastards!"

The thunderous sound of hooves grows steadily louder.

And louder.

And *closer.*

Delphi looks back. She watches the first of the half-breeds emerge from the trees… swiftly followed by many, many more.

And they all have their sights on the unicorns.

Delphi calls out.

"It's a stampede!"

The others hardly have time to process.

With astonishing ease, the half-breeds catch up to them, overtaking their lead.

Now caught in the center of the herd, the unicorns push on, left with few other choices.

A white light flies up from the trees, now even farther behind them. It races across the sky, as if running on air.

No. Not just a white light.

A *being* of white light.

Petunia.

She runs across the sky. Platforms of white light appear under her hooves, vanishing after each step.

Damnation's voices roar once more.

He *leaps* from the forest, sailing into the air. He reaches toward Petunia, arms outstretched.

He misses.

But not by much.

He falls, hitting the ground with a heavy *THUD.*

He *leaps* again, reaching up for her.

Petunia looks down to him. Her horns *flash* for a split second. A massive wall of light stretches out before her.

Damnation collides with it full-force.

The shield of light *shatters* from the impact.

Damnation falls. He lands on the broken roof of the farmhouse, *crashing* through it.

Petunia staggers from the force, knocked aside.

She falls, landing among the trees.

Damnation punches the farmhouse from inside. The wood *explodes* out, splintering into countless little pieces. He steps through the broken doorway and looks around, trying to spot any sign of Petunia.

He doesn't see her.

But he does see the herd of half-breeds running into the hills.

And among them, he spots three unicorns.

And a mercenary.

And a fairy.

His aggression dampens.

He cocks his head, amused.

"Gotcha."

He gallops after them.

The herd runs further into the hills, the unicorns still stuck in the center. Maus looks back. He catches a glimpse of Damnation barreling toward them.

Ka-thump… ka-thump… ka-thump…

Maus shouts to the others.

"He's gaining on us!"

A vibrant red glow overtakes Princess Pipsy's eyes. The energy *crackles* and *pops*. Her horn, too, glows the same. She calls out to the others.

"No better time to fuck him up."

Princess Pipsy drops her speed, falling to the back of the herd.

Delphi notices.

"What is she *doing?*"

Aster's eyes glow bright blue. Her horn, too, glows the same.

"Something stupid."

Aster drops her speed, falling to the back of the herd.

Delphi watches, disappointed… but not surprised.

"Don't go *with* her!"

She groans, frustrated.

Her eyes glow a brilliant yellow. Her horn, too, glows the same. She looks up to Maus, still on her Maus.

"Things are probably gonna get dicey! Get ready!"

Maus grunts.

I'm always ready.

Delphi drops her speed, falling to the back of the herd.

Damnation gallops onward, gaze locked on the unicorns. His voices cackle.

"You cannot escape your Damnation!"

Princess Pipsy scowls.

"Come up with a *better fucking line!*"

KRAAAK!

A bolt of red lightning explodes from her horn. It strikes Damnation's face. He staggers from the impact, nearly losing his footing. The skin at the point of the impact chars just a bit.

The herd continues to run. They wind through the bottoms of the hills, making their way through the landscape.

Aster fires beams of blue light from her horn.

Pew! Pew!

Damnation groans, growing frustrated.

Aster fires again.

Pew! Pew! Pew!

The beams pierce Damnation's body. Purple sparks fly out. He winces at each hit, though he does not slow. If anything, his frustration only spurs him forward.

Princess Pipsy lets another bolt fly loose.

KRAAAK!

It strikes Damnation's orcish arm.

He roars.

"I will wipe you from existence!"

Far behind them now — back at Petunia's, before the hills even begin — a white light rockets out from the tree line. It speeds toward the group at astonishing pace. Its entire form glows with its beauty, almost a challenge to look at.

Petunia.

In their very minds, the unicorns hear her voice.

"Keep him distracted! I need to catch up to you!"

The other unicorns exchange glances, surprised.

Delphi speaks to the others.

"Did you hear that?!"

Maus complains.

"I didn't hear shit…"

Aster responds.

"I think the rest of us did!"

Delphi speaks again.

"What are we supposed to do?!"

Petunia's voice echoes in their minds once again.

"Fuck him up."

Princess Pipsy grins.

Princess Pipsy turns her head back toward Damnation. Another red bolt explodes out from the tip of her horn.

KRAAAK!

It strikes Damnation's chest with a ***BOOM.*** He reels back.

Aster — as steadfast as ever — continues to fire her beams.

Pew! Pew! Pew!

Damnation feels every hit.

Delphi shouts to the others.

"I think we're getting to him! I don't think he looks so hot!"

Damnation presses on, losing no ground.

"Very poor choice of words."

He *huffs* and *puffs*. The purple spark in his mouth fades to orange.

A *very* bright orange.

Embers float out between his teeth, scattering to the wind.

"I am *always* hot."

Heavy flames spew from his mouth. They whip at the backs of the herd. Flames burn into the hides of the unicorns. Several half-breeds cry out from the pain, tumbling to the ground.

Damnation tramples them, stomping them into the soil under the sheer weight of his hulking form. Blood and bone bursts out from their bodies, reduced to nothing more than collections of flesh.

Delphi's yellow glow strengthens.

She turns her head back, pointing her horn toward Damnation. Yellow energy pulses outward, pushing back the flames.

Behind Damnation, Petunia picks up speed, gaining ground. The essence of her glowing horn trails behind her, like the echo of a ghost on the wind.

She's almost here.

But she's not here yet.

The fairy notices the action.

"Hey! No fair! I want in!"

She flies over the herd of half-breeds, the herd still galloping onward. The wind whips at her wings, threatening to blow her away. She focuses, pushing through it. Her wings flap even harder.

She latches onto Delphi's mane.

Delphi glances back.

"What are you doing?!"

The fairy responds.

"Helping out the assholes!"

The fairy presses her hands onto Delphi's neck.

Delphi's yellow glow strengthens even further, far beyond what she's seen herself. She feels the warmth of the energy flow through her, now more apparent. Unmistakable. Her eyes glimmer with recognition.

She shifts focus back to Damnation. The pulses of light from her horn extend further, diverting more of the flames, now protecting the whole of the herd.

Damnation's flames retract, dissipating.

"You will never—"

Aster fires blue beams from her horn.

Pew! Pew! Pew!

Damnation groans.

"You will—"

A thick bolt of lightning explodes from Princess Pipsy's horn.

KRAAAK!

Damnation's voices roar.

Pew! Pew!

KRAAAK!

He shouts, now enraged.

"I will slaughter you all!"

Damnation reaches out, clawing at the unicorns. They adjust their positions, dodging the strike.

He claws at them again, faster now. Several claws dig into Aster's back. His hand pulls away, tearing across her spine. Blood gushes out, carried by the wind.

Aster cries in pain. Her footing falters.

Delphi shifts her focus. The yellow wall of light fades from the back of the herd. A yellow glow appears at Aster's back. The blood remains, but the flesh folds back together.

Aster breathes a sigh of relief.

Damnation's eyes lock on to Delphi.

He takes another swing, reaching for her. His hand hooks onto Maus, throwing him into the stampeding herd.

The princess watches him sail through the air.

"Shit!"

Maus lands on the back of a half-breed. It stiffens, startled by the impact. But it keeps running. Maus grips its mane, pulling himself upright.

He glances behind him.

Dozens of half-breeds separate him and the unicorns.

"Shit."

The herd turns, following the curve of the hills. In the distance ahead of them — still a great deal away, but now visible — craggy rocks gather in masses. Shorter mountains dot the landscape adjacent. Cold, dark grasses stretch beyond.

The mountain pass.

Behind Damnation, Petunia gains more ground, finally nearing the other unicorns.

Damnation doesn't notice.

Aster fires more beams.

Pew! Pew!

Damnation swings at her, his claws about to strike.

A wall of yellow light appears behind Aster. His claws deflect off the light, as if it were a surface. As soon as it deflects the blow, it dissipates entirely.

Aster gives Delphi a firm, thankful nod.

The princess launches another bolt of lightning.

KRAAAK!

Damnation roars once again.

Maus — watching the action unfold from ahead — sits backward on a half-breed near the front of the herd…

…the exact opposite of where he needs to be.

He thinks to himself for a moment.

He looks at the herd running around him.

Then, he sighs.

"I can't believe I'm going to do this."

With careful balance, Maus stands upright on the back of the half-breed.

He takes a deep breath.

He leaps.

He crashes onto the back of the half-breed behind the previous. Like the first, it tenses up from the impact, yet continues to run.

Maus pulls himself upright.

With careful balance, he stands on its back.

He eyes the next half-breed behind.

He leaps.

He lands.

Petunia's form glows brighter. Flashes of white light appear below her hooves. She rises into the air, climbing higher and higher, ascending a staircase of wind.

Maus stands on the back of a half-breed.

He leaps.

He lands.

But the herd turns, following the hills.

Maus slips over the side of the half-breed, sliding under it. He exerts his full strength to hang on. His greatsword dips onto the grass, carving a line in the dirt.

Maus now hangs underneath the running half-breed.

"You gotta be *fuckin'* me!"

Petunia climbs higher, now far above Damnation.

The other unicorns look up, spotting her.

She matches the speed of the herd, following their path in the air.

Damnation takes another heavy swipe. His claws tear into the back of a half-breed. Blood flies into the wind. The wounded half-breed falls, crashing into a hill.

KRAAAK!

A red bolt explodes from the princess's horn. It strikes Damnation's outstretched arm.

He shifts focus.

He swings at the princess.

Delphi's horn *flashes* bright.

Damnation — blinded by the light — misses the swipe. His claws dig into the cold dirt.

Maus struggles to lift himself over the side of the half-breed. He manages to bring himself up just a bit… but he slips. His fingers lose traction. He slides right back under the half-breed, muscles now strained even further.

He looks out at the path ahead.

He spots the numerous clusters of sharp, jagged rocks.

"Gods-fucking-dammit!"

He tries to pull himself up with renewed urgency.

The herd follows the curve of the hills, now approaching the mountain pass.

Damnation's draconic jaw hangs slack. It swings with the wind as he runs. Within it, a familiar purple spark flickers to life. It quickly grows in intensity. A steady *hum* builds.

Delphi shouts to the others, a panic in her voice.

"I don't think I can hold that back!"

A voice echoes down from above, carried on the very wind itself.

"I can."

The purple spark *crackles.*

It *snaps.*

It *pops.*

It explodes.

A pulsing beam of purple energy bursts forth.

It collides with a blinding beam of white.

Petunia runs with the herd, racing through the air above them, now much closer. Her horn — pointed firmly toward Damnation — blasts a steady beam of beautiful white light. Its form holds steady, the power behind it evident.

Damnation's beam warps, its form crackling and erratic. Purple sparks fly off in all directions, scattering into the air.

Petunia's beam keeps Damnation's at bay, its light seemingly *inches* above the unicorns.

The herd continues forward, just about reaching the rocks.

Maus still hangs beneath a half-breed.

"Come on, come on…"

He swings up, trying to clear the side of it.

Not enough.

He slides back down, nearly losing his grip. He hangs below it once again.

The rocks draw ever closer.

But he still holds on.

"Come on!"

With all his might, he swings himself over the side of the half-breed. As he does, it passes over the rocks. Several cut into its underside.

Maus stands on its back.

He leaps.

He lands.

He leaps.

He lands.

Not much farther.

The princess glances ahead, taking her eyes off Damnation. She takes note of the herd's course. She notices the mountain pass, now fast approaching.

Not much farther.

Damnation's purple beam brightens, growing wider. It *pulses* and *thrums* with unstable energy, its *crackles* now violent and frequent.

It begins to push back Delphi's beam.

Her beam brightens as well.

Then a beam of translucent yellow joins hers.

Delphi.

A thin blue beam joins the other two.

Aster.

Crackling red lightning connects with all three.

Princess.

The four beams converge, melding together. The white light burns bright, now accented by flares of yellow; waves of blue; stark streaks of red.

Damnation's beam is forced back toward him.

Rapidly.

He roars through it all, his voices piercing the chaos.

His beam grows brighter still.

But it's not enough.

The white beam of color pushes it further, its strength now even greater. Its colors flare with majesty. It forces Damnation's beam back into his own mouth.

It *explodes* with a violent thunder.

All beams vanish entirely.

Damnation continues to chase.

But he stumbles, now losing some speed.

A thick clump of bone and flesh falls from his head, a portion of his lower face now missing, revealing the purple glow beneath. A deep crack carves across his eye socket. Despite the exterior damage, his purple shell remains wholly intact.

But he absolutely felt that.

The herd clears the last of the Sanctuary's grasses, now running exclusively over craggy rocks and shale.

Princess Pipsy calls out to the others.

"We're almost there! We need to lose him!"

From the half-breed ahead, Maus leaps onto Aster's back.

She yelps in surprise.

"Warn me next time!"

Maus grunts.

Whatever you say.

They continue with the herd.

Damnation swipes at the unicorns with furious speed.

Delphi's yellow glow blocks the impacts.

He swipes again. And again. And again.

Delphi's magic blocks each. Her brightness, however, starts to dim.

"I don't know if I can do this much longer!"

Damnation's voices roar with an incomprehensible rage.

He swipes again.

Delphi's magic blocks it.

But it dims further.

The herd passes a drop-off. They make an abrupt adjustment to compensate. The rest of the herd follows, course still set for the pass.

One half-breed stumbles, her hooves catching on the rocks. She falls over the side of the drop-off. She cries out, rolling into the heavy rocks of the cliff face as she falls. Bones *crack* at every impact, splotches of blood left behind.

Petunia watches her child fall.

Time seems to slow for a moment.

She sheds a single tear. It evaporates instantly from her glow.

She looks to the front of the herd, now nearing the pass, dark grasses stretching beyond. They stumble as they gallop, but they gallop nonetheless.

She looks back to the unicorns, still running. The historian, with her wavering yellow glow; the royal guard, with her tired rider, both losing hope; the princess, steadfast in her anger, yet unable to best such a threat.

Then she looks to Damnation. The twisted monster of wanton destruction, his face now broken and cracked. Her own eye catches a glimpse of Damnation's eyes. His *true* eyes. The eyes of the broken boy inside. The eyes of insanity bent to hatred. The eyes that — even indirectly, by her consequence or not — she helped create.

She speaks to the unicorns, her voice entering their minds.

"If Damnation follows you from here, you will never find your artifact. He must fall back now, or you *will* fail in your journey, and all living things will be killed."

She looks down at the herd.

"My *children* will be killed."

The unicorns glance up at her above them.

Her voice continues.

"I will not ask you to safeguard my children. They are not your responsibility. But I *will* ask you to guide them. Somewhere safe. *Anywhere* safe. Guide as many as you can."

Delphi calls out.

"No! Wait! We need your help!"

Petunia ignores her plea. She speaks into their minds once again.

"Remember me not as a coward, but the saviour that he'll never be."

She faces Damnation.

She stops.

The light vanishes from under her hooves.

She falls.

The herd doesn't stop.

Neither do the unicorns, looking back.

And neither does Damnation.

He sees the glowing unicorn fall in front of him, horns pointed at his chest.

But he has no time to slow.

It's too late.

Damnation's body collides with Petunia's at full speed. Both of her horns dig deep into his torso, their vibrant white glow still apparent.

Damnation shrieks with pain, his voices disjointed and separate.

He stumbles to a stop.

The herd does not.

Damnation looks down at the glowing unicorn protruding from his chest. He grabs her head in his hands, squeezing it between his fingers. The hide of her head *snaps* in several places. Blood seeps out. His clawed thumb digs deep into Petunia's only eye. Its nail scrapes against her skull.

Petunia, too, shrieks.

Her white light strengthens impossibly. Its brightness pulses into Damnation, surging through his inner body. Twisting, vibrant white veins shine across his form. His own magic — the purple glow that holds him together — dims.

Maus and the unicorns are forced to look away.

Damnation tumbles down the cliffside, all arms wrapped around the unicorn in his chest. Chunks of boulders *crack* off as he falls, bringing a landslide of rocks down with him.

The unicorns push to the front of the herd, leading them through the mountain pass, onto the stretch of dark grasses beyond.

Chapter XVI:
Meeting the
Murder

Chapter XVI: Meeting the Murder

Gentle wind blows through the forest.

It's the first thing to reach his ears.

He opens his eyes.

The light of the early morning creeps through the bedroom window. Diffused as it may be, it brightens the room nonetheless.

Time for the day to begin.

The figure sits up. He scratches his head, adjusting his dark feathers with his claws.

Well, *mostly* dark feathers, anyway. What was once a jet-black hue now resembles a much paler shade.

He *plucks* a loose feather from his head. He looks at it for a moment, taking it in. He closes his hand around it, all four fingers holding it tight. He gets up.

Ragged robes hang loose from his body, dyed a mix of earthy green and brown tones. He approaches the window, still clutching the feather in his hand. The claws of his feet scrape lightly across the floor as he walks. His movements are deliberate, but with no sense of urgency.

Krrrt... krrrt... krrrt...

He reaches out with his free hand, pushing against the shutters.

Creak...

They open outward.

The breeze blows in, noticeable, but not uncomfortable.

The forest haze soaks into the town below, as it always does. Ornate wooden buildings — none more than two stories — connect to each other through thin, mossy paths of cobblestone. Fresh dew collects on their layers of prickly shingles. Already, some townsfolk walk the paths, all donned in their usual cloaks. The sun — its rays diffused — gives the town a peaceful, dreamlike presence.

The figure releases the feather.

It floats out through the open window, carried across the wind.

In moments, it disappears from view, sailing into the towering trees.

The figure exhales, contented.

From the floor below, a sound rings out.

KNOCK, KNOCK, KNOCK, KNOCK!

He turns his head toward the sound.

Such an early hour.

He closes the shutters.

He walks back to his bedside. He grabs a set of long necklaces from the wall, placing them around his neck. Their wooden beads *clack* together. Beautiful feathers — not of his own — make up several segments of the necklaces.

From the same wall, he grabs two leather cuffs, a large feather hanging from each. He sets one around each wrist.

KNOCK, KNOCK, KNOCK, KNOCK!

The figure sighs.

He approaches the bedroom door, still closed. A walking stick rests against the corner of the room, its height a foot shorter than he is, perhaps less. He grabs it.

A sense of welcome familiarity washes over him.

He opens the bedroom door and steps into the hallway.

He shuts it behind him.

Wasting no time — but still in no rush — he descends the staircase. His feet scrape across the top of every step.

Krrrt... krrrt... krrrt...

His walking stick *thumps* in rhythm.

Someone knocks at the front door once more.

KNOCK, KNOCK, KNOCK!

A muffled masculine voice — a scratchy, gravelly tone — speaks through the still-closed door.

"Chief! Urgent! Please!"

The chief opens the front door.

Another Varsii — ravenfolk — stands on the other side. Taller than the chief, the black feathers of his body look striking by comparison. He wears a ruffled brown cloak, hood up. Brown cloth hangs down over his legs, more akin to a kilt than true pants. A thick strip of leather holds it tight around his waist.

He cocks his head to the side a bit, one eye staring right at the chief, giving him his utmost attention.

"Sorry. It's early. But urgent."

The chief squints. It takes a second for his vision to adjust. When it does, he recognizes the face immediately. A smirk pecks at the corners of his face.

"Nok. Fitting."

The chief takes a step closer.

"Tell me."

Nok *clicks* a few times, then continues.

"Visitors. Travelers. Many."

The chief responds.

"Interesting. Rare. But not urgent."

Nok shakes his head quickly.

"Horses. A human. And *unicorns.*"

The chief's peaceful expression drops instantly, replaced by a solemn seriousness, as if recalling a hundred bad memories.

He turns his head, his own eye meeting Nok's.

"Take me."

———————————————————————————————

Princess Pipsy walks at the front of the herd. The other two unicorns walk beside her. The light mist of the forest hangs around them. Massive oak trees span all directions, branches jutting out from all sides. The half-breeds follow behind them, each with a vacant expression.

The princess groans.

"This is taking too long. We're losing time."

Aster — with Maus still atop her — speaks.

"If we go any faster, the half-breeds will get lost. They won't keep up in this terrain."

She takes a breath.

"Damnation surely isn't dead. I highly doubt that killed him. But he must be injured badly. That fall would kill most living things. I think we have some time. It's the least we could do for a unicorn."

The princess frowns.

"These are not unicorns."

Aster replies.

"They aren't, but *she* was. And *she* asked us to guide them to safety."

Princess Pipsy looks to Maus.

"Prisoner! How long until we get to the Loftwood?"

Maus shrugs.

"How should I know? I've never been up here before."

The princess mumbles to herself.

"Useless."

Maus grunts.

Whatever.

Delphi speaks.

"Loftwood is the name of the region. I assume it still is, even after all this time. The majority of Varsii live around here, but they never built any cities. Not in the history I studied. Their settlements are… smaller. More nomadic. Like villages more than cities. Since there are so many — and they move location frequently — they aren't on many maps."

She gestures to the forest surrounding them.

"And it's tough to know exactly where you are in this place. Which is pretty integral when it comes to cartography."

The princess responds.

"So we wander in a straight line until we run into something?"

Delphi nods.

"More or less."

Princess Pipsy sighs.

"Great."

Aster speaks, glancing over at Delphi.

"Petunia mentioned them specifically. Surely there must have been more to that."

Delphi shakes her head.

"I doubt it. Varsii scavenge and collect by their nature. Based on the proximity to the valley — and the time that has passed since the Siege — it's just the most likely scenario."

She pauses.

"Well, *technically,* the most likely scenario is that the sword fell into a lake and got buried by mud. Or it fell into some random cave, never to be found again. But I'd rather not think about that."

The fairy rolls out from under Delphi's mane.

"I'm *tired!*"

Everyone rolls their eyes.

Delphi speaks, already annoyed.

"You've been sleeping this entire time. How can you *possibly* be tired?"

The fairy rolls around in her mane.

"I don't know! I'm just *tired!*"

Delphi replies.

"Try bothering somebody else. Or just stop bothering *me.*"

The fairy giggles mischievously.

"But you're just… so… *tickly!*"

The fairy dives into Delphi's mane. Her little fingers dance along the back of her neck.

Delphi twists her head wildly.

"Stop it! Get *off* me!"

The fairy ignores her.

"Tickle, tickle, tickle!"

Delphi shakes harder, irritation building.

"Stop!"

Aster's eyes and horn glow blue. The fairy floats out from Delphi's mane.

The fairy wriggles in the air.

"Hey! Put me down! No fair!"

Aster brings the fairy in front of her.

"Listen when we speak to you. We have kept you around for utility, not for conversation. And *certainly* not for tickles. If your annoyance outweighs your usefulness, we will not hesitate to get rid of you. *Permanently.*"

Aster's glow vanishes.

The fairy falls to the ground. *Thump!*

The unicorns walk on, stepping over her.

The fairy pouts.

"Assholes."

A half-breed nearly steps on her. She yelps, rolling out of the way. She stands up, shaking a fist at the half-breed.

"Watch where you're goin', buddy!"

Another one nearly steps on her.

She flies up off the ground. She rises higher into the air. Now grumpy, having been chastised, she flies *behind* the unicorns, as opposed to directly above them.

She smirks.

That'll show 'em.

The unicorns pay her no mind.

They continue to walk on ahead.

Then the princess's ears perk up.

She hears something.

Her head tilts up slightly, taking note of the distant sound.

Delphi's ears perk up, as do Aster's. They hear it.

Rustling.

Or… running?

Whatever it is, it's approaching the group.

Fast.

All three of the unicorns stop.

The half-breeds bump into them. Then they, too, stop walking. They stand idle behind the unicorns, almost entirely indifferent.

Princess Pipsy says nothing to the others.

She doesn't have to.

Red energy *crackles* to life, overtaking her eyes and her horn.

Aster's blue glow brightens after.

Delphi's, of yellow, comes next.

Maus reaches to the sword on his back. One hand grabs the hilt.

The fairy cocks her head, not catching on.

"What are you looking at?"

Princess Pipsy speaks, projecting as much as naturally possible.

"We can hear you! There is no point in hiding. Reveal yourself. Then we might be able to have a conversation."

The rustling stops.

Dozens of Varsii emerge from behind the trees; from behind rocks; from behind foliage; from everywhere around them.

Each one wears a loose necklace, a design of unknown significance. They each wield a spear, every tip pointed right at the unicorns. Their expressions are firm. It's impossible to read anything more than that.

The unicorns look around, taking in their presence.

Aster speaks.

"Should we kill them?"

Delphi responds.

"No. There's too many. There's no guarantee we'd all live."

The princess, frustrated, speaks.

"*Clearly* they don't want to talk. What the fuck are we *supposed* to do?"

An older voice speaks from ahead.

"Explain. Why you are here."

The chief steps forward. His robes hang *just* above the ground. He carries a simple walking stick of smooth wood in his left hand. Around his neck, large necklaces hang, a design more detailed than the others. The wooden beads *clack* as he walks.

He stops in front of the unicorns.

They can see the very wrinkles in his skin. The very feathers of his face.

He shows no fear.

"We talk. But no magic. Not yours."

The unicorns do nothing.

A tense moment passes in silence.

Princess Pipsy exhales.

Her crackling glow dissipates. Her eyes return to normal.

Aster and Delphi — still uncertain — follow her lead. Their own glows vanish to nothing.

The spears encircling them remain upright, the Varsii behind them unwavering.

The chief smiles.

"Good. Now we talk."

The unicorns walk through the village.

Maus walks alongside them, keeping pace. The fairy flies not far above, staying nearby. At their front, the chief leads them through thin, winding paths laid with cobblestone. At their back, the Varsii guards hold their spears steady, ensuring they make no rash decisions.

All around them, the townsfolk watch on.

Cloaked Varsii peer out between shutters. Others, between cracks of front doors, barely open. Some peek out from corners of buildings. Many stand at the side of the path, staring and taking it in.

Unicorns.

Even walking through the village, it *is* bigger than they thought it would be. But what Delphi said was right: this certainly isn't a city. How they live nomadically at this scale remains a mystery.

The buildings look expertly carved. Fanciful designs are etched into the walls of each one, the walls themselves made of pale brown wood of an odd, muted shade. Several stone stairs lead up to many of the buildings, giving an even more naturalistic feel to the village, despite the archaic nature of their construction. A number of large, mossy stones lean against the bases of buildings, unclear whether decor or utility. Layers and layers of thinly pressed shingles top off each building, reminiscent of the feathers of the Varsii. A light mist hangs over everything, much like the earlier parts of the forest. While far less limiting than the fog of the Shale Plains, it still obscures much in the distance. It makes the village feel more like a dream. Or like an uncomfortable memory.

The chief's claws drag across the moss and stones. *Krrrt... krrrt... krrrt...*

His walking stick *thumps* in rhythm.

Princess Pipsy takes a careful note of everyone watching them. Then, she speaks.

"You haven't told us where we're going."

The chief turns his head slightly. One eye faces the princess. He continues walking forward.

"Somewhere to talk."

Aster glances back at the guards behind them.

"How do we know we can trust you?"

The chief responds.

"You don't. But still. You must."

Aster — looking back — speaks again.

"We don't know who you are. We don't even know if…"

She trails off, struggling to find the proper words. Back from whence they came, she spots the half-breeds walking slowly through the tree line. A number of cloaked Varsii lead them.

"…if those *horses* will still be alive. We have no way of knowing what your word is worth."

The chief grins softly, as if to reassure.

"I am the chief. The eldest. The horses live. They *will* live. The east is safe. The edge is safe. Those guiding are safe. And my word is law."

He turns his head back around, facing forward.

The Varsii around him — those who heard his response — *click* their tongues several times.

Aster leans over toward Delphi. She whispers.

"Do you have any idea what that is? What it means?"

Delphi sighs. She whispers back.

"No, I don't. I studied what history we recorded, yes, but…"

She pauses.

"Our recorded history is largely focused inward. Our writings and books concerning other peoples are… *limited.*"

Aster frowns a bit.

"I see."

She leans away.

The princess hears this. She says nothing.

Maus speaks, eyes fixed on the chief.

"Look, I hate to ask, but how much longer we walking? You won't tell us *where,* only fair you tell us *when.*"

The chief turns his head. One eye looks at Maus.

"I did. We are going to talk. Not far."

He turns back around, facing forward.

Maus exhales, disappointed.

"Gee, thanks."

In a quieter tone, the chief mimics Maus's voice with astonishing clarity.

"Gee, thanks."

Maus blinks, surprised. He whispers to himself.

"…the hell?"

The chief *clicks,* a subtle caw accompanying it.

Is he… laughing?

The chief stops in front of a wide, one-story building. Thin windows line the exterior, not built for the sake of seeing through. It stands noticeably shorter, with most of the village made up of two-story structures, though it carries much of the same aesthetic. At the center of its roof, a chimney rises up. Thin wisps of smoke flow through it, barely discernible from the fog settled all around it.

The chief turns to the others.

"We talk inside. It stays with us. No weapons needed. No guards inside."

He looks to the Varsii behind the unicorns, all still clutching their spears.

One of the guards steps forward. Her voice sounds shrill. Somewhat young.

"Are you sure?"

She cocks her head.

The chief responds.

"I am sure."

The guard continues.

"With respect—"

The chief *thuds* his walking stick on the ground. The speaking guard falls silent. All other guards stand at attention.

The chief smiles warmly.

"No guards inside. I am sure."

The outspoken guard falls back in line. She stares down at the ground, now embarrassed.

The chief continues, gaze still on the guards.

"Stand outside. At the ready. Just in case."

He takes a breath.

"And *relax.*"

The guards, indeed, relax.

Or try to, anyway.

With that command, they nod, dispersing. They each take positions around the squat building, backs to the walls, spears upright.

The chief looks to the unicorns.

"Follow me."

He opens the door and enters the building.

———————————————————————————————————————

Nok was told to wait in the Murmury, so he did. Nok was told to light a small communal fire, so he did.

When Nok asked why, the chief told him that, as the first of their people to witness the unicorns, he might have more insight to share. So Nok waited. And Nok lit the fire. But then — not long after that — Nok did something he *wasn't* told to do.

Nok took a nap.

He leans against the wall of the open space, the edges of his cloak pulled tight around himself, both eyes firmly closed.

The chief enters.

Nok does not awaken.

The unicorns follow.

Then Maus steps inside.

The fairy flies in after.

Still, Nok does not awaken.

The chief gives a nod to the guards outside, then closes the door behind them.

Packed dirt makes up the whole of the floor. Refined as it may be, the princess looks unpleasantly surprised. At the center of the space, heavy stones form a ring. A small fire burns within them. Its smoke rises into the chute-shaped chimney above, floating into the forest air beyond. Several small rooms sit at the back wall, likely storage of some kind. Various supplies sit in loose, unorganized piles atop a long table at the right wall, perhaps for some sort of handcrafting practice. Numerous wooden chairs sit beside it.

Princess Pipsy is the first to speak.

"This is… *quaint.*"

Aster, too, takes in the space.

"That's certainly *one* way to put it."

Maus flicks his head toward the Varsii leaning against the wall.

"Who the fuck is *that?*"

The unicorns turn, noticing Nok.

Delphi speaks.

"That's an *excellent* question."

The fairy cocks her head. She flies a bit closer.

"Looks like a real fuckin' slack-ass!"

Aster glares at the fairy.

"Language."

The fairy groans. She points an accusatory finger at the princess.

"She says that stuff all the time!"

Aster responds.

"She is the Princess of the Unicorns. *You* are merely useful. Do not overestimate your contributions."

The fairy pouts.

The chief steps up to Nok.

He *thumps* his walking stick hard on the dirt.

Nok startles awake at the familiar sound. He *caws* instinctually. He nearly falls to the ground, but manages to regain his footing.

"Chief! Sorry. Resting! I..."

He trails off. He looks at the three unicorns standing in front of him. He falls silent. His chest tightens.

He looks at the gruff human, who crosses his arms. He grunts.

He looks at the fairy hovering behind him. She sticks her tongue out in response.

He looks back to the unicorns.

Then to the chief.

Then to the unicorns.

The chief smiles.

"Let us talk."

Chapter XVII:
Last Thoughts
Down the
Mountain

Chapter XVII: Last Thoughts Down the Mountain

Damnation runs.

Then a unicorn pierces his chest.

Then he falls.

He tumbles. He rolls. And he crashes. His body strikes rocks; they break free. His body strikes boulders; they crack. His body shudders from the brilliant light coursing through it; he *hurts*.

Purple and white sparks fly out with every impact.

His hands, stained with numerous bloods, wrap tight around Petunia's head. The claw of his thumb presses into her socket. The fluid and pus that was once her eye squishes onto his finger. Were they not actively cascading down the cliffside, he would have turned her head to putty by now.

She screams.

But Damnation can't hear it.

He's too busy screaming himself.

His voices cry out, all separate and disjointed.

He tumbles. He rolls. And he crashes.

He impacts the body of a half-breed wedged against rock. It bursts into paste, its blood coating both him and Petunia.

Damnation falls further. He lands on Petunia. He hears — *feels* — a *crack*. Her horns push deeper into him, glowing brighter. Their pulses of bright light continue.

The purple glow of his body flickers.

Damnation impacts another heavy rock.

His orcish arm falls away.

Petunia shrieks with anger. With rage. With pain.

Damnation's voices — disjointed — do the same.

He tumbles. He rolls. And he crashes.

His lower back *cracks* onto the point of a jagged rock. His waist splits from his body. It tumbles off in another direction.

The fall feels like it goes on forever.

But it doesn't.

And — eventually — they reach the bottom.

Damnation falls onto wet earth.

Grass? Mud? It's difficult to tell.

Only now does he realize his vision is blurred.

Petunia breaks away. He feels the horns tear out of him. Purple sparks spew from the holes in his body like blood.

Petunia wails. Now blind, with her head covered in blood — skin and bone broken all over — she falls. Her face plants firmly into the soft, marshy ground. Dirt presses into her coat. Mud seeps into her nostrils. Her magnificent white glow finally dissipates.

Damnation calls out, his voices distorted in discord.

"What did you do to me?"

He does not see her lying beside him.

He calls out again.

"What the *fuck* did you *do* to me?!"

Screeching penetrates his mind. The high-pitched ringing pierces his senses. He falls forward. The uncomfortable magic of the unicorn still burns inside him. Whatever she did, it hasn't gone yet.

For the first time in centuries, he feels his heartbeat — his *real* heartbeat — beating inside his chest. His *real* chest.

The screeching subsides.

He pushes himself off the ground, getting back up onto his hands. His vision — still blurred — begins to focus slightly.

But not by much.

He pulls his hulking form across the spongy ground beneath him.

On his torso, his rotting feminine arm *snaps* under the weight of his body, his magic no longer preventing decay. It falls away. He crawls over it. His body presses it into the ground.

And he crawls.

His voices groan in pain, still disjointed and unorganized. The white magic coursing through him grows weaker. He can *feel* it grows weaker. Yet it still remains, carving through his essence. His purple shell flickers but a moment, almost struggling to maintain its form.

He focuses inward.

The magic holds.

And he crawls.

He is so close to wiping out the unicorns. *So* fucking close. He is *not* going to be beaten now. Especially not by that bitch of a hag.

And he crawls.

His fingers push into the mud. His hands drag his body forward. He thinks about his suffering. He thinks about the unicorns. He thinks about his mission. He thinks about his father. He thinks about his legacy. He thinks about killing *something*. He thinks about grafting it to his body. He thinks about killing the unicorns. He thinks about growing much stronger. He thinks about killing existence itself. He thinks about joy in the slaughter. He thinks about purpose and reason. He thinks about killing the princess. He thinks about killing the unicorns. He thinks about fresh cotton candy. He thinks about killing the unicorns.

And he crawls.

— — — — — — — — — — — — — — — — —

Time passes slowly. Damnation feels every second. How long he has truly been crawling is a mystery. A total unknown. An impossible thing to guess.

How long has it been?

Hours?

Days?

Weeks?

He doesn't know.

But he doesn't care.

It doesn't matter.

So he crawls.

And he crawls.

And he crawls.

— — — — — — — — — — — — — — — — —

Mud and grime coats the front of Damnation's torso. His arms that remain pull him forward. His purple glow flickers. Its intensity greatly wavers.

But it does not fade.

He will not let it.

Not yet.

So he keeps his head high.

He keeps his thoughts sharp. His mind focused.

And he keeps.

Crawling.

Forward.

The forest marsh still surrounds him. The stench of stagnant water still sinks into the ground. He still feels the mud on his bones.

But ahead of him, he sees something new.

Something not like the forest around him.

Something that does not belong.

Behind a cluster of overgrown trees and long-forgotten foliage, a mossy stone pillar sticks out from the ground.

No.

Not a pillar.

A *structure*.

Damnation changes course.

He pulls himself through thick fauna. Vines, leaves, and branches collide with his face. Unbothered, he forces through them, uprooting numerous plants in the process.

The stone structure comes into view.

Crumbled partially, its centerpiece — made up of a stone tower — reaches into the sky. Considerable distance remains between its highest point and the forest canopy. Symbols of various deities of worship encircle its very point, carved into the stone itself. The tower seems no more than twenty feet tall, if not less; its base looks no longer than ten feet in circumference.

Around it, large stone bricks sit in piles, all in various states of ruin. Many of them have already sunk into the ground. The tower, too, looks like it stood taller at one point, though that point was a number of years ago.

Many years ago.

He pulls himself closer.

Beneath his body, he feels rock scrape against him, likely all pieces that belonged to the tower.

The tower, however, has an entrance.

Several large chunks of rubble crowd the entryway, its arch cracked and falling away.

But it still stands.

Damnation stares at it.

Interesting...

He pulls himself closer.

In front of him, a wide, rectangular stone juts out from the ground. Moss and dirt coats the front of it, its layers collected over considerable time.

With his draconic arm, Damnation reaches out. He drags his palm across the stone, wiping the muck away.

It *splats* onto the ground.

With some dirt now removed, he sees etchings.

Writing.

He wipes his hand across it once more, removing another layer of grime. He shakes it off onto the ground.

Splat.

While the stone still shows age, its inscription now shows.

Damnation pulls himself even closer.

He reads the plaque before him.

> *To every soul this message see,*
> *What you are now, so once were we*
> *What we are now, you shall become*
> *To fate we all succumb*

Below it, another thick layer of muck obscures more lettering. He drags his palm across it, too, wiping nearly all of it away.

Now legible, he reads it.

> *The Resting Place of Our Greatest Heroes*
> *Crypt of the City of Zeth*

He stares at it.

He reads the words over and over again.

He traces his nails over the lettering. The tips of his nails glide along each curve, hardly making a sound.

Then he speaks.

"I do not remember this place."

He wishes he did. Not knowing frustrates him deeply.

He crawls away from the plaque, approaching the archway.

He peers through the rubble of the fallen tower. Between the piles of crumbled stone, darkness lies beyond.

The smell of ancient rot seeps out from further within. From deeper below. It coats his mouths, a thick, sickening sweetness. Far different than the taste of fresh unicorns.

The archway remains blocked. The stone and rubble clogs its entrance. Only through gaps of darkness can he sense for what lies below. For how many dead now lie dormant. For how many forgotten sit, silent. For how many folk heroes rot.

So he pulls a heavy stone away.

Then another.

And another.

And another.

Now having been cleared, he stares into the darkness beyond the partially collapsed archway. It looks *just* wide enough to fit him. Or what's still left of him, anyway.

His purple glow strengthens.

Not by a lot, mind you.

But by enough.

Enough to notice.

His voices — more unified — speak.

"I will build myself anew."

Damnation crawls over and through the broken stones. He moves like a spider that's missing most of its legs. Asymmetrical. Clumsy. Revolting in his movements.

He descends into the ruins of the swamp-sunken crypt.

— — — — — — — — — — — — — — —

The corpses in the crypt are decorated like kings.
The stones breathe for the first time.
He can feel them breathing.
The bones of the fallen beg for purpose.
He will give them a home.
Damnation will be built anew.

Chapter XVIII:
The Trouble
with Traitors

Chapter XVIII: The Trouble with Traitors

The chief sits at the base of the fire pit. His walking stick rests across his lap. The fire remains small — controlled — as it was before.

Beside him, Nok paces back and forth, too nervous to take a seat.

On the other side of the fire pit, Princess Pipsy stands, Aster and Delphi on either side of her.

Maus leans against the wall, not unlike Nok did prior, though he carries a much stronger sense of confidence in his posture.

The fairy floats beside him, whispering and giggling to herself. This usually follows with Maus swatting at her once or twice.

The chief looks out to the unicorns.

"Interesting."

He stares into the faint flames of the fire for a moment, deep in thought.

He looks back up.

"All true?"

The princess scoffs.

"Of *course* it's all true."

Aster speaks.

"Why would we bother to lie? We have nothing to prove."

The chief *clicks* his tongue once.

"Then time is short."

Nok stops pacing. He looks at the chief.

"You *believe* them? They could lie. Embellish. Mislead."

The chief shakes his head.

"They speak truths. *Ancient* truths. Passed down in stories. Spoken by our people. Attend Tellings more often. Then you'd know."

Nok recedes, somewhat embarrassed.

The chief turns back to the unicorns.

"You say the valley. How certain?"

Delphi responds.

"We're *not* certain. Not really. But we don't have other options. It's our best guess."

The chief exhales.

"Guesses mean less."

Delphi retorts.

"And inaction means death. Look, we saw what magic can do to that monster. It can hurt him. *Really* hurt him. More than we ever could, even now. But the only unicorn who could access that magic…"

She trails off for a moment.

"She is gone. For the sake of moving forward, we have to assume she is dead. The horses we brought with us… They might be related to her, but they inherited none of her magic. The only other time that kind of magic had *ever* been seen was during a battle that none of us were present for. That sword was used against us. And from what we can gather, it used that same magic. We don't really know *what* kind of magic, but I don't think it matters. It may be the only way to kill Damnation."

The chief opens his beak to speak.

Nok interrupts.

"I don't believe you."

Everyone in the room turns to him at once. He feels all eyes upon him, a nearly suffocating presence.

He exhales, then continues.

"I *do* attend Tellings. Not often. But I do. And they talk of unicorns. Not often. But they do. Stories of violence. Of murder. Of bloodshed. And chaos."

Slightly more confident, he takes a step toward the unicorns.

"*You* are violent. Murderous. Bloodthirsty. Chaotic. Why act any different? Why garner our trust?"

The chief shifts his focus to the unicorns, silently backing Nok's questions.

Maus watches the unicorns *very* carefully.

The fairy sits perched on his shoulder. She leans forward.

Aster, Delphi, and the princess exchange glances.

After a moment, Princess Pipsy steps forward.

"We have no memory of the last several centuries, or however long it's really been. We used to be a mighty people. Strong. Dominating. Nearly *invincible.* But when we awoke, we were stripped of that might. We were robbed of our magic. Only now have we started to get any of it back. We remembered a world that trembled at our breath, yet we stepped into a world that didn't even *know* us. And we found ourselves hunted by a monster we never met. He killed many of us. Those left alive were forced to flee. We don't know where they are now. And he still hunts us. The world might have moved on, but Damnation hasn't. He never will. And as soon as he wipes out the unicorns — *us* — he'll do the same to everyone else."

Aster and Delphi stare, wide-eyed and impressed.

Even Maus seems surprised.

The princess takes another step toward the chief.

"I used to think that superiority meant disregard. That by killing and pushing away all those lesser than us, we would keep our place above them all. But that was before we experienced the true threat of death.

Before we experienced… *weakness*. Now we know what it's like to be weaker. To be *lesser.*"

She exhales.

"Being better than all other forms of life shouldn't mean *slaughtering* them. It should mean *protecting* them."

She steps back, falling in line next to Aster and Delphi.

Aster whispers to the princess.

"That was shockingly eloquent."

Princess Pipsy mumbles a hushed response.

"It *better* be fucking eloquent. Took me thirty fucking minutes to come up with that shit."

Aster and Delphi drop their surprise.

There she is.

At the opposite side of the campfire, the chief stands.

"Then I have decided."

All eyes look over to him.

"We will help."

Nok steps forward in protest.

"Chief. They are *unicorns*. We—"

The chief *thumps* his walking stick on the ground.

Nok quiets. He takes a couple steps back, shrinking away.

The chief *clicks* his tongue. He continues.

"We don't have your sword. But we can look. Quite good at looking. We will help."

He walks around the fire pit, heading for the front door.

Nok, sensing the closure, grabs a small bucket of water nearby. He quickly dumps it onto the whimpering embers. They extinguish with a *hiss*. The steam rises up through the chimney.

The chief arrives at the door.

"We have a party. Scavengers. They leave often. Weekly. They look for supplies. Objects of interest. You will go with them."

Delphi, despite standing next to her, avoids looking right at the princess. Not to an excessive degree, but enough for the princess to notice.

The chief opens the door. It *creaks*.

The Varsii guards beside the door bolt upright. Those stationed around the building rush over. They all peer inside, unsure what to expect.

One at the front calls out, almost on instinct. "Chief!"

The chief steps through the doorway. He *thumps* his walking stick on the ground.

The guards take several large steps back, giving him ample space. They stand at attention, their spears pointed to the sky.

The chief speaks.

"We will help them. Travel with scavengers. They won't stay. Leaving soon."

The guards breathe a collective sigh of relief, some more obvious than others.

The chief continues.

"Respect them. No trouble. My orders."

The guards nod out of sync.

The chief walks forward, traveling along the village path once again.

Krrrt… thump… krrrt… thump… krrrt… thump…

The unicorns follow. Their hooves *clack* against the mossy stone. A number of guards avoid eye contact.

The princess stares intensely at one guard in particular.

She *huffs*.

The guard jumps.

The princess grins. She walks off, keeping pace with the other unicorns.

Maus and the fairy follow after.

Nok trails behind, leaving last.

The Varsii guards walk with the group, never letting the chief out of sight.

———————————————————————

Numerous Varsii figures — no more than a half-dozen — pack supplies into satchels and backpacks. Woven baskets and open crates sit around them. Off to the side, a tarp stretches out between two branches, tied to each. It offers some shade and shelter to the table of tools just below it. The silhouettes of the village's buildings blend into the fog, barely visible. Tall trees pack tight all around them, though this larger patch of space provides contrast.

The Varsii in the clearing mumble amongst themselves, their conversations too distant to discern.

The chief approaches from the fog.

Hunched over a crate, one Varsii notices. A long scar runs down the side of his face, exposing the pale hue of his flesh. His feathers look rougher; less uniform; more unkempt. While still cloaked like the others, his cloak looks more ragged, and in dire need of repair.

He speaks, his voice raspy and taunting, his cadence elongating every word.

"Oh, look. Here comes the chief."

The other Varsii straighten up, noticing the chief.

From beside the first, a female Varsii comments, donned in a brown, earthy cloak. A short sickle hangs from her belt.

"That is our chief. Show some respect."

The scarred Varsii turns to the second.

"I prefer not to."

Behind the chief, a number of other shapes emerge. As they step beyond the threshold of the fog, the Varsii can make out more details.

Unicorns.

Other figures, too, follow behind, though they don't demand the same level of attention.

The scarred Varsii leans forward.

"How... *interesting.*"

A handful of guards walk with the chief. They fan out, standing idle, each ready if called upon.

Nok stands at the back, not really sure what to do with himself, nor his own hands.

The unicorns step a bit closer, all getting a look at the space.

The Varsii within the encampment stare in awe.

Princess Pipsy speaks.

"I hope they're more prepared than they look."

The human behind her — Maus — grunts.

"This looks fine."

The princess responds, quieter.

"It looks like shit."

The chief greets the encampment.

"Good evening. I bring guests. Fellow scavengers. Looking for something. Rare. Dangerous. To help slay a monster. To help protect all. They will tell you."

The scarred Varsii speaks.

"We leave soon. *Very* soon."

The chief responds.

"They will join you. Travel down south. Hundrian Valley. Do not delay."

The scarred Varsii *clicks* his tongue.

"We *will* delay. You double our size. Do not expect speed."

The chief *thumps* his walking stick.

The scarred Varsii continues.

"You force this upon us. Do not expect speed. There *will* be delay."

The chief *thumps* his stick once more.

"Enough."

The scarred Varsii continues.

"Your word is not law. I speak when I please. Your age has made you a fool."

The chief gives a single, firm nod to the closest guard.

In an instant, the guard rushes over. He throws a single, heavy punch. It connects with the scarred Varsii's face. He falls.

The guard walks back to his place beside the chief.

The chief speaks, addressing the fallen Varsii.

"Remember your place."

Maus exhales.

Sounds familiar.

The chief turns to his 'guests' behind him.

"That is Kra, Traitor of Keep. He is not respected. Greedy by nature. Stabber of backs. Prefers to cause trouble. He has hatred. But skill. Owes us his life. Keep him close. Keep him watched."

The fairy cocks her head, curious.

The chief walks into the encampment.

Maus and the unicorns follow.

The fairy does not.

Standing before the array of various tools, one Varsii clips a thin hammer to her belt. It *clinks* softly against her sickle. She spots the chief approach. She stands at attention.

"Chief."

The chief nods.

Her posture relaxes.

The chief gestures to her.

"This is Flin. She leads the journeys."

Flin responds.

"We leave soon. We're nearly prepared. But…"

She trails off.

The chief notices.

"Speak."

She does.

"Toll cannot make it. Still injured. He wanted to. I said no. Not healthy. Not safe. Not for him."

The chief grins. He looks back to Nok, standing not far behind him.

"Nok will suffice."

Nok looks shocked. He *clicks* his tongue.

"Chief! I must—"

The chief *thumps* his walking stick. His smile drops.

Nok silences.

The chief stares at him.

"You wanted to join. Now you join. Consider it… training."

He smiles.

Nok exhales, already exhausted.

The chief walks on, pointing out other Varsii to the unicorns. Maus follows behind, arms crossed.

The fairy flies over to Kra, just now getting up from the ground. She hovers in front of his face.

"What the fuck is up with *you?*"

Kra's pained expression gives way to a mischievous grin.

"Why, hello there. Who might *you* be?"

He gets up to a crouch, staying level with the fairy.

The fairy puts her hands on her hips.

"I'm asking the questions here, buddy! You answer *me* first!"

Playful, Kra responds.

"Oh? *Or what?"*

The fairy crosses her arms.

"Or you're an asshole."

She frowns.

Kra holds back a chuckle.

"I am Kra, Traitor of Keep. I chose greed over family. Got my family killed. Too good to let go. So they keep me. They use me. Feed me little. Make me work."

He leans closer.

"Your turn."

The fairy blinks a few times, like she wasn't expecting him to answer.

"Well, I'm a fairy."

She gestures to herself dramatically.

Kra exhales, playfulness fading.

"I can *see* that. But who are you? What is your name?"

The fairy shrugs.

"I dunno. Don't have one, I guess. Plus, *they* never bother to ask."

She points very obviously to the unicorns — and Maus — still being led through the encampment.

Kra responds.

"Then what should I call you?"

The fairy thinks for a moment.

"I dunno. Whatever you want."

She feigns a yawn, fooling no one.

"You're starting to bore me, buddy!"

Kra grins again.

"My sincerest apologies. Let's give you a name?"

The fairy speaks, still looking bored.

"Yeah. Sure."

Kra leans in even closer.

"How about… *Dinner?*"

The fairy tilts her head, confused.

"What? That sounds like—"

Kra lurches forward. His beak *snaps* around the fairy. Still grinning, he swallows.

Then he exhales.

"Much better."

Flin approaches him from behind.

"We're ready. Let's go."

Kra stands, saying nothing. He walks off toward the unicorns.

Flin speaks, walking after.

"No misbehaving. No trouble."

Kra looks back to her. He feigns a smile.

"Wouldn't dream of it."

He turns back around. The smile drops instantly.

The chief spots his approach. He addresses Maus and the unicorns.

"It is time."

He continues.

"Stay safe. Stay wise. Stay alive."

He bows to them.

The guards around him do the same.

"Good luck."

Princess Pipsy nods.

The chief walks off.

"You will need it."

The guards walk along with him, all heading back to the village.

The unicorns furrow their brows, surprised by his final comment.

The princess speaks.

"Like *that* wasn't way fucking ominous."

Then Aster.

"I was thinking the same."

Then Delphi.

"Glad it wasn't just me."

Kra and Flin, both in hiking gear, take their places at the front of the unicorns. Three other Varsii tail after, Nok nervously among them.

Kra faces the unicorns.

"Three days. Four nights. Camp at dusk. Rise at dawn. No break until camp. We leave now."

Maus holds up a hand.

"Hold on. You're skipping a *lot* of details. What do we eat? When do we rest? How are we getting there in the first place?"

Kra responds.

"We eat what we find. We rest when we sleep."

He leans closer, already savoring his next few words.

"And we *walk.*"

With that, he turns back around. He walks on through the forest. Flin and Nok join him, as do the other two Varsii, each with supplies of their own.

Maus sighs.

"Figures."

He follows, walking behind.

The unicorns do the same.

Aster steps up beside him. She looks over.

"If you truly can't bear it, you would be permitted to ride. *Briefly.* Only to safeguard your strength."

Maus considers it for a moment.

"I think I'll pass for now. But thanks."

Aster pulls away.

"Suit yourself."

Suddenly, Maus starts looking back and forth, eyes pointed up toward the canopy.

The unicorns watch with confusion.

Delphi speaks.

"What's the matter? Are we being watched?"

Aster exhales.

"If we were, I would know it."

The princess chimes in.

"He better not have some disease."

Still walking, Maus looks back to them.

"Where's the fairy?"

Simultaneously, the unicorns notice her absence.
Aster comments.
"Huh. That *is* strange…"
Delphi next.
"Good riddance. She hardly helped us at all."
Then the princess.
"I agree. Let her wander off to the next interesting thing. If she comes back, great. If not, we'll be fine. Watch your feet."
Maus raises an eyebrow.
He trips over a large root in the dirt. He falls forward with a *thud.*
The Varsii ahead stop their march. They all turn around, seeing Maus in the dirt.
Kra sighs loudly, making a point.
"Watch your step. Do not fall behind."
He turns back around, as do the other Varsii.
Maus gets up. He dusts the dirt off his palms.
The unicorns walk around him.
He stands there for a moment.
"This is going to be a very long three days."

— — — — — — — — — — — — — — —

Maus leans back against a tree. His greatsword, too, leans against it. In front of him, the Varsii clear a patch of forest floor, moving large sticks and stones to the side.
Evening light further dims. Stars peek through the darkening sky above, peering down through the gaps of the canopy.
Maus keeps a close eye on Kra.
Kra notices.
He smiles at him.
Maus says nothing.
Kra returns to his work.

Maus continues to watch.

Farther off — but not *too* far off — the unicorns stand in a group.

Aster looks over to the Varsii.

"I don't trust them."

Delphi watches them clear out the area. Pass out supplies.

"Neither do I. But we don't have a choice. All we can do is hope *we* find *it* before *Damnation* finds *us.*"

The princess exhales.

"Agreed."

No one else speaks after that.

— — — — — — — — — — — — — — — — —

Princess Pipsy shivers. The morning air feels cold and moist. The mossy ground squishes like a throat beneath her hooves.

Aster and Delphi walk alongside her. Maus walks ahead. The five Varsii lead them all onward, Kra at the front. Flin watches him closely.

The princess speaks.

"This ground feels *disgusting.* I hope we aren't walking into a swamp."

Aster responds.

"*Around* one, perhaps. I highly doubt they'd take us right *through* one."

— — — — — — — — — — — — — — — — —

The unicorns walk through a swamp.

The shallow water feels warm and unwelcome. Bits of algae stick to their skin. The fog of the Loftwood still hangs in the air, now joined by the rotten smell of wet plants.

Princess Pipsy exhales slowly.

"This is the worst fucking day of my life."

— — — — — — — — — — — — — — — — —

Nightfall.
The party rests atop a large stretch of flat rock, still well within the swamp. Maus lies on his back, hands behind his head, eyes closed. The Varsii rest on crudely fashioned bedrolls. Nok tosses and turns a bit, never quite getting comfortable. Kra sleeps further out from the group.
Aster and the princess stand together, both deep in their sleep.
Delphi stands further away. Her eyes are closed, but she remains conscious. At least for now. The stakes have never been higher, yet — in this brief lull of the journey — she can't help but think of the alleyway.
She winces.

— — — — — — — — — — — — — — — — —

Early morning.
Nok panics.
"Where did she go? Where is Leke?"
He approaches Kra, marching right up to him. Flin walks behind.
Kra raises his hands innocently.
"I know nothing."
Flin steps closer.
"And Lis? Did you *kill* them?"
Kra chuckles.
"I'm shocked. I would *never.* I feel quite offended."
Maus and the unicorns watch from nearby, all keeping a close eye on Kra.
Flin reaches toward the sickle on her belt.

"No games. No tricks. No misbehaving."

Two Varsii emerge from the tree line. They rejoin the group.

The one with a heavy pack slung over her shoulder — Leke — speaks.

"Sorry. Morning search. Awoke early. Should have spoken."

The one next to her — Lis — adds on.

"Went for food. Nothing grand. Nothing fruitful."

Kra looks back to Flin. He grins.

"Told you before. Wouldn't dream of it."

Flin walks off, momentarily satisfied.

Nok hurries after, not wanting to be close to Kra for too long.

Kra speaks loudly, addressing them all.

"Everyone is accounted for. No time to waste. Let us depart."

He walks past the unicorns. He flashes a taunting smile.

"Don't fall behind."

Princess Pipsy scowls.

— — — — — — — — — — — — — — — —

The firm dirt under the princess's hooves feels familiar. Far more comfortable terrain than the marshlands were, that's for certain. Despite the brevity of their passage through, she very much hated each second, and she very much hopes to never return there again. Even now, she can feel algae wedged into her hooves.

Sunlight beams down from above, illuminating the forest.

The fog feels thinner here. *Is* thinner here. The air feels a bit richer, too. None of them realized before —

not even Maus — but, in retrospect, it *was* tougher to breathe further north.

At the front of the group, Nok, Leke, and Lis whisper among each other. Several times, they point to Kra.

Kra looks back to them. He says something that the unicorns can't hear. Maus can't either. The Varsii are too far away.

Kra, facing forward, addresses the party.

"We clear Loftwood by nightfall. Close to the valley. Getting closer. We march on. No delays."

The princess exhales. She speaks to no one in particular.

"I really hate that bitch."

Maus speaks.

"Don't think it really applies to him."

The princess rolls her eyes.

"Anyone can be a bitch. Swearing has no limitations. That's what makes it beautiful."

Maus grunts.

Whatever.

He shifts focus back to the path ahead.

The princess watches Kra lead them. Subconsciously, she frowns.

"I hope he gives us a justifiable reason to kill him."

Aster responds.

"We shall see."

Delphi says nothing.

— — — — — — — — — — — — — — — —

The Varsii sleep on their lackluster bedrolls, all below clusters of trees. The forest is, indeed, thinner, though tight groupings of trees still appear.

Maus slumps against a stump, exhausted, but conscious. He maintains careful focus on Kra, keeping watch.

Princess Pipsy and Aster stand together, both asleep, not too far from the Varsii.

Delphi stands farther out, a deliberate distance away.

— — — — — — — — — — — — — — — —

The forest continues to thin.

The party continues to march.

The morning sun brightens the sky.

In the distance, they now spot the grasslands.

Beyond it, they *just* make out the valley.

Other kingdoms and settlements pepper the horizon.

Kra leads them.

They follow.

— — — — — — — — — — — — — — — —

The Varsii sleep in a deep alcove in the rock of the hillside, barely wide enough to fit all of them. Kra, even sleeping, still smiles. Flin stands a few feet away, keeping watch.

Maus leans against the rock of the hill, not too far from the Varsii. Aster stands beside him, deeply asleep. Delphi, as before, stands further away.

She does not sleep.

Not yet.

The princess notices.

She approaches.

"What's the problem?"

Delphi turns to her.

The princess continues.

"Don't act like we haven't noticed. Being dark and mysterious doesn't suit you. Assuming we're even successful, we have a dangerous battle ahead. I suggest you spit it out, before it gets you killed."

Delphi looks offended.

"You beat me to death not one week ago."

The princess responds.

"Yet you're fine. You're here now. And you have *magic.*"

Delphi steps closer.

"You didn't *know* that. You didn't *know* I'd be fine. You didn't *know* I'd have magic. You beat me to death over an off-handed comment that I made out of frustration."

She looks into the princess's eyes.

"And you *still* can't admit you were wrong, let alone say you're fucking *sorry.*"

She walks off.

The princess frowns.

She says nothing.

— — — — — — — — — — — — — — — —

Kra leads the group over the grasslands.
They follow the slope of the land.
They descend into the mouth of the valley.

— — — — — — — — — — — — — — — —

Hills rise up on either side of them. Grasses and bushes paint the valley. Nary a tree can be seen, barring those beyond the lip of the valley. Tiny speckles of stone dot the valley floor ahead, an obvious contrast from the green all around it.

The valley itself stretches a great distance. From wall to wall, it could easily take one a half-day to cross, not to mention the physical prowess it would require.

The valley curves slightly, bending off to the right. Its farthest end touches the horizon, its green slope instead a gray-blue.

To travel the full length of the valley could take half a week, if not more. It's no wonder the great Kingdom of Man was once built here.

The air feels… quiet. Like the valley itself has been waiting for something. Like the valley itself is *still* waiting for something.

No birds chirp in the distance.

No animals nip at the plants.

No predators stalk behind bushes.

No rivers run.

No brooks babble on.

The valley feels empty.

Unwelcoming.

Vulnerable.

The wind carries through, doing little to ease the eerie stillness. The strange, haunted silence fills the air in a suffocating way.

Not literally, of course.

Though it might as well be.

The Varsii walk at the front. Kra leads them. Maus walks behind. The unicorns trail at the back.

Still facing forward, Kra speaks, addressing the party.

"Welcome to the Hundrian Valley. Don't be fooled. It is beautiful. But nothing lives here."

He walks on.

The princess mumbles.

"I'm starting to think *all* these people are fucking ominous by default."

Maus grunts.

Agreed.

Delphi spots the stone shapes in the distance.

"There. Dead ahead."

She gestures to it with her snout.

"I think that's the Kingdom of Man. Or what's left of it, anyway."

Aster speaks.

"I had never seen it myself, but I always thought it would be a bit more… *deserving* of its reputation."

The princess replies.

"I don't give a damn about its reputation. That sword is all that matters. Assuming we can even find it."

Delphi looks to Aster, ignoring the princess.

"Our perception of time is skewed. It doesn't *feel* like that long ago. But remember, in reality, it's been much longer. We *still* don't know how long it's been. Not exactly. And, honestly, it's safe to assume it's been even longer."

Flin turns her head slightly. One eye looks back toward the unicorns.

"We camp soon. Set up gear. Tools. Edge of the ruins. We're close. Not there. But close."

She points to the speckles of stone further ahead, reaffirming Delphi's suspicion.

So the Varsii continue to walk, and the unicorns follow behind.

— — — — — — — — — — — — — — — — —

The sun bends toward the horizon.

The evening arrives.

The Varsii stand beside an ancient pillar at the edge of the ruins. Foliage sprouts from the cracks in the stone, the material itself yellowed with age. Vines crawl down its side, reaching down toward the grass. The pillar stands no more than ten feet tall. Shorter stones branch out from its base, possibly foundations for some ancient wall or building.

The bags and satchels of the Varsii sit in a loose pile against the pillar. Kra and Nok tie knots in a long rope, preparing something to fit around the pillar. Nok deliberately avoids eye contact with Kra. Leke and Lis organize tools along the shorter stones, using them as makeshift tables. Flin stands further back, supervising everything… and keeping a *very* close eye on Kra.

The rest of the ruins stretch out before them. As Flin promised, their base of operations sits right at the very edge. A worn path of coarse dirt and matted grass winds through the ruins proper. Still — even from here — it looks to be more of the same. Nothing but long-broken pillars and overgrown piles of rubble, once-gray stones discolored by the unwavering passage of time.

Maus stands not far from Flin, also keeping a close eye on Kra.

Kra meets his gaze.

He flashes an eerie smile.

Maus says nothing.

Not even a grunt of acknowledgment.

Kra returns to his work.

The unicorns stand behind Maus, paying only partial attention to the Varsii.

The princess looks to Delphi.

"Alright. We're here. So — while they're still doing… whatever it is they're doing — how the fuck are we supposed to find this thing?"

Delphi responds.

"I don't know, but—"

Aster cuts her off.

"You *don't know?*"

The princess speaks as well.

"What the *fuck* do you mean?"

Delphi furrows her brow. She doesn't back down.

"Let me *finish* my gods-damn fucking *sentence.*"

She glares at the other two.

Aster's expression immediately softens.

The princess's doesn't.

Delphi continues, cooling down.

"Since the sword vanished not long after the Siege, we never had a chance to study it properly. Our knowledge of it — what it can do, how it behaves — is limited. Based on what I *have* studied, Petunia's magic seemed like a pretty close match, but…"

She pauses.

"…well, we didn't really have the time to ask questions."

Aster replies.

"I don't understand why it matters. *Magic* is *magic.*"

Delphi shakes her head, frustrated.

"No, you *don't* understand."

She exhales, calming back down.

"*Our* magic is tied to emotion. It's why we don't have control until adolescence. Same reason why the three of us got magic back at all, incomplete as our powers may be. But Petunia's magic was *different*. It wasn't tied to emotion. It was tied to something else."

Aster speaks.

"How do you know?"

Delphi looks to her.

"Because it *felt* different. That's the only way I can explain it. Didn't you feel it, too?"

Aster and the princess think to themselves for a moment.

They did.

The princess breaks the silence.

"Back to the question at hand. How are we supposed to find it?"

Delphi responds.

"The Varsii are known scavengers. Looters, in some cases. But they're good at what they do. Our records may not have described *what* they do, or *how* they do it, but I know what they do yields results. And with Petunia gone… we don't really have other options."

Delphi looks solemnly to the Varsii.

Aster does the same.

Looks like they're almost done.

The princess approaches the Varsii.

"How long do you think it will take?"

Flin answers without hesitation.

"Three days. Best guess. Maybe five. If it's here."

Princess Pipsy takes a deep breath. She feels her heart beat faster. She feels her muscles tense.

"We don't have three days. We don't have five days. We're lucky we had the last few it took to get here."

Flin takes a step forward.

"*You* arrived unannounced. *You* made us travel. Our chief showed trust. I still disagree. But *you* met *us*. Traveled with *us*. We'll search as able. But *you* don't lead. *You* don't command. Treat us with respect."

The princess feels her chest tighten. She forces a long, slow exhale.

"The monster we face will not show you respect. He will rip out your throat with his teeth. Snap your spine the first chance he gets."

The princess steps closer to Flin.

"You are *real* fuckin' lucky that we need you on our side, because any one of us could splatter your guts across this valley in a *second.* But that doesn't mean we have to be *nice.* The stakes here are *way* beyond niceties."

She takes a breath.

"Let me explain it in a way that you'll understand."
She leans forward. Her upper lip rises noticeably.
Flin feels the warmth of her breath on her feathers.
But she does not back down. Instinctively —
unbeknownst to either — she reaches toward her sickle.
The princess speaks.
"Get your shit together, or we're *all* gonna fucking
die."
Flin stares back at the princess.
The princess steps away.
Flin says nothing. She turns back around, keeping
an eye on the other Varsii once again.
Maus gives the princess a disapproving look. It
catches her off-guard.
After a moment, he, too, turns back around.
The princess feels… *something*.
She isn't sure what.
But it's there.
And it wasn't before.
Is this… shame?
A hint of regret?
She doesn't have time to dwell on it.
Not far off — further toward the heart of the ruins
— a sound carries over the edge of the valley.
No. Not just *one* sound.
Many sounds.
Distant impacts. Like footfalls on dirt. Muffled
voices — or, more accurately, their echoes — shout in
rhythm. Less like chaos. More like deliberate orders.
The shouting is evident, but the words are too distant to
make out.
The princess turns toward the noise.
She doesn't say anything.
She doesn't have to.
Because everyone else hears it, too.
Their eyes all lock on to the side of the valley.

And they watch.

For a few moments, nothing happens.

Then a shape crests over the lip.

A horse.

It stumbles wildly. It sprints ahead at full speed, its footing misplaced and erratic, like it can't truly see where it's running.

It doesn't slow down.

It tumbles over the side of the valley. Its body impacts the steep decline. Its cries of pain carry on the wind. It rolls. And it *thuds*. And it *cracks*.

Its body looks beaten and broken. Red stains nearly cover its white coat beneath, layers of dirt and dried mud on top of it.

Each impact leaves a splash of red on the greenery.

The horse falls to the floor of the valley. As it does, its features become more visible. Before anyone can react, it rolls into the center of the ruins.

Petunia.

Princess Pipsy races to the spot where she fell.

Aster and Delphi do the same.

Flin, now confused, turns to Maus.

"What is that?"

Maus replies.

"Our best fuckin' shot."

He runs after the unicorns. His greatsword *clinks* on his back as he runs. His heavy boots *thump* on the ground.

Flin *clicks* her tongue. The other Varsii turn to her.

"Trouble. Get ready."

Kra grins.

"Always ready for that."

He drops his end of the rope. He looks to Nok, still holding the other end.

"Finish up."

He walks off, joining Flin. Leke and Lis follow after, leaving Nok on his own.

He sighs.

The unicorns rush through the ruins. The *clack* of their hooves echoes through the valley. They weave through the remnants of structures long gone, careful to maintain their balance.

Petunia lies bleeding on the ground. Blood and dirt cover her body; it's impossible to tell where her wounds even *are*. It's impressive that she could even stand before the fall. Tearful moans escape her throat, though she has no tears to cry. As soon as the unicorns reach her, they notice the mass of dark scabs in her eye socket.

Her eye has been fully gouged out.

She writhes on the ground. Her legs twitch, her body too weak to move properly.

The sound of running grows louder from over the wall of the valley.

Delphi's eyes glow a radiant yellow. Her horn does the same.

A similar glow appears around Petunia's body. She whimpers in pain. She feels the breaks in her flesh fold back together. Yellow light mends the muscle and skin. Her broken bones *snap* into place. The fractures in her skull realign. She feels the pieces *push* and *turn* under her skin.

Her gouged eye, however, remains.

The golden light fades from her body. She breathes heavily, exhaustion quite evident.

The glow fades from Delphi as well.

The sound of running grows closer. Not an army, no, but certainly *something*. And far more than one person.

Aster speaks.

"Petunia! We thought you were dead!"

Petunia coughs. Dark blood sprays from her mouth.

"They're coming!"

She stands. Her ears scan the space, trying to pinpoint the direction of the noise. Were she able to see, she'd be looking around.

Delphi can't take her eyes off Petunia's scabbed, empty socket.

Why didn't it work?

Aster steps forward.

"How did you get here? What's going on?"

Petunia turns to her. Her words are as frantic as she is.

"I felt it. A pull. I can't see. He took out my eye. I can't see. But I felt it. My head hurts. But I ran. And they found me."

She moves her head around, trying to face where she thinks the unicorns might be.

"You have to *kill* them!"

Princess Pipsy steps closer.

"Who?"

Petunia responds.

"The Legion."

— — — — — — — — — — — — — — — —

The sound of running draws even closer.

Maus and the Varsii catch up, joining the group. Nok hurries over, closing the distance between himself and the others.

Princess Pipsy turns to Delpi.

"You've got ten fucking seconds to give us a history lesson on just who the fuck we are dealing with."

Delphi nods, sensing the urgency. She projects her voice, addressing them all.

"Before the First Casualties, the Legion were trained unicorn hunters. Formed to wipe out our people. They were the reason the Siege happened in the first place. The Queen said she wiped them all out."

The princess snarls.

"Well *clearly* she fucking embellished."

Aster looks to Delphi.

"What *exactly* are we dealing with? Be specific."

The footfalls continue to approach.

Delphi responds.

"It's been *hundreds* of *years*. I have no fucking idea."

Petunia speaks, regaining some composure.

"They followed me from somewhere. I don't know where. I couldn't see. The pull brought me there. I always felt it a *little*, but…"

She pauses.

"Damnation took my eye. Then I felt it more."

Maus speaks.

"How many? Do you know?"

Petunia replies.

"A couple dozen. Maybe more. Not an army. But enough of one."

She steps closer to where she heard his voice.

"We need to kill them all."

Princess Pipsy's horn *crackles* with electricity. It emanates a bright red glow. The same glow overtakes her eyes. Thin sparks flick out from her pupils.

She faces the wall of the valley.

"It would be my absolute pleasure."

The wind kicks up around her. It carries the scent of a storm.

Maus climbs onto Aster's bare back.

They exchange not a word.

They don't have to.

He unsheathes his greatsword from his back. He holds it steady, muscles tense and ready to swing.

Aster's eyes and horn glow bright blue. Ripples of barely visible light pulse out from her horn, a similar shade.

She faces the wall of the valley.

Delphi's vibrant yellow glow returns. Its shine overtakes her eyes and her horn.

She speaks, her focus on Petunia.

"Can you protect us without sight?"

Petunia nods.

"My magic has been less reliable since my eye. But I will try."

Her two horns glow a bright white. A slight shimmer appears on her body. White sparks fly out from her scabbed-over socket. A subtle glow pulses from behind the wound, as if the light wants to escape from her head.

Delphi and Petunia face the wall of the valley.

Flin pulls the sickle from her belt.

Nok stares, frozen in fear.

Leke and Lis each pull a small axe from their back.

Kra chuckles nervously.

"This is *above* us. Needlessly dangerous. We should flee."

Flin turns to him.

"You disappoint our people. Be my guest."

Kra smirks.

"As you command."

He ducks out of the way, hiding behind the crumbled remains of a stone wall.

The sound of the running crescendos.

Horses gather at the lip of the valley. Each one supports an armed rider. Their clothes appear mismatched and scraggly, though their armor bears more uniformity. Scratches and scuffs are apparent.

Every piece of their armor shows age, as if passed down through each generation. A worn, painted symbol adorns the front of each chestplate, something akin to a diamond shape, but far more stretched, and pointed at the ends. Many wield crossbows. Those that do hold them at the ready.

They all appear humanoid. Many do, in fact, look human. But among them are elves. Dwarves. Orcs. Ottesh; otterfolk. Frillen; lizardfolk. Even some Varsii are stationed among them, though they've not seen those in the valley before.

Nearly three dozen riders are gathered.

For a few moments, both parties simply stare at each other, neither side breaking the tension.

The colored glow of the unicorns shines from the floor of the valley, their magics bright and foreboding.

The riders part.

A lone rider walks on. He stops at the front of the group. He stares into the valley below. His bulky, orcish frame shows through his armor. His tusks poke out from his bottom lip, a number of symbols carved into them. A large, heavy blade rests on his back, yet unsheathed. His voice projects easily over the wind.

"Unicorns!"

His voice echoes.

"We have followed your kin from the west. Her irreverence killed three of our best. For their deaths — and for the deaths of those who came before us — we gather here to complete our lifelong quest, the very same that our ancestors gave us."

He reaches behind him, grabbing the hilt at his back. He pulls the massive blade from its sheath, the weapon nearly six feet in length. A subtle hum emanates from the blade. Runes — seemingly forged into the metal itself — glow white with a tense magical power.

The unicorn's eyes widen.

Delphi vocalizes what every unicorn is thinking.

"We're *fucked.*"

Aster speaks.

"Good news, princess."

She turns to her.

"I think we just found it."

The orcish man at the front of the Legion — the captain — speaks again.

"By the power of Silver Seal, Lucent Blade That Slays the Unicorns, you will be ripped from existence."

The captain scans the group in the valley below. His eyes lock onto Maus. He stares briefly, then cocks his head. There's a glimmer of recognition in his eyes.

"You."

He points the tip of the blade at Maus.

"For abandoning our quest, you will be slain alongside them."

Princess Pipsy turns to Maus.

"What the *fuck!*"

Maus clenches his jaw.

"Talk later. Fight now."

The princess looks back to the Legion. She hates that Maus is right.

The captain gestures to the valley with Silver Seal.

The Legion descends.

Chapter XIX:
When the
Mountains
Move

Chapter XIX: When the Mountains Move

The sound of the Legion rattles the valley like thunder.

The horses race down the ramp-like decline of the valley wall, their footing impressively steady. Those with crossbows let their bolts fly.

Choom! Choom!

Choom!

A bolt sinks into Maus's shoulder.

Shunk!

He recoils.

Blood burbles out from the hole.

He ignores it.

Princess Pipsy fires a bolt of her own.

KRAAAK!

It impacts the wall of the valley. Rock and dirt fly into the air. One horse at the front stumbles. It trips over itself, falling down into the valley. It lands on its rider with a wet, meaty *crack*. The rider falls limp. Both roll down into the valley.

The others continue to charge.

KRAAAK!

The princess fires another red bolt.

It misses.

Aster joins in.

Pew! Pew! Pew!

Her brilliant blue beams pierce through the bodies of numerous riders, leaving sizable wounds. Unfortunately, none fatal.

The riders continue to charge.

Aster and the princess continue to fire at the Legion.

KRAAAK! Pew! Pew! KRAAAK!

It does little to slow their approach.

Delphi turns to Petunia.

"It's not enough! We need you!"

Petunia steels her resolve.

She steps forward, taking her place at the front of the unicorns.

"By my light, they will come no further."

Petunia's glow strengthens. The intensity forces Delphi to look away. A white shimmer sparkles across Petunia's body. Then — above them all — a barrier of light brightens into existence.

The captain shouts to the Legion.

"Do not fall prey to her parlor tricks! *Do... not... yield!*"

At his command, the Legion runs on.

Their front lines reach the barrier.

Their horses run across it, as though it were a solid surface.

Because it *is*.

Maus looks up.

The unicorns look up.

The Varsii look up.

Above them, the Legion's forces race across the bubble of light, approaching its downward curve.

The princess turns to Petunia, her eyes forced to squint.

"Drop it."

Petunia replies.

"So be it."

The magical barrier shimmers. Then — as soon as it appeared — it dissipates, fading into nothing.

The Legion falls.

Delphi shouts.

"Look out!"

Horses whinny. People scream. And they fall.

The Varsii scramble to avoid getting crushed. Horses *crunch* with heavy impacts. Several *crack* their heads against the ruins, red splotches left behind. Some fall onto their riders, crushing their legs. Their chests. Their heads.

The unicorns scatter, their eyes on the sky. Legion continue to fall. Petunia, unsure where to go, tails the princess.

The captain falls. His horse lands directly on Leke. Her spine *snaps* from the force. Feathers and blood explode outward. Her body caves in on itself. The horse lands on its neck, *snapping* bone.

The captain stands, Silver Seal in hand.

He looks down at the body of the crushed Varsii below. Her limbs twitch and convulse. Her head wriggles erratically. Blood pours from her mouth, falling over the sides of her beak.

The captain raises Silver Seal.

"If you stand with them, you die with them."

He swings downward.

The blade of Silver Seal strikes Leke's head. The sheer weight of it bursts her skull like a rotten fruit. Blood and pulp scatters everywhere. Her feathers fly out in wet clumps.

All through the ruins, a number of Legion succumb to their injuries.

Those that do not, stand.

More crossbows fire at the unicorns.

Choom! Choom!

Princess Pipsy calls out to the others.

"We *cannot* leave without that sword!"

Aster replies, firm understanding in her voice.

"Then we kill them all."

She breaks away, circling back to the center of the ruins.

Princess Pipsy nods.

"Kill them all."

She calls out to Petunia.

"We circle back! Follow me!"

And she does.

Aster runs back through the ruins. The Legion nearby charge on foot.

Maus swings his greatsword. Its blade cleaves through the arm of a stout human man. Blood sprays into the air.

Maus winces. He struggles to support the weight of his weapon. Instinctively, he reaches toward the bolt in his shoulder.

Delphi catches up to them. She looks to Maus, her yellow glow still vibrant. She shouts.

"Tear it out!"

Maus exhales. He knows he has to.

"Fuck me."

With one hand still on his sword, he wraps his fingers around the protruding wood. And he *pulls*.

He feels the pointed metal *scrape* and *dig* against his flesh in the wrong direction. Its metal tip carves against the grain of his muscles. He cries out in pain. He pulls harder.

The bolt tears free, both it and his hand covered in blood. He tosses the bolt to the ground. It *clatters*.

Delphi's eyes lock onto his injury.

His shoulder glows with a golden light. He feels the torn muscle mend itself. He feels the light fold his skin back together. And it *hurts*. But it heals.

The yellow glow fades from his body.

He exhales.

Back to it.

His strength now returned, he brings his sword to position. Aster races past another Legion member, this one a younger elf woman. Maus swings along with the momentum. His blade cuts right through her face, her bloody jaw sent flying.

More crossbows fire at the unicorns.

Choom! Choom!

Princess Pipsy fires back.

KRAAAK!

It strikes the torso of a Legion. His shoulder *explodes* in a burst of bone and blood. His arm — still clutching his crossbow — falls.

Hearing all the chaos, Kra peeks out from behind a stone wall. Then he *sees* the chaos.

"Not my fight. Time to go."

He sneaks away, running off.

He doesn't get very far.

He runs directly into a towering orcish figure. In his hand, the figure wields a massive glowing greatsword.

Kra barely has time to process.

The captain swings Silver Seal into him. It carves into his chest. Blood flies out from his mouth, painting over the front of his body.

The captain raises his leg. He plants his boot firmly against Kra's bleeding chest. He pushes, prying the blade free. Kra falls back, dead before he has a chance to hit the ground.

Further off, Flin fights against two Varsii members of the Legion, both wielding battle-worn shortswords. She fends off their blows with her sickle. Metal scrapes against metal. Their swords *clash* and *clang* against her weapon, each strike masterfully deflected.

One swordsman stumbles, open for a strike.

Flin rushes up to him. With astonishing speed, she digs the curve of her sickle into his eye. Before he has a chance to scream, she forces it deeper. It *cracks* his skull and pierces his brain. He falls.

The other swordsman rushes her. She frees her sickle just in time to deflect the blade.

Nok runs frantically through the fight, not paid attention to by anyone.

Another crossbow bolt sails through the air. It brushes past his head.

Nok screams.

Princess Pipsy fires another bolt of lightning.

KRAAAK!

It strikes a cluster of Legion swordsmen. Blood scatters into the air with bits of pulpy flesh. They fall.

Several blades swing out, striking Petunia's legs. She crashes to the ground. As soon as she falls, she cries out to the others.

"Help me!"

Delphi shouts back.

"Hold on!"

Three swordsmen tower over the fallen Petunia. They raise their blades high. The one at the center — an ottesh man with graying fur — speaks.

"You get what you fucking dese—"

Petunia's glow *flashes* bright.

A protective barrier appears…

…right through the mouths of the swordsmen.

Their bodies slump to the ground, tongues still attached to the back of their throats.

The tops of their heads *slide* off the barrier, leaving a thick trail of blood.

Delphi closes the distance. She looks down at the dead swordsmen.

"Looks like you got it covered."

Petunia exhales.

"Seems like it."

Delphi takes off, racing back to the heart of the ruins.

"Come on!"

Princess Pipsy fires another bolt of lightning.

KRAAAK!

It strikes the head of another Legion, knocking the flesh from her elven face. She falls. Her blood soaks into the ground.

The captain looks around, taking in the carnage.

"So much chaos. So much wanton destruction."

His eyes lock onto the unicorns.

"You deserve death."

He swings Silver Seal through the air. Its runes glow brighter. A massive arc of white light flies out from the edge of the blade. It sails through the air, heading right for the princess. The bottom tip of its curve digs through the dirt as it flies.

The princess turns around just in time to see it.

"Shit!"

She lurches to the side, evading the brunt of it. The edge of the light cuts her skin as it sails past. Blood trickles out.

The arc of light crashes into a stone tower adjacent. Dust and debris fling into the air.

The princess calls out to the others.

"We can't deal with them all when *that's* coming at us!"

Aster responds.

"We can't *all* go after him! We'll be swarmed!"

She fires off another thin blue beam.

Pew!

Then another.

Pew!

Both impact Legion fighters.

Maus — still riding atop her — speaks.

"Take me to him."

Aster grunts.

Will do.

She changes course, splitting off from the other unicorns.

Delphi calls out to her.

"What are you *doing?!*"

Aster doesn't waste time replying.

Nok runs around a crumbled corner of the ruins.

A Legion swordsman does the same.

The two stop. They lock eyes.

The swordsman raises his blade.

Nok turns to run.

He trips over a cluster of weeds.

The swordsman swings his blade.

Lis rushes in, blocking the blade with her forearm. It sticks into her bone. Bleeding, she turns back to Nok.

"Run!"

Nok scrambles to his feet.

Choom!

A crossbow bolt flies through the air. It *thunks* into the side of Lis's head. Feathers fly out from the impact. She falls.

Nok runs.

The captain stares at Aster, watching her approach. He tightens his grip around Silver Seal's hilt.

Humph!

He swings the heavy blade through the air. Another curve of brilliant white light leaps out. Aster bears to the side, dodging it. The light *crashes* into more ruins behind her. Stones crumble to the ground. Dust scatters into the growing wind.

Aster skids to a stop.

Maus leaps off her back. He lands on one knee, his greatsword still in his hands.

Aster races off, returning to the other unicorns.

Maus stands.

He locks eyes with the captain, raising his weapon.

The captain smirks.

"Mine's bigger."

They charge at each other. The two blades collide.

Flin backs into a stone corner. The swordsman in front of her swings his sword recklessly, pushing her into the wall. Her sickle barely deflects his assault. Her movements slow. The swordsman's do not. She pants, each breath labored and strained.

She feels the stone press against her back.

Nowhere to go.

The swordsman brings down his blade.

Her sickle is too slow.

The sword cuts into her shoulder, tearing her cloak. She cries out.

The sword *rips* out from the wound, taking bloody feathers with it.

From across the way, a bolt of red lightning arcs out.

KRAAAK!

It strikes the cheek of the swordsman. Bloody chunks of his face splatter across Flin's. His left eye reduces to mush. With the deep meat of his face now revealed, he falls.

Flin catches a glimpse of Princess Pipsy racing back to the other unicorns.

She exhales, grateful.

She slumps to the ground, dropping out of sight. She breathes slowly, putting pressure on the wound. Maus and the captain *clash* blades once again. Maus grits his teeth. His eyes scan the captain for any sign of weakness. Any opening he can exploit.

He finds none.

The captain speaks.

"I never forget a face."

He pulls Silver Seal away. In the same motion, he swings it back around.

Both blades *clash* together once more. Tiny white sparks fly out from Silver Seal.

Maus tightens the grip on his hilt.

"I never forget a bullshit cult."

They both pull away. Each one takes several steps back. They slowly circle each other at the center of the battlefield, each wanting the other to strike. Blood taints the stone all around them. The corpses of Legion litter the ruins.

The captain speaks.

"Look around you! Our forebearers were right. Their writings were true. This is the first time we have seen them in person, and look at the chaos they've caused."

He gestures to the carnage all around them. He doesn't take his eyes off Maus.

Farther off, the unicorns continue to strike down the Legion.

KRAAAK! Pew! Pew! KRAAAK!

Maus replies.

"You brought the fight to *them.* Only *idiots* wouldn't defend themselves."

The captain scoffs.

"They are not idiots, no. But they *are* violent. They *are* dangerous. They kill who they like when they please."

Maus grunts.

"As blind and ironic as ever."

The captain stops moving.

"Perhaps you need another lesson."

He looks at Maus's face.

"Perhaps it's time I finish that nose job."

He charges forward.

Maus does the same.

Another crossbow fires at the unicorns.

Choom!

Then another.

Choom!

The first collides harmlessly against a crumbled wall. It *clatters* to the ground.

Princess Pipsy calls out to the others.

"There aren't many left! We—"

The second pierces through Princess Pipsy's cheek. She chokes on her words.

Its sharpened, bloody end sticks out on the other side.

She wails.

Delphi spots the final two Legion members. They stand atop a fallen pillar nearby, each wielding a massive crossbow.

Delphi shouts.

"I'll handle it!"

She races toward them.

Aster replies.

"What about the princess?!"

Delphi shouts back, charging onward.

"Just get that thing *out* of her!"

Aster and the princess stop running.

Princess Pipsy feels the blood gather in her mouth. Its warmth coats her tongue. Sticks to her teeth. Rolls down the back of her throat.

Aster looks to her. She watches the blood fall from her lips.

"Hold still!"

She bites down onto the metal tip of the bolt. Her teeth clamp down hard. And she pulls.

The bolt makes a horrible *squelch*. It pulls slowly. The friction scrapes the holes in the princess's face. Delphi runs up to the fallen pillar. Both Legion members take aim.

Delphi leaps onto the pillar. She lowers her head. Her horn spears through the first Legion's head with a wet *shunk.* It digs deep into his brain, killing him instantly.

The second Legion member fires another bolt.

Choom!

It impacts the corpse of the other, still dangling from Delphi's horn.

The final Legion member takes off, racing toward the mouth of the valley.

Delphi watches him run. With an adult corpse stuck to her horn, there's no point in chasing. She would never be able to catch him.

Slowly, he makes even more distance.

Her eyes lock onto him.

Her yellow glow brightens.

An identical glow appears around the fleeing Legion's body. Panicked, he runs faster.

Delphi concentrates.

Thick tumors grow in his throat, distorting the shape of his neck. He starts to choke. Instinctively, he paws at them. The tumors expand, pushing against the inner wall of his throat. His neck bulges out in disgusting, irregular lumps. Small globs of blood fall from his mouth. His eyes widen, bloodshot and strained. His breath weakens to nothing. He clutches his neck, feeling the painful lumps that clog it.

His running slows to a stumble.

He falls.

Delphi pulls the corpse from her horn.

Aster pulls harder.

The bolt rips free.

She drops it to the ground.

Princess Pipsy spits blood.

Delphi joins them.

"Hold still."

Her glow brightens for a moment. The same glow appears around the princess's face. The holes in her cheeks mend back together. The glow around her head dissipates.

She gives Delphi a firm nod.

"Thanks."

The princess hesitates for the briefest second, as if to say something else. But she doesn't.

Delphi looks over to Maus and the captain.

"We're not done yet."

She runs toward them.

"Come on!"

Aster and the princess run after. Petunia, not far off, hears the running. She changes course, joining back with the others.

Maus and the captain lock blades once again. Each one studies the other.

The captain spots the four unicorns approach from afar.

"I hate to cut this short, but I have business to attend to."

He looks Maus in the eyes.

"You really shouldn't have left."

He kicks Maus in the chest.

Maus stumbles back.

The captain takes a wide swing, aiming for the unicorns beyond. Another brilliant curve of light arcs out, sailing through the air.

Maus rolls out of the way at the last second. The edge of the light cuts into his leg. He winces.

The unicorns step to the side, dodging the light.

Except for Petunia.

Her glow strengthens. A wall of shimmering light appears in front of her, following her movements.

The arc of white light impacts the barrier. Both *shatter* like glass, crumbling into a thousand little fragments that instantly fade into nothing.

The captain smirks.

"Impressive."

He raises Silver Seal to the sky. Its runic inscriptions *hum* with a building energy.

Princess Pipsy's horn *crackles* louder.

Aster's magic emits a pulsating *hum* of its own.

Delphi's yellow glow shines bright.

Petunia's body starts to shimmer.

They continue to charge.

Maus crawls away, getting distance.

The captain shouts.

"By the power of Silver Seal, Lucent Blade That Slays the Unicorns, you will plague this world no longer."

He stares at them with fury in his eyes.

"DIE!"

He brings down Silver Seal with all his might.

A massive beam of pulsing white energy rips through the air, tearing into the ground. *This* beam, however, is constant, stemming from the point of the blade.

Petunia halts. Her own white glow brightens even more. The beam from Silver Seal connects with her horns. She absorbs the attack, holding the beam steady in front of her. She cries out with exertion, angry and guttural.

The runes of Silver Seal pulse. The beam holds.

The captain grins.

"Thanks for holding that for me. *Much* appreciated."

The captain takes a step forward.

The force of the beam pushes Petunia back. Her hooves dig into the dirt.

The captain takes another step, still holding tight to Silver Seal.

Petunia pushes back further.

She shouts to the others.

"I can't hold this back for much longer!"

The horn at the top of her head — her *real* horn — cracks.

"RUN!"

The other unicorns stand behind her, unable to look away.

Princess Pipsy stares at the captain. She watches the pulse of the runes. Sees the smug look on his face. Feels her chest tighten. Feels her heat rate rise. Feels her breathing turn deeper. More deliberate.

She scowls.

"No."

*KRAAAK-**KOW**!*

A massive bolt of red lightning *explodes* out from her horn. It *crackles* and *snaps* with violent energy. It connects with the white beam ahead. Its jagged lines of electricity dance up the side, connecting back to Silver Seal itself.

The captain feels the electric burn dig into the skin of his hands, flaying flesh. Blood seeps into the hilt of the sword. It drips from his fingers. He feels the force of her magic push against him.

He does not yield.

With effort, he takes another step forward.

Petunia pushes back.

So does Princess Pipsy.

Petunia's horn cracks further.

Aster steps up to the opposite side of Petunia. She fires a steady blue beam from her horn.

PEW!

It melds into the beam from Silver Seal, tainting its color with a warping blue hue.

Petunia's other horn — the one buried in her eye socket — cracks.

Delphi stands next to the princess. Radiant yellow light *blasts* out from her horn. It joins the colorful fray, pushing its golden color through the center of the beam. Red and yellow sparks fly out in all directions. Waves of translucent blue energy flow into the air.

The captain feels himself being pushed back. He feels his heels dig into the dirt against his will. The torrent of magic travels down the blade of Silver Seal. It whips at his hands — his arms — cutting him deeply. He feels the blood seep out from his wounds. He feels the electricity burn into his flesh. He feels a steady, painful energy seep into his very bones. He feels the golden magic strengthening the others. He feels the skin of his hands meld together.

He stares back at the unicorns.

He feels the force of their magic push him back.

He feels himself losing more traction.

"So we were destined to rest here. At the site of the very beginning."

He inhales.

He exhales.

"So mote it be."

He drops Silver Seal.

Its glowing runes dim.

Its steady beam dissipates.

The combined magics of the unicorns impact him simultaneously.

A thunderous *CRACK* echoes through the valley.

The captain falls.

— — — — — — — — — — — — — — — —

Everyone's ears ring.

Everyone's.

It takes a few moments to pass.

Maus puts a hand to his head, coming to.

The unicorns — at least those with eyes — blink a few times. Their magical glows have already vanished.

Petunia speaks.

"…what happened?"

The others look to where the captain stood.

And they do see the captain, farther off.

Surrounded by blood all his own, he lies against a cracked wall, having been blown back from the explosion.

Maus and the unicorns approach.

Only a fraction of the captain's face remains intact. His right eye bulges from its socket, bloodshot. It hangs loose. His left, entirely absent, is nothing more than a wet glob of pus. His cracked cheekbone protrudes, glistening red in the evening's light. A dark, bloody tunnel sits at the center of his face. All across the exposed flesh and muscle, tiny, fibrous strands twitch at random, nearly obscured by blood. With his cheek torn away, most of his teeth *would* be visible, were they not all knocked out of his mouth, save a few. His right tusk remains. His left does not. Bulbous tumors sprout beneath the little skin that remains, many having spread to his body. His tongue, slick with gore, wriggles. Deep wounds carve into his chest. His breathing is slow. Shallow. Deliberate.

Only upon reaching him do they realize his arms are both missing.

The muscles of his face convulse. Their spurts of blood slow slightly. With painful effort, he turns his head just a bit. His eye locks with those of the princess.

He inhales a raspy breath.

He speaks, his voice strained and wheezing, his cadence now slow and methodical.

"You cannot kill us all."

The princess steps up to him.

"I beg to fucking differ."

The captain speaks again, hardly moving.

"We go on. We—"

Princess Pipsy stabs her horn into his eye socket.

Shunk!

Blood spurts out from the impact. It splatters her horn. She feels thick nerves tangle at its point. She digs deeper. The captain falls limp.

She *rips* her horn back out. It catches on the fibers of his face, tearing bits out along with it. His eye, too, rips out with the motion.

Princess Pipsy steps back. She glares and the mangled face below her. The eyeball dangles from the tip of her horn. Meaty strands wrap around its ridges, holding the eyeball in place. Blood and mucus coats her horn, almost none of its silver still visible. The blood trails down her face. She feels its unwelcome warmth. The putrid stench of iron fills her nostrils. The entire ruins give off that same sickly smell. The blood rolls down the ridge of her nose. It splits at the base of her muzzle. Collects under her jaw. Drips onto the grass.

"You should've learned when to shut up."

Aster looks among the others.

"Is everyone alright?"

Maus grunts. He stands.

Aster, Delphi, and the princess turn to him.

The princess stomps over.

"You've got some *real* quick explaining to do. I suggest you get to the point before I blow off your head."

Maus frowns, unafraid.

He takes a single step toward her.

"First of all, *you* kidnapped *me*. I didn't say shit 'cause *you* never asked. So don't act all fucking surprised."

He takes another step.

The princess backs up to accommodate. She does not realize she does.

Maus continues.

"And *that* piece-a-shit fucking *cult* tries to rope in whoever they can. I'm *calling* it a cult 'cause it *is*. They promise the hunt of a lifetime, then they bog you down with this ancestry crap."

He takes a breath, calming down a bit.

"Joined for the promise of glory. Stayed 'cause of nowhere to go. Got into a fight with the captain. Fucked up my nose. Then I left."

He curls into himself ever-so-slightly at the mention of his nose. No one notices but him.

Princess Pipsy relaxes her posture, seemingly satisfied with his answer.

Maus glances over to the corpse of the captain.

"Guess there was truth in the bullshit. Since you're real. Don't know how they found us, though. Maybe they learned some new tricks."

Delphi turns to Petunia.

"How *did* they find us? What happened?"

Petunia turns to face her. Or where she thinks Delphi is, anyway.

"When I awoke after losing my eye, I just ran. I don't really know where, specifically. As I said, I felt a pull. It was strong. Strong enough to follow. So I followed it. The Legion caught a glimpse of me when I got too close, and, evidently, I was a tantalizing target. I simply took off after that. But they were already mobile when they found me. Something else drew them out first."

Everyone goes silent. Not because of Petunia, but because of something else. Something they all feel simultaneously.

The feeling of being watched.

Princess Pipsy turns. She notices a silhouette at the lip of the valley, unclear how long it's been present.

She furrows her brow.

"We've got company."

The others all turn, taking note.

The princess approaches the figure.

The silhouette comes into detail.

Not just any silhouette.

A *unicorn's.*

Battle scars cover his body. His back looks misshapen, yet he stands nonetheless. His short, dark gray mane blows in the strength of the breeze. His coat looks dirty and unkempt, as though it's been unwashed for weeks. His hooves look beaten to shit, a number of deeper cracks visible.

He looks down at the princess below.

He bows.

"A pleasure to see you again, Princess Pipsy."

The princess stares back for a moment.

"General?"

— — — — — — — — — — — — — — —

The general descends into the valley.

— — — — — — — — — — — — — — —

The unicorns gather around him. Maus, too, watches close.

The general looks among them all.

"I never thought I would see any of our people again. I really did think I was done for."

The general's wandering gaze stops at Petunia. He tilts his head ever-so-slightly, reaching for long-distant memory. He hesitates to speak, still unsure if he's even correct.

"…Petunia?"

Petunia nods.

"Hello, general. It's been quite some time."

The general studies her. He notices her… *accentuated* height. How she stands a bit taller than she naturally should. How her mane has grown terribly long. How her skin is now weathered with age. How both of her eyes have been taken.

"You look… *different.*"

Petunia takes a moment to reply.

"I presume you do as well, though I honestly have no idea."

Aster then speaks.

"We are quite glad to see you as well. It's good to see you escaped."

The general shifts focus. He replies.

"I've been looking all over for you. Searching everywhere. For *weeks.* I saw the smoke when that forest burned down, but after that, I lost the trail. Figured I'd keep heading east. Guess I brought a hunting party along for the ride."

Delphi steps toward him.

"It was horribly reckless, incredibly stupid, and could've gotten us killed."

She pauses.

"…*but,* if it weren't for you, indirectly speaking, we wouldn't have the sword. And I don't know if we can kill Damnation without it."

She continues.

"I don't know if we can kill him *with* it, either. But I like our odds much better."

The princess examines the general's back.

"How did you survive? I watched you die."

The general responds.

"Didn't break all the way. Got *real* fucked up, though. Healed bad, so I can't feel much of my ankles."

He shows his beaten front leg to the others.

"Still standing, though. And running when I need to. So I'll take it."

Delphi, too, looks at his back.

"We could try to heal you."

The general shakes his head.

"You of all unicorns should know it wouldn't work. My body already healed itself. Healed it *wrong*, yeah, but it doesn't matter. We'd have to break it if we want to try something like that. And I don't think it's worth the risk."

Delphi looks away in solemn understanding.

Maus steps closer to the group.

"I hate to break up the reunion, but — speaking of that sword — I think it's time we go fuckin' *get* it."

The others look around.

They see the captain. The blood around his corpse.

But they don't see the sword.

Delphi mutters under her breath.

"Shit…"

Princess Pipsy speaks.

"Fan out. Form a search party. That explosion probably knocked it away, but it can't be too far."

The others nod. They split off.

Petunia inhales.

Petunia exhales.

Petunia's horns glow the faintest bit white.

She calls out to the others.

"I feel it."

— — — — — — — — — — — — — — — —

Petunia stands before a pile of freshly collapsed rubble. Maus and the other unicorns stand around her. Buried beneath the bricks, the hilt of a weapon sticks out, barely visible.

Aster's eyes and horn glow bright blue.

Several large chunks of rubble glow the same. They float off to the side.

Maus pulls away smaller pieces.

With enough debris moved, more of the sword becomes visible. The runes forged into the blade are unmistakable, even without their white glow.

Silver Seal.

Maus grabs the hilt of the sword. He pulls it from the lingering bits of rubble. Tiny stone fragments fall aside.

The sheer weight of the sword forces Maus to use both hands. He stares at it, simply taking it in.

"Before today, I had never even *seen* this before. A legendary weapon, long before my time. One that few people have even heard of."

He pauses.

"I'm keeping it."

He looks to the unicorns.

"Unless there are any objections."

Delphi replies.

"You're the only one with hands."

The princess, too, responds.

"In any other circumstances, we'd kill you for even *suggesting* to keep it. But, as we all know, these are not any other circumstances. Should you survive, consider it a gift."

She steps closer.

"But if it *ever* falls into the wrong hands, you better hope it's because you were killed."

Aster chimes in.

"Just… take care. Use caution. And — just in the spirit of clarity, though I'd hope it's already understood — do *not* use that sword on *us.* "

She pauses.

"We *will* kill you."

She takes a breath.
"Just to make that clear."
Maus responds.
"Crystal. But when all this is over, I am *not* your fucking prisoner. I go free."
Aster, Delphi, and the general look to the princess.
The princess stares at Maus.
She hesitates.
She furrows her brow.
She groans.
"Fine."
Not far off, small rocks audibly *tumble* and *clack*.
Everyone turns toward the noise. The unicorns pin their ears back.
Nok and Flin hobble out from behind a wall. Flin leans on Nok for support, one hand still clutching her shoulder. Both Varsii look scratched up and damaged.
The unicorns relax their posture.
Nok and Flin make their way to the group.
The general speaks.
"Who are these two?"
Nok replies.
"Friends."
The princess clarifies.
"Temporary allies."
She takes a breath.
"But I'm glad you weren't killed in the fight."
Her expression softens, unbeknownst to anyone else but Nok. Not even herself.
Flin speaks.
"Others… less lucky."
She pauses.
"Only Nok. Only me. That is all."
Nok looks to Maus. Then to the sword.
"Found it, I see."
Maus grunts.

We did.
Nok continues.
"Then we should return. Go back home."
Princess Pipsy speaks.
"Your assistance has been much appreciated."
Flin looks up at her.
"Never have us… assist you… again."
Then she nods.
"You are welcome."
Aster looks to Petunia.
"Should you teleport them back?"
Petunia shakes her head.
"Teleportation is extremely taxing. It wears out my magic much quicker. Beyond that, I can only teleport to places I've seen. And, well…"
Everyone looks at her gouged eye.
She continues.
"I've never tried it with someplace I've never been. I have no idea what it might do."
Nok quickly replies, very nervous.
"We're okay. We can walk. Please do not."
Flin adds on.
"We will go. Tell the chief. Tell what happened."
She pauses.
"Good luck. You will need it."
They turn to walk off, heading back toward the mouth of the valley.
Petunia steps forward in protest.
"Wait!"
Nok and Flin turn back around. They wait for her word.
She continues.
"Are my children safe?"
Flin thinks for a moment, then speaks.
"They were gathered. Brought to the east. Edge of the Loftwood. I did not see. Not myself. But I trust it."

Petunia struggles to form a reply.

"Is it beautiful?"

Flin nods.

"It is."

Petunia recedes. Her legs wobble just a small bit. Her upper lip quivers gently. Not a tear falls from her eyes. She has none.

Flin turns back around.

Nok picks up on the cue.

Time to go.

The two Varsii trek back through the ruins, their path set for the mouth of the valley.

Stones *tumble* and *clack* nearby.

Princess Pipsy rolls her eyes.

"Give us a *break.*"

They all turn to the source of the noise.

Lying face-down on the grass — surrounded by a thick pool of blood and matted feathers — the body of Kra twitches slightly.

Everyone approaches, intrigued.

Aster, still staring, speaks warily.

"Is this some kind of undying magic? Perhaps he's been brought to undeath…"

Delphi shakes her head.

"I don't think so. If it was, it'd be obvious. Plus, I don't see any purple. And that stuff is usually purple."

The ground beneath Kra twitches. Or Maus shifts his weight. One of the two.

Then the head of Kra lurches out. The throat emits an odd *squelch.*

Then it lurches again.

And again.

Everyone leans close.

Except for Petunia, who can't see.

The beak of Kra's carcass flies open.

A wet ball of dim blue light tumbles out.

The fairy.

She stands. Viscous slime drips from her body, some rank mix of blood, saliva, and stomach acid.

She smells *bad.*

Even at this distance, Maus and the unicorns recoil.

Petunia scrunches her nose.

"What is that horrible stench?"

The fairy shouts.

"I have been *in there*... for *THREE DAYS!*"

She angrily points to the body of Kra behind her.

Its beak droops.

The general gets a close look.

"What the fuck is *that?*"

The fairy looks up at him.

"Who the fuck are *you?*"

Maus sticks a foot in front of her.

"Knock it off."

The fairy pounds against his boot.

"You're lucky he's holding me back!"

Princess Pipsy addresses the general.

"That's our fairy. Hitched a ride from the forest. She's a huge pain in the ass, but she helps boost our magic."

The fairy looks up at her.

"My *name*... is *DEENA!*"

She spits a glob of *something* on the ground.

Absolutely vile.

The wind picks up.

Then the air shifts.

Not in any specific way. Not that the unicorns can place. Not that Maus nor the fairy can place.

But it shifts.

And they feel it.

Delphi's voice breaks the eerie stretch of silence.

"I feel something."

Aster comments.

"As do I."

Princess Pipsy looks around, confused. Concerned. And — truth be told — a little bit angry.

"The *fuck* is going on?"

The valley itself starts to rumble.

Very, very slightly.

But it rumbles. Like a thousand miniature tremors shaking the earth. Like the very ground is beginning to breathe.

The rumbles — ever constant — continue.

The princess grumbles.

"We can't see *shit* down here."

Petunia steps forward.

"Allow me."

Her horns glow a brilliant white. Her hooves, too, glow the same.

She walks over to the wall of the valley, feeling her way with her hooves. She steps up. More platforms of light appear beneath her hooves. The ones behind her, however, remain. She continues to climb. Each step brings her closer to the lip of the valley. And as she moves on from each step, a staircase of white light builds behind her.

Princess Pipsy follows.

"I got a *bad* fucking feeling about this."

She ascends the stairs of light.

Aster walks after.

"We *all* do. I suspect you just wanted to swear…"

She ascends the stairs of light.

Delphi next.

"And I thought the *princess* stated the obvious."

She ascends the stairs of light.

Deena, still wet and unable to fly, feebly climbs the very first stair.

Maus and the general, paying no mind, share a glance.

Maus gestures to the staircase.

"Please. After you."

The general grunts in acknowledgement.

He ascends the stairs of light.

Maus comments to himself.

"I like that one."

Maus slips Silver Seal into the now-empty sheathe on his back. It barely fits — and he can feel the weight of it pulling down on his shoulders — but it fits well enough.

He ascends the stairs of light.

He also scoops up Deena.

She protests.

"Hey! Watch the merchandise!"

The two ascend the stairs of light.

Maus — Deena in hand — steps onto the lip of the valley. As he does, the stairs of light dissipate behind him. He feels the rumbling beneath his feet once more.

The unicorns stare off in the distance, all gathered a few paces ahead.

Maus joins them.

"What is it? See something?"

Aster squints.

"Not yet."

Her eyes search the horizon.

Nothing but the sun's slow decline. That, and the clouds gathering in the distance. But nothing out of the ordinary.

Deena pipes up.

"What are we even *looking* for?"

The princess replies.

"Anything."

For a few moments, there's nothing.

Nothing other than the wind.

The unicorns.

The soft, steady rumbling.

Then there's something.
A sound.
Or, rather, *hundreds* of sounds.
Thousands.

The uneasy snap of a forest of trees, falling one by one, all in a rapid succession. And — far to the north, what must be a week's journey out — they can barely make out the sight of the falling trees. *Mighty* ones, judging by their size at this distance.

Aster silently gasps.

"That's a *forest*... "

All those who can do so look closer.

The trees aren't just being broken.

They're being *uprooted.*

The ground below the trees begins to swell.

A hill begins to rise.

The rumble beneath their feet — their hooves — grows stronger.

In the distance, the hill continues to rise. The dirt of its surface cracks and falls away. Its grasses tear asunder. Thick spikes of dark rock pierce out from beneath its soil.

All manner of animals race out of the forest, the specificity of which can't be discerned at this distance.

The air feels the slightest bit thinner.

The sound of innumerable landslides echoes on the wind.

And the hill continues to rise.

Petunia speaks above the distant, echoed chaos.

"What's happening? What do you see?"

Aster replies, hardly believing her own words.

"The hills are beginning to move."

Delphi shakes her head.

"No. Not hills."

She pauses.

"Mountains. "

Were Petunia not pale, she'd turn white.

The rest of the hill falls away. It tumbles across the distant land, scattering heavy debris all over. Even more dark rock is revealed. And the dark rock continues to rise.

Large segments of land tear upward, leveling the rest of this distant forest. The sound of such heavy destruction echoes through the sky.

From around that distant forest, crowded flocks of birds take off, fleeing in all directions.

And the dark rock continues to rise.

What emerges is shaped like a head.

A very *particular* head.

A very *familiar* head.

Its appearance resembles something vaguely orcish, with its wide eye sockets and extended cheekbones, but it looks… *off* in its proportions. Wrong in a way that *feels* wrong. Like it shouldn't even exist. *This* head, however, is adorned with a pair of marvelous black horns, each made from that same jagged rock. A violent purple light shines where the eyes would be. That same light pokes through gaps in the rock all over the head, like it's peeking through cracks in its shape.

The unicorns — and Maus — and Deena — are speechless.

All they can do is stare.

Other people do the same for miles.

From beside the head, two massive sets of claws emerge. They, too, are made of the same dark rock. A slight purple glows from within. Boulders and trees are sent flying in a horizontal landslide. Almost all of the escaping animals are caught in its wake. Their shapes disappear under the flowing rush of land.

The mountain crawls out from beneath the ground.

It continues to rise.

Even from here, they can feel the sudden rush of wind.

But the wind isn't merely strengthening, *the very air is being displaced.*

The mountain steps onto one foot.

The impact of its single step shakes the land. They feel it under them. They watch the dirt ripple like water beneath its foot, just for a second.

Then they hear the sound of it.

THOOM!

They recoil a bit from the shock. The vibration rattles in each of their chests.

They're not just *seeing* this.

They're not just *hearing* this.

They're *feeling* this.

The mountain tears its other leg free from the ground, sending out a second landslide. The echoes of it carry on the wind.

The mountain straightens its second leg.

THOOM!

The vibration rattles in their chests once more. In their very *bones.* It is unwelcome.

Then the mountain stands.

The thousands of *creaks* and *cracks* of its body sound like an avalanche. It straightens its posture slowly. Not because it *wants* to move slowly, but because it *physically cannot move faster.*

Its entire body is made of the same ancient rock, its form riddled with cracks. Its bright purple glow shines within. Its clawed hands hang low, resting just below its knees.

It exhales.

Its breath flows into the wind.

It whips around the manes of the unicorns.

And the mountain breathes.

Princess Pipsy breaks the silence.

"Delphi?"
Delphi responds.
"Yes?"
The princess continues.
"Just *what* in the *gods-damn* everloving *fuck* are we looking at?"
Delphi says nothing.
Petunia speaks instead.
"Damnation."
She pauses.
"Our Damnation."
Slowly, the mountain turns its head.
The air around it whips at the clouds.
It looks down to the valley beyond.
Its head stops moving.
It looks directly at all of the unicorns.
Princess Pipsy groans.
"You've *gotta* be fucking *shitting* me."
The jagged rock at the corners of its mouth *cracks* and *breaks* and *bends.* A number of large pieces fall off. And it smiles.
It opens its mouth to speak.
And it does.
They watch its jagged lips twist and curl, forming words. Countless little bits of dark rock break off, falling downward.
But they do not hear it.
Not right away.
They feel the rumbles in the ground.
But the rumbles aren't in the ground.
The rumbles are in each of their chests.
They *feel* his words first.
Then they hear them.
Thousands of voices speak all at once, each in perfect unison. The deep thrum of the speech rattles

them further, both in body and in spirit. The words carry on the wind, only the echoes reaching their ears.

"Found... you..."

Damnation's grin spreads further, a smile just barely too wide. More bits of dark rock fall from his face. They tumble below, striking soil.

Damnation takes another step.

Chapter XX:
Showtime

Chapter XX: Showtime

THOOM!
Damnation moves slowly.
But he *does* move.
Deena stares, as wide-eyed as the others.
"Whelp. We're fucked."
Delphi speaks, too.
"What are we supposed to *do?*"
They all stand idle, frozen in horror and awe.

The princess's eyes drift to the displaced earth beneath Damnation's stride. To the landslides he caused upon emerging. She can't help but think of all the animals that were killed. That she *just saw* get killed. And she dwells on the true scale of his evil. The true magnitude of his festering hate.

Then she spots something else in the distance. Not *exactly* where Damnation is, though it may be quite close to his path, if not within it.

A city.
A kingdom.
It's tough to make out the details, but she can still see it, out there in the distance. She can still see its grand stone walls. She can still see the tops of some buildings within. And she can see little specks now scramble around it.

People.
She stares at the kingdom. Not at Damnation.
Then she speaks to no one in particular.

"They're all going to die."
She pauses.
"*All* of them."
Aster follows her gaze. She takes note of the kingdom.
"There's nothing we can do. That city is — *at minimum* — several days of travel. Likely more. We'd never make it in time."
Delphi speaks, hardly processing Aster's words.
"He's going to kill *everything.*"
Her voice chokes briefly.
"Just like he said."
Petunia speaks next, ever solemn.
"Then I suppose this is it."
A sad, still moment lingers.
The general frowns.
Then he turns to the others.
"Do you lot even *hear* yourselves?"
The others, in turn, turn to him.
He steps to the front of the group.
"Pull yourselves together! You are *unicorns!*"
He looks to Maus and Deena.
"Except for you two. But you live in this world, too. You don't have a fucking excuse."
Maus and Deena say nothing. They simply take in his words, as do the rest of them.
The general continues.
"*Neither do the rest of you!* And neither do I."
He takes a breath.
"We have lost *too fucking much* to go down without a fight. We have worked *too fucking hard* to keep our people safe. And we have lived through *too fucking many* insurmountable odds to die now. The very same thing is true for *every single fucking unicorn* that came before us."
He paces in front of them like a true general.

"For *years,* we have faced impossible challenges. For *years,* we have dominated *all* conflict. And for as long as this world has lived, our people have lived along with it. Do you *really think* our ancestors would allow their legacy to extinguish? Do you *really think* they would allow themselves to lay down and *die?"*

Delphi mutters, somewhat guiltily.

"No."

The general turns to her.

"What did you say?"

Delphi speaks up.

"No."

The general steps closer.

"I'm sorry, I *can't fucking hear you!"*

Delphi, more energized, shouts back.

"I said *NO!"*

Her intensity surprises everyone. Even herself.

The general mirrors it.

"NO! They would *never* give up. They would *never* take losses in strides. And they would *never* allow *their* world to be crushed by some low-life, piss-stained, power-hungry corpse of a gods-damn bloodthirsty *child!"*

Princess Pipsy looks impressed by his verbiage.

Not bad.

Damnation's next step lands.

THOOM!

The general looks to his monstrous approach.

"If we stand and do nothing, that undying bastard will slaughter us all. Wipe our people off the map. Our legacy will fade into nothing. There won't even be a world left to forget us. And everything — *everything —* will die."

He turns back to the others.

"I will not allow you to stand and do nothing!"

From deep within his chest — from underneath his bent, misshapen back — a subtle green glow comes to life. His eyes are overtaken by a magnificent glow of impossibly brilliant green. His horn, too, glows the same. He stands tall before the unicorns, a beacon that serves to inspire.

"I will not allow our people to fall!"

From the tip of his horn, strands of green sparkles — clusters of shimmering light — reach out to the unicorns in front of him. The magic audibly *pulses,* almost musical in tone.

Each strand connects to each horn. Its brilliant sparkles flow into them.

Princess Pipsy feels a surge of energy rush through her body. She feels strength return to her being, the likes of which she didn't know she had. She feels… *power.*

So does Aster.

So does Delphi.

So does Petunia.

They inhale deeply, each feeling the might now within them.

Maus watches the light show unfolding before him.

Deena claps and cheers, still in Maus's hand.

The green strands dissipate. Their countless green sparkles scatter into the wind. They rise into the sky like a field of verdant stars. Their color melds into the evening's final light. Then they fade into nothing, disappearing far beyond.

The general's green glow remains.

He looks among the unicorns.

"You aren't the only ones who got some magic back."

He locks eyes with the princess.

"Do you want to save our people? Do you want to save *those* people? Do you want to save *all* people?"

The princess hesitates.

The general steps closer.

"That was not rhetorical! *Answer me!*"

The princess shouts back.

"YES!"

Her eyes flash a bright, blinding red. They *crackle* and *snap* with violent electric energy. Her horn, too, does the same. She glows even brighter than before.

The general grunts, impressed.

"You have your mother's ferocity."

The princess's fearsome expression wavers but a moment.

Only she and the general notice.

The general turns to the group.

"With my magic, I have made you all mighty. Even mightier than you were before. It will not last forever, but it will last long enough."

THOOM!

The general steps over to Maus.

"He who carries Silver Seal, the blade that slew our people. Do you stand with this world? Do you stand with us?"

Maus nods.

"Aye. I do."

The general steps over to Petunia.

"She who lived beyond her days, who has lived through impossible odds. Do you stand with us?"

She nods slowly.

"I do."

Her horns brighten with brilliant white.

The general steps over to Delphi.

"She who has guarded our knowledge, who has brought back those who would die. Do you stand with us?"

Delphi furrows her brow. Her eyes glow a bright, golden yellow. Her horn, too, does the same.

"I better."

The general steps over to Aster.

"She who has guarded the princess since birth, who has guided our people for years. Do you stand with us?"

Aster nods.

"I do."

She takes a deep breath. Her eyes glow a radiant blue. Her horn, too, does the same.

The general steps over to the princess.

"Princess Pipsy. She who is destined to one day lead our people, who has stood against Damnation itself. Do you have what it takes to fight? Do you have what it takes to lead us?"

She nods, eyes and horn still *crackling*.

"I do."

The general stomps his front hoof. His ears pin back. He shouts at the top of his lungs.

"Say it like you mean it!"

The princess shouts back.

"I FUCKING DO!"

Arcs of red lightning *snap* out from her horn. Everyone feels a split-second flash of heat. More storm clouds collect in the darkening sky high above.

Deena leaps off from Maus's hand, springing into the air. Her wings, now dry enough to fly, keep her aloft. She cheers.

"YEAH! Give him hell, assholes!"

The general smirks, eyes still on the princess.

"Good."

He steps aside.

"Then take your place and lead us."

He falls back.

Princess Pipsy steps up to the front of the group as the wind whips over the valley, blowing her mane back behind her.

Maus takes his place atop Aster.

Aster glances back, acknowledging his presence.

Maus reaches to the hilt on his back. With both hands, he pulls Silver Seal from its sheathe. The weapon feels warm in his grasp. A soft *hum* emanates from its blade as the white glow of its runes brightens to life.

Damnation does not wait.

THOOM!

The princess speaks to the others.

"On my mark, we make way to that kingdom. Damnation will try to attack us the second we get any closer. *Do not let him hit you.*"

The unicorns nod.

Maus whispers to Deena.

"I get the feeling you'll want to hold onto something."

She blinks.

"What?"

Then—

"Oh! Shit."

She flies over to Petunia, grabbing onto her mane.

"Hey, hot stuff! Mind if I hitch a ride?"

Petunia responds with the slightest hint of irritation.

"Be my guest."

Deena giggles.

"Ooh, this is gonna be *fun!"*

Deena hugs Petunia's mane, unconvincingly feigning an emotional breakdown.

"If I die, tell my nieces I love them!"

Petunia responds with… confusion.

"I don't even know who you are."

The princess continues.

"Escort whoever you can. Push out civilians. Evacuate all those in the city. If we don't, not only will Damnation kill them, but they'll get in our way."

She squints at them all.

"So don't take too fucking long."

She looks back to the massive approaching Damnation, eyes narrowed.

"When that's done, we take the fight to him."

Damnation looks down at them all, still grinning. Still miles away. Still approaching.

Princess Pipsy shouts back to the others.

"Everyone ready?"

Delphi exhales.

"As much as we'll ever be."

Aster agrees.

"I think we are."

Petunia concurs.

"Then we are."

Maus grunts.

Ready.

Deena cheers. Her tiny, shrill voice pierces the wind.

"WHOO!"

The general, too, agrees.

"At your command, Princess Pipsy."

He looks into her eyes.

"It's been an honor to serve in your name."

The princess gives a single, firm nod.

She turns back toward Damnation, her gaze fixed on the horizon and the distant kingdom that sits upon it.

She inhales.

She exhales.

She feels ready.

She feels determined.

And she feels *angry.*

"Showtime."

Princess Pipsy takes off with impossible speed. An electric red glow trails behind her.

Delphi complains.

"That was our fucking cue?!"

She, too, takes off, her own speed equally impossible. Her brilliant golden light trails behind her, as Pipsy's did with her.

The general smirks. He chases after, his own green glow stretched behind him.

Petunia speaks aloud for her own sake.

"May our magic bring down that monster."

Deena throws a triumphant little fist in the air.

"Hell yeah!"

Petunia takes off.

Deena barely hangs on.

"Oh SHIT!"

Aster briefly looks back to Maus.

"Hang on!"

She takes off. The blue glow of her magic flows behind her.

Maus feels the wind whip at his face. It's an intensity — a speed — that he's never felt before. The air rockets through his hair. It soars across his body. He feels Silver Seal push back from the force. He quickly adjusts, maintaining his grip. Were his legs not as strong as they are, he'd be blown free from Aster's back. And a fall like that — at *this* speed? — would most certainly kill him, let alone *anyone*.

It takes a few seconds to get used to the movement. It's not often he rides on a steed that runs faster than most men can comprehend.

Not far ahead, the other unicorns race across the grassy landscape in a stalwart V-formation. Their colored glows paint the air behind them, if only for the briefest time.

Princess Pipsy leads the charge, her red glow *crackling* fiercely. Petunia and the general run on either side of her. Delphi follows the others at the left tail of the formation.

Aster catches up. She takes her place on the right. Her blue glow adds a welcome coolness amid the shine of the others.

Petunia glances over toward Maus and Aster. But she *doesn't* glance. Not really. She has no way to see.

It's almost like… she *sensed* them. Like she knew where to look, could she see.

Maus notices.

Petunia focuses ahead.

The unicorns charge on.

Princess Pipsy feels the ground skip out from under her with every step. With every split-second moment of each lifted hoof, it feels like she's flying… until the split-second after that brings her back down to the ground, only to cycle all over again. She doesn't even have time to process the imperfections of the land she's running across. By the time she realizes she stepped on a rodent — trampled a shrub — nearly kicked rocks — she's already hundreds of feet ahead.

It doesn't feel like she's running. It feels like the ground is running underneath her.

She really hopes none of them trip.

The landscape around them zips by. It looks like it's running just as fast in the opposite direction.

The air around them howls in their ears as they rush across the land.

The kingdom does, indeed, draw closer.

And at this rate, they'll make it in minutes.

But it's still a great distance away.

And it's going to take more than a few minutes.

Damnation's abominous form looms in the ever-shortening distance. He turns his head. The cloud above his horns whip into a momentary whirlwind. His gaze falls on the unicorns.

He stops smiling.

Boulders fall from the edges of his lips.

His lips form words.

And he speaks.

The vibrations reach them first. They feel their chests rattle, even now.

Then they hear the words.

"You… will… die…"

He takes another step.

THOOM!

He towers in the distance, now much closer.

The unicorns race on.

Aster shouts to the others.

"I don't think he'll be able to reach us!"

Damnation shifts his weight.

Tremors shake the land.

The very ground vibrates beneath them.

Damnation leans down. Fragments of his body break and crumble. Hundreds of fragments of rock hit the ground.

Princess Pipsy looks over.

"What the *fuck* is he doing?!"

Delphi quickly replies.

"Trying to reach us!"

Damnation's dark claws sink into the ground.

The ground *cracks* around his hands.

He pushes deeper.

The grasslands tremble.

The hills quake.

Damnation pushes his claws forward.

The ground tears away from itself.

The roar of a thousand crumbling rocks fills the air.

Massive chunks of the land fly upward.

Outward.

Toward the unicorns.

The gargantuan tidal wave of boulders and soil barrels toward them. It quickly closes the distance. Fragments of dirt and rock fly out in all directions.

Princess Pipsy screams out.

"Petunia!"

The wave of land approaches.

A deep, rhythmic pulse shakes the sky.

Damnation is laughing.

Deena's tiny hands glow blue. Still holding on to Petunia's mane, she presses her hands against her neck.

"Good thing I picked *you!"*

Petunia's white glow brightens.

She feels her power grow.

"By my light, *we will be safe!"*

Her horns *screech* with a shrill magical energy.

Beside the unicorns — and matching their speed — a translucent wall of brilliant white light appears. It stretches far beyond the length of their formation, towering at what must be more than fifty feet above them.

The rushing wave of land *smashes* into the barrier of light.

The sound of the wave breaking apart is nearly deafening.

Excess earth spills over the top of the barrier. It falls into the path of the unicorns.

They have almost no time to react.

Princess Pipsy shouts instinctively.

"Fuck!"

She barely dodges clumps of falling dirt and rock. Many still strike her back, breaking skin.

Small bits of stone hit the others, doing no severe damage.

Another large chunk of rock falls through the air. It strikes Petunia on the shoulder, drawing blood. She recoils.

Petunia stumbles a moment.

Deena nearly falls.

Petunia regains her footing.

But the barrier dissipates.

Previously held back, the piles of debris *pound* against the land, thankfully hundreds of feet behind them now.

Damnation takes another step.

THOOM!

The ground trembles once more.

He's getting closer.

Delphi calls out to the others.

"We won't have much time once we get there! It's gonna be close!"

Aster responds.

"It's *always* close!"

Then—

"Look out!"

A house-sized boulder soars through the air. Its jagged points cut through the wind as it flies. It arcs above them, momentarily blotting out the setting sun.

It falls into the ground a few miles ahead of them.

CRASH!

They have very little time to adjust.

Princess Pipsy fires a bolt of lightning from her horn.

KRAAAK!

Small chunks of rock break off. But the boulder remains.

Aster fires beams into the rock.

Pew! Pew! Pew!

Yet the boulder remains.

Maus straightens his posture.

"Get out of the way!"

Princess Pipsy bears to the side.

Struggling to keep a firm grip on Silver Seal, he brings the weapon high above his head. He swings it down.

An arc of white light rockets out of its edge. The arc *strikes* the boulder, leaving a heavy crack along the side.

But the boulder does not break away.

Maus groans.

"Shit!"

The general speeds to the front of the group.

"Watch out! It's gonna get rough!"

His horn brightens. It casts a vibrant green glow over the front of his body. Its magic *pulses* and *hums*. The green light under his hooves, too, grows brighter.

He lowers his head.

He picks up more speed, gaining ground.

His hooves *thump* with a deep, powerful echo.

The general pierces through the boulder.

The boulder explodes.

Its remnants scatter to the sides. A number of pieces fall from the sky.

The unicorns rush through its absence. Chunks of falling rock beat at their skin, tearing wounds. They each feel flecks of their own blood fly into the wind.

But they keep running.

The general drops speed. He grunts in pain, but wills himself through it. The rest of the unicorns catch up to him.

He falls back into position.

He gives Princess Pipsy a nod.

She returns it.

Damnation takes another step.

THOOM!

The unicorns rush on, cresting over a hill.

Ahead of them, the stone walls of the kingdom come into view. From somewhere within it, warning bells ring out.

Gong! Gong! Gong! Gong!

Petunia shouts above the chaos.

"Are we going to make it?!"

Aster responds.

"We're almost there!"

The princess glares back at Damnation. His form now crests over the landscape behind them.

Princess Pipsy replies.

"Well so the fuck is he! So *move!*"

No one objects.

Damnation takes another step.

THOOM!

Townsfolk flee from the kingdom, a number already long gone. Many run on foot. Couples and families cluster together. A handful of horses rush out from the gates, their riders' expressions of panic. Most pay little mind to the unicorns. Most are far too busy screaming.

The unicorns draw closer.

Heads turn, more aware of the approaching streaks of light.

Civilians start to run out of the way. Some dive.

The unicorns arrive at the kingdom.

But they can't slow down.

Princess Pipsy — concerned — calls out.

"Why can't we slow down?!"

Delphi replies.

"Because we're moving too fast to—"

The unicorns crash into the stone wall of the kingdom.

— — — — — — — — — — — — — — — —

Princess Pipsy comes to in a pile of rubble. Bits of cracked stone push into her body. Blood trickles out from all over. Her red glow has vanished entirely.

Screams echo all around her, some much closer than others.

THOOM!

The ground shakes. It brings her back to reality.

She scrambles to her feet.

She now stands on the other side of the grand stone walls. Massive chunks of it lay strewn about, all cracked and broken. She looks back.

A gaping hole sits in the wall, an entire segment of it — nearly twenty feet across — broken away.

Maus crawls out from beneath rubble. Deep scrapes and scratches cover his body. He coughs.

"Fuck me…"

He pulls Silver Seal out with him. Its runes have gone dark. He stands.

More rubble falls away. Petunia stands. Her head looks badly beaten. Her horns do not glow.

Princess Pipsy looks to her.

"How long were we out?"

Petunia responds.

"I don't know. Not long. Maybe no more than a minute or two."

Princess Pipsy steps back through the hole in the wall.

Behind her, the others emerge from the rubble, all still alive. Their glows, however, have faded.

The princess's hooves *crunch* and *clack* over broken stones.

She stares out into the distance.

Damnation is *much* closer.

She can feel the rush of air displaced with his every movement.

He takes another step.

THOOM!

Princess Pipsy runs back to the others.

"We're running out of time!"

Petunia's white glow reignites.

"We never had time to begin with."

She leaves through the hole in the wall.

The princess shouts to her.

"Where are you going?!"

Petunia speaks without turning back.

"I am going to do what I can. I may not be able to *see,* but I can *sense.* And that's enough."

She steps onto the grass of the hill.

Princess Pipsy stares out.

"Good luck."

Petunia doesn't hear it.

The princess turns to the others, all looking to her.

"Come on!"

She races into the city.

The general follows.

Delphi runs after.

THOOM!

From under a pitifully small rock, Deena crawls out, coughing.

"That sucked *ass!*"

Maus grabs her.

"We're not done yet."

He tosses her at Aster. Deena plops onto Aster's mane. She grabs hold of it.

Maus swings a leg over Aster's back. He adjusts himself, putting both hands back on the hilt of Silver Seal.

Aster takes off.

The city seeps chaos. Sparse crowds scream and run, seemingly with no direction. Aster's hooves *clack* across the cobblestone streets, hardly audible amid the panic and distant destruction.

Aster catches up with the others.

Princess Pipsy's red glow *cracks* back to life.

The general's green glow *hums* into being.

Delphi's brilliant yellow shines once again.

Aster's blue glow *snaps* back to full brightness.

The runes of Silver Seal glow white.

The princess calls out to the others.

"Lead out whoever you can! Split up and cover more ground! Don't die for these people, but don't let them all die because of us!"

The general replies, a bit of surprising enthusiasm in his voice.

"I haven't felt this good in *years!*"

He breaks off from the group, racing down the street adjacent.

Delphi turns to the princess.

"Try not to get us all killed!"

The princess frowns.

Delphi breaks off, running down a parallel street.

Aster splits from the princess, circling back to the wall they came in from. She shouts out as she runs.

"This'll make one hell of a history book!"

Aster runs out of sight.

Princess Pipsy charges on. Her hooves *clack* as she runs.

Then — somehow, over all the constant chaos — she hears a frantic sound.

Mrow! Mrow!

She stops running.

She turns to the source of it.

There — trapped at the top of a half-crumbled balcony — stands a frazzled cat with disgusting matted fur. Whether it's brown from grime or genetics is unclear.

"No fucking chance. Priorities."

The princess races past.

Mrow!

Damnation takes another step.

THOOM!

Petunia faces him. Her horns glow bright.

His form — that which she can't see — looms high above the landscape. She feels the wind whip through her mane, air displaced with each of his movements. His bright purple sockets stare into the kingdom behind her, still some distance away. He watches trails of color rush through the emptying streets.

Then he notices the glowing white shape that stands in front of it all.

He sees Petunia.

She doesn't see him.

But she can sense him.

And that's enough.

White light shimmers across her body. The glow of her horns brightens further, shedding substantial light on the space all around her.

More civilians flee from the kingdom.

Petunia speaks, her voice magically enhanced.

"I will not allow you to live *any* longer! By my light, *you will fall!*"

Her two horns audibly *pulse.*

Damnation inhales.

The wind recedes.

His lips form words.

He speaks.

But this time — being much closer — the sound has little delay.

"I… disagree…"

Damnation exhales.

The wind returns.

He takes another step.

THOOM!

Petunia charges forward.

FLASH!

A massive wall of light appears in front of Damnation's face.

He frowns. Rocks tumble from his lips.

He reaches up with one arm.

Petunia feels her mane pull in his direction.

He swats at the barrier of light.

A dangerous gust of wind blows toward Petunia.

The barrier *shatters* with a horrible sound, like a million panes of glass. It breaks into fragments, each one vanishing before it hits the ground.

Petunia runs closer.

FLASH!

Another barrier of light appears in front of Damnation, this one substantially thicker.

Damnation reaches up once more.

He swats at it.

The barrier *shatters*, as before.

Damnation inhales.

The wind recedes.

His lips form words.

He speaks.

"Parlor... tricks..."

Petunia continues to run.

FLASH!

FLASH!

FLASH!

Three barriers of light appear in front of Damnation's path, each one thicker than the last. Their light is all that separates this lumbering behemoth from Petunia below.

Damnation brings up his arm again.

But he doesn't swat at the barriers.

He reaches through them.

Petunia feels the torrent of wind rush at her.

SMASH!

His outstretched hand breaks through the first barrier.

Petunia mumbles.

"Shit."

SMASH!

His hand breaks through the second.

FLASH! FLASH! FLASH!

Petunia brightens more barriers of light.

SMASH!

His massive, jagged claws reach for her.

She exhales.

"Shit!"

His hand reaches further.

SMASH!

SMASH!

SMASH!

Bits of rock fall from his fingers, his hand still outstretched. Were Petunia not blind, she'd see ancient, mangled corpses woven into the rock of his body. Petunia's horns brighten further. An intense *hum* quickly builds.

"Shit!"

The edge of Damnation's hand rips into the dirt.

His fingers bend around her.

FLASH!

His fingers clasp around… nothing.

He tilts his head, confused.

Then he sees a bright, white light fall in front of him.

Petunia screams. Her long mane whips helplessly around her. Her legs kick and flail, touching nothing but air.

She has no idea where she is.

Damnation watches her fall. Then—

FLASH!

She teleports again.

Damnation spots her. She tumbles through the air to his right. He shifts his weight, preparing to reach for her. The ground *trembles*. Weaker buildings in the kingdom fall.

FLASH!

Petunia teleports again. She now falls at his *left* side.

Before he can reach for her—

FLASH!

She teleports again.

She doesn't stop screaming in terror.

The kingdom shakes from Damnation's constantly shifting weight.

Princess Pipsy races through a familiar street when—

Mrow! Mrow!

She looks.

The balcony actively crumbles from the vibrations in the ground. The cat backs up into a corner. Stone bits of it continue to fall away.

The princess sighs.

"Fuck me."

At the other end of the city, an elderly ottesh woman — not five feet tall, her fur flecked with gray — falls to the ground. Her grandson — holding her hand — falls with her. They both lie on the ground, wind knocked out of them. Behind them, a tall, stone watchtower buckles.

Maus — still atop Aster — watches the watchtower fall. He points to it instantly.

"There!"

Aster's eyes narrow. Her blue glow strengthens. She rushes toward it.

The bottom of the watchtower folds into itself like wet clay. It becomes nearly horizontal in moments.

SHOOM!

Vibrant blue light appears around the collapsing tower. It floats a few dozen feet off the ground.

Aster struggles to hold focus on such a large object. Loose bricks fall out, *cracking* apart on the street.

Maus hops off. He quickly sheathes his weapon. He rushes over to the elderly woman, helping her up.

Larger chunks of stone fall from the tower, the magic losing some of its potency.

Aster's footing falters. She barely catches herself. Panicking, she calls out.

"Hurry!"

Maus rushes them both to Aster.

He quickly helps them climb onto her.

More bricks fall from the tower.

Maus, himself, climbs atop her.

He shouts.

"GO!"

Aster turns around. She takes off.

The blue glow fades from the watchtower.

It falls.

The boychild looks back behind them, watching the rest of the tower fall as Aster just *barely* outruns it.

He screams.

And so does Petunia.

FLASH!

She teleports once more.

Damnation can't get a look at her for more than a few seconds before she teleports away.

FLASH!

And he grows irritated.

Aster runs out of the city. She stops beside the gates. The two civilians step off.

Maus looks to them.

"Go. Run. As fast and as far as you can."

They say nothing.

They flee.

Aster stares out at Petunia. At Damnation.

The general — green glow still shining — runs over to Aster.

"That everyone?"

Aster turns to him.

"Yes. I believe so."

Delphi leaps over a pile of rubble. She lands next to the general.

"It fucking *better* be."

She looks out at the towering form of Damnation, glad that *he* hasn't seen *them.*

Deena peeks out from Aster's mane, a little too excited.

"Did I help?"

Aster responds.

"So that *was* you."

Deena scoffs.

"Of *course* it was!"

The general corrects.

"If you recall, *my* magic would be responsible."

Deena shakes her head.

"Nuh-uh!"

Aster steps in front of the general.

"You can argue about this *later.* Where's the princess?"

Delphi groans.

"She's clearly not here *now.* Why does it matter?"

The general frowns, disappointed.

"Because we need all the help we can fucking get."

Delphi looks off at the constantly falling Petunia, vanishing and reappearing all around Damnation's head.

Delphi speaks.

"She better get here soon. Petunia won't be able to distract him forever."

From behind Delphi, the voice of Princess Pipsy —
somewhat muffled — speaks.

"She doesn't *need* to distract him forever. Just for
long enough."

Everyone turns.

The princess — eyes and horn still *crackling* —
steps out through the hole in the wall. She holds the
scruff of a grimy brown cat in her mouth.

She drops it. The cat scampers off, fleeing west.
Princess Pipsy rejoins the group.

She notices Petunia falling. And teleporting. And
falling. And teleporting. And falling.

She narrows her eyes.

"What the fuck is she doing?"

Aster replies.

"Something that's *working*. At least for now. She
clearly knows what she's doing."

Damnation swats at Petunia.

He misses.

Petunia shrieks.

FLASH!

She teleports again.

The general takes a deep breath.

"Well, unicorns… I think now's the time."

Delphi focuses on Damnation.

"A good a time as any."

Maus grunts.

What she said.

Deena merely giggles.

Aster, too, fixes her gaze on the monster ahead.

"Are you sure that we're ready for this?"

The princess shakes her head a bit.

"No. But we don't have a choice."

She glares at Damation.

"Let's fuck him up."

Princess Pipsy rockets forward. Her *crackling* magic trails behind her.

Aster follows.

Then the general.

Delphi exhales.

"We better not lose."

She launches after them.

Damnation swings his hands at Petunia, still teleporting around him. Her teleports begin to stall at times, then pick back up in urgency.

She continues to shriek through it all.

The motions of Damnation's hands — his arms — his *body* — tear through the air. Violent gusts of wind cut across the landscape. Weak trees tear up from their roots. Rocks scatter at high speed, constantly shifting.

The unicorns approach.

They feel the tremors in the ground intensify. And — as they do get closer — they see the trail of monstrous footprints behind the towering monster before them.

Maus feels a pulse at his back. Even sheathed, the piercing white glow of Silver Seal is evident. He clenches his thighs for stability. He reaches back, grabbing the hilt of the sword. He pulls it from its sheathe.

The wind nearly knocks it from his grasp.

"Shit!"

He fights against the current, taking control.

Deena hangs on to Aster's mane for dear life. She squeals.

Princess Pipsy flashes a glare at Maus.

"Do *not* lose that fucking sword!"

Maus — a touch irked — shouts back.

"I wasn't fucking *planning* on it!"

FLASH!

Petunia teleports again.

The unicorns continue to approach.

Despite extreme vertigo, Petunia turns her head toward them.

Toward Maus.

Toward Silver Seal.

She can sense it.

She knows they're coming.

She cries out, voice magically enhanced.

"Help me!"

FLASH!

She teleports again, appearing just behind Damnation.

Damnation — now with a clear field of view — spots the unicorns below.

A deep, rhythmic pulse rattles the sky.

He's laughing.

The rocks of his lips form words.

He speaks.

Each one of his thousands of voices resonates in everyone's chest for miles.

Everyone's.

"So... be... it..."

He shifts his weight.

The world trembles beneath him.

He takes a step.

THOOM!

The vibrations nearly knock the unicorns off their feet. They struggle a moment, but they steady their footing.

The unicorns draw ever closer.

Princess Pipsy shouts over the roar of the wind, her voice just *barely* audible.

"Split up as soon as we reach him! Attack from all sides! Do whatever you can!"

Delphi calls out in response.

"Are you *sure* it's a good idea?"

Her voice isn't strong enough to break through the chaos.

Nobody hears her.

The others begin to split up.

Delphi grumbles.

"Fuck."

She, too, bears away from the group.

The unicorns near the front foot of Damnation. The massive, cracked form of it *hums*. Its purple glow peeks through the cracks. Throughout his foot — throughout his entire body — mangled bones and corpses are packed and crushed into it, they themselves a dark and ancient color. They almost look like—

Realization hits Maus and the unicorns.

Damnation's body *isn't* made of rock.

It's made of thousands of corpses.

His figure towers over them. The unicorns continue blazing forward.

They gain ground.

Their magics trail behind them.

Damnation's foot is a mere few hundred feet out.

Princess Pipsy shouts.

"GO!"

The unicorns split up. Each one runs in a different direction, but all at incredible speed.

Petunia continues to teleport, still left with no other option.

FLASH! FLASH! FLASH!

She feels her own mental clarity blur.

She fights to stay conscious.

She's losing.

Damnation pays her no mind. His attention falls to the unicorns below.

Princess Pipsy's horn *crackles* louder. Large arcs of red lightning *snap* out of it. Her eyes, too, do the same.

Energy *hums* and *builds* at her horn.

In the darkening sky above, storm clouds thicken from nothing. They gather slowly overhead. Little red *snaps* and *jolts* of electricity flick between them.

Aster runs laps around Damnation's front leg, giving a substantially wide berth. From her horn, piercing blue beams fire.

Pew! Pew! Pew!

Each one impacts. Each one sends bits of bone and debris flying. But Damnation is massive. It's not enough.

Maus shouts above the wind.

"Let's give *this* a shot!"

He swings Silver Seal. The weight — the *wind* — nearly knocks him off Aster. The runes of the sword flare with the swing.

An arc of sharp, brilliant light jettisons out from the edge of the blade.

FWOOM!

It strikes Damnation's foot with a heavy CRACK! Bone and debris fall away. But with the scale of his body — the sheer *mass* of his form — the damage isn't substantial. It isn't enough.

He shouts.

"Fuck! What do we do?!"

Aster shouts back.

"Whatever we can!"

Maus nods.

He swings Silver Seal again.

FWOOM!

More bone breaks and flies off.

Delphi races behind Damnation's backside. Staring up at him, she complains.

"The fuck am *I* supposed to do?!"

The general races past. He shouts at her.
"Whatever you *fucking* can!"
Damnation — looking down at them — speaks.
His words rattle their chests.
"Bye... bye... bugs..."
He shifts his weight.
The landscape quivers.
Vibrations rock the ground.
He lifts his back leg.
He brings it in front of him.
Maus and the unicorns stare up, momentarily stalled by the sight of him.
Fuck.
Damnation lowers his foot.
Princess Pipsy screams out.
"RUN!"
They can barely hear her at all.
But they don't need to.
Everyone is already running.
Damnation's foot lowers further. *Faster.*
Petunia shouts amid teleports, voice still enhanced, though it strains.
"Fuc—"
FLASH!
"—king—"
FLASH!
"—help—"
FLASH!
"—me!"
FLASH!
"PLEASE!"
Damnation's foot stomps the ground.
THOOM!
The ground shatters under his foot. The land quakes around him. A heavy shockwave tears through

the dirt. Cracked segments of rock jut out from the impact.

Every tree within close proximity tears up from its roots.

A dust cloud rushes out.

The sound rips through everyone's ears.

Only Petunia's don't ring.

The general's bleed.

Those on the ground fly several feet into the air.

Princess Pipsy barely catches herself.

Aster stumbles over her feet. Maus and Deena nearly fall. Aster loses considerable speed, but managed to stay upright.

Delphi — vision obscured by the dust — falls.

The general trips over now-exposed rock.

The general falls.

High above, storm clouds continue to gather. They darken and fatten with moisture.

Delphi — ears loudly ringing, having been knocked far away — scrambles to her feet.

Aster looks back to Maus. She shouts.

"Are you alright?"

Maus shouts in reply.

"Wouldn't matter if I *wasn't!*"

Aster picks up speed. She circles back around, making her way back. Damnation.

Princess Pipsy feels energy build in her horn. Its *crackles* and *snaps* grow violent. Erratic. *Angry.*

The ringing begins to subside.

She loops back around, her course set once again for Damnation, still looming above them all.

The dust starts to settle.

Visibility returns.

The general lies unmoving, not a hundred feet from Damnation's front foot. His green glow flickers and wanes.

The princess sees him.
Aster sees him.
Maus sees him.
Delphi sees him.
Damnation sees him.
Damnation shifts his weight.
The ground trembles.
He lifts his front leg.
Princess Pipsy picks up speed. She screams in rage, her voice magically enhanced.
"NO!"
Thick bolts of lightning *explode* from her horn.
KRAAAK! KRAAAK!
Each one strikes Damnation's leg. Large chunks of bone break away.
But — like before — the damage still isn't enough.
Thunder *rumbles* within the dark clouds. Strands of red electricity flick between them. More clouds slowly gather, further widening the storm. *Forming* the storm.
Light rain begins to fall.
Princess Pipsy lets more lightning loose.
KRAAAK! KRAAAK!
From behind her, Aster fires her beams.
Pew! Pew! Pew!
Bones break off.
But it isn't enough.
Damnation lowers his foot over the general.
The general struggles to stand.
Delphi races in his direction.
Princess Pipsy screams at her.
"Heal him!"
Delphi screams back.
"Give me a fucking *second!*"
The general wobbles to his feet.
Damnation's foot lowers further.
Princess Pipsy reaches the general.

She mumbles to herself amid the chaos.

"This better fucking *work!*"

Her horn *crackles* louder. Massive arcs of lightning *snap* out of it, striking dirt. An audible *hum* builds. More and more thin flicks of electricity *pop* with quick jolts.

In the sky above, red lightning leaps between the clouds.

Rain continues to fall.

Aster continues to run.

Delphi continues to run.

Damnation lowers his foot.

Princess Pipsy's glowing eyes surge with intensity.

The *hum* of her horn goes silent.

*KRAAAK-**KOW!***

A *massive* beam of pulsing red *explodes* out from the princess's horn, made of hundreds and hundreds of *crackling* bolts.

KSSSSH!

The beam of lightning pushes back against Damnation's foot, not thirty feet above them.

Bits of broken bones fall from it.

Aster arrives.

She turns her focus to Damnation's foot. She fires beams into it.

Pew! Pew!

Maus hops off her back. Eyes locked on the jagged foot above them, he swings Silver Seal.

FWOOM!

Its arc of white light *crashes* into Damnation's foot. More bone splinters off.

It's still not enough.

But it's holding him back.

Delphi reaches the general. Her golden glow brightens.

The same glow appears around the general's body, completely overshadowing his flickering green. He breathes heavily, regaining composure.

Princess Pipsy's beam holds steady.

KSSSSH!

Aster continues to fire.

Pew! Pew! Pew!

Maus continues to swing.

FWOOM!

Damnation forces his foot further down.

It pushes against the princess's beam. Her hooves grind into the dirt. The foot lowers by several feet. Still, her beam pushes against it.

She screams out to the others.

"Hurry the fuck up!"

Delphi screams back.

"I'm *trying!"*

The general looks to Delphi, coming back to the present moment.

"What's going on?"

Aster stops firing her beams. She turns her head toward Deena, still tucked into her mane.

"Help her!"

Deena pokes out.

"I thought I was with you!"

Aster shouts again, angrier.

"Go!"

Deena frowns.

"Fine! Fucking asshole."

Deena zips out of Aster's mane, flying toward Delphi.

Damnation pushes his foot further down. It lowers another few feet.

The wind kicks up at the sudden jerk of movement.

The gust sweeps Deena away.

Her tiny voice shrieks.

Then she's gone.

The wind carries her high into the sky. *Much* higher than she's ever been before. Her body twists and tumbles in the rain. Her wings — now soaked and fighting against an onslaught of wind — are useless.

She feels herself swept higher and higher into the air. The cold rain pounds against her. She spins and spins and spins around.

She vomits.

The general feels the cuts in his body fold back together. Fractures and minor breaks — ones he didn't realize he had — *snap* back into place. He doesn't wince.

His back, of course, remains misshapen. But his ears stop bleeding.

He feels *much* better.

The yellow glow vanishes from around his body. The strength of his green glow returns. He looks around for the briefest moment, remembering where he is. What's going on.

He looks to Delphi.

"Can't hear shit. Pretty sure I just lost it for good. Always knew it would happen at some point."

Delphi frowns.

Not good.

Princess Pipsy screams at him.

"You fucking *what?!*"

Maus swings Silver Seal once more.

FWOOM!

More bones break away, falling down.

He shouts to the princess.

"He can't *hear* you!"

The general shouts to the others.

"Come on! *Move!*"

He runs out from under Damnation's foot.

Delphi does the same.

Damnation forces his foot further down. It lowers by *many* more feet.

Princess Pipsy stares up at it. She can make out the clusters of skulls and bones within it.

Maus swings a leg over Aster. He pulls himself onto her.

Aster takes off.

She shouts back to the princess.

"Come on!"

Princess Pipsy takes several steps back. Her violent beam holds steady.

Damnation's heel dips lower, less magic now pushing against it.

Princess Pipsy exhales.

"Fuck!"

She focuses.

KOW!

An *explosion* of lightning bursts out from her horn. It impacts the front of Damnation's foot.

Her steady beam dissipates. Her red glow remains.

She sprints away.

Damnation lowers his foot.

THOOM!

The ground rattles.

Thanks to the princess, that wasn't a stomp.

Damnation exhales, frustrated.

The wind picks up dramatically.

Deena falls prey to its whim. It pulls her in every direction, lifting her higher and higher. She feels the air steadily thin.

She can almost make out the form of Damnation's head through the black and purple blur all around her.

Wait.

That blur *is* Damnation's head.

Yikes.

Then—

FLASH!

Petunia teleports in front of her.

Deena collides with her neck.

Pap!

Deena groans. She holds tight to Petunia's mane.

The two of them tumble and fall, dropping through the wind and rain around them.

Petunia — speech slurring dramatically — speaks.

"What is that…?"

Deena shouts back.

"Hey, hot stuff! Long time no see!"

Petunia forces more speech.

"Please… help…"

Deena — strategically tying her arm to Petunia's mane — nods.

"You got it!"

She gives a thumbs up.

Petunia continues, consciousness actively slipping.

"Get… ready…"

Deena cocks her head.

"Ready for—"

FLASH!

They teleport away.

Damnation watches the unicorns race around him below. They're chaotic. Unbalanced. Unorganized.

Perhaps he gave them too much credit.

Princess Pipsy sprints along the scarred stretch of land around Damnation's feet. Delphi catches up to her.

Before Delphi can utter a word, the princess turns to her, furious.

"What the fuck was that? Try some *urgency* next time! You could've gotten us killed!"

Delphi looks taken aback. She responds.

"Magic can't solve *everything!* It has its fucking limits!"

The princess shouts back.

"We don't have time for limits! *Get your shit together!*"

Damnation inhales.

The wind recedes.

His lips form words.

He speaks.

"You... are... pathetic..."

He shifts his weight.

Tremors shake the land.

The countless *cracks* and *snaps* of his body sound like a landslide.

He reaches down toward Delphi and the princess.

Aster and Maus attack his hand from a distance.

Pew! Pew!

FWOOM!

But it's not enough.

The general — hearing nothing — runs the opposite way.

Delphi glances behind her and the princess.

"Shit!"

The princess shouts.

"Divert!"

She takes a hard turn, running laterally.

Delphi shouts back.

"Divert?!"

She takes a hard turn in the opposite direction.

Damnation's hand follows her.

It starts to close the distance.

Delphi picks up speed.

But it's not enough.

Aster changes course. She charges toward Damnation's outstretched hand.

"Delphi! We're coming!"

She fires.

Pew! Pew! Pew!

It doesn't do much.

Maus swings Silver Seal.

FWOOM!

Its arc flies out into the night. It misses.

Princess Pipsy catches a glimpse of the hand.

Of Delphi's futile sprint.

She exhales.

"Fuck me."

She turns back around, galloping full speed toward Damnation's hand.

In the sky above, thunder echoes. Red lightning flickers between the clouds.

Rain continues to fall.

Damnation's jagged fingers start to curl.

Delphi feels the constant rush of wind at her back.

She hears the ominous *creak* of the monstrous body behind her.

Aster screams out.

"DELPHI!"

The princess's lightning *crackles* erratically. From her horn, a *hum* quickly builds.

Damnation's hand draws closer. His fingers creep into Delphi's field of view, now impossible to ignore.

She mutters to herself.

"No, no, no, *no!*"

His fingers curl further. They start to block off her path. The edge of his palm *rips* through the dirt.

Delphi cries.

"No…"

The princess picks up speed.

Damnation's fingers close.

Thunder shakes the sky.

Princess Pipsy races through his fingers as they close.

In an instant, a *massive* bolt of red lightning arcs down from the clouds. It connects to the princess's horn.

She lurches forward.

KOW!
The air *sizzles* with energy.
Damnation's thumb breaks off.
His hand idles the briefest moment.
Delphi looks… surprised. Her ears ring.
Princess Pipsy looks into her eyes.
She opens her mouth to speak.
Blood launches out of it; Damnation's fingers grab *her* instead. Her eyes bulge out of her sockets. She feels her chest *crack* in his grip.
He lifts her high above the ground.
He doesn't even say a word.
His weight shifts.
The ground rumbles.
He lifts his other hand.
Princess Pipsy — face leaking blood — stares into the face of her Damnation. For the smallest moment, each one stares at the other.
Then the moment ends.
His other hand blocks her view.
Its massive fingers wrap around her upper body. She feels its jagged bones rip into her flesh.
Damnation pulls.
Her spine *snaps* in a microsecond.
Her lungs *explode* in her chest. Her heart ruptures. Her organs smear into paste.
Skin and muscle *rips* apart. Strands of sinew *snap* away.
Blood sprays out with the force of an ocean. Her mangled innards taint the wind. Clumps of loose meat fall from her body.
Damnation drops the two halves of her form.
Her allies — her *friends* — scream for her.
She doesn't hear them.
Her red magic fades as she falls.
Princess Pipsy dies.

Chapter XXI:
Master of
the Universe

Chapter XXI: Master of the Universe

Where am I?
What is this?

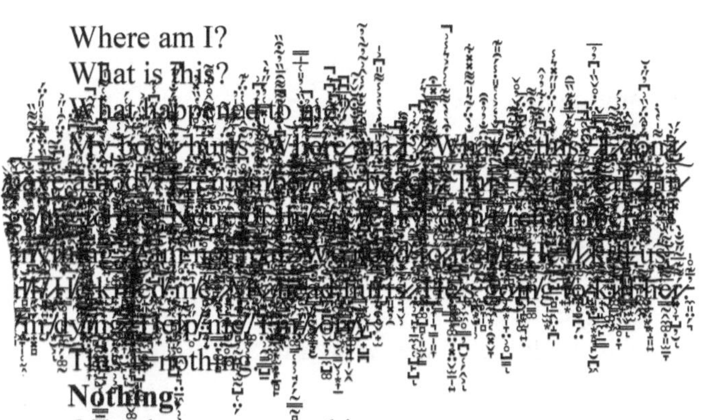

Or perhaps… *not* nothing.
It is calm.
It is cool.
It is quiet.
There is nothing here.
But there *isn't* nothing here. Merely unbeing.
Unbeing is here.
That's not nothing.
Princess Pipsy is dead.
But she *isn't* dead.
Not yet.
She could be, if she wanted to.
She doesn't want to.
Does she?
What happened?

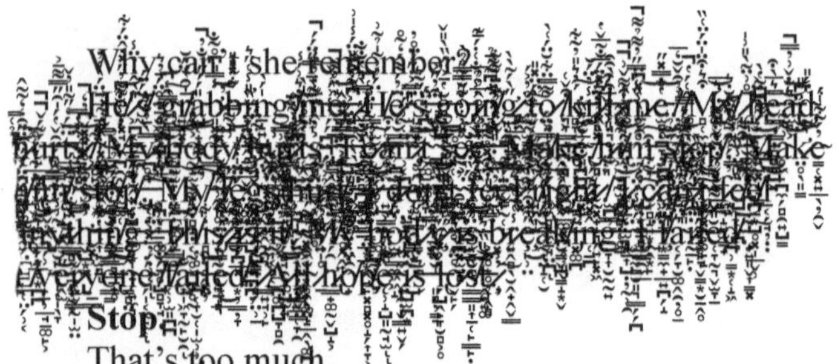

That's too much.

Focus on the absence.

Princess Pipsy *is* dead. That is an unchanging fact. No matter how strongly you feel, facts will not yield to your will. Facts do not give in to demands. Facts are unchanging and true.

Princess Pipsy *is* dead. Only fragments of fragments linger on in separation. Fragments of fragments of fragments of fragments of unknowable parts of her being.

But she isn't gone.

Not yet.

She could be, if she wanted to.

She does *not* want to.

She will not.

Others have felt so before. Been *here* before. Been *this* before. And others will again. Existence is cold. Ruthless, when it needs to be. And it *is* loving, to an extent. But it remains uncaring all the same. There is a place for everything, and everything — *everything* — returns to this place. This nothing.

But it's *not* nothing.

But it *is*.

Fucking semantics. It *isn't*.

This is not nothing.

It is merely unbeing.

Princess Pipsy *is* dead.

But she isn't gone.

Not yet.

Not until she chooses to be.

And she — like all others — will eventually choose to be.

Fuck you.

Princess Pipsy *is* dead.

But she isn't gone.

Not yet.

She is merely undone.

Unwound.

Unfinished.

A reflection of an echo of a memory.

Memory.

She remembers what happened. She awoke at morning's first light. She ran to her mother. She remembered the day before. She was foolishly excited at such a benign, simple thing. And the next day, she remembered remembering yesterday. And the next day, she remembers remembers remembers remembers remembers—

No.

That's not right.

That's too early.

She remembers… the beach. She remembers the gingerbread man. She remembers the dream. It happened so, so many times. She remembers—

No.

That's not right.

Still too early.

She remembers… memory.

She remembers the concept of memory.

She remembers what memories are.

Everyone has memories.

Even *she* has memories.

What *are* her memories?

She remembers Damnation.

She *hates* Damnation.

She *remembers* hating Damnation.

She feels anger stir inside her.

But there *is* no *her.* There *is* no anger. There *is* no memory to recall. These are all merely echoes. They reverberate infinitum in this place of nonexistence.

Big fighting words for a gods-damned fucking *concept.*

Princess Pipsy *is* dead.

But she isn't gone.

Not yet.

Not until she chooses to be.

She will *never* choose to be.

So here she unexists.

So be it.

Princess Pipsy *is* dead.

But she isn't gone.

Merely undone.

Unwound.

Unfinished.

What are her memories?

She remembers…

She remembers…

She remembers…

Damn.

Nothing.

Not nothing. Merely the absence of being. Unbeing.

Fuck you.

Princess Pipsy *is* dead.

But she isn't gone.

Merely unfinished.

What are her memories?

She remembers… that she *was.* That she *is.* Or… isn't. Not anymore. But she *was.* And still *is,* to some degree. But it's different. Not nearly the same.

What *is* she?

She isn't *anything.*

What *was* she?

She remembers herself. Not in whole, but in concept. She remembers the *concept* of herself. Of one's self. She remembers that she was once herself. She remembers that she was once a unicorn.

She was once a unicorn.

Hell yes.

She instantly loses the trail.

Fucking gods-damn bullshit fucking piece of shit bitch-licking useless fucking—

She remembers.

She remembers… *something.*

It *did* fade away, the thread. But now it returns. A memory of a memory. An echo of an echo. And perhaps it is here the echoes remain, in this place — in this *state* — of unbeing.

Fuck that.

The something surges into her, its roots in sheer vulgarity.

She remembers.

She remembers *herself.*

Not just the *concept* of herself.

Herself.

Princess Pipsy.

Princess Pipsy *is* dead.

But she unexists less every minute.

There *are* no minutes here. There *is* no here. There is only unbeing unending. There is only undoing eternal.

Fucking semantics.

Princess Pipsy remembers herself.

Not just the *concept* of herself.

Herself.

Remembrance rebirths itself.

She remembers Damnation.

She remembers the fall of her city. The fall of Unicornicopia. The slaughter of her people. She remembers feeling powerless. She remembers feeling weak. She remembers feeling angry.

But there *is* no anger. There *is* no memory.

Princess Pipsy remembers feeling angry.

She remembers the forest. She remembers the hills. She remembers the city. She remembers the bar. She remembers the cart she remembers the cell she remembers the fight she remembers her leg she remembers the house the chase the pass the trees the walk the talk the birds the breeze the fight the sword the doom the chase the fear the sprint the help the city the cat—

That cat tasted *awful.*

It was hard *not* to taste it. Not like she had any arms. Her options were fairly limited. It *was* a last-minute scramble, after all.

But why didn't she use magic?

There's a nothingness.

Or, rather, an *unbeing.*

Then—

Fuck. Yeah. That would've been smart. Why didn't she *think* of that?

She remembers why.

It was a scramble.

They were scrambling.

All of them.

She remembers herself. Princess Pipsy. Heir to the Queen of the Unicorns.

She remembers Aster. Right hand to the queen. Unwavering honor and loyalty.

She remembers Maus. Prisoner. *Was* a prisoner. Now an ally. *Was* an ally. She remembers resenting him. She remembers respecting him. She remembers both simultaneously.

She remembers the fairy. Gave herself a stupid name. She remembers not wanting to use it. She remembers wondering where she went.

She remembers Petunia. Mostly quiet. Always stoic. She remembers feeling grateful. She remembers feeling conflicted. She doesn't remember why.

She remembers the general. She remembers seeing him die. She remembers seeing him return. She remembers his unbroken spirit.

She remembers Delphi. She remembers lashing out. She remembers feeling bad. She remembers feeling regret. She remembers feeling shame. She doesn't remember why.

She remembers Damnation.

She remembers the fight.

She remembers the sacrifice.

She remembers the crushing and the breaking.

She remembers the pulling and the tearing.

She remembers it being too late.

She does not remember being dead.

But she remembers *being* killed.

She remembers being killed by Damnation.

She remembers *being*.

She remembers herself.

She remembers *all* of herself.

I remember myself.

Everything fractures.

Who am I? Where am I? Why am I here? I've been killed. I've remembered. I am. I am. I am. It's only you. Only me. Only—

This is all that will ever be.

No.

That was wrong.

This is right.

The balance is delicate. It always has been. It always will be. Nothing but the utmost deliberation will yield anything more.

She remembers… herself.

She remembers *all* of herself.

Her remembrances steady.

Her consciousness steadies.

She balances fragments of herself. The balance is delicate. It always has been. It always will be. But she remembers herself. And she can be *very* deliberate.

Yes. She remembers herself.

She remembers *all* of herself.

Her memory steadies.

Her consciousness steadies.

Where is she?

What is this?

She remembers herself.

She remembers her life.

She remembers her death.

She remembers it all.

Princess Pipsy becomes self-aware.

She opens her eyes.

She doesn't. Not really. She doesn't *have* eyes. She doesn't have a body at all. It merely *feels* like she opens her eyes. It is merely an echo of what she remembers it feels like.

But it doesn't matter.

She *feels* like she opens her eyes.

She *feels* it.

In a place of unbeing infinitum, she feels something.

In an unknowable expanse of unknowable unbeing, she *feels* something, which should not be possible.

But it is.

It continues to be.

She remains self-aware.

It is a delicate balance. It always has been. It always will be.

She's met worse.

Princess Pipsy *is* dead.

But she is not gone.

Not yet.

She feels a brief flash of panic. Of uncertainty. Not quite terror, but unease absolute. She does not know where she is — *what* she is — and she knows that she does not know.

There is it again.

Feeling.

In a place that, by its very nature, should have none.

But it does.

And she feels it.

Then she feels… curiosity. Intrigue. Interest. Enamorment. Sanctity. Quietness. Peace. Appeal. A pull. An offer. An option. A mandate. An absolute. A desire. A need.

No.

She is not meant for this place.

She *is*.

Fine. Then she *is*. But not yet.

Not right now.

She feels herself calm. She remembers feeling panic moments ago. Feeling uncertainty. Curiosity. Intrigue. All the other things that come with it.

But she doesn't feel all of these *now*. Not anymore. She merely *remembers* she felt them.

For a place wholly absent of feeling, she's doing quite a lot of feeling.

She remembers a few things.

She remembers a lot of things.

She remembers *everything*.

She knows that to focus on this place — to dwell on unbeing itself — is to unmake herself once again. She can feel it tug at whatever is her.

So she remembers.

She remembers *everything.*

And she feels something.

Something… *new.*

Something… *familiar.*

She feels anger.

Energy rises inside her. Which is *very* strange, considering there *is* no her. There *is* no energy. There *is* nothing else — *could be* nothing else — other than whatever comes next. That, and the endless expanse of unbeing.

Princess Pipsy, of course, has no regard for what *should* be. That's not her fucking problem.

She remembers what Damnation did to her people. What he did to her allies. What he did to her *friends.*

What he's *still fucking doing* to her friends.

And she feels *angry.*

She remembers the memory of what her chest felt like when it tightened. She remembers the memory of what her heart felt like when it quickened. She remembers how her upper lip raises. How her right eye twitches. How her brow furrows. How her muscles tense. How it feels to be *angry.*

Energy rises.

She remembers how it feels to breathe slower at first. Deeper. Deliberate. She remembers how it feels to be restless. How it feels to have the unyielding pressure of anger simmer inside her.

Energy rises.

She feels angry.

No.

She doesn't just *feel* angry.

She *is* angry.

For the first time since she died, she *is* something.

In an instant, she feels watched. She feels observed. She feels an endless collection of near-endless fragments of fragments of fragments. She feels them observe. She feels them regret. She feels them yearn.

But that's too bad.

That's not her fucking problem.

She remembers the pain. She remembers the adrenaline. She remembers the fury. She remembers that gods-damn fucking piece of shit monster that dares stand against the greatest fucking civilization to ever walk the gods-damn fucking piece of this plane of fucking existence.

Suffice to say, Princess Pipsy feels *very* angry.

Is very angry.

Is.

Energy rises.

Continues to rise.

And she only gets way fucking angrier.

She feels a current all around her. It flows like a web of electricity. She feels it tingle.

She feels it tingle.

This is not a memory. This is not an emotion. This is an *actual, physical feeling.*

In a place of eternal unbeing, Princess Pipsy has willed a new feeling into existence.

Not a memory.

Not an emotion.

An actual, physical feeling.

She continues to feel it. The tingles — the jolts — reach deep into her very being, whatever it may be. She feels them pierce the very concept of herself. She feels them push into the center of her identity.

Is she even a being?

Truthfully, it doesn't matter.

Because — right now — she *is.*

She knows it.
And she is very, *very* angry.
Princess Pipsy.
That title — that *name* — carries weight.
She's the *gods-damn* fucking *princess.*
Time to fucking act like it.
She feels the tingles grow stronger. Like thick electric pinpricks all over her body.
All over her body.
She feels electricity wash over her body.
Through her body.
It *is* her body.
It is *not* fucking *calm.* It is *not* fucking *cool.* And it's sure as hell *not* fucking *quiet.*
KRAAAK!
She hears the impact of lightning. She doesn't know how. She doesn't know where. But lightning doesn't care what she knows. The sound of it reaches her ears nonetheless.
The sound of it reaches her ears.
KRAAAK!
Lightning strikes out once again.
She feels electricity burn at her skin.
It burns at her skin.
Energy rises even further. It *pulses* and *hums* and it *crackles* and *pops* through whatever is her being. And it reminds her that she is *very* angry.
She feels moisture. It becomes very cold very quickly. She *hates* the cold.
KRAAAK!
Her eyes shoot open.
Really shoot open.
She sees nothing but red.
She *is* red.
She *is* anger.
She *is* fury.

She *is* rage.

She is Princess Pipsy, heir to the Queen of the gods-damn fucking Unicorns, and she *will not* allow some childish, piece of shit *abomination* fuck up the rest of existence just because he throws a *gods-damn fucking temper tantrum.*

KRAAAK! KRAAAK!

Lightning grows violent around her.

She feels her chest tighten.

She feels her breathing deepen.

She feels her upper lip raise.

She feels the bottom of her right eye twitch *just* slightly.

She feels the freezing cold condensation collecting on her skin. In her mane. Across her entire body.

Crackling energy rises.

She feels it rise within her.

She feels the storm around her.

She commands the lightning.

She enslaves the thunder.

She *is* the storm.

KRAAAK! KRAAAK!

The electricity fuels her ferocity.

Princess Pipsy is *not* dead.

But she *is* very angry.

Very, *very* angry.

She feels. And she breathes. And she *snarls.*

And though no one can hear her — for the first time since her death — she speaks.

"I'm gonna blow his fucking head off."

KRAAAK! KRAAAK!

KRAAAK!

The storm grows more violent. Erratic. Constant arcs of red lightning leap through the air. Deafening thunder rips across the sky.

She is a unicorn.

She is a princess.
She is aggression incarnate.
Princess Pipsy is not dead.

472

Chapter XXII:
Showtime
(Reprise)

Chapter XXII: Showtime (Reprise)

Delphi looks into the princess's eyes. She watches her open her mouth to say something. But she doesn't get the chance to say it.

Blood flies out of her mouth. It splatters onto Delphi's face. Damnation's fingers wrap around Princess Pipsy instead.

He lifts her high above the ground.

He doesn't even say a word.

His weight shifts.

The ground rumbles.

Delphi sprints away. She has to. She *must*. She *needs* to get away from him.

Aster and Maus stand idle. Both stare up at Damnation.

Delphi reaches them.

"What are you doing?! We need to *move!*"

Aster and Maus say nothing.

Aster looks *petrified.*

They continue to stare.

Delphi — now a safer distance from the monster — turns around.

She, Aster, and Maus watch Damnation's other hand wrap around the princess's upper body.

They watch Damnation rip her in half.

They watch blood and viscera surge out of her.

They watch Princess Pipsy die.

Damnation drops both halves of the corpse. They *splatter* onto the ground.

Delphi mutters.

"Fuck…"

Maus holds his solemn expression.

Aster remains speechless.

A deep, rhythmic pulse rattles the sky. It resonates in each of their chests.

He's laughing.

The wind recedes.

Damnation inhales.

His lips form words.

He speaks.

"Child's… play…"

His weight shifts.

The ground rumbles.

Damnation takes a step toward them.

THOOM!

The chase begins anew.

Storm clouds hang above. Arcs of red lightning *crack* and *flash* within them. Rain continues to pour.

Maus and the others stare in shock.

Damnation takes another step.

THOOM!

Delphi snaps back to the present moment. She shouts to Aster.

"Come on!"

Delphi takes off. Her yellow glow trails behind her. Aster stands frozen. She can't take her eyes away from the mangled corpse of Princess Pipsy in the distance.

Maus leans forward. He looks into one of Aster's eyes. His solemn look gives way to something more urgent.

"Snap out of it, or we're *all* going to die!"

Aster doesn't budge.

She doesn't even look at him.

She can't take her eyes away from the mangled corpse of—

The general races toward them. He sees Aster frozen in place. He shouts, voice magically enhanced.

"Move!"

He blazes past her, running onward.

Aster shakes her head frantically. She blinks, coming back to reality.

THOOM!

She panics. With quickening breath, she turns around, running full speed after the others.

Maus — still facing forward — turns his upper body toward the *very* close Damnation. He swings Silver Seal.

FWOOM!

Its brilliant arc rockets out. It collides with Damnation's front leg.

CRASH!

Heavy chunks of bone break away.

But — as before — it isn't enough.

Aster races on.

Delphi — keeping pace with the general — turns to him.

"Where the hell is Petunia?!"

He doesn't respond.

He notices her gaze. He shouts back in reply.

"I can't *hear* you! Remember?"

She does now.

She mutters to herself.

"Shit…"

The general continues.

"I'll do what I can! Just don't bother talking to me! Do whatever you need to! I'll catch on!"

He focuses back on the landscape ahead.

Delphi begrudgingly does the same.

Damnation takes another step.

THOOM!

Aster catches up to them. She looks confused. Shaken. Distraught.

Delphi turns to her.

"Where is Petunia?!"

Aster takes a moment to process the question, like her brain is lagging behind.

"What?"

Delphi repeats herself, louder.

"Where is Petunia?!"

Aster struggles for words.

"I don't know!"

The general looks back, noticing Aster. He shouts to her.

"Stay with us! We *cannot* afford to lose anyone else!"

Aster gives a weak, curt nod.

Damnation takes another step.

THOOM!

The wind recedes.

He inhales.

His lips form words.

He speaks.

"Nowhere... to... run..."

Above them all, the storm grows terribly violent. The clouds — swollen and dark — blot out the stars. Thunder *rumbles* within them. Flashes of red flicker and *crack*. The rain continues to fall.

Damnation's movements only strengthen the wind even further.

Far in front of them — way out in the dark — a white *FLASH* catches Delphi's attention. It vanishes the moment she sees it.

She calls out to the others.

"There!"

Maus and Aster scan the horizon. Nothing but dark trees and hills in the distance.

FLASH!

The white light appears once again. Still far away, but much closer now. Even the general sees it.

He mumbles to himself with pleasant surprise.

"Son of a fucking bitch…"

FLASH!

It vanishes again.

THOOM!

Damnation draws closer.

FLASH! Petunia teleports beside the group. She runs alongside them. Her legs wobble a bit — like her balance is off — but she keeps pace nonetheless.

Deena pokes out from the base of her mane. She waves enthusiastically to the others.

"Hiii!"

Delphi looks over.

"Glad you're okay, but where the *hell* have you been?!"

Deena scoffs.

"Asshole."

Petunia shouts in reply.

"I'm lucky I'm standing at all! I still—"

She wobbles. Her footing falters. She quickly makes up for it.

She continues.

"Something's not right in my head. On the inside. But I'm fine for now, thanks to Deena. She's been my eyes. Helped me get down."

She pauses.

"Sort of."

Deena nods.

"Rough landing, that was! At least *someone* appreciates me."

She glares at the other unicorns, as if to stir up any feelings of guilt.

They ignore her.

THOOM!

Damnation draws ever closer.

The unicorns are fast — certainly moreso than the average horse — but they don't have the same impossible speed that they did before.

Which means Damnation gains ground with every step.

He shifts his weight.

The ground trembles.

He leans down. He wraps his fingers around the base of a tall, mighty tree. He *rips* it from the ground. Dirt scatters to the wind.

He stands upright.

The ground trembles.

He wields the tree like a spear.

The wind recedes.

He inhales.

His lips form words.

He speaks.

"Try… dodging… this…"

He throws the tree at the unicorns.

Maus glances behind them. He instantly spots the approaching projectile.

"Incoming!"

Petunia's glowing horns flare.

Behind the unicorns, an arced wall of glimmering light appears. Its glow sheds light on the space all around them.

The tree collides with it.

SMASH!

The barrier shatters into countless dissipating pieces.

Aster shouts to the others.

"Brace yourselves!"

The tree collides with the ground. It loses none of its speed, sailing across the land. It carves through the dirt with its speed.

Its approach sounds like a landslide.

It crashes into Aster and Maus, launching them forward. Its wood *splinters* and *cracks*.

The displaced dirt lurches under everyone's hooves. It sends them flying.

The tree — broken in numerous places — skids to a halt.

KRAAAK! KRAAAK!

Lightning strikes out from the storm. Thunder rumbles through the sky. Rain falls down all around them.

THOOM!

Damnation draws ever closer.

Maus groans in pain. He struggles to stand. The moment he puts weight on his right leg, he falls.

"Fuck!"

Aster, too, struggles to stand. Thankfully — though her gashes *are* deep — she doesn't have any breaks. Merely flesh wounds.

Petunia wobbles to her feet. Immediately, she speaks.

"Deena. Are you alright?"

Deena flops out from her mane, tongue sticking out. *Dead.*

Petunia repeats herself.

"Deena? Hello?"

Deena drops the act. She looks disappointed.

"Yeah, yeah. Forgot you were blind. What a bummer."

Petunia thinks for a moment. Dryly, she responds.

"My condolences."

The general stands. He looks out to their approaching Damnation.

"We won't go down without a fight. I swear it."

Delphi stands. She feels a break in her front leg. Without hesitation, her golden glow appears around it. The bone *snaps* back into place. She cries out momentarily. Then it's over. The glow fades, and she stands.

She rushes over to Maus. She speaks.

"Hold still. I'll go as fast as I can."

Her golden glow appears around his leg.

Maus responds.

"What do you—"

SNAP!

His leg clicks back into place.

He cries out in pain.

"Ah! *Fuck!*"

The glow around his leg disappears. He stands, looking to Delphi.

"Thank you."

Delphi nods.

THOOM!

Damnation draws ever closer.

Everyone turns to him.

The storm rages on.

For that moment, they stare, saying nothing.

And for that moment, Damnation — the mountain that he is — stares back.

KRAAAK! KRAAAK!

Red bolts of lightning strike out from the storm. Damnation's horns just barely pierce its clouds.

Thunder rattles the sky. Its sound melds with the tremors in the ground, nearly impossible to distinguish.

Then they hear a voice.

A very *familiar* voice.

It shakes the sky harder than the thunder. It emanates from the very clouds above.

And it does *not* sound happy.

"DAMNATION!"

KRAAAK! KRAAAK!

Thick bolts of red lightning strike the ground.

Damnation shifts his weight.

The ground rumbles.

He looks up into the storm.

A deep vibration rings out.

He's growling.

Everyone looks to the sky. The freezing rain peppers their faces.

Maus speaks.

"No fucking way…"

Aster follows.

"It can't be."

Petunia corrects.

"It *can.*"

The storm grows wilder still.

And the voice — *Princess Pipsy's* voice — continues.

"You are *disgusting.*"

KRAAAK!

A *massive* bolt of lightning strikes the ground at his feet.

"You are *pathetic.*"

KRAAAK!

Another bolt of lightning strikes. It connects with his foot, blowing off a *considerable* segment.

"You're nothing but a big fucking amateur."

KRAAAK! KRAAAK!

Lightning strikes out. It knocks large pieces free from his torso.

"Leave my friends the *FUCK* alone!"

*KRAAAK-**KOW!***

A red bolt strikes out from the center of the storm, nearly thirty feet in diameter. It carves through Damnation's chin. More than half of his jaw breaks away. He stumbles back.

Thud… thud… thud…

The impossible bolt connects with the ground in front of the unicorns.

Dirt explodes from the impact.

Ears ring.

Debris scatters.

Then it clears.

Standing on the spot where the lightning struck — the *exact* spot — is Princess Pipsy. Her red glow seems *more* red than before. It shines brightest from her eyes and horn… but it *also* shines from her body, though subtle. What *isn't* subtle, though, are the streaks of electricity *crackling* through her mane.

She's not just *harnessing* the lightning anymore.

She's *creating* it.

The others stare at her, awe-struck.

Deena cheers.

"Like a phoenix from *fucking* fire!"

Princess Pipsy locks eyes with Delphi.

"I'm sorry."

Delphi doesn't know how to react.

The general speaks.

"Glad to have you back."

The princess looks to him. She nods.

She turns back to Damnation. So do the others.

He clutches the break in his jaw.

He looks down at the unicorns.

At Princess Pipsy.

She stares back at him. The very air *crackles* around her. Even from such a great distance, he sees it.

Suffice to say, she is *very* angry.

Damnation inhales.

His lips form words.
He speaks.
"*You... should... have... stayed... dead...*"
The other unicorns fall into formation.
Petunia — with her white — stands left.
"I feel much better about our chances."
The general — with his green — stands right.
"Let's make sure we *actually* fuck him up this time."
Aster — with her blue, and her rider's white — takes her place beside the princess.
"*Please* try not to die. Again."
Delphi — with her golden glow — stands opposite.
"Thank you."
Princess Pipsy stands at the front of the group. Violent red electricity *crackles* all around her. She holds steady eye contact with Damnation.
She speaks.
"Showtime."

— — — — — — — — — — — — — — — — — — —

Princess Pipsy takes off with a confident speed. Her electric red glow trails behind her.
The other unicorns rush after.
All except Delphi.
"I still think we need a *better fucking cue!*"
She gives chase.
Damnation stares down at the unicorns' approach. The storm above him *cracks* with flickering red.
He shifts his weight.
The landscape trembles.
THOOM!
He steps toward them.
Delphi catches up to the others. She shouts above the rage of the storm.

"What's the plan?"

She looks to Princess Pipsy.

So does everyone else.

She responds, words cutting through the rain.

"Split up as soon as we get to him. *But stay fucking close.*"

She stares ahead at Damnation.

She snarls.

"We're gonna knock him on his ass."

Maus nods.

"Aye, princess. I think we can do that."

The ground trembles.

THOOM!

The unicorns near his front foot. They begin splitting off from each other.

Maus swings Silver Seal.

FWOOM!

Its arc of light *crashes* into Damnation's leg. Chunks of bone fly outward.

It isn't enough on its own.

But it doesn't need to be.

Aster's horn *hums* with building energy.

Pew! Pew!

Her beams penetrate deep through the cracks of Damnation's form.

The ground trembles.

Damnation shifts his weight.

He stares down at Aster and Maus.

He brings up a hand, preparing to swing at them, when—

KRAAAK!

A bolt of red lightning strikes his other leg. Distracted, he turns his head. He watches Princess Pipsy gallop past, her very form still *crackling*.

The wind recedes.

He inhales.

His lips form words.

He speaks.

"Princess… fucking… Pipsy…"

She circles back, running toward him once again.

She furrows her brow.

"You're gods-damn right."

*KRAAAK-**KOW!***

A thick bolt of lightning *explodes* out from her horn. It strikes Damnation's shoulder. Chunks of bone blast away. He recoils from the impact.

His focus locks on to the princess.

The ground trembles.

He steps toward her.

THOOM!

The ground — sufficiently soaked — sinks *just* a bit deeper under him.

Petunia gallops behind him. The glow of her horns flares bright. She calls out to Deena.

"Ready?"

Deena presses her tiny, glowing hands onto Petunia's neck. She shouts back, ecstatic.

"Ready!"

Petunia gallops on.

She breathes.

She focuses.

And she *senses*.

SHOOM! SHOOM! SHOOM!

Towering walls of light — nearly twenty feet tall — appear behind Damnation's legs.

He sees them.

But he doesn't care.

He takes another step toward the princess.

THOOM!

Deena grumbles.

"Shit! I *really* thought that would do it!"

Petunia's horns flare once again. The walls of light vanish. She speaks.

"No matter. We simply try again."

She steels her resolve.

"By our light, this monster *will* fall."

Princess Pipsy sprints toward Damnation. She fires another red bolt from her horn.

KRAAAK!

It strikes Damnation's knee. Segments of bone break away.

The ground rumbles.

He shifts his weight.

He reaches for her.

The *creaking* and *cracking* of his body sounds like an avalanche.

The horn of the princess *hums* and *snaps* and *crackles* with building energy.

Damnation's heavy hand draws closer.

Closer.

Then—

*KRAAAK-**KOW!***

Another massive bolt — nearly a dozen feet in diameter — *explodes* out from the tip of her horn. It strikes Damnation's hand, cracking the bones of his pinky. Sizable chunks blast away.

Damnation retracts his hand.

His pinky falls off.

Delphi and the general gallop together, cresting past Damnation's left side.

They both glance up.

Damnation's pinky plummets.

CRASH!

It lands directly in their path. Dozens of rocks — small chunks of bone — fall around it.

Delphi prepares to turn back.

The general shouts.

"No! I got this! Do not yield!"

His horn — his eyes — flare bright green. The light under his hooves, too, grows brighter. He picks up considerable speed.

Delphi — wisely — falls behind.

The general lowers his horn.

He picks up more speed.

His hooves *thump* with a deep, powerful echo.

The general pierces the crumbling finger.

It explodes.

Heavy fragments whir past Delphi's head, just barely missing. She yelps.

The general looks back.

"Next time, stay behind me!"

Delphi mutters.

"Please don't let there be a next time…"

Aster curves around the front of Damnation. She passes the princess. The two exchange a single, firm nod.

Damnation shifts his weight.

The ground rumbles.

He lifts his front foot.

Aster sprints under it. She shouts back to Maus.

"Fuck him up!"

Maus grunts.

"With pleasure."

His muscles tense. With all his might, he swings Silver Seal toward the sky as Damnation lowers his foot.

FWOOM!

Its arc *crashes* into the bottom. Heavy segments break off, tumbling down. Aster deftly weaves through them.

Damnation retracts his foot. He takes a step back.

THOOM!

From the ground, Delphi *FLASHES* the glow of her horn. Its light is nearly blinding. The general can hardly look at it.

Damnation can't.

He takes another step back.

THOOM!

His foot sinks *just* a bit deeper than before. Petunia races past his rear once again. She calls out to Deena.

"Now?"

Deena — a little *too* excited — shouts back.

"Kick it!"

Petunia's horns flare once again.

She breathes.

She focuses.

She senses.

SHOOM! SHOOM! SHOOM!

Walls of white light appear behind Damnation's feet once again.

Aster and Maus charge at his front. Aster fires her beams into his face.

Pew! Pew! Pew!

Damnation raises a hand, blocking the strikes.

The wind kicks up in response.

Maus swings Silver Seal as hard as he possibly can.

FWOOM!

Its arc rockets out. It *crashes* into the shin of Damnation's front leg, knocking even more fragments away.

Delphi continues running alongside the general. Her horn *FLASHES* over and over.

Princess Pipsy races back to the front of Damnation, joining the others. Her commands cut through the chaos of the storm.

"Petunia is ready! Hit him with everything you've got! *Do… not… YIELD!*"

Her horn quickly charges with energy.

The violent storm above *pulses* red.

KRAAAK-

Lightning strikes out from it, connecting with the tip of her horn.

-KOW!

A massive beam of pulsing red *explodes* from the princess's horn, made of thousands and thousands of *crackling* bolts.

KSSSSH!

It blasts into Damnation's torso, scattering heavy chunks of bone. It *pushes* against his monstrous form.

And he *feels* it.

The wind recedes.

He inhales.

His lips form words.

He speaks.

"You… cannot… kill… me…"

Maus hops off of Aster's back. He steps up to Princess Pipsy's side. Eyes locked on Damnation, he takes a wide swing with Silver Seal.

FWOOM!

"I beg…"

FWOOM!

"…to fucking…"

FWOOM!

"*…DIFFER!*"

Each arc *crashes* into the front of Damnation's body, pushing against his form.

Princess Pipsy's beam holds steady.

KSSSSH!

Maus feels his muscles burn. He continues to swing.

FWOOM! FWOOM!

Aster stands beside Maus. Her glow flares bright. Then — from the tip of her horn — a pulsing blue beam fires outward. It melds into Pipsy's, the strength of both combining.

It pushes harder against Damnation's chest.

Delphi stands on the opposite side of the princess. Her glow flares bright. Then — from the tip of her horn — a translucent yellow beam blasts out. It melds into the other two, each color still distinct.

It pushes even harder.

Damnation takes a single step back to steady himself.

THOOM!

It shakes the ground.

His back heel scrapes against Petunia's walls of light.

And they hold.

Petunia — still positioned behind him — shouts to Deena.

"How's it look?"

Deena shouts back.

"Like we should *run like hell!*"

Petunia nods. She takes off, making as much distance as she can.

Maus continues to swing wildly.

FWOOM! FWOOM!

His muscles burn. His body slows. But he *does not* stop.

The general stands beside Delphi. His own glow flares as well. Then — from the tip of his horn — violent, erratic green sparkles burst forth in a marvelous steady beam. It sounds almost musical in tone. It melds into the others, its sparkles spread throughout.

The combined beam *pulses.*

It *hums.*

And it *expands.*

The colors mesh together at the far end of the beam, its color there a dazzling, brilliant white.

More heavy chunks of bone break away from his chest, exposing more of the glowing purple shell beneath.

It pushes harder against Damnation.

Much harder.

Damnation starts to lean.

Princess Pipsy's hooves dig deep into the wet earth, feeling the push back of her own magic beam. But her footing *does not* falter.

She screams above the very storm.

Her storm.

*"Do... not... **YIELD!**"*

Deena stares at the marvelous light show from a distance, eyes wide, jaw slack. She is utterly speechless.

The beam pushes further against Damnation's chest. *Into* his chest.

Krrk...

His purple shell cracks.

Krrk... krrk...

The beam forces him further back. He takes another step back to steady himself.

THOOM!

Both heels push against Petunia's walls of light.

The barriers hold.

The wind recedes.

Damnation speaks.

"You... will... fall..."

Princess Pipsy snarls.

"Poor choice of fucking words."

Her magic surges.

The collective beam surges.

Krrk...

Krrk...

Sound cuts out for a moment.

Then—

*THRA-**GOOM!***

A gargantuan explosion rocks Damnation's chest. Large chunks of bone *fracture* and *crack.*

Maus and the unicorns fly back from the shockwave of air — of sheer *force* — it creates.

The collective beam dissipates.

Damnation touches the massive hole in the front of his chest. He feels the break in his purple shell. And he stumbles back. This time, there's nowhere else to go.

Petunia's barriers of light catch his heels.

The brunt of his weight pushes against them.

They *shatter* into a thousand dissipating pieces.

But it doesn't matter.

Their work is done.

Damnation falls.

Petunia races to the others. Her horns flare. A dome of white light appears around them all, shielding them from what could truly be an actual deafening sound.

The fall sounds like that of a mountain.

Because it *is.*

Thankfully, none of them hear it.

Dirt and debris pushes hard against the barrier. *Hard.*

But it does not break.

It does not yield.

Petunia does not yield.

Rain washes over the barrier.

The dust settles.

The storm lingers on.

And — far, far in front of them — now truly
resembling a mountain of the land — lies the massive,
unmoving body of hard, ancient bone.

Damnation has fallen.

———————————————————————————————

But he is not dead.

Not yet.

That's the very first thing they all notice.

Then, of course, they notice the crater around him.

He lies on his back, facing the sky. His head —
half-buried in the mud — is stuck to the side, unable to
move.

His body is broken and fractured, *especially* his
torso. The pulsing glow of his purple shell is quite
visible, as is the jagged hole at the center of his chest.

But the purple shell remains.

His *magic* still remains.

That's how they know he's alive.

The unicorns approach, Maus on Aster once again.
Even lying on his back, his form still towers over them,
at least a hundred feet tall. *Almost a quarter of his
standing height.*

The unicorns gather within view of the head.
Maus hops down from Aster, still holding tight to Silver
Seal. His arms struggle to support the full weight of the
weapon, but he does not sheathe it. He refuses to. Not
until all this is done.

The storm in the sky rages on.

The cool rain continues to fall.

Aster speaks first.

"I don't understand. We hit him with everything we
had. He should be *dead.*"

Petunia exhales.

"Damnation is, if nothing else, resilient."

Lightning *cracks* in the distance. Thunder echoes through the sky.

Delphi responds.

"Then how the *fuck* do we kill him?"

They all turn toward the wall of his torso.

The general speaks.

"I don't think he's dead. Which begs the question, how do we—"

Delphi bumps his shoulder to get his attention. She shakes her head gently.

"Wha— oh. Got it. Understood."

Princess Pipsy addresses the group.

"Clearly we need to get inside. And that means we need to climb."

Deena — still in Petunia's mane — gasps in horror.

"You want to go *inside* the big scary monster?!"

Everyone ignores her.

The princess steps up to Petunia.

"Care to assist?"

Petunia replies.

"Gladly."

Her horns flare.

A white glow appears beneath her hooves.

She ascends Damnation's body, leaving steps of light behind her.

Princess Pipsy follows.

Then Aster.

Then Delphi.

Then the general.

Then Maus.

The wind — while having calmed somewhat — continues to blow.

Maus feels it push against him. Feels the rain wash across his body. Each drop splatters against the stairs of light.

He continues to ascend.

He can't help himself.
He glances down.
His footing slips.
He—
The general catches the back of Maus's armor in his teeth.
Maus breathes heavily.
The general speaks, voice muffled.
"Careful, son. That's a *long* way down."
Maus regains his footing.
The general releases him.
Both continue up the stairs of light.
Lighting *cracks* the distant sky. Thunder rumbles through the air.
Maus and the unicorns step onto the torso of Damnation. Here, the sense of his scale sets in. Atop his torso, *it's as wide as the distance they just ascended.*
The ground — or, more accurately, his *body* — feels rough and jagged under them. Cracks and breaks of varying depths riddle the body all over. Every step, if not careful, could be a wrong one.
Purple light flickers from below.
It emits a soft, subtle *hum*, hardly discernible amidst the storm.
Princess Pipsy stops at the bottom of the chest.
The other unicorns join her. They all stare down at something.
Maus, too, joins the group. He follows their gaze.
There it is.
At the top of his chest — right where the top of the sternum would be — sits a charred, gaping hole. Sharp edges of his flickering shell poke in a bit further, having been damaged less than his exterior. Even still, the hole itself is easily the width of a house.
Below it is something… *wet.*

Not that the rain isn't helping that fact. But it looks just a bit more… organic. Moreso than his ancient exterior, that's for sure.

And it smells *bad*.

At this point, Maus and the unicorns have been through worse. None of them flinch at the stench.

Deena vomits into Petunia's mane just a little. She hopes she doesn't notice.

Petunia does. She simply elects not to mention it.

Princess Pipsy addresses the others.

"I'm willing to bet he's inside there. Whatever's *really* him. Even if we can't kill *this*, I think we can probably kill *that*."

Petunia takes a step forward.

"In that case, it only makes sense to—"

The ground rumbles beneath them.

Damnation rumbles beneath them.

His lips *twist* and *crack*.

They form words.

And he speaks.

"You… have… not… won… yet…"

Every syllable shakes their core. Their chests all tighten on instinct.

And he continues to speak.

"Death… is… all… around… you…"

Delphi responds.

"What does he mean by that?"

The purple glow beneath them pulses. Surges. *Flares.*

The rumbles worsen.

Delphi shouts.

"What the *fuck* does he mean by that?!"

Portions of his body *crack* and *break*, jutting out.

No.

They aren't breaking.

They're *rising*.

Clawing out of him.

Ancient bones begin to rise up from the very body they create.

They *creak.* They *crack.* They *rattle.*

And they *stand.*

Those with skulls attached have small purple flames in their sockets.

And — one by one — they approach the unicorns.

Princess Pipsy exhales.

"You've gotta be fucking kidding me."

Aster fires beams from her horn.

Pew! Pew! Pew!

Each one strikes a skeleton, shattering its bones.

But there are a *lot* of skeletons.

And — one by one — they continue to unform his body, approaching the unicorns.

Maus steadies Silver Seal. He grunts in pain.

"Here we go again."

Exertion setting in — and fighting through it — he swings the blade.

FWOOM!

Its arc of light rockets out, striking a cluster of skeletons. They *snap* and *break* apart.

But there are a *lot* of skeletons.

Princess Pipsy wastes no words.

KRAAAK!

Red lightning leaps from her horn. It tears through another cluster of skeletons. Their bones *clatter* to the ground. The ground of which even more skeletons rise from.

Delphi — unsure what to do — fires her own golden beam at a skeleton.

Shoom!

The bones of the skeleton burn, evaporating the rain around it. The skeleton collapses under itself, falling to pieces.

Delphi silently gasps.

"I can *do* something! I can finally fucking *do* something!"

She fires more beams.

Shoom! Shoom! Shoom!

She laughs.

"So *this* is how it feels!"

The general smirks. His green glow flares. The light under his hooves strengthens.

"I've always wanted to do this."

He charges into the skeletons with reckless speed.

They *explode* into pieces as he crashes through them.

Aster continues to fire into the slowly amassing horde.

Pew! Pew!

Maus — pushing his limits — continues to swing.

FWOOM!

He sweats. He breathes shallow. His body burns with a painful exertion. But *he does not fall.*

He swings once more.

FWOOM!

Delphi, too, fires into the skeletons.

Shoom! Shoom! Shoom!

And the general — unusually giddy — smashes through even more groups of them.

But there are a *lot* of skeletons.

More crawl up the torso, joining the fray.

The unicorns are barely holding them back.

Petunia stands nervously behind the others.

Princess Pipsy fires into the horde.

KRAAAK!

She breathes. Then—

KRAAAK!

She calls out to the others.

"This doesn't make sense!"

KRAAAK!
Maus pants.
"You're damn fuckin' right."
He forces another swing.
FWOOM!
Princess Pipsy shakes her head.
"No! I mean—"
KRAAAK!
"—this is too easy!"
Petunia's head jerks toward Damnation's.
"I sense something."
She faces the princess.
"I don't like it."
Damnation's lips *twist* and *crack* yet again.
They form words.
And he speaks.
"I... am... your... Damnation..."
His massive jaw — the half that remains — *pushes* and *SNAPS* out of place. It digs into the mud, forcing itself wide. *Unnaturally* wide.

Deep in his mouth, a bright cluster of purple sparks *flickers* and *crackles* to life. It builds an audible, ominous *hum.*

Maus catches a glimpse. He shouts.
"Looks like we're *really* fucked this time."
FWOOM!
He continues.
"Been almost nice knowing you."
FWOOM!
Princess Pipsy shouts.
"Delphi!"
KRAAAK!
She continues.
"How bad is it?"
Shoom! Shoom!
Delphi responds.

"Judging by the size of him, and assuming that his beam scaled along with the rest of his body…"

Shoom!

She continues.

"Yeah. We're *really* fucked."

Shoom!

She turns to the princess.

"So stop wasting time and *kill* this son-of-a-bitch, before he vaporizes half the fucking continent!"

The ominous *hum* grows louder. Previously drowned out by the storm, it now starts to overpower it.

Princess Pipsy shouts above the chaos.

"Unicorns! Petunia comes with me! Maus comes with me! The rest of you, *keep fucking fighting!"*

Petunia's horns flare. The light under her hooves does the same.

She turns her head toward Deena.

"You'll be more useful here. Stay with them. Do whatever you can."

Petunia continues.

"And *please,* stop calling me *hot stuff."*

Deena unties her arm from Petunia's mane. She flies out.

"No promises!"

She zips off toward the other unicorns.

The *hum* continues to build. The sparks in Damnation's mouth grow brighter.

Petunia quickly descends into the chest hole, leaving stairs of light behind her.

Princess Pipsy hurries after.

Maus wordlessly follows.

The sickly sweet stench grows much stronger. Now inside, the glows of the unicorns — and of Silver Seal — illuminate the space.

While the exterior was made of hardened, ancient bone, the *interior* is not nearly as ancient.

Damnation's interior is made of rank, rotting flesh.

No organs. Just cavernous space, and the flickering magic shell that holds it together.

Maus looks around.

"Good thing I'm too burned out to vomit."

Princess Pipsy rushes onward.

"We're running out of time! *Come on!*"

Petunia and Maus run after.

Outside of the hole, the others fight on. With less offensive power, the skeletons push closer in. They nearly surround the hole.

But they haven't reached them yet.

Aster fires into the horde.

Pew! Pew! Pew!

Delphi, too, fires beams into them.

Shoom! Shoom!

Camaraderie — and deep respect — flows between them both.

The general plows through more skeletons. Their bones *clatter* and fall.

Deena zips through the shuffling figures, eyes locked onto the green blur crashing through them.

"Oh, *general!* Whatever your name is! I'm here to *assist* you!"

She's no match for his speed, especially in the wind of the storm.

She flies after him anyway.

The ominous *hum* continues to build.

Inside Damnation, Princess Pipsy races ahead. Petunia and Maus trail behind. Their steps *squish* into the wet, fleshy ground. It slows their speed somewhat, but not enough to make a difference.

The flesh tunnel narrows.

And narrows.

And narrows.

It forces them to proceed single-file. The slimy residue of the walls brushes across the sides of their bodies.

Still, they press on.

Deena flies after the general. Each time she gets close, he takes a hard turn, rushing off again.

She groans.

"General! I'm trying to *help* you! Come here!"

She flies past the edge of the torso.

A skeleton climbs up over it.

Deena sails right into its eye socket.

The skeleton steps onto the torso. It claws at her with its long, bony fingers.

Deena pushes herself into its deepest point. She whimpers.

Princess Pipsy presses on. The other two follow closely.

The tunnel widens out to a large chamber, this, too, lined with similar rotten flesh.

This isn't the head, but it's *very* close to it.

At the center of the chamber — embedded within a cocoon of swirling purple magic — the jawless, limbless body of a ten-year-old boy dangles, suspended by thick branches of flesh.

Princess Pipsy enters, as do Maus and Petunia.

The voice of Damnation — the *real* voice of Damnation — speaks into their very minds. The voice sounds like that of a child's, but one that's been burdened with wisdom.

"Welcome, Princess Pipsy. And behold, the Damnation your people have wrought."

Deena pushes herself deeper into the socket. She tries to flatten herself against it. The skeleton continues reaching in for her. Clawing at her. The jagged tips of its fingers scratch her body. She cries.

Her blue glow attracts more skeletons.

Many more skeletons.

Aster notices.

Pew! Pew!

She shouts to Delphi.

"Deena's trapped! We can't let her die!"

Shoom! Shoom!

Delphi responds.

"We don't have a fucking *choice!*"

The skeletons continue to surround them. Both unicorns take several steps back, inching toward the hole.

More skeletons crowd around Deena. They all reach for the glowing blue socket, clawing at her. Scratching her. Nearly climbing over each other.

She wails.

The general *crashes* through more skeletons. They continue to gather. He circles back around, planning to make another pass.

He sees the blue glow of a skeleton's socket.

He does not hesitate.

He barrels toward her. Bones *crack* and fly into the air. Even more skeletons emerge, some directly from under him. They scratch and tear and dig at his flesh. But he doesn't care. He runs on, eyes locked on his target.

Deena curls into herself.

Then a cacophony of bone *shatters* in front of her.

She catches a glimpse of a vibrant green blur. She takes note of the shrapnel and bone in the air. Then she feels a heavy *tug*. The entire skull lurches.

The general bites down on the skull. He rips it free from the body with a loud *SNAP!*

All of the nearby skeletons turn to him.

They claw at his skin, tearing through it. He bleeds heavily. But he doesn't care.

With all of the strength left within him, he hurls the skull toward Aster and Delphi.

It sails through the air and lands with a *crack* beside Delphi's hooves. It splits open. Deena crawls out, scratches and cuts on her body.

Skeletons surround the general on all sides. He has no space to run. No way to plow through them. They dig into him. His blood flies into the wind. Light reflects in every drop, mixing with the rain. It rises to the sky like a field of glimmering sparkles.

He closes his eyes.

The skeletons surround him completely. They pile on, wholly obscuring him from view.

His green glow fades away. Not in a fit of violent combat, nor a cataclysmic event, but in a moment of wordless atonement.

The general dies.

Delphi nearly cries.

Aster does.

They fight on.

The skeletons do the same.

Princess Pipsy stares into the ancient, yellowed eyes of Damnation. She snarls.

"You are *so* fucking dead."

Her glowing horn *crackles* and *pops*.

KRAAAK!

Red lightning *explodes* out from it. The bolt strikes Damnation's magical cocoon.

It does nothing.

Not a mark.

Not a scratch.

Nothing.

Damnation's voice echoes in their minds.

"Nothing can break through this magic. Not here. Not now. Your *teamwork* was merely a *fluke*. A *mistake*. A *very* lucky chance."

He goes on.

"It's too late for you. Try whatever you like. You won't—"

Maus charges forward, screaming like a madman. He swings Silver Seal with *every single ounce of strength he has within him.*

"I'm—"

FWOOM!

"—calling—"

FWOOM!

"—your—"

FWOOM!

"—fucking—"

FWOOM!

"—BLUFF!"

Every arc of light strikes the swirling purple magic. It *shatters* into nothing. The final arc cuts through his flesh tethers.

His body falls with a barely-audible, pitiful *plop.*

Maus drops Silver Seal.

He collapses from exhaustion.

He looks up at the princess, barely conscious.

"Make sure you fucking kill him."

The traces of purple glows throughout his body — his *massive* body — flicker into nothing. Beyond the hole, the skeletons crumble and fall. The ominous *hum* fades to silence.

Princess Pipsy approaches Damnation.

He *gurgles* helplessly, face-down in the muck of long-since-rotten flesh.

She kicks him over.

His body rolls, his front now facing the ceiling. His breathing is strained. Shallow.

The princess towers over him.

Her eyes, horn, and mane *crackle* with erratic, violent energy.

Damnation wheezes. He stares up at the princess. With exceptional effort, he speaks into her mind once again.

"I am your Damnation. I was birthed of your very arrogance. By your arrogance, I will be born again. You cannot kill me in any way that matters."

The princess puts a hoof on his chest, pinning him down.

Damnation's heartbeat quickens.

She leans in close.

Very close.

Damnation feels the heat of her breath. The moisture it carries. He can see the rage in her eyes. He can feel the painful *crackling* of her energy. It burns at what skin he has left, charring the edges.

The princess's red glow brightens. Her electricity builds. It *crackles* and *pops* even louder. Its brightness burns Damnation's eyes. But he can't move. He can't look away. And — for the first time in a *very* long time — he feels afraid.

Princess Pipsy scowls.

"I beg to fucking differ."

Lightning explodes from her horn.

Damnation's head splatters into paste.

Epilogue I:
The Burden
of Greatness

Epilogue I: The Burden
of Greatness

The sound of gentle, rolling waves enters the chamber from the open window. Princess Pipsy peers out of it, looking out to the city below.

The sun rises high into the sky; the mark of early afternoon. Its light reflects off the wondrous curvature of buildings below. Tall stretches of scaffolding hug the exterior walls of numerous buildings. Unicorns walk across the supports, stopping to exchange words before going back to business. They examine each building closely, focused on completing repairs.

On the streets below, many more unicorns mill about, all with their own days to attend to. Among them, a very, *very* sparse number of people — *not* unicorns — slowly wander the city. Jagged lines of beautiful silver carve and wind through most of the main roads, having been used to fill in any cracks.

Around the city, a fortified wall of metal and stone — now *heavily* reinforced at its base — forms a protective barrier. At the far end, two massive metal gates remain open. A handful of unicorns walk through, some departing, and others arriving. A long, descending stone bridge — its texture mismatched throughout — touches down to the beach of the shore.

A handful of unicorns below catch a glimpse of the princess. They give a firm, thankful nod.

She returns it.

—— —— —— —— —— —— —— —— —— —— —— —— —— ——

Princess Pipsy descends a beautiful staircase of near-white stone. The *clack* of her hooves echoes slightly.

Aster stands at the bottom. She locks eyes with the princess.

"*There* you are. I was beginning to worry."

The princess continues her descent.

"You're *always* beginning to worry."

Aster replies.

"You said this would likely take time, but it's been—"

Princess Pipsy butts in.

"It's been a *few months,* Aster. I don't know how long it'll take to fully recover. Power often balances exhaustion. And I am still *very* exhausted."

Aster exhales.

"Yes. I know."

The princess meets Aster at the bottom of the stairs.

"I'll be back to normal eventually. I appreciate the concern… mostly."

She and Aster walk on.

She speaks again.

"Any more news of other unicorns?"

Aster shakes her head.

"None yet. We still find an isolated few every so often, but no other cities have risen. Those that *have* were already contacted."

The princess — reluctant — looks to her.

"Any word of the queen?"

Aster replies.

"None yet. But we'll find her eventually. I'm sure of it."

The princess moves on.

"And what of re-education? Any more hiccups?"

Aster grimaces.

"Successfully mandated, as you requested. It's quite the cultural shift from what they're used to. Some unicorns are more… *receptive* than others. But they always come around. Even if they think they won't, we keep them *very* much in check."

The princess replies.

"Good. Let's *really* hammer down on keeping murders to a minimum."

Aster speaks.

"Already accounted for. It's the very first thing we tell them."

The two enter the wide atrium of the building's main floor. A long wooden table sits at the center of the room. Banners line the walls, each one a masterfully patterned color: red, yellow, blue, green, and white. Displays of armor line the walls. Centered among them — and prominently displayed — are the twisted, broken remains of Princess Pipsy's armor.

A reminder.

Aster steps up to the heavy doors of the chamber.

The princess speaks.

"I take it they're done by now. Guess we should get to the square, then."

Aster nods.

"Unless you have any objections, princess."

She shakes her head.

"None at all. I'm sure they've been getting *quite* antsy."

Aster's horn glows blue. The same glow overtakes her eyes. And — beyond that — the very doors in front of them.

The doors open, creaking gently.

Both step out into the city.

———————————————————————

Unicorns greet them as they walk through the streets. Some glance at them with unease or reluctance, clearly more new to the city.

Ahead of them, the princess spots Petunia walking in their direction, albeit fairly off-balance.

The princess calls out to her.

"Petunia!"

Petunia's head turns in her direction. She smiles as she approaches.

"Afternoon, princess. It's good to see you."

Realization hits. She corrects.

"It's good to *hear* you, anyway."

Aster speaks.

"Your balance is off. Where's Deena? Is she not with you?"

Petunia sighs.

"No, unfortunately not. Delphi wanted to borrow her, and, well… you know how eager she can get. I'm on my own for the day."

She grumbles.

"If not the next *few*… "

The princess speaks.

"We're heading to the square to check out the statue. You're obviously more than welcome to come along, though I can't promise it'll be very exciting."

Petunia responds.

"The marvel, I'm sure, will be lost on me. But I would be happy to join you."

———————————————————————

The city square — having been completely rebuilt — radiates beauty and splendor. Short walls of white-and-gray stone form a series of wide planters;

each houses a number of flourishing exotic flora. At the center of the city square, a fountain of white stone — an intricately carved unicorn atop it — burbles endlessly.

Not far off — and still *technically* within the center of the square — a long gray cloth covers what is very clearly a statue underneath.

Two gray unicorns argue with Maus, the three standing directly in front of it. Maus's hair remains short, though it *does* look a bit cleaner. Silver Seal — no longer glowing — rests in the sheath on his back.

Princess Pipsy approaches. Aster and Petunia walk alongside her.

Maus and the two unicorns turn to face them.

The two unicorns bow. One acknowledges.

"Princess."

Maus rolls his eyes. He looks to the princess.

"These two knuckleheads have been fighting me all morning. If you got here a minute later, they would've skipped the dramatic reveal."

One of the two steps up to Maus, considerably taller.

"The word of the princess is *law*. But I'm not one to keep such a sculpture from the people. And we were *never* officially told to delay it."

He steps closer to Maus.

"You are here as a guest, *not* a citizen. Remember your place. Or do I need to mention that I'm much bigger than you?"

Maus scoffs, unfazed.

"I've seen bigger."

Princess Pipsy clears her throat.

Everyone turns to her.

She speaks.

"Just reveal the fucking statue, please."

The gray unicorns nod.

The one that was talking to Maus replies.

"Right away, princess."
Maus shakes his head.
The two unicorns look to the cloth. Their horns
turn a dim blue. While not quite as bright as Aster's, it
clearly does the job. The cloth, too, starts to glow.
The princess seems somewhat impressed.
"Looks like Delphi's lessons are actually working.
I didn't think she had it in her."
The cloth pulls free. It falls to the ground.
Before them stands a grand statue of a unicorn,
carved from a textured marble. It stands atop a high
pedestal, seven or eight feet off the ground. Its front
hoof raises up. Magnificent stone curls form its mane
and tail.
The pedestal itself bears an inscription.

*In remembrance of all unicorns who lost their lives
when our city was attacked,
and in the memory of General George,
who gave his life to save another,
may this statue remind us all
that Damnation is never the end.*

Maus speaks quietly to himself.
"So he *did* have a name…"
He takes a breath.
"I fuckin' knew it."
Princess Pipsy turns to the two gray unicorns.
"It's beautiful. Thank you. You're dismissed."
They both bow, then walk off.
The princess watches them leave.
Waits for them to step out of earshot.
Then—
"This is the *ugliest* thing I have ever seen. And it
looks *exactly the same* as everything else! This was

supposed to be *unique!* What kind of idiot *approved* this?!"

Aster blinks.

"Uh… *you* did, princess."

The princess continues, losing no momentum.

"Well, who *allowed* me to approve this?"

Aster replies.

"I suppose that's technically me."

The princess rambles on.

"As soon as you can, scratch 'marble' off the list of ceremonial statue materials. I mean, *look* at it! It's literally *no fucking different* than the one that's right over there! How is that *ceremonial?* This is one of the worst fucking…"

Her passionate critique goes on.

Aster nods along, only following somewhat.

Petunia speaks.

"Sounds like I'm not missing much."

Maus responds.

"Nope. Not much at all."

Epilogue II:
The Burden
of Knowledge

Epilogue II: The Burden of Knowledge

Delphi stands before a grand room of unicorns, not unlike a lecture hall. While there aren't *technically* seats, many of the available spaces are filled. The unicorns attending are a wide range of colors and ages (all within the realm of natural possibility, of course). A handful seem to be disengaged, but the vast majority are very attentive.

Delphi addresses the class.

"Alright, everyone. Seems like we're missing a few today, but it's not an issue. We'll carry on. That being said, I hope you've all been practicing, because today we'll be going through some exercises."

Some students perk up. Others groan.

Near the front, a unicorn with a chestnut coloration raises her horn.

Delphi spots it.

"Yes, Perri?"

Perri naturally projects her shrill, youthful voice.

"Will our guest be a part of the exercise?"

Delphi quickly responds, almost panicking.

"Now, class, I *told* you our guest can get *very* excited, so please try not to—"

Deena zips out from her mane. She flies high into the air, looking out to the class. And, of course, her blue glow remains.

"Listen up, fucknuts! Class is in session! Today, you're gonna *learn!*"

Delphi watches.

"Oh, boy…"

Deena flies up to a unicorn in the front row. Her wings flutter audibly.

The unicorn — a yellow dun coloration — looks alarmed and surprised.

Deena jabs a finger toward her.

"Are you ready to do whatever it takes to follow in your teacher's footsteps? Huh? Are you ready? *ARE YOU?!* Answer me!"

Deena flies *very* close.

Uncomfortably close.

The unicorn in question leans away just a bit. She hesitates, uncertain how she's meant to respond.

"Uh… *yes?*"

Deena slaps her snout.

"I don't believe you! Get out of my class!"

Delphi steps forward.

"No, no. You don't have to do that."

She looks down at Deena.

"Don't hit my students."

Deena flies over to her.

"Hey, don't worry! I won't hit *any* more of *our* students!"

She elbows Delphi's shoulder.

Delphi sighs.

"This might've been a bad idea."

Then—

KNOCK, KNOCK, KNOCK, KNOCK!

Delphi looks to the door. She groans.

"Just a moment, everyone. We'll get things going shortly."

Delphi walks over to the door.

Deena flies after.

From the crowd of students, one quietly mumbles.

"Is this class ever going to start?"

Delphi's eyes and horn glow pale blue. The same glow appears at the door.

The door opens. The glow dissipates.

Standing on the other side is a small group comprised of humans and elves. All seem to be fairly young, though certainly adults. Like some kind of younger adults.

As soon as the door opens, Delphi speaks.

"Wrong building. City hall is three blocks away."

She prepares to close the door.

The front most figure — a human man dressed in shabby yet scholarly attire — takes a step forward.

"Actually... I think we *are* in the right place. Are you Delphi?"

Delphi narrows her eyes.

"I am. Why?"

The members of the group exchange uncertain glances. After a moment, the front most human continues to speak.

"Well… we were hoping it wasn't too late to enroll in your class."

The unicorns behind Delphi chuckle quietly.

She shoots them a stern look.

They instantly quiet.

She looks back to the group at the door.

"I'm sorry, I thought it was clear in our announcements. This is a class for *unicorns. All* of our classes are for unicorns. Visitors and diplomats are welcome, but that doesn't mean everything's for you."

She prepares to close the door once again.

The front most figure reaches out.

"Wait! Please!"

Delphi exhales.

"Look, I respect the drive. I really do. But I have a class to get back to. The eastern magic schools are probably more your speed. The study of emotion is its own brand of academics. Besides, you're not unicorns. You'd never get anything out of this class, let alone any of the others. You don't have horns to utilize."

The members of the group exchange glances once again.

The front most figure speaks.

"Actually... we do."

He reaches deep into his pocket. The others do the same.

Each one reveals a masterfully carved wand, made from a rich, elegant wood. The top half of the wand curves around itself and into a single point, mimicking the length and shape of a unicorn's horn.

Deena stares, thoroughly impressed.

"Well, I'll be damned! *Come on in!*"

A look of relief washes over the group. They push past Delphi, entering the chamber.

Delphi opens her mouth to protest.

She immediately gives up.

The new students file in.

She magically closes the door.

Deena rubs her hands together mischievously. She giggles.

"Like illiterate lambs to the educational slaughter..."

Delphi addresses them.

"Ignore her. Please, find a seat. At the back of the class, thank you."

The humans and elves walk to the back, six of them in total. The unicorn students give them all sorts of odd, unwelcome looks.

They file into an empty row at the *very* back. There are no chairs — nor are there any *anywhere* — so they elect to stand.

Whispers spread among the class.

Delphi exhales, collecting her thoughts.

"Alright, everyone. It looks like we have some new students joining us today. So don't bully them too hard. And *behave yourselves.* You're *unicorns,* so act like it."

The class settles down.

Perri scowls at the new group in the back.

The group members nervously look away.

Delphi continues to speak.

"Now, if there are no more interruptions, we can—"

KNOCK, KNOCK, KNOCK!

Delphi mutters.

"For fuck's sake…"

Some of the students quietly 'ooh' in a steadily rising key.

Delphi magically opens the door.

"If you lost your group, they already—"

An *incredibly vile* smell assaults her nostrils. The sheer shock of it ends her sentence. It reeks like a wet rag left in the sun, but somehow exponentially worse.

She looks down to the source of the odor.

Standing at less than five feet all — if not *four* — maybe less — is a pale, lanky figure with four arms and long, spider-like fingers. Not a single piece of its clothing matches any other. It wears a large, singular goggle over its bald head. Its oblong, beady eye — its *only* eye — stares right into Delphi's.

The creature smiles, revealing rows and rows of countless little teeth.

"Pleasure to meet you. Hm. Ready to learn."

Delphi responds.

"Absolutely not."

She magically slams the door.

All of her students breathe a collective sigh of relief.

She takes her place at the front of the class. *Finally,* she addresses them all, ready to begin.

"Let's get started before the whole city walks through the door. For the sake of our new additions, I hope you all *actually* practiced. I guess we'll all find out shortly."

A handful of unicorns look a little nervous.

Delphi continues.

"Who'd like to volunteer first? Or will I have to call one of you up here?"

Epilogue III:
The Burden of Matronage

Epilogue III: The Burden of Matronage

In a land far to the south, nestled in the Saven Wood, the ground rumbles and quakes.

A city rises up from beneath the trees, uprooting a number of them.

Those who spot it say it wasn't there before.

But it *was* there before.

Just a very long time ago.

— — — — — — — — — — — — — — — —

Its denizens begin to stir.

— — — — — — — — — — — — — — — —

Queen Marika opens her eyes.

The first thing she does is take a breath.

She exhales slowly.

Clarity returns.

Then she examines the space around her.

Stark white stones make up the walls. Sunlight illuminates the room through a series of thin, vertical windows. The room itself is just about thirty feet across. A wooden table sits in the center of the space, filling a good portion of it. Banners of varying ages and qualities decorate the walls, many stained with old, dark splotches. One in particular bears a diamond shape, though far more stretched, and pointed at the ends.

War trophies.

She feels a welcome sense of relief.

This is *exactly* where she left off.

At the other side of the table, an all-black unicorn — his horn a deep purple — comes to consciousness. His long black mane drapes over his shoulders. Thin scars along his body taint his otherwise well-kept appearance.

He blinks a few times.

Then he breathes.

Then he locks eyes with the queen across from him.

He bows.

"My queen."

He looks back into her eyes.

"I take it your plan was successful."

The queen responds.

"In part, absolutely. We're still here. In whole… I'm uncertain. If that bitch of a child is finally dead, I'll consider the plan a success."

The other unicorn responds.

"He *must* be dead by now, surely. Not even those with magic can withstand the march of time. Everything has its limit."

He thinks.

"Do we *know* how much time has passed?"

The queen replies.

"We don't. In truth, it shouldn't matter. I highly doubt that any mortal can match our power, even now. And if the world has forgotten us, so be it. We can just as easily remind them."

She walks to the door of the chamber.

"But, to clarify, it *would* be incredibly helpful to know. So I intend on finding out."

She focuses her attention on the door in front of her.

But nothing happens.

She looks… alarmed.

"What?"

The black unicorn walks over to her.

"What is it? What's the matter?"

The queen focuses on the door once again.

A moment passes.

Still, nothing happens.

Queen Marika looks to the black unicorn. The confusion in her eyes surprises even him.

"My magic is gone."

— — — — — — — — — — — — — — — — —

Queen Marika walks through the city streets with her head held high. The black unicorn walks alongside her, keeping pace.

The city streets are built with familiar white stone, as are most of the buildings, though some appear to be made with a different stone material. A number of unicorns walk through the streets, almost all of them looking confused and concerned.

The moment they see Queen Marika pass, they stop to bow.

She pays them no mind.

"Lupin."

The black unicorn — Lupin — looks to her.

"Yes, my queen?"

The queen continues forward, not so much as glancing in his direction.

"Have any of our knights awoken?"

He responds.

"I'm sure some of them have by now. If not, they'll be awake soon."

She speaks once again.

"Find whoever you can. More is best, but even a few will suffice. Meet me at the city gates as soon as you're able. I think it's time we get some answers to our questions."

Lupin bows.

"As you command."

He trots off, immediately barking orders at the unicorns around him.

Queen Marika heads for the gates.

Time to see what they've all woken up to.

— — — — — — — — — — — — — — —

The trees of the Saven Wood aren't necessarily thick. They aren't necessarily clumped together, either. While there is *some* variation, most of the trees are a fairly even distance apart. That — coupled with the fact that the canopy blocks much of the sky — means that it's *very* easy for someone to get lost. Even the most hardy survivalists can find themselves turned around. The same can be said for any family taking a hike farther out than they should, especially when their youngest daughter is only seven.

Rila — the young elven girl in question — stares down at her feet as she walks. She kicks up leaves with every step, watching them fall back down.

Ahead of her, two older men lead the walk, both of them elven themselves. One — with a long brown beard — holds a poorly maintained map in his hands. Beside them, a younger boy walks, though he seems to be more of a teen.

Rila hums to herself as she walks.

One of the older men at the front glances back, noticing Rila's meandering gait. He calls out to her, his voice scratchy and gruff.

"Rila! *Please* don't wander off again. Silly times are over. We're trying to get *home* now."

He turns his attention back to the map in his hands.

Rila doesn't even acknowledge him. Truth be told, she hardly even hears him.

The elven boy scoffs at her lack of awareness.

"She's gonna get stuck out here forever. Or get killed by a wild animal."

The man without the map slaps the boy upside the head.

"Do not say such things about your sister. Fate is not one to be tempted."

Rila slows her pace, kicking up more of the leaves.

Then—

Rustle...

Rustle...

Her head perks up. Not far off — just a *little* ways away from the path — she hears the sound of a rustling bush.

It continues.

Rustle...

Rustle...

She gasps quietly.

"A *squirrelly*... "

Moving slow — careful not to make a sound — she steps away from the forest path, eyes wide and looking for squirrels.

She follows the rustling.

Rustle...

Rustle...

She steps through a prickly bush. A thorn catches her finger.

"Ah..."

It draws blood. But no matter. She wipes it on her clothes, walking further out.

Then — directly in front of her — she sees it.

The face of a beautiful white horse peeks out from a bush. Little leaves and tiny twigs stick to her pretty black mane.

Rila gasps again.

"A *horsey...*"

She takes a step closer.

The horsey smiles.

Rila watches her emerge from the bush. She is a *very* tall horsey. And so, so beautiful. So beautiful, in fact, that it takes a moment for Rila to notice the long silver horn on her head.

Rila whispers to herself, positively awe-struck.

"A *unicorn...*"

The unicorn takes a step closer.

Rila, too, slowly approaches.

The unicorn leans down, bringing her head — and her *very* pettable muzzle — closer to the little girl's level. All the while, she continues to grin.

Rila takes another step.

She reaches out her hand.

— — — — — — — — — — — — — — — — — —

Rila's screams echo through the forest. Birds scatter at the sudden noise.

Her dads and brother whip around in panic. Fearful expressions take their faces.

They sprint in the direction of her shrieks.

— — — — — — — — — — — — — — — — — —

It doesn't take long to find her.

They shove through a large, thorny bush, stepping into a small clearing of sorts.

Queen Marika stands over Rila, pinning her to the ground with a hoof on her chest. Her lips drip red.

Rila cries, trying to force herself to be silent.

She can't.

Her hand — while still attached — is broken, and bleeding profusely.

Around them, four other unicorns stand, Lupin among them.

Queen Marika's voice booms.

"If you take one more step, I *will* kill her."

Rila continues to cry.

Her family members do the same.

The elven boy speaks first. His voice quivers.

"Please… let her go. She doesn't—"

The queen interrupts, a deeply commanding tone.

"Quiet, child. Adults are talking."

The boy shuts up.

The bearded man speaks.

"Whatever you want, it's yours."

The queen replies.

"Do you know who I am?"

He does not immediately respond.

She presses more weight onto Rila's chest.

Rila screams.

The queen repeats the question.

"Do you know who I am?"

The other man forces a reply.

"Yes! Yes! You're a unicorn!"

He breaks down.

"I don't understand… She said not to worry…"

Queen Marika stares at him.

"Who said not to worry? About *what?* And *do* try to be specific. For your daughter's sake."

Rila continues to cry.

The man continues.

"The princess! I don't remember her name. She said… unicorns used to be cruel! That they're not anymore! I don't know! She said a lot of things!"

The queen looks… amused.

In some sick, twisted way, she's *amused*.

She speaks again.

"And did you know of us before then?"

He responds.

"No. No. Only stories. Please, let her go…"

The queen ignores his plea.

"How *very* interesting."

She turns to Lupin.

"As soon as we're done here, I want you to leave for Unicornicopia. I assume that my daughter's still there. I can't imagine *what* has gotten into her head, but it sounds like she went soft for these… *lessers.*"

She takes a breath.

"It seems the princess needs a reminder of who she really is."

Lupin bows.

"Yes, my queen."

She looks back to the teary-eyed family before her, as if she forgot they were there.

"Oh. And kill the three of them."

The unicorns do as instructed.

Rila opens her mouth to scream.

Queen Marika caves in her face with a single stomp. Blood and mucus explodes from the impact. Her screaming — reduced to a gargle — fades in an instant.

The queen wipes her hoof on Rila's clothes.

The other unicorns waste no time in tearing the wailing family to shreds.

Blood arcs through the air, staining the forest around them.

Queen Marika watches the carnage before her.

And she smiles.

BEFORE EVERYTHING, THERE WAS NOTHING.
AND BEFORE NOTHING, THERE WERE UNICORNS.

Hunted by a creature called Damnation for the sins of her mother, Princess Pipsy, the last known member of the royal family, embarks on a bloodthirsty quest to rekindle the magic of the unicorns... and to slaughter all who stand in her way.

Cover illustrations by Jesús Bey
Map illustration by Alberto Garcia
Chapter illustrations by Katherine C. Neal

ISBN 979-8-218-68287-3